UNDERGROUND

Also by Andrew McGahan

Praise
1988
Last Drinks
The White Earth

ANDREW McGAHAN
UNDERGROUND

ALLEN&UNWIN

This is a work of fiction. Nothing in it is meant to be taken as fact.

First published in 2006

This project has been assisted by the Commonwealth Government through the Australia Council, its arts funding and advisory board.

Allen & Unwin
83 Alexander Street
Crows Nest NSW 2065
Australia
Phone: (61 2) 8425 0100
Fax: (61 2) 9906 2218
Email: info@allenandunwin.com
Web: www.allenandunwin.com

National Library of Australia
Cataloguing-in-Publication entry:

McGahan, Andrew.
   Underground.

   ISBN 978 1 74114 931 9.

   ISBN 1 74114 931 2.

   I. Title.

A823.3

Set in 12.5/15 pt Granjon by Bookhouse, Sydney
Printed and bound by Griffin Press in Australia

10 9 8 7 6 5 4 3 2 1

UNDERGROUND

PART ONE

ONE

Its name was Yusuf.

Probably a joke by someone in the Department of Meteorology. Or maybe that's just official policy now. A state of emergency decree from the government. If something looks big and dangerous, then find a means to link it to Islam.

Either way, it was surely the biggest cyclone to hit that part of the Queensland coast in decades—a great-granddaddy of a tropical storm. Category five. Winds gusting over two hundred and ninety k; walls of horizontal rain, like Allah himself was pissing in your face; and a storm surge that had lifted the Pacific Ocean by twenty murderous feet or more.

I was right there in the middle of it all. Six storeys up, my belly on the tiles and one arm wrapped around the balcony railing, hanging on for dear life as I peered over the edge, nearly deafened by the unearthly shriek of the wind. My face stinging. My slotted eyes agonised. The rest of me drenched. With a whisky glass clutched in my free hand, holding more sea water now than alcohol.

Below me, three years of work was being steadily destroyed. The artificial beach had been the first to go. Huge waves loomed there now, their crests torn into a brown froth that streaked ahead wildly. I couldn't even tell where the beach had *been* anymore. Hundreds of dump trucks had emptied thousands of tonnes of white sand down there (it cost a fortune) but now it was all just part of the raging ocean.

Even drunk and half-terrified as I was, I could appreciate the irony. Leave the mangroves alone, the environmentalists had said. Leave the dunes behind them alone. They had protested and petitioned and chained themselves to bulldozers—and gone to prison for their troubles. But what did I or my investors care? We wanted a pristine beach for the punters, not mudflats. We wanted open ocean views from the rooms, not the backs of old dunes covered with scrub. So I'd let the construction company loose to rip out the mangroves and level the frontage.

Three years later, the environmentalists were all long gone, no doubt locked up for good these days, but Yusuf was teaching me a lesson. The storm surge had drowned most of the resort. The beach and, behind that, the lawns and gardens and pathways that led to it. Wreckage floated everywhere. The four-acre pool was underwater, with its cabanas and bars, as were the tennis courts, the croquet pitch, and, from what I could see, a fair percentage of the championship links golf course. But what was truly awesome was that the great muddy waves were rolling clear over the lot of it, two hundred metres or more from the normal coastline, and slamming like thunder into the resort's main buildings.

Up in one of the penthouse suites, I could feel the hotel wing shake with every watery detonation, solid concrete or not. From the floors below came the sloshing din of shattered glass and broken furniture rolling about. And squinting into the storm I could see that the other buildings were faring worse. The luxury villas, off in their private gardens, were inundated up to the gutters. The restaurant/reception centre was roofless, a mass of papers and tablecloths and curtains, whipping away into the wind. And the great big block of the two-thousand-seat convention centre was crumbling with each wave, like a sandstone cliff collapsing into the sea, filmed on video over millennia and set at furious fast-forward.

'Come on,' I yelled at the sky. 'COME ON!'

I was enjoying myself, actually.

In fact, the cyclone was doing me the biggest favour possible. That is, the cyclone, and an insurance policy that was a good month yet from lapsing. Because, to be frank, the Ocean Sands Green Resort was the white elephant of all white elephants. Despite all the money we'd spent, despite all the work we'd done, the place had never opened to the public. And it never would have, storm or no storm. World events had put paid to any hope of that. So I, managing supervisor and public face of the project, was free to cheer and sob and laugh myself sick as it dissolved away like a sandcastle.

The cyclone whooped and sobbed and laughed along too.

It was time for another drink.

I let go of the handrail and allowed the wind to drive me back through the shattered glass doors into the suite proper. I was bleeding from that glass, and from other flying debris, but none of the cuts were serious. Indeed, I felt invulnerable. And why not? God knows how much scotch I'd tossed down or how many grams of dodgy cocaine I'd snorted by that stage. I crawled about the room, a jumble of overturned chairs and empty bottles and filthy plates and torn bed sheets, praying there was still some alcohol surviving somewhere.

Of course, the room had been like that even before the cyclone hit. Julie and I had been living it up hard. For the resort had actually welcomed *two* guests before its untimely demise. Me, and my assistant publicist, Julie Favmore—twenty-eight years old, cunning as the devil, and horny as all hell. The pair of us had set ourselves up in one of the suites—indeed, the only one that had been properly fitted out, for display purposes, before financial reality sank in and construction ceased. All that time and effort deserved at least one party, I'd decided.

And what a time we had, with the whole place to ourselves. Oh, Julie ... I wonder where you are now? My old balls are still aching from the things you did to them. It was less than a month ago, after all. And yet you were the very last fuck of my life, it looks likely.

But Julie was long gone by the time the storm really got going. She cleared out as soon as the first warnings came. She was a sensible local lass, for all her sexual depravity, and had seen cyclones before. So I was alone. True, there was a security team on station at the main gate, but they were under strict instructions to let no one else in and, more importantly, not to disturb me. No doubt I should have hauled out of there too, but I was hardly the man to let a mere storm get in the way of a promising bender. Besides, my career was in the toilet once again and, an empty resort aside, I had absolutely nowhere else to go.

Anyway, I found a bottle at last, then sat spreadeagled on the wet marble floor, grinned at the fury out there on the ocean, and drank.

The next thing I knew, everything got quiet. The wind, the noise, the rain—in just a minute or two, it all faded away.

'Ah!' said I.

I'd been hoping for this. It's not every day that you get to see the eye of a cyclone. I lurched to my feet and went back to the balcony to look.

Now I've heard that sometimes in the eye of storms people have seen clear blue skies. I didn't. There were still clouds above. But they weren't like any clouds I'd seen before—they were a creeping, glowing grey. And they capped a gigantic bowl of warm, faintly misty air, drifting between towering walls of cloud that curved off into blackness. Five miles across, ten, it was impossible to gauge distances. So vast and calm, and yet the atmosphere thrummed with an electric sense of threat. And while there was no rain or wind, the ocean was still sending breakers across my resort—their sand-stained crests glassy now, and all the more ominous for it—and shuddering booms still quaked through the building.

It felt like the end of the world, and I don't know how long I stood there, gazing up. But finally a new sound grabbed my attention. It was the crack and splash of something large falling into the water. I peered down over the railing. Several storeys below, the balconies of the lower floors were breaking away from the building and toppling into the sea.

Through the drunkenness and the hum of chemicals, some alarms finally sounded. It was time to get out of there. I was more than happy for the hotel to collapse, but not with me in it. I looked up. The walls of Yusuf's eye reared in every direction, almost unmoving at a glance, and yet swirling with the slow hypnotism of ferocious speed, seen from far away. Or maybe not so far away. But a carelessness still possessed me. As if I had all the time in the world, I hunted out the bottle again, then reeled off lazily through the bare hallways.

Moisture dripped everywhere, and awful echoes rang up and down the stairs. I descended to the first floor and found it awash up to my knees—and this was still a good fifteen feet above ground level. I paused to open a door that led to a seaward-facing suite. It was a horrible sight, like gazing out from the back of a cave, a tangle of broken concrete and glass, and only the ocean beyond. Even worse, a monster was rolling across the water towards me. From above, each wave had looked big, but now, from sea level, I saw an evil, dirty-brown wall. The water in the room receded to meet it, and in horror I slammed the door. An explosion seemed to erupt behind it, and water jetted through the cracks like twenty fire hoses.

I staggered away to the other side of the hall and entered a suite on the leeward side of the building. Here, there was much less damage. I waded to the balcony. These would have been the cheaper rooms, for instead of facing the ocean they faced the low coastal hills. Staring out now, I could see that the front car park and landscaping were drowned deep, but perhaps less than one hundred yards away rose a muddy hillside of storm-ravaged scrub and trees. Dry land.

Truth to tell, I hadn't given much thought to my escape, until then. I'd probably assumed that I would be driving to safety. But my Mercedes was somewhere down in that car park, or sailing halfway to Tahiti by now. I would have to swim. I considered the water—it was relatively calm, here in the lee of the hotel— but it still had a malignant look, with all sorts of debris tossing in greasy undulations. I swigged from the bottle, mustering my resolve, but then the water in the room surged and lifted, and I didn't so much jump off the balcony as float off it. The bottle was gone from my hand and I was swimming.

I am not a fit man, even for a fifty-nine year old. But fat, they say, makes you buoyant, and I have plenty of that. And while there were probably all sorts of treacherous currents and vortexes in the water, somehow I avoided them all. I do have one memory of staring down into the murky depths and seeing a golf cart tumbling beneath me. But then there was something solid under my feet. Not mud, but bitumen. And thus I waded, completely unharmed, out of the cyclone's deadly ocean, and onto the resort driveway.

I was laughing. Nothing was going to kill me today. I knew that half a kilometre along the driveway was the front gate, and the security complex, built as solidly as a bunker. I could ride out the storm there. Maybe, if the guards had any sense, there would even be something to drink. I consulted the sky. The walls of the cyclone loomed with their surreal fixity, and a haze covered the sea—but somewhere out there the other side of the eye was rushing towards me. I took one last look at my resort, the final folly of an age when things like holidays and tourism had seemed to matter. Then I nodded farewell, and turned to the road.

And saw the most unlikely sight of all, on that insane day. A bright red Australia Post van was grumbling down the hill.

Was I hallucinating? There was certainly enough alcohol and cocaine in my system. But no, the vehicle was real enough, a jarringly everyday sight amidst all the chaos. My first thought was—so what were the security guards doing? How had the van got through the gates? The lazy bastards must be hiding away in the office. My second, and far more rational, thought was—what the fuck was the van doing out in a storm like this anyway? The dedication of the postal service was one thing—but no mail was *that* important.

And yet, why the hell not?

Nothing could surprise me anymore.

The van halted in front of me, and two postmen climbed out. Bizarrely, they seemed to take no note of the sky, or the sight of the swollen ocean consuming a resort. Their eyes, under their caps, were fixed steadfastly and seriously upon me, as if we'd arranged this very meeting, long ago. One of them held a package about the size of a shoebox.

'Mr Leo James?' the man with the package asked.

'That's me.' Could they possibly be for real? Of course it was me, and I doubted there were many people in Australia who wouldn't know that. The craziness of it all was overpowering. I even found myself giving a little bow.

Neither one responded, or smiled.

They were odd looking posties, I decided. Their uniforms were untidy, somehow. Ill-fitting. And then I noticed that the package was lying empty on the road, a soggy heap, and instead, the first man was holding a gun.

'Get in the van, please,' he said.

I stared. Since when did postmen carry weapons? Was this another state of emergency decree? (I mean, who can keep track of them all?) But in any case, why on earth was he pointing it at me? And from behind now I could hear a sound above the boom of the waves—a rushing and howling that could only be one thing. The armed mailman blinked, a fraction of his weird calm draining away. He was facing the ocean, of course, and could see what was coming.

'In the van,' he repeated. 'Now.'

I gawped at him. And a sudden breeze tugged urgently at my back.

'I *will* shoot you,' he stated.

Abruptly the wind was there again, a savage gust of it that made me stagger forward to my knees. Something silver flickered past my eyes, moving so fast it was only a blur, and at the same moment the air was full of noise and water again.

But I was staring at the postie. I'd never seen a man decapitated before—well, not right in front of me, anyway. But that's cyclones for you. Nothing is more dangerous in high winds than a loose sheet of tin.

The other mailman was gawping now. His colleague's headless body took a few odd steps against the wind, and then fell over.

'Ha!' I cried above the cyclone. 'Fuck you, prick!'

Nothing was going to kill me today.

Then the back doors of the van popped open, and two more men jumped out, and these guys hadn't even bothered with the pretend uniforms. Together, the three of them set to and proceeded to beat the shit out of me. After which they threw me in the back of the van. But I suppose I can't blame them for panicking a bit. One of them was dead, and that cyclone really was a scary thing, even if it turned out to be on their side.

TWO

But no, on second thought, that isn't going far enough back. My troubles began long before the cyclone. I'll have to start this again.

For that matter, why am I even bothering to write this down? I know perfectly well that it will never be read by anyone. Except, that is, by *you*, my dear interrogators. You, and maybe a few of your superiors. That's not much of an audience. And besides, it's not as if you people need to hear all of this over. You've already made me tell you everything. Admit to everything. Confess to everything.

So why?

Well, because here I sit, at this big, empty table, locked away in this giant, empty room, with nothing else to do. And despite the fear and the anger, and the occasional pain, I'm also, mostly, just very bored. No proper books in here, no TV, nothing to pass the hours between our little talks. Nothing to do but wait, and worry, and stare at my surroundings.

I'm getting very sick of the colour green.

Green leather, green carpet, green walls.

Everywhere I look.

So to occupy myself I've decided to commence my memoirs. One thing I do have is plenty of wastepaper and pens. The previous occupants very thoughtfully left them behind. And it seems, too, that I have the time...maybe even enough to get this finished, before the inevitable comes to pass.

But how far back should I start? I could go back years and years, no doubt. My current fate, after all, is linked to a much wider history. I could go all the way back, ten years and more, to September 11 and the Twin Towers. (And who'd have ever thought that we'd reflect on *that* particular day as a happier, saner, safer time?) Truth is, I could go back even further than that. But I won't. I'll go back just over two years. I'll start with the dreadful events in Canberra.

I was there when all that happened—as I'm sure I've told you. An eyewitness, by chance, to the greatest disaster of the age. It was also the last time I saw my brother. And you know who he is, of course. None of this nightmare would have happened at all, if I wasn't his less famous sibling. I would never have been kidnapped, yet alone ended up in this curious dungeon of yours. So I guess I have to start with him too.

The Honourable Bernard James, Prime Minister of Australia.

My twin brother, fraternal, I should say.

THREE

In fact, Bernard was the only reason I ever went to Canberra. I didn't much like the place, but for a developer and real estate entrepreneur of dubious repute, like myself, to have the Prime Minister as a brother ... Well, you can imagine the opportunities. Because of him, I was known the country over, and got to stalk the corridors of power with the best of them. Of course, I had absolutely no power of my own, and everyone else in those corridors loathed the sight of me. Indeed, I was usually being escorted out of those same corridors by overly polite security guards. But access is access—or the illusion of access anyway.

For instance, the day before it all went haywire, I was in town on business, trying to tie down some investments for the resort. The potential investors were a consortium of Fijian politicians who were visiting the capital to negotiate an aid package—their country is sinking—from the Australian government. Much of that package was never going to go anywhere near Fiji, obviously. The delegation fully expected to reinvest the cash portions of it into various money-making ventures of their own—my resort amongst them. God only knows what happened to the poor bastards. They never did get their money. Now probably half of their islands are underwater at high tide, and there sure as hell isn't any foreign aid around anymore.

But on that day at least, they were junketing in Canberra, and I, the PM's cherished brother and confidant (according to my own PR) was showing them a good time. We spent the afternoon boozing and schmoozing around the city's finest restaurants and bars, with me assuring everyone constantly that I was on the best of terms with a whole raft of government ministers and planning agencies, state and federal. My resort was thus a mortal lock of an investment. None of which was exactly true, but it was all part of my trade—to be a recognisable face, a player who looked connected and sounded influential. And the Fijians obediently lapped it up.

None of us had a clue that we were drinking through Canberra's last day of normality. Still, by about nine that night (and lunch had started at midday) everyone was well and truly lubricated and I'd been promised wads of cash. Satisfied with my efforts, I packed the Fijians off to one of the better brothels, and swayed drunkenly back to my hotel room.

But even before I took off my shoes, the phone rang.

It was Bernard.

Now, admittedly, I'd just been telling the Fijians that I spoke to my twin all the time, that I had his ear, that he trusted me and *listened* to me. The truth was that in those days a phone call from my brother was a rare event indeed.

Okay, the fact is, we hated each other, and hadn't spoken in months. I'll go into all the history of it later, if I can bear to, but to put it briefly, I thought he was a pompous worm, and he thought I was a walking, talking embarrassment to his position. And we were both right. Still, publicly, it was in our interests to pretend to be civil. So I'd always supported him, the faithful familial booster, on those occasions when reporters sought me out during election campaigns and the like. He was my meal ticket, after all. And in return, Bernard turned a blind eye to the more questionable activities of mine that traded on our relationship. It was, in the best political tradition, a win–win thing. Or so *I* thought. But I was never glad to hear from him.

I said, 'How'd you know I was around?'

'How could I not know?' he replied, coldly. 'You and the Fijians have been thrown out of half the bars in town today.'

'But how'd you know I'm here at Rydges?'

'You always stay at Rydges.'

Well, Canberra was a small city, so he might've been telling the truth. My own suspicion was that he had ASIO keeping tabs on me, but I was too drunk to argue.

I said, 'You gonna give those guys their aid package?'

He ignored the question. 'I want you to come to The Lodge for dinner.'

'No thanks. I've eaten.'

'Not since lunch, I'm told.'

'I'm not hungry,' I insisted, watching the room spin before my eyes.

'There's a car waiting for you, outside the lobby.'

'Why? What's so important?'

He had hung up, the little prick.

(By the way, I reserve the right to insert 'little' before any term of abuse that I throw at him in the following pages. I don't mean 'little' in terms of 'short', because he isn't. I mean it because he's my 'little' brother. I was born fifteen minutes earlier. And resent it though he does, there's nothing the little shit can do about it.)

But I made my way to the lobby, all the same. You don't refuse a call from the country's leader simply on a drunken whim, family or not. And besides, it would only impress my backers all the more if I could say (honestly, for once) that I'd dined with the PM just the night before.

The car was waiting as promised, a government limousine. The driver was expecting me, and we whiffed off into the Canberra night. It wasn't far, just over the lake and then around the parliamentary circle and up Adelaide Avenue to the front gates of The Lodge. Security men peered hard through the windows, and demanded my wallet for identification—as if they didn't know who I was. Then they looked underneath the car for bombs, and in the boot too, and finally waved us on. More security waited for me at the front door, with a pat-down for weapons, and scans by metal detectors, and anthrax detectors, and lord knows what else, and at last, cleared of everything, I was ushered through to the inner sanctum.

Of course, Bernard would not have been in Canberra, yet alone in residence at The Lodge, if it wasn't the middle of a parliamentary session. He hated the house, just as, everyone knew, he hated the whole city. He preferred (like many a PM before him) the much grander vistas of Kirribilli House, on the harbour in Sydney. But there he was, waiting for me in the study, very much the Prime Minister after hours, his coat and tie removed, and his sleeves rolled up. Not that this made him look relaxed at all, or casual. He was a man born to wear suits. So bland and nondescript a figure that he might have been a low-grade book-keeper, not the most powerful man in Australia. He isn't exactly ugly, I suppose. But to me he's always had one of those gloomy, stubborn faces. An aggrieved face. A bully's face. A reflection, in other words, of all that lies in his heart.

I've always been thankful, therefore, that we aren't identical twins. And in our younger days, I was the better looking, no question. Taller, sharper, more hair, more friends, more girls, and far, far more sex. I wouldn't claim any of that to be true in later years—except maybe the sex, for Bernard was never a womaniser. But I haven't aged well, what with my indulgent lifestyle. My brother has always been more careful about his health, in that deadly dull way of his, and has no vices that I know of. Plus, by the time he ascended to the leadership of the Liberal Party, he had a personal trainer and was being groomed immaculately by experts. So he passes. And the raw stench of power, of course, is better than any plastic surgery.

'I've ordered you some coffee,' he said.

'A drink would be better.'

'You've had enough already.'

I fell into a chair, disgusted. A more self-righteous man I have never met. And he had no reason to be self-righteous—not considering the opinion polls around that time. Bernard was a Prime Minister in trouble. True, the Liberal Party had been in power for so long it seemed the country had forgotten how to vote for anyone else—but most of that had been with John Howard, the man of steel himself, at the helm. Bernard was the second leader since Howard's departure, and the gloss was wearing thin. The various wars overseas were a mess, Australian troops were dying in droves, car bombs were exploding on home soil, and the economy was in free fall. My brother's personal approval rating was the lowest ever of any sitting PM, and on a two-party preferred basis, Labor was leading by nearly twenty points. But if Bernard was worried, he didn't show it. He seemed a little tired, perhaps, and a little stressed, but emotions of any kind were not his strong suit.

'The family in town?' I asked him.

'No.'

I hadn't seen his wife, or his two adult children, in years. For that matter, I hadn't seen much lately of *my* three ex-wives, or my own three children, either.

We made small talk for a while. Awkwardly, because we had nothing whatever in common. But eventually I said, 'So what did you want me for?'

'You have to sign these.' He slid some papers across the desk to me. 'It's the final settlement of Mum's will,' he told me, as I read.

Our mother had died six months before—our father having preceded her by several years. There was nothing all that special to deal with, regarding the estate. Just the old family house and some investments. Bernard and I had both been named as executors, but I'd left it up to Bernard to arrange. When it came to dreary legal stuff, he was the expert.

'There's a cheque there, too,' he said.

I took up a pen and scribbled my signature. 'You could have mailed this to me,' I said, when I was done.

'I thought we should finish this in person.'

There was something about the way he said 'finish' that caught my attention. 'Finish what?'

'Us. This deal you seem to think you and I have.'

I was smiling. Bernard tried this on every few years. 'C'mon. It's just been two brothers helping each other out, hasn't it?'

'When have *you* ever helped *me* out?'

And he had me there. 'Doing you damage, am I?'

'You always have.'

'So why the fuss now? What, you're gonna lose the next election and suddenly you think it's due to me?'

'I'm not worried about the next election.'

'You bloody well *should* be.'

But even that bounced off him. 'You're on your own from here on in, that's all I'm saying. No more cashing in on my position. If I hear that you're telling people you have my special confidence, then I'm going to contact them myself and tell them that I give you no backing whatsoever.' He tapped the documents. 'Mum and Dad—they always asked me not to stand in your way. So as a favour to them, I didn't. But they're both gone, finally, so enough.'

'Sounds like you couldn't wait for them to die.'

'That's a disgraceful accusation.'

'Christ, everything is a disgraceful accusation to you, Bernard.'

'It is when it's not true.'

'Nothing is ever true, either, when it comes to you. You even tried to deny it that time I caught you wanking in the back shed. Dick in your fucking hand.'

A dead smile broke out on his face, and from there I probably would have received the usual lecture about responsibility and hard work and so on, and that would have been that. We were family, we'd argued like this for decades. But whatever he might have replied, he never got the chance, because right then the doors burst open and security personnel flooded the room. Bernard stared in angry surprise, and then a man was whispering in his ear. I hadn't moved, and was amazed to see my brother's eyes go wide with shock.

'It can't be for real,' he said.

The man shrugged. 'That's what we have to find out.'

Bernard struggled to regather himself. 'Leo, you'll have to go.'

I rose, our argument forgotten. Was he actually scared? 'A problem?'

He only shook his head, distracted.

The security men had me outside before I could say anything else. The Lodge seemed to be exploding into life. Phones were ringing everywhere, and personnel were dashing back and forth. My limousine and driver were waiting, and I was bundled inside. As we roared up the drive I was astonished to see an army truck pulling up at the front gate—loaded with soldiers.

Then we were back on Adelaide Avenue and racing towards the circle again. Away from the residence, the rest of Canberra seemed as quiet as ever. The giant Australian flag flapped high above Parliament House, and orange lights glittered in the still waters of the lake.

Minutes later, I was back in my hotel room, sobered and bewildered.

Must be something serious, I decided.

But it wouldn't be until next morning that I found out just *how* serious. That's when my brother went on TV to address the nation.

FOUR

I don't remember much about how Cyclone Yusuf ended. My abductors didn't exactly beat me unconscious, but by the time they threw me into the postal van I was bruised and bloodied and dazed, with my hands tied. Two of the men climbed into the back with me, while the third got behind the wheel. From there we drove for a time, the rain and wind buffeting the vehicle while the driver swore ceaselessly. They were *all* swearing— unnerved and furious about the decapitation. But I don't recall anything particular they said. Only their desperation, and their eyes watching me hatefully from under dripping wet hair, as the van rocked and swayed.

It might have been about an hour that we drove, and I don't know in what direction, or where we finished up. My resort was north of Bundaberg, so if you want to know (you hear me, interrogators?) look at the map and work out the possible locations yourselves. A bunch of shitty little towns is all you'll find, somewhere between Gladstone and Gympie.

One thing I can tell you, I sobered up a lot in that hour and, even knocked silly as I was, started to get scared. These guys were obviously terrorists of some sort, and I knew as well as anyone the unhappy fate of hostages in this day and age. I had no desire to be blindfolded, dressed up in orange and ritually beheaded. (But lord, how weird was that flying piece of tin!) And yet, right from the start, I could tell there was something strange about my captors. For one thing, they were very young. Not much more than boys really. But much stranger, they didn't look at all Arabic or Asian, nor did they speak with any sort of accents. They looked like typical anglo-Aussies to me. Of course, if they *had* looked or sounded Islamic, then they wouldn't have been there in the first place. They'd have been safely detained in the ghettos, along with all the rest.

And they hadn't blindfolded me. That was either a very dire sign for me, or it was a sign of incompetence on their part. And I suspected the latter. Honestly, what sort of half-arsed caper was this anyway? To grab the Prime Minister's brother in the middle of a frigging cyclone? I'll admit that the postal van was cute, it normally would have blended in quite anonymously, but when you're the only vehicle on the road during the mother of all storms, you're going to look suspicious, mail or no mail. But then again, who else would be on the roads to see them? Not only would there be no traffic, none of the usual roadblocks or checkpoints would be manned either. When better, then, to kidnap someone? Perhaps my captors were actually masterminds. But somehow it didn't feel that way to me.

Indeed, when we finally stopped there was more confusion. One of my guards popped open the back door, but then his companion was yelling at him and slamming it shut again.

'Dickhead! You want him to see the house?'

So they'd wised up at last. *Then* they whacked a bag over my head. The doors opened again, and I was manhandled across some sort of muddy yard. The rain was still pelting down, and the wind was blowing, but the deeper violence was gone from it now. Either the cyclone was in decline, or we'd driven some distance inland; I couldn't say which. They dragged me up a

short flight of stairs, and we were indoors. The floor was wooden.
For a moment, anyway, then it was down a longer flight of stairs
and onto dirt. They dumped me there, then I heard them clump
away up the stairs, still muttering and swearing, and leaving
me, apparently, alone.

I lay motionless for a while, catching my breath. The bag
was a loose cotton thing, and not tight. After a few minutes
of listening—footsteps and voices from above, but nothing
nearby—I decided it was just me in there. My hands were still
tied behind me, but by dragging my head across the ground
and then shaking it wildly (and painfully) I managed to get
the bag off. I was in a basement, or maybe a storage cellar,
small and dim. The walls were made of concrete blocks, the
floor was raw earth, and a single bulb hung down from the
ceiling. There was no furniture, no decoration, only a staircase
climbing to what looked like a very solid door. I assumed it
was locked fast. My abductors might be rattled, but that stupid
they couldn't be.

I lay there, breathing.

Kidnapped.

It's such a sign of the times that it's almost a cliché, and yet
of course you never think it could actually happen to *you*. And
there's no need here to get into the terrors and doubts I felt in
those moments. (We all know I didn't end up dead, right? Not
then, at least.) Either way, I could think of nothing that might
help me, no clever escape plan. Getting the bag off my head was
one thing, but my hands were tied hard, and no amount of
wriggling made a difference.

I waited. Staring. Listening.

A long time seemed to pass. Above me, the footsteps and
murmured voices went on. At some stage I heard doors slamming,
and then a new round of arguments broke out, quite fierce.
I gazed at the ceiling and could discern, to my surprise, the shrill
voice of a woman rising angrily above the rest. Then everything
fell quiet again.

And after that, believe it or not, I must have fallen asleep.

Maybe it was the drugs and alcohol still in my system. Maybe it was shock. Or maybe it was that deeply ingrained human thing that refuses to believe something this bad could really be happening, so let's close our eyes and wake up when it's all over.

But when I woke up it wasn't over. I was still in the basement, and things had become strange indeed. A chair had been brought down to my prison, and seated upon it was a woman dressed in a black, full-length burqa—nothing of her visible at all except a pair of eyes staring out from a narrow slit in her veil.

I blinked at her in disbelief.

She said, 'You are being held by forces of the Great Southern Jihad.'

Christ. Well, I'd suspected all along that these people were Islamic terrorists, and that name, and the burqa, only confirmed it. Still, she didn't sound at all foreign. Her accent was sharply Australian. And there was something about her eyes. They were a very pale blue, and the skin around them was powder white, almost albino-looking. Certainly not Middle Eastern.

Odd, too, for Islamic extremists to send a woman to guard me.

She might have been reading my mind. 'I'm in command here.'

I struggled for a futile moment against the ropes, then lapsed again. 'That doesn't make any sense at all,' I croaked, my throat very dry.

The freakishly white eyebrows lifted. 'You don't think so?'

'Men are in charge with you lot, not women.'

'The men do what I say.'

'Tell them to let me go then.'

She didn't reply, only watched me. Burqa or not, I could sense that she was tall, even when seated, and slender too.

'You're thinking about my body, aren't you?' she said. Her tone was convinced and utterly humourless. *She's mad*—that was my first real thought about her. 'You're wondering if I'm naked underneath, and what my breasts look like.'

Oh dear . . . Barking mad.

'What do you people want with me?' I asked.

'*I* didn't want you at all.'

'What's that supposed to mean?'

She shifted in her seat, leaning back and crossing her legs, a position that looked incongruous in the burqa. I could see now that she was wearing black leather boots, long ones that disappeared up into her robes. That was incongruous too.

'I was away,' she said. 'Those idiots upstairs did this on their own. Without any instructions from me. They were supposed to be lying low for the time being, but they got wind that the Prime Minister's brother was staying nearby, all alone at his empty resort, and then with this cyclone clearing the roads . . . Well, you know the rest. It's very annoying. I had other plans for the postal van and the uniforms.'

'So like I said, let me go.'

'You're certainly a problem to me, I'll admit that.' But there wasn't any hint of impending freedom in her statement. There was only an implication that some problems can simply be disposed of, not solved.

'I don't get it,' I said. 'You can't be an Islamic group. They're all locked up. They got all of you.'

She shook her head. 'No one knows we even exist.'

'But you *are* Muslims?'

'We are. We're warriors for Allah.'

'Warriors? You lot?'

She leant forward again, those pale eyes flaring. 'Don't think we won't kill you. We've killed before. Our hands are red with blood.'

'What use am I to you dead? I assume your men grabbed me so they could bargain with my brother. He'll want me alive. And unharmed.'

'Your brother hates you. My men might not know that, but I do.'

And that really did scare me, because it was perfectly true, but I'd been praying that no one else was aware of the fact.

I swallowed drily. 'I could use some water, you know.'

She considered. 'Yes . . . I don't think we need to make any decisions right this minute, and in the meantime we may as well let you live.' She called out, and I heard the door at the top of the steps open. 'Bring him some food and water!'

There was a bustle from the upper floor, and then my original three abductors trooped down the stairs carrying bottles of water and sandwiches and guns. They all looked even younger, suddenly, and abashed, avoiding their leader's glance.

'Untie him,' she instructed, 'but keep a gun on him.'

'What about the hood?' one of them asked.

'Forget it. He's already seen your stupid faces.'

The boy nodded, going red. In minutes the ropes were off, and I was gulping water gratefully. (The hangover had settled in now, well and truly.) I was sitting against one wall, and the gang watched me from the other side of the room. Three nervous boys with guns pointed my way.

'They're certainly a fine-looking team,' I said to the woman.

'They've made a mistake,' she corrected. 'But don't judge us by these three here. Or by their deceased brother back at the resort. We are a deadly organisation, and we have powerful friends. The most powerful in the world.'

'Oh, right.' I was shaken in all sorts of ways, but I couldn't just lie down and accept this stuff unchallenged. 'You're the local al-Qaeda chapter, I suppose.'

'Something like that.'

'And you talk to bin Laden's ghost.'

'Maybe.'

And I could swear she was smiling at me now.

'You're fucking crazy,' I said.

That was too much for the boys. They muttered in fury, and one of them advanced across the room, his gun aimed.

'Leave him be,' the woman snapped. She rose from the chair, and stretched, arms above her head, as if she'd gone stiff from sitting. And it was the weirdest thing, but for a moment the burqa draped closely about her in a way that I'd thought burqas were never supposed to, showing off far too many curves, and damned if it didn't seem that she really *was* naked underneath, apart from those leather boots that appeared to go right up past her knees. And her men weren't watching me anymore. They were watching her. Hopelessly. Desperately.

Her arms came down, and she was covered in shapeless black again. 'You'll see how sane we are, soon enough.'

'Sure,' I said, throwing out my last barb. 'You and your three little friends. You're the great destroyers.'

Her voice went low. 'We are.'

And she was leaving now, sailing serenely towards the stairs.

'For a start—we're the ones who nuked Canberra.'

FIVE

Poor old Canberra.

How did that joke go, afterwards?

What if they blew up the capital city, and nobody noticed?

Well, it wasn't quite like that. And I was there, remember.

I woke up in my hotel room, after the night with my brother, to the sounds of yelling and hurried movements throughout the building. I switched on the TV and there it was, blazing across the news on every channel. An Islamic terrorist group, who gave no name, claimed to have planted an explosive thermonuclear device somewhere in Canberra. More than just 'claimed'. They had sent photos of the bomb, and blueprints of it, to the Federal Police and to all the media, just so people knew it was for real. And it was set to detonate seventy-two hours after the first warning.

I hardly need describe the bedlam that ensued.

Mind you, it struck me at the time how forbearing the terrorists were being. Why give the three-day alert? Why not just nuke the place and be done with it? They weren't even making any demands, like the release of al-Qaeda prisoners or the withdrawal of troops from the Middle East. It was just the blunt warning— in three days we press the button. Strange. And there were certainly plenty of people who thought the whole thing was a bluff. But while the police and the army searched madly for the bomb, and my brother made defiant speeches about not being cowed by terrorist threats, there was no choice but to evacuate the town.

And the thing was, three days was plenty of time. I don't mean that there wasn't panic in the streets, but if ever a city was made to be abandoned quickly, it was Canberra. (That was another of the jokes, even on the first morning.) A mere three hundred thousand people, spread across sprawling, spacious suburbs, surrounded by wide empty freeways and native bushland. And for all that the city was almost a hundred years old, it wasn't really a place that many residents had a *history* in. Primarily, it was only ever a garrison town for the public service, and like troops decamping from a military compound, people loaded up and got out fast.

So overall, the evacuation was surprisingly orderly. I made my own escape late on the first night, crawling patiently along in my car amidst tens of thousands of other vehicles, all of them jammed with people and property. There were only three routes to choose from: north-east along the Federal Highway to Sydney, south-west along the Hume to Melbourne, or dead south into the hills, along the Monaro. I opted for Sydney, where, by decree, every hotel room and dormitory had been thrown open, free of charge. And as I crept along in first gear, I watched an unbroken stream of commandeered trucks passing by in the opposite lanes. They were heading *into* Canberra, destined for the National Gallery, or for the National Museum, or for various government archives, or for any other such place where the national treaures and records might be in need of rescuing.

Staring at those trucks, a dark part of me found the whole thing hilarious. Paintings by dead artists, relics of dead racehorses, old bats belonging to dead cricketers. How bizarre are the things we value? And once we'd saved the family jewels, well, sure—blow up Canberra by all means. I didn't mind. It was such an *inconvenient* place. Off in the middle of nowhere. Stinking hot in summer. Freezing in winter. And totally soulless, all year round. Still, there were one or two decent restaurants I would miss, and what would happen to the nation's sex industry, once the mail order warehouses and porn studios of Fyshwick had been vaporised? That, at least, was a grim business.

Either way, after forty-eight hours of the most frenzied activity imaginable, Canberra was stripped of virtually everything that mattered. By then, it was populated purely by soldiers and police, some still searching for the bomb, but most of them sweeping through the suburbs, house by house, to make sure everyone was gone. The last evacuee left Canberra just fourteen hours before the deadline. And who do you think that person was? It was my brother, of course.

The footage is famous. The Prime Minister waiting bravely until all his subjects have reached safety ahead of him, and then the farewell from the grassy lawn atop Parliament House. The solemn lowering of the flag, the final salute, the official party wafting away by helicopter, eastwards, fading into the ironic sunrise as hope and beauty die. Not a dry eye on the house. My brother—forever after to be known as Bernard 'Last Man Out' James.

What bullshit. They left a cameraman behind to film that chopper flying away, for one thing. So maybe *he* was the last man out. Or most likely it was some anonymous soldier, performing a final sweep. And no doubt there were a few crazy loners who never left at all, hidden away cleverly from the evacuation teams—those who either refused to believe there really was a bomb, or those who were bent on looting until the last possible minute, or those who simply decided to martyr themselves in the fireball. Whoever the last man out was, it wasn't the Prime Minister.

Anyway, with an hour to go the army had pulled back to a fifty-kilometre radius from the city centre. Nine p.m. was zero hour. The highways were barricaded, the airspace over the town had been cleared. There was nothing to do now but wait and watch. I was safely ensconced in a Sydney bar by this stage, drinking up big for the occasion, eyes glued to the TV screens. Camera crews were filming from vantage points near Yass, a half-hour's drive north of the capital. It was, without question, the most highly rated moment in television history—throughout the world, not just here in Australia. A live nuclear explosion was news, even if it was in some unheard-of little city far away down-under. The only frustration was that nothing of the actual town could be seen. From fifty k out there was little visible but hills and sheep paddocks and scrub.

The explosion wasn't bad though. It went off five minutes late, no doubt for the sake of good drama, and then the night sky lit up, white and stark and shocking. (The bar around me went dead silent.) For a moment after that there was only darkness, but then the cloud rose majestically over the hills. I'm told that to observers on the fifty-k limit, the fireball was in fact disappointingly small. They were just too far away. But for those of us in that bar, and for the billions of viewers around the globe, the television cameras zoomed in and it was an awesome sight, boiling and evil, and an indisputable sign that the world had changed forever, yet again.

It sure as hell changed Australia. True, we'd been fighting the war on terror for years, and we already had some of the toughest security laws in the world, but this was Armageddon on a whole new level. And for Bernard in particular, it was his finest hour. He was unpopular, dull, and as lame-duck as they came. But when the crisis was actually upon him, he stood forth and calmly took control. The state of emergency, for instance—suspending all normal due process and individual freedoms, and replacing them with martial law—that was his idea. So was the decree that effectively outlawed Islam, and began the process of rounding up all believers into the camps and the cultural precincts. Parliament, grateful and impressed, further empowered him to act unilaterally for the duration of the crisis, without reference to either of the Houses, and without having to call the election that was soon due. Stability was needed now, not a panicked country milling about the polls.

I ask you. Could the little bastard have been any luckier? A month after the bomb, his approval rating was at seventy-five per cent!

Of course, the state of emergency was only supposed to last until things settled down again. But here we are, two years later, and it's still in force. My brother remains in command, the election remains on hold, and nothing has settled down at all. It's like Canberra was only the starting gun—just look at the endless spate of terrorist attacks we've witnessed ever since. Car bombings. Assaults on oil depots, and the communication networks, and sporting crowds. Not to mention all the kidnappings and assassinations of public figures. The Deputy Prime Minister—captured and beheaded, and the video screened across the nation. Then it was the Governor-General—shot. Then it was the Leader of the Opposition—blown up. Then it was a High Court judge—beheaded. Then it was a state Commissioner of Police—beheaded again. The list goes on and on.

And the security responses just keep getting tougher. All these laws and decrees. The massive enlargement of the Federal Police, and of ASIO, and of the armed forces. The mushrooming of roadblocks and security checkpoints throughout the streets. The issuing of identity cards to all citizens, along with loyalty oaths. All the new prisons. All the new ghettos. All the new wars we've declared.

Nothing is the same.

And yet, do you know what strikes me as weirdest about it all?

It's this. For a country whose capital has ceased to exist, we've carried on with remarkably little civil inconvenience. Not a soul died in Canberra—that anyone knows of, at least. Our national treasures are all safe. The government departments have established themselves happily in Sydney or Melbourne, right where they would've always preferred to be. And Parliament? Well, there it was in Melbourne, just two weeks after the bomb, making itself at home, appropriately, in the Royal Exhibition Building where it first sat back in 1901.

My brother, meanwhile, moved straight into Kirribilli House, and announced that it was now the official Prime Ministerial residence. Which was not to suggest that Sydney was therefore to be the new capital city. Nor, indeed, was it to be Melbourne. Quite simply, there *is* no new capital city—a solution which neatly avoids the kind of pointless argument that led to Canberra being built in the first place. And the fact that Parliament and the Prime Minister are now situated a thousand kilometres apart doesn't seem to matter much to anyone. My brother has increasingly little to do with Parliament anyway. The truth is, since the state of emergency legislation was passed, he's had no need of Parliament at all.

So the administration of the country sails on—the assassinations aside—and for all the outrage and fury and breast-beating and avowals of revenge, it seems to me that Canberra is genuinely mourned by very few. Only a small amount of footage has ever been shown of the ruins—the pictures, shot from the air, are considered bad for morale—but the destruction looks rather final. There, for all to see, is the bent and mangled flagpole over the scorched lump of Parliament House. There's the High Court building collapsed into rubble. There are the black poisoned waters of Lake Burley Griffin, from which the Captain Cook fountain will never rise again.

The bomb, we're told by experts, was situated in the suburb of Yarralumla, only a kilometre from the city centre. Why it wasn't found by the searchers, no one can say. How the terrorists built it, or from where stole it, no one can say either—although man hunts continue to this day all around the world. In any case, the device was apparently in the order of three to four megatons, over a hundred times that of Hiroshima or Nagasaki. And worse, it was particularly dirty in terms of radiation. Canberra, we are informed, will glow in the dark for decades to come.

So there has never been any talk of rebuilding. Instead, the ruins have been declared a national shrine, to be left untouched in terrible desolation forever, a memorial. Roadblocks and fences have been built all the way around the city in a huge circle, so that no wanderer or ghoulish tourist can ever defile the ruins. Just to make sure, the army now patrols the perimeter, working from their giant new base at Yass—the base itself being a symbol, according to the military chiefs, that Australia will never be defeated. Why, the very airspace above the city has become a forbidden zone. It's on the direct flight path between Sydney and Melbourne, true enough, but planes are diverted far around it, so that even from ten thousand metres passengers will be spared the horrible vision.

You see what I mean? We've cut poor old Canberra out of our lives like it never existed. I suppose that once you take the people out of a city, it just becomes a collection of buildings with no purpose or value. But to be simply erased—could there be a worse fate for a town?

And there was me, a prisoner now of the group responsible.

SIX

I don't know how long I was down in the cellar. It must have been a couple of days at least. They treated me well enough— gave me food and water and a bucket to shit in. But I didn't see the burqa woman again for some time. It was just the boys, still angry and waving their guns around in embarrassment. Or was it sexual frustration? I know that these holy war types get the seventy virgins and all that when they die, but in the meantime— well, surely holy warriors don't play with their dicks. No doubt all the poor bastards had to keep them going at night were dreams about pale eyes in a veil, and fantasies about leather boots that went up Christ only knew how far.

I did try to talk with them occasionally, but aside from frowns and the odd kick, they ignored me. So no, I can't tell you a thing about them, interrogators. Not their names, not their backgrounds, nothing. You could ask them yourselves, except that of course all three of them are dead and with the virgins now. Good luck to them, too.

By my guess it was about the third day when the burqa floated down the stairs again. And for me it had been three days of fairly intense thought. Could any of it be true? It was one thing to imagine these guys as some lunatic little terrorist cell. But part of a group with the clout to mastermind a nuclear bomb? That was something else. True, the specific terrorists who blew up Canberra had never been found or identified. But my mind baulked at believing it was this lot.

And, I won't deny it, I was thinking about those boots too.

Then there she was, sitting on the chair in front of me again. Her three lovesick henchmen lined up behind her, sweaty guns all erect and at the ready.

'Have a name, do you?' I asked.

She said nothing, a black ghost with white eyes.

And it was hard to meet those eyes. I babbled somewhat. 'You ever take that thing off? I mean, I've already seen the others' faces, so what does it matter? Or is it a religious thing? You're not allowed to be seen by males or something?'

'No one here is allowed to see me.' That voice—so cold. She might have been a priestess invoking a ritual sacrifice. Then she shrugged, practical. 'It's not a religious thing. We're Muslims, but we're not in the Middle Ages. It's a security measure. The men in this cell have never seen my face. That way, even if they're caught, there's no way they can identify me.'

Ah. No wonder they were scared to death of her.

She watched me. 'We've decided what to do with you.'

'Who has?'

'Me. And my superiors.'

'So you're not the boss of all this?'

'Oh no.' Once more, it sounded like she was smiling. And you know, people have got it wrong. A burqa doesn't stop a man lusting after a woman, if that's what the burqa is supposed to do. No—instead it drives a man mad wondering what the hell is under there, so after a while you're just *itching* to yank the damn thing off and see. But maybe that was the whole idea. Maybe we didn't understand the Muslim world at all. Maybe it was all about sex for them too.

'No,' she repeated, as I imagined lips as white and severe as her eyes, 'I have people above me.'

'And who are they?'

'I couldn't tell you their names, even if I wanted to. But they're rather concerned about your capture. It wasn't planned, as I said. And they don't like things that aren't planned. Especially now. These are very delicate times.'

'Why delicate?'

She didn't answer.

'Did you guys really nuke Canberra?'

'You don't believe me?'

'It's kinda hard.'

'Why? It happened. Someone did it. Why not us?'

'Where the hell did you get the bomb from?'

'Somewhere. A place we can get more, if we want.'

'And how did you get it into the country?'

'In a shipping container.'

'Bullshit. They have detectors for that sort of thing. They have screenings.'

'No one screened this container. From there it was put into a van and driven to Canberra. It was hidden in a house.'

'That's way too simple. It couldn't have worked.'

'Obviously it did.'

'Why give the three-day warning then? Your sort have never cared about killing people before. You didn't even make any ransom demands. So why risk it being discovered in those three days? Why not just detonate it?'

For the first time since meeting her, I saw the certainty in her eyes go cloudy, the blue fading out of focus. 'That wasn't my decision.'

'So you *wanted* to kill three hundred thousand people?'

No response.

And it suddenly struck me that her willingness to tell me this—to tell me everything—was a very poor sign indeed for my long-term survival.

I was all out of conversation. 'What are you going to do with me?'

She stood up. 'We're taking you for a drive.' She nodded to one of the men, and he produced a familiar-looking hood, and some ropes.

A drive? Fuck. I knew what that meant. I should have struggled, I suppose. But there were three of them, and they already didn't like me much. No doubt they'd have killed me there and then, given any sort of excuse. And maybe a drive didn't have to mean death. You never knew. I was the Prime Minister's brother. Surely I had some use to them alive.

They tied me up and put the hood over my head. Then it was back outside to the van. My senses were heightened now, in the way they are when you think you're about to die, drinking in every last moment. It was very quiet. No sound of traffic or people nearby, only a bird singing sweetly (at that stage, a crow would have sounded sweet) and, somehow most heart-rendingly of all, the clock of an axe against wood, somewhere far off. And it was hot. I could feel the sun on me, the rain and the cyclone long gone, although there was still the smell of mud about. And damp grass, and gum trees steaming, and old manure. If you want my guess, they'd held me in some sort of farmhouse, one of those little properties in the tangled Queensland hinterland. With hippies and gun nuts and bitter old dairy farmers for neighbours, all of whom would diligently mind their own bloody business. I didn't even bother yelling for help.

They threw me in the back, and we were on our way. It sounded like all four of them were there, the driver up front, and the woman and the other two guards with me in the rear. I wondered a moment—why wasn't she sitting up forward? But then I realised. A burqa in the front seat of a postal van? Nothing suspicious about *that*.

Still, they couldn't be planning to take me far. With the cyclone gone, the roadblocks would be back in force, and even an Australia Post van couldn't rely on getting through them without being searched. Sure, there were always the back roads, but it would

be impossible to get near a town of any size without identity
checks and vehicle inspections. Then again, if their aim was
merely to find the first bit of dense bush in which to dump a
body, what did it matter?

We drove, and I dwelt upon the shabby facts of my life.

Was I a good man? Not really. I couldn't think of a single
thing, right then, that I'd done for someone else's sake. And my
ex-wives, and my daughters—well, I knew what they would say.
A successful man? Hardly. Oh, I'd always scraped out a living.
I always had money. Lots of it, at times, from a dozen different
careers. But none of those careers were what you would call
honourable, and three quarters of them were only a step above
outright fraud. A shark-like existence, that's what it had been,
always in motion, always hungry. So...a man who would be
mourned by his friends? Ha. What friends would that be?

But it was the only life I had, *my* life, and there had been
some fine wine in there, and good food, and the sun on beaches,
and bright lights in casinos, and even some wild nights of fucking
that I would never forget.

And oh boy, I did not want to die.

'You don't need to kill me,' I said, trying not to actually beg,
but feeling very low. 'If you let me go, I wouldn't tell anybody.'

The woman answered. 'That's the problem with you faithless
people. When your time comes, you can't even face it with dignity.'

An insane thought came that maybe, if I promised to convert
to Islam, then they would let me live. But it seems that even in
terror, my hypocrisy stretches only so far. I could feel my mind
going a deathly blank colour. And tears were close.

Then all calamity broke loose.

The van was screeching to a halt and we were all flying about
the cabin, the air filled with yelling. For a moment I was sure
my head was up against a female breast. Then there was a
booming, tinny voice outside. Someone on a megaphone. More
yelling, from inside the van and out. And then shooting. Lots
of it. Metal ripping. Thuds. Shrieks. The name of Allah, taken
in vain.

An explosion like a grenade. Then silence.

I lay there, wide-eyed and panting. And not, by the feel of it, riddled with bullets. The back door of the van was torn open and I was dragged out. Hands fumbled at my ropes and lifted the hood from my head. Sunlight dazzled me. I saw a narrow country road. Scrub all around. The postal van, parked askew, bullet holes in the side, two of its tyres deflated. Dead bodies, male, my young abductors, one sprawled half out of the driver's seat, the other two contorted in the back. The smell of shit and piss. A car blocking the road in front of the van. Another behind it. Gas drifting from a canister in the gutter...

This was no normal roadblock. This was an ambush— I recognised it even then. And uniformed men were everywhere. Federal Police. Such a wonderful, wonderful sight.

A man was shaking my shoulders.

'Leo James,' he said.

'Yes.'

'Federal Agent Spencer, sir. Glad we weren't too late.'

And above it all, the sound of a female voice I knew, screaming.

SEVEN

The Australian Federal Police.

You know, I can remember a time when they must have numbered less than a thousand. You hardly noticed them, outside the Capital Territory. Now—between the massive recruitment since Canberra, and the subsumption of all the state police forces into one body—there's over eighty thousand in the AFP. Backed up by the all-powerful state of emergency laws, and answerable to only one man. The Minister for Freedom. Who happens, of course, to be the Prime Minister.

Some cynical folk call them Bernard's private army. His black shirts.

Right at that moment, ambush complete, I called them my saviours.

Indeed, the commander of the rescue squad, Federal Agent Spencer, looked every inch like one of the new breed. He couldn't have been more than thirty. Clean-cut to the point that you could nick yourself on his jaw, taut, compact and fit, resplendent in his blue combat fatigues, and smelling impressively of gunpowder, aftershave and adrenaline sweat.

I smelt somewhat less pleasant, hunched by the roadside after an attack of vomiting, trying to get my breath back. Agent Spencer crouched casually beside me, sympathetic, patient, and smiling at his men as they cleaned up the aftermath.

'Thank you,' I managed to say eventually.

He tipped a finger to his cap. 'No worries, sir.'

It was a glorious, sunny day. Not a cloud in the sky, and everything a riot of green. But I couldn't really see much of the surrounds, for the ambush had taken place where the road passed through a cutting, heavily overgrown. Now there were about a dozen agents busy on the scene. An unmarked van had driven up, and my erstwhile abductors were being tagged and body-bagged and loaded into the back of it. The burqa woman had stopped screaming. For the moment they had her locked in the disabled postal van. From time to time a thump and a shriek came from inside, but nothing else.

I waved an unsteady hand at it all. 'How did you know?'

Agent Spencer was chewing a stalk of grass. 'Information received.'

'My security people, from the resort, right?' It suddenly seemed rather obvious to me. Help had been coming all along. 'They must have reported me missing. And of course, you would've found the body, in a postman's uniform . . .'

He glanced at me coolly. 'Your people at the resort reported you dead.'

'What?'

'Decapitated. During the cyclone.'

'That wasn't me! That was one of these bastards.'

A shrug. 'Hard to tell, with no head. They still haven't found it.'

'What about the uniform?'

'The body was just mincemeat, after the storm. Who's to say what it was wearing?'

'You really mean people think I'm dead?'

'They must. It was on the news.'

Jesus Christ. 'But you guys knew I wasn't, right?'

'It came to our attention.'

'And my brother. *He* knows, doesn't he?'

'Yes, sir. This operation took place under his direct orders.'

Well, what did you know! It seemed I owed Bernard one.

A yell went up from the other men, and laughter. They were lifting the last corpse. The young man had been shot through the neck—by something big enough to obliterate his spine—and his head lolled from his body by the merest shred of flesh. Even as they lifted him it dangled elastically for a moment, and then came away completely, rolled off a distance, and halted face down in the dirt. The agents laughed again, and one of them gave it a kick, sending it skidding across the road. Another man kicked it back towards the first, soccer style.

'Hey,' I said.

Agent Spencer watched on. 'What?'

'They shouldn't be doing that, should they?'

'Why would you care?'

'But you're the police!'

He spat the stalk of grass from his mouth. 'Right. And those men just saved your life, sir. They've been in the line of fire, for your sake.' Then he sighed, and raised his voice. 'All right you lot, time's important here. Get on with it.'

The men subsided, and the head was stuffed into a bag.

But questions still rattled around my mind. Three dead bodies, just like that. 'So, what, did you have these guys under surveillance or something?'

'These are security matters, sir. I can't discuss them.'

'But...look, they told me things. I think they were planning to kill me, so they didn't care what I knew. They're called the Great Southern Jihad.'

'You'll be fully debriefed, sir.'

'No, listen, they said they were the ones who nuked Canberra.'

He gave me a somewhat pitying look, then cleared his throat politely. 'I expect a lot of people say the same thing.'

'What?'

'Take it from me, sir. When it comes to terrorist groups and what they claim ... well, every man and his dog nuked Canberra.'

'Hey, seriously, they told me how they did it.'

His expression was setting firmly now. 'Sir, this is really none of your concern.'

'Not my—? They *kidnapped* me!'

'Yes, but we've resolved that situation.'

I stared at him.

'Ah,' he said, looking along the road.

A long, black car was approaching slowly. Time was, you saw very few black cars in Australia. Now they seem to be everywhere. With darkly tinted windows. Just like this one. It pulled up beside us, and Agent Spencer rose to greet it. A rear window rolled down, and looking out was an older man's face, expressionless behind sunglasses as mirrored as the windows.

'Status?' he inquired.

'Green, sir,' Agent Spencer replied.

'Excellent.' The sunglasses turned towards me briefly. 'And the package?'

'Undamaged.'

'Even better.'

The man in the car was American, his accent southern and lilting, almost slurred. He was dressed immaculately in a black suit, his countenance lean and lined, with a wave of grey hair. But the left side of his face did not seem to move. A stroke victim, perhaps. And one of our bosom allies, I assumed, from the CIA— or from some other such secret service.

'I'll inform the interested parties,' he told Agent Spencer. 'And the status of the target participants?'

'Three terminally degraded, sir. And one in detention.'

The man frowned, a distorted twist of half his lips. 'Oh?'

'It's the woman, actually.'

I glanced towards the postal van, and was alarmed to see a white face, bloodied and furious, staring out at us from the rear window.

'I understand,' the man in the car said, and he was looking

at the face too. His infirmity made him sound drunk in some genteel fashion. 'Well, you have your orders.'

'Yes, sir.'

'I'd like to borrow some of your men, if I may. We should sterilise the house.'

'Yes, sir. We're nearly done here.'

'Four should be enough.'

'I'll have them follow you.'

'Well done, agent.'

'Thank you, sir.'

The window rolled up, and the car pulled away. Agent Spencer turned to his men and barked a string of orders. Four of them climbed into a car, and drove off in pursuit. That left only six, and the whole area was looking different now. The smells of gas and gunpowder were gone, as were the bodies. Only the bloodstains remained, darkening slowly towards black.

'So who was that?' I asked Agent Spencer.

'Look, sir, you can ask all these questions when we get you home to base.'

'And where's that?'

'Classified, sir.'

'You can't even tell me where I'm going?'

But he seemed to have lost interest in me completely. He walked over to the postal van and opened the rear doors, looked in. 'Get her out,' he told his men.

Two of them reached in and dragged the woman forth. They'd already removed her burqa, and it turned out that underneath she was simply wearing black jeans and a red T-shirt. And the boots, after all, only went up to her knees.

Still, she came out like a wildcat, kicking and cursing, a whirl of long limbs and tangled white hair. I don't think she was an actual albino, she was just one of the palest people I had ever seen. Eventually the agents got her upright between them, and she stood there, glaring at us. And Christ, she really wasn't much more than a girl. A tall, wild girl, with a livid bruise on her forehead and blood on her hands and arms.

'Fucking cunts,' she breathed to us all.

Agent Spencer was unperturbed. 'Was she armed?' he asked his men.

'Two handguns, loaded,' one replied, 'and a knife.'

'There might be more. Strip her.'

Another struggled followed, and it took four of them to do it. I looked away. I know that she had planned to kill me, but still, I didn't need to see this.

'There's nothing else,' I heard one of the agents say.

'Cavities too,' Agent Spencer ordered.

Screams ensued, female, then the sounds of blows, and laughter from the men.

Then, 'She's clean, sir.'

'Okay.' His voice became formal. 'Your name is Nancy Campbell?'

'Fuck you!' she yelled back.

And despite everything I thought—Nancy Campbell? Her name was Nancy? I'd been kidnapped by a terrorist named Nancy? You had to be *kidding*.

'Also known as Aisha Fatima Islam?'

Well, that was more like it...

'You have no fucking right!' she raged.

Agent Spencer paid no attention. 'Nancy Campbell, you are charged with consorting with a known terrorist organisation, and of conspiring to, and committing, criminal acts against the people and government of Australia. How do you plead?'

'Not guilty, shithead!'

'You have been found guilty as charged. Under the authority of State of Emergency Decree 44, I am empowered to impose sentence and implement same. The sentence is death by execution, to be carried out forthwith.'

I spun around.

Nancy Campbell (and I was still struggling to believe that was really her name) hung naked and exhausted between the two agents. Her nose was bleeding, and her white body looked defenceless amongst all those uniformed men.

I said, 'You're gonna kill her?'

Agent Spencer was as collected as ever. 'It's the law.'

'But right here, right now?'

'She's a killer herself.'

'But surely you've got to interview her. Interrogate her. Find out what she knows, and who she works with. I told you, these guys did Canberra!'

'We already know all we need to about her. And her group.'

One agent was tying her hands while two of his colleagues held her. The other three men had formed a line and were checking their weapons.

I couldn't believe it. 'But you can't just gun her down!'

'Shut up, Mr James.'

'You think you can just do this? I'll tell my brother about it, believe me. And not only him—I'll tell anyone who'll listen.'

It was like lightning. Agent Spencer's arm shot out from his side, and suddenly the barrel of a pistol was hard against my temple. 'I'll tell you one last time, sir. Shut up.'

'You wouldn't dare.'

'Mr James, let me explain. As far as anyone in the outside world knows, you're already dead. I can make that a reality, very quickly. Now, your brother has indicated that he would prefer you alive. But he only said *prefer*. Because, frankly, you're more of a problem than anyone needs right now. And the main condition of your continued survival is that you forget everything that has happened to you in the past few days. That you forget everything you have seen here. And that you never mention a word of it to anyone else. All of this will be made abundantly clear to you during your debriefing, and trust me, you will not be released until you have fully agreed. But for the moment...shut...the fuck...up.'

I gaped. And said nothing.

Agent Spencer lowered his gun. 'Right,' he said to his team, 'step clear of her.'

The men holding the woman shoved her to her knees and moved away to either side. She knelt there on the road, pathetic, hands behind her back, nose still bleeding. But she was taking her impending death better than I had.

'Pray to Allah, girl, if you want,' Agent Spencer said.

She spat out blood. 'I hope your dicks rot off.'

'Squad, take aim.'

I looked away again.

Shots spluttered out, even though no one had said 'fire'. Then there was screaming, male this time, and more shots. Something exploded and I was thrown to the ground. Looking up, I caught a glimpse of figures leaping down from the top of the cutting. Federal agents were falling, bloodied and agonised, and smoke was billowing into the air.

Fuck, I thought, in a kind of weary amazement, three times in as many days.

Here I go again.

EIGHT

I really wasn't born for such excitement.

Me, a child of the placid 1950s.

Mind you, in my youth, we did have the cold war. And looking back, that really *was* a war. Two monolithic powers, evenly matched, slugging it out for control of the whole world...or at least the mutual destruction of it. It was a different scenario from today, believe me. The Russians were something to truly fear, an enemy who actually had the capability to win. Who would have thought that, sixty years later, the evil empire would be long forgotten, but we'd all end up twice as terrified of nothing more than a few thousand stateless terrorists? Or that, in the name of eradicating them, we'd be fighting a dozen different shitty little wars across the globe? Stalin would have been thrilled to cause half as much alarm, and he had a fully equipped army five million strong behind him.

I'm sure that my parents, securely enclosed in the great swathe of white middle-class Australia, and fighting the good fight against the red peril, had no idea what oddities the future held.

We had the house in suburbia, we had the picket fence, we even had Mum waiting on the couch with a cocktail for Dad to come home from work. We were proof that democracy worked, and we knew that, once the Russians finally admitted defeat, all would be right with the world.

What on earth did Islam mean to any of us?

This was Melbourne. We lived in Camberwell. Leafy streets, green lawns, and a 'dry' zone. Not even a pub in sight to disturb the peace, let alone a mosque. (In fact, last time I visited the suburb nothing much had changed, the odd AFP checkpoint notwithstanding. When Camberwell gets rowdy, well, that really will be the end of western civilisation as we know it.)

My father? He was a public servant, Department of Mines and Energy, upper middle grade. My mother didn't work, and Bernard and I were the only children. The good life was all ours, so much so that looking back it seems like a fairytale now. Actually, a rather boring fairytale, for very little of my earliest years seems to stand out in my memory. Playing in the backyard, watching TV, walking to primary school, holidays at the beach. Bernard was always there too, of course. Did we get along then? I don't recall hating him. But not really liking him either. He was my brother, he was just around all the time.

But as we grew older, to about age nine or ten, two things became clear. Bernard was more timid than I was—quieter, less adventurous, less daring. But on the other hand, he was far more stubborn than me. Say there was a gang of us kids throwing rocks at the windows of an empty factory over Collingwood way. I'd be in there amongst it, and when the windows were all broken I'd be the first to suggest we creep inside and see whatever secrets there were to see. But Bernard, if he was tagging along, would frown at the rock-throwing, and refuse point-blank to break and enter. Even when the rest of us mocked him and called him a girl and chanted other horrible things at him, he still refused. Shaking his head all the while and growing red in the face—but red with angry defiance, not embarrassment. He never ran away, or burst into tears, or backed down.

And it's not that he was simply law-abiding. He wasn't at all. He could be downright sneaky when it came to disobeying our parents. Stealing biscuits, or avoiding chores around the house, or cheating off my homework. But if the law-breaking was public and dangerous, then he wasn't interested. It was a matter of risk assessment, of investment versus return, of calculating the odds. In every other way he would grab whatever he could, legal or not—as long as he was certain of not getting caught. The other kids were completely baffled by him, but they caught on, eventually, to that stubbornness in him, and eventually gave way before it. He was never as popular as I was, but he was tolerated and respected in a grudging kind of way. A super-cautious little prick, everyone agreed, but certainly clever.

Me, I changed my mind about everything twenty times a day. And while I'd charge off on any caper that was going, well, as soon as it went wrong I'd hightail it out of there just as fast. And I had no problem whatever in backing down if the other kid was bigger and meaner than me, or worse, if it was the school principal. I'd throw in fulsome apologies too, as lengthy and inventive as they were insincere. Christ, it was only for a laugh, so what did it matter?

You can tell which one of us was destined to be PM, can't you?

Our education was private. We weren't at the best schools in town, but they were far from the worst. Church of England— sport, God, buggery and the Queen. Well, okay, no buggery, not in my case at least, and nor, as far as I know, in Bernard's. To be fair, not so much of God or the Queen either. And while neither of us were geniuses, we got by all right, academically. Me, I think, on native intelligence, breezing along without really trying, and Bernard more by rote learning and by an innate grasp of how to work the system. He was one of those kids who always pinned the teachers down on exactly what part of a lesson would be in exams and what wouldn't. One of those kids who always had a good excuse as to why he should get an extra two days to finish an essay. One of those kids who always demanded his test papers be reassessed, and who would fight over every half mark. A ready-made lawyer, one teacher called him. An annoying little twerp, said another, while wearily changing a C into a B minus.

No, by the time we were teenagers, I really didn't like my brother very much.

And we were going our separate ways already. I'd discovered girls, for instance. Not to mention all sorts of useful, entertaining things to do with erections. The underside of my mattress became the repository for a growing collection of racy paperback novels and stolen issues of the quaint, softly pornographic magazines of the day. Thankfully, Bernard and I had our own bedrooms by this stage, so what sort of stash he had I don't know. Perhaps he didn't have one at all because there was nothing under his mattress. On the other hand, he would never have hidden it somewhere so obvious. Indeed, as I've already mentioned, he did that kind of thing in the garden shed.

Real girls, meantime, while not actually taboo, were still dangerous and foreign things to boys from an all-male private school. The other lads and I hung out at milk bars and cinemas and studied them like novice game hunters amidst a pack of lions. It was a time of heavy-breathing trysts behind cricket sheds and the sheer trouser-straining ecstasy of touching female lips, arms, legs and (oh my God!) breasts. I was no Lothario, but I had my share. Bernard, however, took no part. He never lingered on his way home from school, he never snuck out at night, he never, as far as I saw, even spoke to a girl who wasn't either a relation or a family friend.

Shit, now that I think of it, his wife is the daughter of a friend of our mother's! They were set up, Bernard and Claire, by their respective maters, when they were both in their early thirties and apparently heading for eternal spinsterhood.

I was already over my first divorce by then.

Anyway, I don't think it was that the young Bernard didn't like girls. What seemed to bug him most about the rest of us horny teenage boys was the *disorder* that sex brought into our lives. The shrieks, the futile moans of passion, the furtive swapping of magazines under the desks. It was too wild, too likely to bring the authorities down upon our heads. And his attitude persisted even after we'd finished school and enrolled in uni. By then, he was free to do pretty much whatever he liked (it was the late sixties, for fuck's sake), but I still never saw him with a girlfriend. Oh, he had female acquaintances. Dour-looking girls from his economics tutorials, and stiff blue-blooded daughters from the Young Conservatives Society that he joined and later chaired. But a woman he was fucking? A woman who might ruin his life and cast shame upon the family name? No way.

But, man, let me repeat, the late sixties!

I was in my element. I moved straight out of home into a filthy share house in Carlton and took gleefully to drink, drugs and debauchery. I have to say that I never really bought into the philosophy of those times. I was never a hippie. I was never into incense, meditation or gurus. But I was certainly into free love and good times. Bernard could have his dreary business degree, I was a free-wheeling arts undergraduate, out to impress the chicks. I grew my hair long, packed myself into the tightest, widest-flared jeans available, stuck some anti-establishment badges on my denim jacket, and posed as a tall dark radical sex god. It was bullshit, mainly, and I failed utterly in my studies, while Bernard succeeded in his stolid way... But then Bernard hadn't even moved out of home.

That's right, he stayed with Mum and Dad for his entire university career. (I know that this is the done thing for kids now—but in those days, it was unheard of.) And we had rather different attitudes to our parents, Bernard and I. For all that I thought they were a little dull, I did have genuine affection for them. And they returned it, despite my evil ways. Indeed, from both of them I detected the merest whiff of envy for the way people my age had it so swell. A hint that my father, given a chance, might have liked some similar sort of fun in his day. And a wistful look in my mother's eye, as if she were considering other lives she might have lived, given the pill and permission to burn brassieres. But maybe I'm just making that up, maybe they just tolerated their wayward son for love's sake. Still, they were no arch conservatives, even though they voted for Menzies and Co all the way through.

In theory, they should have approved of Bernard more. He was the good son, the earnest son, the son with his eyes on the future. And yet I think they were dimly appalled by him, skulking quietly around their house. Surely parents want a *little* rebellion from their children. (I was always quite proud when my own various offspring told me to bugger off out of their lives. The misery of it aside.) And who knows, left to an empty nest, my mum and dad might have loosened up a bit and really *swung,* man. Other people their age were doing it, getting with the times. But with Bernard always frowning about the place, what chance did they have? He *did* see them as arch conservatives, and expected them to remain that way forever. They, and their generation, who fought the war and rode the boom and obeyed the rules, written and unwritten, who never complained or marched or caused trouble—they were his fixed inspiration.

So forgive me if I declare I was the better son. Sure, I didn't call, I hardly visited, they had to bail me out with money time and time again. Indeed, I was a shame to them in nearly every way. But ah, how their faces lit up when I entered the room! Bernard, I think, suspected all this, and resented it.

But then, he resented almost everything he saw. Nothing had changed since school really, and the same kids who had mocked him for not smashing windows were now long-haired layabouts mocking him for his neat hair and sensible clothes, for his sobriety and his work ethic, for being pro the Vietnam War and for his membership of a right-wing political society—they even mocked him for the virginal state of his dick. He suffered it all with his usual stubborn silence, but I knew he hated them for it, and hated everything about their lifestyle. To no one's surprise, when he finished his degree he joined an accountancy firm. Moreover, he joined the Liberal Party. And yet he *still* hadn't bothered to move out of home.

Me—after failing arts, I started an architecture degree, in which I managed to scrape passes for two years. Not out of any genuine interest, but it was better than conscription for Vietnam. Thankfully, the Whitlam government came along in 1972, and I could safely drop out of uni to take up intermittent pub work, or work waiting tables, or labouring, or whatever else looked like easy money for a while. I didn't have a clue about what I really wanted to do with my life. In fact, apart from my disastrous first marriage—childless, thank heavens—I don't think I took a damn thing seriously for the rest of the seventies.

Bernard... Well, I don't suppose he had his life planned out exactly either. But deep in his gloomy dreams he must have yearned for authority. He could see the world going to pot even as he emerged into it. And like many a long-suffering conservative all around the world in those wild and free days, no doubt he was even then plotting his revenge.

It was a while coming, but oh lord, when it did come...

NINE

Another day, another basement.

I was becoming a connoisseur of them—and this one, I had to admit, was much better than the first. No bare walls or dirt floor or dingy light bulb. This room was large and carpeted and well lit, with comfortable couches and a bathroom off to one side. There was even a studded leather bar in the corner, vintage 1970s. The shelves behind it were empty, alas, but the wall did at least boast a neon beer sign. ('Brisbane Bitter' it said, which to my knowledge hasn't been brewed in several decades.)

It was someone's snooker room. Sans table. Which was fine, really, because there was no one down there for me to shoot pool with, apart from Nancy Campbell (sans burqa), and I doubt that she would have been interested. Not that I would have trusted her with a cue in her hand anyway.

And where was this place, you ask, interrogators dear?

Good question.

It was the same old story. The men who carried out the

ambush were all masked with balaclavas. (I'm talking about the second ambush here, the one in which the AFP were the ambushees, not the ambushers. Ludicrous, really—I don't think even back in the bushranger days had one road cutting ever seen so much action.) Then, in all the shooting and screaming and confusion, me and the naked Nancy Campbell found ourselves bundled into the back of the van (the AFP van, now appropriated, not the postal van) and driven at breakneck speed for maybe half an hour to who knows where. They'd put bags over our heads right from the start. Professionals, these boys.

At the end it seemed that we pulled into a garage. Then we were hurried through a house and down some stairs and, when the bags came off, there was the 'Brisbane Bitter' sign to greet me. And five men, dressed in civilian garb, but still in balaclavas, still with their guns. They dumped some clothes on the floor for my burqa-less friend, and then left, locking the door behind them. All throughout I'd been yelling questions at them—who were they, what did they want, what the fuck was going on? Not one of them had spoken a word.

So there we were. Me and my would-be executioner.

'Well then,' I said, after prowling about the room for a time, and verifying that there was no escape, no alcohol, and nothing else to do but talk. 'Nancy.'

She was slumped in a beanbag. (This room was strictly retro.) The clothes they had given her were not her own—those were presumably still lying on the road where the AFP had dropped them. Instead she seemed to be wearing a man's clothes, several sizes too big for her. Her wild white hair was tied back into a bun, revealing a pale, narrow neck, lividly bruised.

'That's not my name,' she said, staring at the floor.

'You're not Nancy Campbell?'

'Not anymore.'

'Oh right, you've got that other fancy Muslim name.'

Her head lifted. 'Aisha.'

And the hate still smouldered there, amidst the blood and the cuts. She might have looked like a waif in those clothes, but only a fool would have considered her to be harmless or beaten. There was no one called Nancy in there, that's for sure.

'Okay, Ay-eesha, do *you* know who these guys are?'

She shook her head, unblinking.

She was in shock, I supposed. After all, it was only her first time being kidnapped or ambushed or otherwise caught up in an assault, while this was my third. And her compatriots were dead. Gunned down right in front of her. She had been right on the verge of death herself.

'Are you okay?' I heard myself ask, amazingly.

In answer she rubbed savagely at the wounds on her face, raising fresh blood, then lifted her reddened hands, her eyes on me all the while. My incipient pity died. She was telling me she didn't give a fuck about pain or death or sympathy.

'You really *are* crazy,' I told her, and left her alone.

For a while anyway. But hour followed hour, without any distraction, and there was no ignoring her presence. An albino terrorist on a green velour beanbag. At the most, she couldn't have been more than twenty-five years old. Hell, my own eldest daughter was twenty-eight. And the only things Rhonda seemed to be interested in were money and clothes and parties with her friends. The world might be going to hell and new wars breaking out every day, with half of Australia locked down for security's sake, but she had a social life to get on with. The spitting image of her mother, in fact. (Okay, maybe the spitting image of her father, too. Even though she made it clear that she despised me, and men in general—her rampant promiscuity aside—and I'll be needing that cheque *now*, please, Daddy.)

But this Aisha creature. I couldn't see *her* hanging around with my daughter's crowd. Parties would fall silent as soon as she walked into a room, and most boys would run screaming from those eyes. All right then, she was a different sort of youth. Someone very serious and very angry. But where on earth had she come from? I watched her as surreptitiously as I could. She didn't fidget or squirm or yawn. Once she rose and went to the toilet, but otherwise she just sat there. Was she meditating?

Was that even the right religion? And that was another puzzle. She wasn't of Middle Eastern descent, that was for sure. She had to be pure Viking stock, cursed to live under a burning Australian sun. So where did Allah come into it?

The silence got to me in the end.

'Don't you have to pray or something?'

She glanced my way as if I were a silverfish.

'You're a Muslim, right? I thought you guys prayed five times a day. Don't you have to get down on the floor and face Mecca every now and then?'

No answer.

'Not that you could tell which way Mecca was down here, right?' I was rambling on for my own amusement as much as anything else. 'It's in Saudi Arabia, isn't it? So from Australia I guess you just face roughly north-west? Yes?'

She rolled her eyes, in an 'are you really so stupid' sort of way, and for a split second she *could* have been my daughter.

Still, she had me there. On this topic, I was pretty stupid indeed. Not that she was the first Muslim I'd met. Back in the old days, before the camps and the ghettos, I'd dealt with investors from the Islamic community often enough. I'd even schmoozed the occasional international Arab banker. And as far as money and business went, they were pretty much the same as anyone else. God wasn't the issue. The only trick, from my point of view, was to work out whether a particular Muslim was worried about the drinking thing or not. And plenty of them weren't. Especially if quality scotch was on offer.

I'd never actually seen one pray, however. Nor, come to think of it, had I ever dealt closely with a Muslim woman.

'Women do pray too, don't they? I mean, I've seen pictures of mosques and people on their knees and all that, but it only seems to be men.'

The boredom must have been getting to her as well, because she spoke finally. 'You're the same as everyone else in this country. You don't know a thing about Islam.'

'Well?'

'Women are perfectly welcome in mosques.'

'Really? I must have seen the wrong photos.'

Her lips tightened. 'In some countries the women prefer to pray at home. It's a personal choice. Men and women. You can pray wherever you like.'

'And you? Obviously you don't go to mosques, they're all shut down. But what about right now? You're just doing it there on the beanbag, are you?'

Her chin went up. 'You wouldn't ask another Christian questions like that.'

'Another Christian? You think *I'm* a Christian?'

'Aren't you?'

'Red-blooded atheist, babe.'

She made a spitting sound. Then she pointedly shuffled the beanbag around and turned her back to me.

Well, what did I expect? Muslims, I knew, had at least some respect for Christians and Jews, even if everyone was at war right now. Maybe they even saw some worth in the Buddhists and Hindus and Sikhs, too. But the utterly godless? Especially fat, semi-alcoholic, dirty-old-man, several-times-divorced, washed-up, cowardly types like me? Not bloody likely.

In any case, we were saved further pleasantries, because at the top of the stairs the door opened, and one of our captors descended. He was wearing a balaclava, but had no weapons that I could see. Instead, rather strangely, he carried a small television set with a rabbit-ears aerial.

'About fucking time,' I declared.

He glanced my way, then held up a finger—wait. Wordlessly, he set up the TV on the bar, plugged it in and switched it on. I watched with growing outrage and impatience. He played with the reception for a time, and when the picture cleared it revealed a game show. The volume was turned down, but it was 'The New Price is Right'. Not far from the end. So now I knew that out there in the normal world—away from all these basements and masked faces and clockless walls—it was about five minutes to six on a weekday evening.

Satisfied, the man took a seat. He leant back, hands behind his head, and considered us both at leisure. 'The Prime Minister's brother,' he said at last. 'And a cell leader from the Great Southern Jihad. I gotta say it—you two are a real mystery.'

I looked at Aisha. She was glaring across the room at him, but didn't seem inclined to speak. 'Um,' I said, 'I'm not *with* her, you know.'

'Oh?'

'She was holding me hostage. Just this morning. She was probably going to kill me.'

'Really?'

'Yes! Look, for fuck's sake—'

He laughed. 'Okay mate, relax. I get the general idea.'

I sat back, staring. It was hard to guess his age. Maybe late forties, going by his hands, and by a solid frame that suggested the beginnings of a middle-age spread. Grey eyes, through the holes in the mask. A patient, confident voice.

I said, 'So who the hell are you people?'

'We're the ones who rescued you.'

'I'd already *been* rescued, before you came along.'

He barked another dry laugh. 'Believe me, you needed rescuing. Both of you. Whether you knew it or not.'

'Fine. You've done it then. Now let us go. Or at least let me go. I don't give a shit about her.'

'That wouldn't be in your best interest, trust me.'

'*You* know what's in my best interest?'

He nodded. 'Right now, I'm your only friend.' He was watching Aisha. 'The same goes for you, little lady.'

'Stick it up your arse,' she responded.

And I could tell the man was amused by the crinkle of his eyebrow. He turned to check the TV screen. 'The New Price is Right' was running the credits. The final contestant had been playing for prizes valued at half a million, including a fully armoured family sedan, with the complete anti-terrorist defence attachments, tear gas and all. But she hadn't won. He turned back to us.

'Before we talk, I want you to watch the news. It should give you some idea of what's going on here.'

He moved his chair around, and we all sat there, facing the screen.

I was interested despite myself. It must have been a week— way back before the cyclone neared the coast—since I'd seen any news. These days, a week was an eternity. And the way the man was talking, perhaps something momentous had occurred. Another Twin Towers, another nuke—who could tell?

But there was none of that. The news, at least the first two minutes of it, was solely about me. And the fact that I was dead.

'Forensic tests have finally confirmed,' said the newsreader, 'that the body found at the Ocean Sands Green Resort near Bundaberg is indeed that of Leo James, the twin brother of Prime Minister Bernard James. The state of the remains had until now led to doubts about the identity of the deceased, but authorities have today made the death official. The Prime Minister himself reportedly donated a DNA sample early yesterday to aid with the identification process.'

I was staring at the wreckage of my resort on the screen, bathed now in sunshine, shot from a news helicopter. And then I was listening to an obituary, outlining my sad and sorry life in a well-censored lack of detail, while old photos of me flashed across the screen. Bernard and me as children. Me at my second wedding. Me with Bernard in his Prime Ministerial office. (The friendly pose belying the fact that he was probably dressing me down at the time.) Me in a silly hard hat on the site of some construction project I was trying to fund.

'The Prime Minister has expressed his great sadness at his brother's passing, and has said the occasion is a reminder that even in these troubled political times, we must not forget the dangers and tragedies with which nature herself presents us. He also expressed deep sympathy for others who have lost loved ones or property as a result of Cyclone Yusuf.'

'Fuck him!' I said to no one, disbelieving.

The man held up his finger again. 'There's more.'

'In other breaking news,' read the host, 'the Federal Police have reported a successful raid on a terrorist cell in south-east Queensland. After lengthy investigation, several members of a group calling themselves the Great Southern Jihad were ambushed and eliminated by AFP agents. Police warn, however, that the cell commander remains at large.'

And suddenly there she was, large as life on TV. It was one of those surveillance-type photos, taken as she was crossing a street somewhere, in normal clothes, her head turned slightly away from the camera. But it was Aisha, sure enough.

The genuine article was blinking at the screen.

'The AFP report that Nancy Campbell is armed and extremely dangerous. Members of the public are advised not to approach her, but to inform police immediately if she is sighted. Campbell is wanted dead or alive, and a shoot-to-kill order has been issued. Extra AFP forces have been deployed to south-east Queensland, and increased roadblocks and other security measures will be in force. Returning now to the clean-up of Cyclone Yusuf...'

The man reached over and switched the television off.

'They aren't kidding about the AFP reinforcements. It's a madhouse out there. Not just the AFP, but the army too, trucks and troops everywhere, roadblocks all over the place.' He nodded towards Aisha. 'They really want you dead.'

'Is that any surprise?' I interjected. 'She's a terrorist. More than that, she's one of the ones who nuked Canberra.'

'Who told you that?'

'She did.'

He laughed. Stared at her for a moment. 'Got tickets on yourself, haven't you, girl?' He shook his head. 'Either way, she steps out the door and someone will gun her down. As for you— your own brother has declared you dead, when he knows perfectly well you aren't.'

'It's some sort of mistake...'

'No mistake. From what we've heard, the AFP has secret orders to shoot *you* on sight as well. The story is that you and her work together, and always have, but supposedly it's all being kept quiet to avoid embarrassing the PM.'

I was shaken. 'That's not true.'

'We know. But even so, by government decree, you don't exist anymore. Indeed, the government seems to be shifting heaven and earth to make sure that neither of you exists. Do you understand what I'm saying? The only reason you're both alive is because we've got you safely hidden down here.'

My mouth was dry. 'Who *are* you?'

He hesitated, picked at the hem of his balaclava. 'I guess you should be told. The fact is, you two don't have any choice but to trust us, if you want to stay alive.'

Then to my astonishment he pulled the mask off. I saw a round, ruddy face. A dishevelled mass of sandy hair. And a wry, lopsided smile.

'My name is Harry. Welcome to the Oz Underground.'

TEN

So now I was a captive of the OU.

And I know that you bastards don't believe me—not if the interrogations are anything to go by—but until that very moment I had never in my life had a thing to do with them. Until that moment, in fact, I wasn't even sure that the Oz Underground really existed. Yes, I'd heard the rumours. Yes, I'd seen the graffiti. But I never once read their name anywhere in the media. I never once heard any law enforcement agency decry their activities, or issue warrants for their arrest. So what was I supposed to think? And when, on occasion, I'd raised the question with the odd government official who crossed my path, I was always blithely assured that there was not now and never had been an Underground. They were a fantasy, a chimera, just the wishful thinking of a few left-wing crazies. Forget all about them, Leo, old son, and have another beer.

Lying motherfuckers.

Meanwhile, down in the empty snooker room, Harry was folding his balaclava neatly and trying to point out that I wasn't a captive at all. (And no, I don't know his last name. Or if Harry was even his real first name. And why am I bothering with denials? You'd know more about it than me. You're the ones who killed him, and you're the ones who have his body.)

'You see what I'm saying?' He was looking earnestly from Aisha to me. 'There's no point hiding my face. I know you two won't betray me. There's no one you could betray me *to*. We're the only refuge you have left.'

'The Underground?' I said, still in disbelief. 'You're telling me that the Underground is real, and that you're it?'

He smiled. 'Well, a part of it.'

He sure didn't look it. Of all the gun-wielding idiots I'd met in the last few days, he seemed the least likely to be part of a militant resistance movement. With his beer belly and open face and receding hairline, he looked like he should be sitting on a beach with a stubbie in one hand and a battered old trannie tuned to the cricket in the other, ogling topless girls who were twenty years too young for him.

He asked, 'You've heard about what we do?'

'Yeah.' I glanced at Aisha, then back to him. 'More bloody terrorists.'

'We're not terrorists.'

'No?'

His expression had grown serious. 'We don't wish any harm to Australia, or to any western society.' Aisha gave a cough of cynical laughter, and he stared at her levelly. 'Or to any other society, for that matter. Certainly not Islam. But we *are* prepared to fight, to save this country.'

'Save it from who?' I asked.

'From itself. Or at least from its government. This police state they've set up.' The smile again. 'In particular, we're trying to save it from your brother.'

'Good fucking luck.' What did this bloke expect—that just because I hated Bernard I'd be impressed by a bunch of would-be revolutionaries trying to overthrow him? 'And you can just leave me out of it, okay?'

'Even when your brother has ordered your execution?'

'So you tell me.'

'What do you think that news report was about?'

And there was nothing I could say to that.

At the same time, a list of stories about the OU was running through my head. How they supposedly had a secret network throughout the country. How they had members from all strata of society—public servants, farmers, doctors, mechanics, priests, IT workers, dock workers, lawyers, teachers—any sort of people you cared to name. How they were waging a hidden campaign against the security laws, against the detention laws, against the US bases, against our involvement in all the wars— in other words, against just about everything that had happened in Australia over the last decade, all the way back to the September 11 attacks. How they had hundreds of safe houses from city to city, and ferried all kinds of illegal persons between them. How they had reportedly sabotaged US army vehicles, or ambushed AFP roadblocks, or broken imprisoned dissenters out of jail. How they scrawled their catchcry on billboards and brick walls and battleships, only to have it hastily painted over by the authorities. 'Free Australia!' The words always accompanied by the drawing of an upside-down Southern Cross.

Phantoms. Except, here was one of them.

I said, 'Okay, if I'm not your prisoner, what exactly *do* you want with me?'

'First of all, to keep you alive.'

'Why?'

'Because the government wants you dead.'

I puzzled this through. 'But how did you know about me in the first place? I mean, that I'd been kidnapped?' I nodded towards the brooding Aisha. 'And how did you happen to show up just when they were about to shoot her?'

'Ah...' Harry pondered the question for a moment. 'I only know so much myself, you understand. I get orders and information from above, and I don't always ask for explanations.

But the Underground has contacts everywhere. Even, dare I say it, in the ranks of the AFP itself.'

That *did* impress me. 'Someone in the AFP tipped you off?'

'Yes. But the truth is, this isn't the first we've heard of our lady terrorist here and her group. We've been watching them for some time now.'

Aisha's eyes narrowed. 'Bullshit.'

'Sorry luv, it's true. And we're not the only ones. It's like this. About a year ago now our sources let us know that the AFP had become aware of a group called Great Southern Jihad. Our informers are only low level, admittedly, but they were confused, because no one in the AFP seemed very worried about these particular terrorists. In fact, orders came down from above that agents were to subject GSJ to only light, intermittent observation, with no interference. And that's unusual. Sure, sometimes the Feds might watch a terrorist group for a while, to see who its contacts are, but this was different. These were "keep your hands off" sort of orders. Which is all pretty suggestive. So the Underground started its own surveillance of GSJ cells, wherever we could find them. We wanted to know what was really going on.' He smiled at Aisha. 'Your little cell was one of the first we started to track. We didn't actually see you nab Leo, but we heard about it from our AFP sources, quick smart.'

Aisha glowered at that. 'The abduction was a mistake.'

'Yes, I'm sure it was. But the question you should be asking is—how did the AFP themselves know about it? And so fast? I doubt that they were out in that cyclone, watching it happen. So who tipped them off?'

She opened her mouth. Shut it again.

'Exactly. Something stinks here. Our own AFP operatives don't know the answer, but they said things went beserk when the news came through. People high up were angry. Not so much because Southern Jihad had kidnapped someone important. No offence, Leo, but to the AFP you really *aren't* important. Or haven't been, until now. But what really seemed to piss the powers off was that now they had to rescue you. Take action against

Aisha and her boys. And that, apparently, was the last thing they wanted to do. For whatever reason, up until a few days ago, GSJ was not a target.'

Aisha found her voice. 'No. That isn't right. We've always been a target. We're at war with all of you.'

'At war? You people?' Harry turned back to me. 'That's what we can't understand. I don't know about *all* the GSJ cells, but the ones we watched were hardly big-time terrorists. Apart from a lot of talk, the most they've done in the last few months is let off the odd pipe bomb that killed hardly anyone. They're mainly just kids. We're not even sure they're really Islamic.'

Aisha sparked up again. 'We are fucking so.'

'Then you're pretty damn weird about it, from what I've heard.'

'They've done serious things too,' I said. 'I told you about Canberra.'

'These knuckleheads could never have done Canberra.'

Aisha was getting quite furious. 'Yes we did!'

Harry eyed her. 'You personally? You brought in the nuke?'

'No, but—'

'I suppose someone higher up in your organisation told you all about it, said it was your comrades that did the deed. Is that the gist of it?'

Aisha subsided, not answering.

'I thought as much.'

Now I was really baffled. Aisha's crowd *hadn't* nuked Canberra? I said, 'You still haven't told me how we ended up here.'

He nodded. 'Okay, we knew you'd been kidnapped, and we knew that the AFP was setting up an ambush to rescue you. Just for interest's sake, I took a party of our own along to observe. Covertly. And things went very strange out there on that road. First they blow the fuck out of the postal van, like they don't care whether anyone survives, even you. Then the American secret service puts in an appearance. Then the PM's brother is getting a gun pointed at his head. And finally, the girl terrorist is about to get shot in the street, without any interrogation, after she's been safely captured and neutralised. That's not the way things usually work. That's a sign that something else entirely is going on here. Something that the big boys really don't want known. And that means the Underground *wants* to know. So I made the call, and we went in, guns blazing.'

'Killing God knows how many Federal policemen.'

His gaze turned flinty. 'The AFP have killed hundreds of *us*, Leo. It's a war out there, even if you've never heard anything about it. And to be completely bloody frank, it's a war that the Underground is losing.'

'It didn't look like you were losing out there on the road.'

'We got lucky today. Everywhere else, we're on the back foot. We're the AFP's prime target these days, not the damn terrorists.' He shook his head. 'Except for now. Suddenly *you two* are public enemy number one. Why? What on earth for? A burnt-out hack developer, and a brat terrorist. What the fuck is so important about you two?'

And amidst my complete confusion, what bugged me the most, perversely, was that he kept seeming to imply there actually was an 'Aisha and me'—that we were linked somehow. I mean, I was sick of the sight of the woman.

'It's not me,' I said. 'I don't know a thing.'

'Maybe not. Maybe you don't even know what you know.' He was staring at Aisha. 'But her, on the other hand, she must have *some* idea.'

We both considered her.

She sat up stiffly on the beanbag. 'I have no idea what you're talking about. And even if I did, why would I tell you?'

Harry threw his arms wide, exasperated. 'Don't you get it? We aren't your enemy.'

'Everyone is my enemy.'

'Fine! Get up and go then. Walk out the front door and just see how far you get. Everyone else in your cell is dead. There're troop carriers on every street corner out there, roadblocks every two miles, your face is on every TV in the nation.' He was pointing to the door at the top of the stairs. 'Go on. Get out.'

For a moment Aisha did indeed stare at the door, her lips pressed tight, her legs seemingly tensed to rise. But in the end she didn't move.

Harry sighed. 'Look, you of all people should know the old saying, the enemy of my enemy is my friend. This government wants you dead, and it wants us dead as well. So, at least for the moment, can we agree to cooperate a little?'

Aisha bit her lip, still right on the edge, and then lowered her eyes.

'I'll take that as a provisional yes.'

'I still don't know anything,' she said dully.

'We'll see about that...'

I broke in. 'Am I free to go as well?'

He gave a bitter laugh. 'Of course. You've got no money, no identity papers, no transport, you're officially dead, and unofficially a shoot-to-kill target. Sure. Go where you like.'

'What's *your* plan then?'

'First thing—get the both of you out of the area. Things are way too hot around here just to keep you hidden in a basement.'

'You mean travel? I thought you said—'

'I know. But we have ways. For a start, we can get you new identity cards that will stand up to most scrutiny. Enough to get you out of Queensland anyway. The real problem is your faces. We can't hide them forever, and you two are pretty recognisable. Aisha here sure as hell doesn't blend in.' He studied her glumly. 'I guess first thing we do is cut the hair. Shorter, but not too short, they'd be expecting that. We'll give you some sort of bob, and dye it, and colour your eyebrows. I don't know what the hell we can do about your skin.'

Aisha lifted her eyes again, a flash of anger, but said nothing. I didn't for a minute think that she was really prepared to cooperate with all this, any more than I was. But I assumed that, like me, she was at least ready to wait and watch a while before making a run for it.

Harry looked back to me. 'But *you*, Leo, you're half-famous. Sure, we play around with the hair, and you've got a beard going, which is good. But that face is too well known. Especially when it belongs to a dead man.' He was out of his chair and walking around me, musing. 'We really need some sort of plastic surgery. I'm not kidding. There are people in the Underground who could do it. We've got contacts in hospitals. Surgeons. But not in this part of the world. Still...' He came to a decision. 'Stand up a minute, would you?'

I got out of the chair. He was peering at my face.

'Sorry about this,' he said, 'but it's the best I can do here and now.'

He drew back his fist and slammed it straight into my nose.

'Ow!' I yelled, agonised, hands to my face. 'Fuck!' And it wasn't just the pain. I was outraged. Despite the various beatings and rough handling over the last few days, my nose was one feature that had escaped any damage. 'Jesus Christ!'

He was all concern. 'I really am sorry. C'mon, give us a look. Is it bleeding?'

Gingerly I took my hands away.

'No,' he sighed. 'Not enough.'

And the prick hit me again.

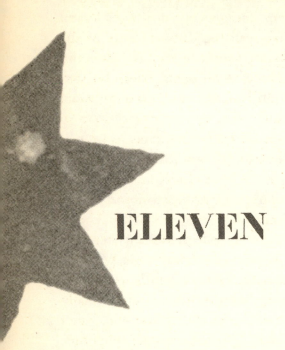

ELEVEN

It astounds me even now.

My brother wanted me dead.

You might be wondering, interrogators, how I could have sat by passively in that snooker room and let someone else tell me how my life was going to be from now on. But you have no idea what it's like to hear that your own flesh and blood has ordered your execution. Not that I ever doubted the truth of it. I was hurt and angry, and I didn't understand right then *why* Bernard was doing this, but I never thought that it couldn't be so. I didn't wonder, for instance, whether this Harry person might simply be lying to me, for reasons of his own. I didn't question whether the news footage I'd seen might have been an elaborate fake. I didn't decide that I should put my trust in my brother rather than in a complete stranger.

No. Deep down, it was all too easy to believe. After all, Bernard didn't get to the top of Australian politics without being prepared to make the brutal decisions.

It's strange, though. If you look back to the dawn of Bernard's career, there were few hints that he would rise so high. When he first joined the Liberal Party, his local branch was in the federal seat of Streeton, in Melbourne's eastern suburbs. Streeton being a safe Liberal electorate, the branch membership boasted some of the party's brightest young talents—but, take my word for it, Bernard wasn't one of them. He was *so* dry, *so* dour, *so* flat, that the only role anyone could see for him was as branch treasurer. And as branch treasurer he remained, apparently content, working away quietly at the books for nearly ten years.

Hardly a stellar beginning. Still, it was a fatal appointment on the part of his colleagues. You don't give a devious operator like Bernard any sort of position—however mundane it might appear—without grave risk. Especially an administrative position, because it's in the *details* that real power often lies. Bernard plotted in the backroom until the sitting Member for Streeton finally retired, and nominations opened to preselect a replacement. Then he struck, putting his name forward against three other hopefuls, all of whom were more experienced than he was, and far more highly regarded by the branch membership.

Not that Bernard was worried. He disposed of the frontrunner by finding a technical hitch in the man's Liberal registration papers, effectively dismissing him from the party for several months. (The mistake could have been overlooked, but Bernard had stacked the registration committee with party hacks as petty and pedantic as himself, and they gleefully refused to waive the issue.) The next contender he maligned by digging into the minutes of ancient meetings and discovering a motion the man had once put, in 1968, that the party adopt a platform backing a new design for the Australian flag. (A flag men had fought and died for! The infamy of it!) And his last rival he disgraced merely by spreading the story of a messy divorce in her youth, involving infidelity and an abortion—an incident Bernard learnt of by noticing a change of last name in her old membership records.

So he was the only one left unsullied, and he was such an obscure and pallid individual that no one else had any dirt on him. Puzzled, and rather disappointed, the branch made him their official candidate. At the ensuing federal election of 1983, the seat of Streeton voted Liberal as always, and thus Bernard James, my own little baby brother, ascended to the House of Representatives—one of the youngest MPs of the day. It was a sad irony for him that the Liberals actually lost government in the same election, and wouldn't regain it for another thirteen years, but still, he was on his way.

Not that he made much of an impression, early on. His debut speech in Parliament gained notice only because he made references to the problem, as he saw of it, of declining birth rates amongst the anglo-European population, the simultaneous growth in Asian immigration, and the imminent destruction of Australian culture—sentiments seen as somewhat out of step for an age when multiculturalism was official policy. The party whip told him to pull his head in, and for the next ten years or so, even though Bernard held onto his seat, he was chiefly known as a reliably conservative but deadly dull nonentity.

It was the seventies, as I said earlier, that had fixed his attitudes—the social chaos of that decade, and the madness of the Whitlam Labor government, hog wild with ideas like free education, universal health care and generous unemployment benefits. The accountant in Bernard was outraged; who the hell was paying for all this? The taxpayer, that's who. No, said my brother, if people had to struggle and save to get to university, well and good—then they wouldn't waste their time marching and protesting and causing trouble once they got there. The same with the dole—if it wasn't so easy to get, then there'd be no hippie communes or artist collectives cluttering up the country, and the unemployed would move heaven and earth to get jobs, just as they should. As for universal health care, well, quite frankly, the most advanced treatments cost a fortune, and if that meant the best care was only accessible to the rich, so be it, all the more motivation for the population to become wealthy themselves. Private sector, user-pays, that was the principle.

The government's true role, according to Bernard, was to

formulate high policy, and to maintain the social order. The latter meant no undue toleration of drugs, or homosexuals, or refugees, or land rights for Aborigines, or militant feminism, or greenies, or rampant abortion, or power-hungry unions, or... Well, you get the picture. Put simply, he had settled upon those two most basic (and to outsiders, oddly contradictory) of conservative tenets. Namely that, in their private lives, people should conform strictly to the rules and be financially responsible for themselves, but that for the corporate world, there should be no limits or responsibilities at all. Nowadays, of course, this is standard conservative fare the western world over. But back in the 1980s, when Bernard was cutting his teeth as a young MP, it was cold and dreary stuff, even for the Liberal Party.

It certainly wasn't the philosophy of the eighties Labor government, so the decade was a grim period for Bernard. Casting about for better models, he ended up spending a lot of time overseas. Many of his Liberal colleagues were enamoured with Britain, and with Margaret Thatcher's way of doing things, but not Bernard. His inspiration was the USA. If there was a fact-finding mission to the States, or a deputation sent over there for some diplomatic reason, then he made sure he was on it. And liking what he saw, he began, in his public pronouncements, to extol the virtues of the US system. He pointed to America's military and economic authority, to its leadership in the overthrow of the USSR, and to its decisive history in defence of democracy. Australia, he insisted, had a responsibility to follow that sort of example. To bind ourselves to it. True, his faith was dented a little by the end of the Reagan era, and by the ascension of Clinton. But he maintained his friendship with the Republicans. Their day, he knew, would come again.

In the meantime, he married Claire. Their only courting engagements, as far as I know, were Liberal Party fundraisers. There were no wild nights out drinking, no afternoons fucking in motel rooms. Bernard's single requirement in a wife seemed to be the woman's ability to fit in with his political career. Claire proved to be polite, sociable and correctly aligned to the right, so my brother declared himself in love and the date was set.

After the wedding, the happy couple moved into a house only a few blocks from our family home in Camberwell. And for the little that his life changed, Bernard might as well have stayed at home. Claire cooked and cleaned for him just as well as our mum ever had. Not even for one day did he have to get out on the street and get dirty, fending for himself. How he later claimed to understand the plight of the working poor, or the social problems of the battlers in the outer suburbs, or the difficulties of running a small business, I'll never know.

Me, I was on a different track altogether.

I'd long since cut the apron strings. The eighties were my decade. Money was just *everywhere*. And luckily, I'd dropped all my leftie pretensions and my aimless drifting at precisely midnight, 31 December 1979. I woke up on 1 January and could literally smell the new age. I could also smell the mould and the filth of my little rented flat—home since my first divorce—and decided I was heartily sick of it all. I realised that I wanted to be rich. I'd been working as a surveyor's assistant for the previous months, laying down new residential developments in Melbourne's outer 'burbs, and it suddenly struck me just how damn easy it was for developers to make money. And so I borrowed a wad of cash (my parents going guarantors), bought a few suburban-fringe horse paddocks on the cheap, put in some cul de sacs and drainage, set up the bunting and a tented sales booth on site, and six months later I'd sold the lot at over one hundred per cent profit.

Voila! I was an entrepreneur.

Okay, it wasn't quite that simple, but it *almost* was, and I didn't look back. In the following years I built more housing estates, and then moved on to hotels and resorts, each project bigger and better than the last, and each one funded by bigger and better loans. Cash? I never really had any, but who cared, you didn't need it back then. Everyone remembers the eighties tycoons, and I was typical of the breed, right down to the ex-hostie second wife with the tanned skin, white clothes and chunky jewellery, and a hopelessly spoiled daughter to boot, the aforementioned Rhonda. There was only one golden rule to understand, and it was this—the larger the debt, the safer you were. If you owed a bank a hundred grand, say, and couldn't pay it back, then the bank would shut you down in an instant. But if you owed a bank a hundred *million*, and couldn't pay it back, then the bank itself was in danger, and so would do absolutely everything to keep you afloat, including throwing more money at you. And not only banks—state governments would jump in too. Because if you folded, and the bank folded, then that was a crisis, and people lost jobs, and MPs lost votes.

So you couldn't go wrong. Debts got shuffled and hidden, annual reports got fudged, shareholders got deluded and ripped off, and the long lunches got longer and drunker and ever more desperate. Until the whole house of cards collapsed, of course, and then everyone was rooted. Suddenly it was a recession and half the country had lost their savings and the other half was out of work. Welcome to the 1990s. Ah, but we all had fun, right? And I didn't do so bad out of the crash. I ended up broke, but I didn't go to jail like some of my colleagues. It wasn't that I was any more honest, or that my schemes were any less dodgy, but I was (I'm forced to admit) one of the smaller players of those days, and by the time the really big boys had been humiliated and imprisoned, no one much cared about me.

Plus there was Bernard. He was still only a minor figure in the Liberal Party, but he had connections all the same, and none of the party powerbrokers wanted a sitting member embarrassed by a corporate criminal brother. So administrators and commissions and judges were talked to and soothed and intimidated, and I sailed away from the bankruptcy proceedings a free man. Privately, of course, Bernard was disgusted with me. Me, and my whole tycoon ilk. We'd given the private sector, the love of his life, a bad name. Sullied something pure. It was like he had a teenage sister, and we'd got her pregnant.

Still, he protected me. And as the nineties progressed, his star finally began to rise. With the economy in extremis the long-serving Labor government was on the nose, and so was multiculturalism and welfare and the environment and anything else to do with minorities. Mainstream Australia had had enough of pipe dreams. All they wanted were jobs and low interest rates. Bernard began to make a name for himself, returning to old themes, and bashing the government on immigration and Aboriginal land grabs. He was not an exciting speaker, but that stubborn insistence of his was there, a sort of *I may be dull, but I know what's right* persona which, year by year, more people came to respect. By 1995 he was in the shadow cabinet, with the (albeit minor) portfolio of Local Government. And then at the 1996 election the Liberals stormed into power, John Howard became the new PM, and suddenly my own little baby brother was a federal government minister.

It was a happy day—the dawning of an age in which Bernard finally felt not only comfortable, but in tune, in the *right*. He was a fervent admirer of John Howard—another life-long politician who had mastered the 'drab, dour, but honest' schtick even more proficiently than Bernard himself had. Indeed, Bernard's only source of frustration was that Howard's first term was relatively lacklustre. No great conservative agenda was proposed or pursued. Fact was, the Liberals had come into government with few actual policies. They hadn't needed any, what with Labor so profoundly unpopular. Even more perplexingly, in their last few years of power, Labor had themselves adopted market reform and deregulation, the only real policies the Libs espoused, so it took a while for Howard to cut any new ground. Bernard might rail about the dangers of missed opportunities, but as he was only the Minister for Local Government, no one really gave a damn about him.

I gave a damn, however. Local Government meant town councils, and town councils controlled property development. My palms were already getting itchy, thinking about the possibilities. The nineties had not been very kind to me. During all the legal action of my bankruptcy, I went through my second divorce, an expensive exercise for a man already in financial trouble. Then I was banned from the property market for three years. I got around that particular ruling by marrying a third time—to a man-eating, alcoholic, long-legged real estate agent, the mother of my other two daughters. But when that marriage inevitably went sour I was in even more trouble, seeing that all my new projects were in the bitch-wife's name. So 1996 found me single yet again, poor, and with a whole mess of alimony and child support payments due. I was eking out a living as the assistant manager at a Gold Coast resort that I had once owned—well, on paper anyway— but that was no life for a high-flyer like me. I wanted back in, and with a brother in charge of the grants system that helped fund every town or city council in the nation, how could I fail?

The only difficulty was that, by the 1996 election, I hadn't spoken to Bernard in some years. He hadn't forgiven me for dragging his name into the bankruptcy courts, and I hadn't forgiven him for all his tedious lectures while bailing me out. But suddenly I felt overcome with fond feelings for my little brother. How could I have let things slide for so long? We were family! On the other hand, I didn't even know his home phone number. But the new Parliament was sitting, and he had to be in attendance, so I jumped on a plane to Canberra. It was my first visit there, oddly enough. My earlier dealings had often involved the state governments, but never the federal. A dreary-looking town I thought it, too. Still, there was power in the air, no doubt about it, so I checked into Rydges and dialled up my brother's department. Leo James calling, I declared, and I'm coming in to see Bernard.

They put me on hold for five minutes. Then they came back and asked me if I had an appointment. I'm his fucking brother, I replied. They put me on hold for five more. Then I got his personal secretary. And damned if I couldn't hear Bernard's own voice muttering angry instructions in the background. He knew it was me calling, all right. But the woman just said that he was a very busy man and really the only way to see him was to set up a meeting.

Fuck, I said, shaken. Okay, when can I get in?

In the end, the little bastard made me wait two weeks.

TWELVE

I don't suppose that the residents of a police state really grasp the truth about their nation until they become *fugitives* within that state. But it opens your eyes, let me tell you. Suddenly, all those security roadblocks that you used to sail through—annoyed at the delay, perhaps, but unscathed, and certainly aware of the necessity, given the unstable times—they become hundred-foot-high walls, impossible to clear. Suddenly those identity papers that you had to renew every year, queueing up for hours—another annoyance, but no different from a driver's licence, surely—the lack of them leaves you feeling like you're naked in a crowd. And all those police and soldiers on the streets—a sight that you found slightly distasteful maybe, but also rather comforting, given that they were there to protect you—now every single one of those uniforms is your enemy.

Bad enough if you're actually a terrorist on the run. But when you're completely innocent, then it's something else again.

Luckily, with the Oz Underground I was in the hands of experts when it came to security evasion. And by the time I got to look in a mirror, I had to admit that I barely recognised myself. It was many days since I'd seen my old reflection, and then the face staring back at me had been smooth and round and well fed (if a little raddled) under a full head of dark hair. Now I had a dirty blond crew cut, huge shadows around my eyes, a certain gauntness about the cheekbones, some freshly healed scars on my chin, and a swollen nose bent a good ten degrees from true. It was still me, and yet not at all the typical me. Certainly I didn't look like my photos on television—but was it really enough? A beard might have been more camouflage still. Or at least a moustache. But Harry had changed his mind about that, and ordered me to shave. And when I'd suggested some fake glasses, or an eye patch, or a wig, he'd only laughed.

Aisha, on the other hand . . . Well, I'd never been that familiar with her appearance in the first place, so it was hard to tell whether she was recognisable or not. But Harry hadn't been kidding, they really had taken her long hair and cut it into a sixties-style bob. They'd dyed it, too, from white to dark red, with accompanying work on her eyebrows. Then they'd adorned her with some dangling clip-on earrings and make-up and a bead necklace and, finally, dressed her in neon green tracksuit pants and a sweatshirt. The transformation was quite freakish—from pale terrorist to suburbanite fashion victim. Not that I was any better. They'd given me a button-up short-sleeved shirt, brown shorts, long socks and (God forbid) a pair of sandals. It made no sense to me. Surely someone dressed like a lay preacher from the 1970s would *attract* attention rather than blend in. But Harry, with some particular plan in mind, was content.

Plus we had papers again. Harry presented me with a worn old wallet that held—besides a small amount of cash—the standard Australia Safe identity card, a driver's licence, several credit cards, frequent flier cards, and even some memberships cards for gyms and the like. All in a new name, and all bearing a photograph of my new face. A complete life, bogus address and occupation (hardware supplier, in my case) included. Aisha received the same, wrapped in a handbag. And those papers were my first clue to just how powerful the Underground's contacts were. Because they weren't merely clever fakes. They were real. The Australia Safe card came straight from the Department of Citizenship. Which could only mean that the OU had an operative in the department. Someone highly enough placed to take my new photograph and plug it into the database, attached to an electronically created false identity. Impressive. (Very impressive, obviously. Otherwise, interrogators, you wouldn't have been so interested in this part of my story during our chats. But I've told you everything I know on that score. Several times, as I recall. Once courtesy of cigarette burns.)

Anyway, we were ready to face the great outdoors.

Or at least to leave the snooker room.

'Our first objective,' Harry told us before we climbed the stairs, 'is to get you out of the immediate area. We're aiming for Brisbane on our first leg.'

I said, 'You haven't told us exactly where we are *now*.'

'I haven't? You're in Hervey Bay.'

Ah. So in all my recent travels I hadn't come far at all, and Brisbane was still three hours to the south. Not that I knew Hervey Bay very well. It was a tourist town of sorts, but too sleepy for my tastes. It had a nice enough beach strip, and some whale-watching tours in the bay itself, but otherwise it was just a sprawl of retirement housing and caravan parks. The surprising thing to me was that the Underground had safe houses here. If the OU was active in such a backwater, then the movement had to be a widespread thing indeed.

'So how do we travel?' I asked.

Harry smiled. 'We've got something special in mind. And we'll need it. There are roadblocks on every road out of town, and then more on the highway all the way to Gympie. That's about as far as they think you two could have made it.'

'And if we get to Brisbane?'

'We'll move on again. We need you right out of Queensland in the end. A safe house in New South Wales or Victoria where there'll be time for a proper debriefing.'

A depressing thought struck me, standing there in my long socks and sandals. 'And after that? I mean, what sort of outlook is there for either of us? How long, exactly, are we going to have spend in hiding?'

The smile was gone. 'The foreseeable future, anyway.'

'What's the point then?'

'The point is that until this government is gone, half the damn country has to live in hiding too. So give the self-pity a miss for a moment, okay?' He glanced at his watch. 'Come on. Our ride should be here soon.'

We followed him up into the house proper. The snooker room must have been a male retreat, because upstairs was a female place, going by all the frills and floral patterns. The owners were waiting in the kitchen. A wizened little old man, and a round old woman, sitting silently over their cups of tea.

'Our hosts,' said Harry, as we trooped through. 'I won't introduce you.'

The old couple sipped from their cups and ignored us.

Then we were in the living room. Harry went straight to the window and peered through a gap in the curtains. 'Make yourselves comfortable,' he told us.

I sat on a plastic-covered couch, stared about at cabinets full of china plates, and at plastic fruit in a bowl on the coffee table, and at faded photos of children and grandchildren, and I wondered about who and what these people were, and why they were willing to help.

Aisha was sitting on the edge of a recliner rocker, colours all clashing violently. I thought about her real name again. Nancy. At least she looked like one now.

I said, 'What sort of name is Aisha anyway?'

And despite the bob and the make-up, her glance could still be withering. 'It's the name of the Prophet's wife.'

'Mohammed? His wife?'

'Actually,' Harry commented from the window, 'just one of his wives.'

'His most important wife,' Aisha retorted. 'She helped create

Islam itself. After the Prophet's death, she even led an army against the false fourth caliph. She's the prime example of how important women are in the faith.'

Harry was nodding. 'But that's the problem, isn't it? She was part of the cause of the whole Sunni/Shiite split. A lot of Muslims hate her. She's one reason some say women should never be involved in the high matters of Islam.'

Aisha sniffed. 'They're wrong.'

I looked at Harry. 'How do you know all that?'

'Oh, I've met a few Muslims in my time.' He was still staring through the glass. 'It's certainly a controversial name. Especially for an Islamic convert to choose. What was your thinking behind that, I wonder?'

But Aisha only watched him with renewed suspicion.

Then Harry straightened. 'Here we go.'

I stood up. 'Now?'

'Now.'

He led us to the front door, and out into the first open air and sunlight that I'd seen in days. It should have felt wonderful— a big blue sky, a warm breeze with the hint of salt in it, and off in the distance the sparkle of the sea.

Instead, I felt acutely visible, and acutely vulnerable. We were only walking out onto a front lawn in an average small-town street—houses, parked cars, pushbikes in driveways—but it was an average street in an Australia at war with terror, an Australia nothing like the old one. Every window, every closed curtain— who was hiding behind them, and what could they see? And who did they report to? Everyone knows that it's more than just the AFP and ASIO and the other security forces these days. There are informers, too. Some paid to do it, some blackmailed, others who simply like to point the finger. Report Anything Suspicious, demand the television advertisements. Anything and anyone. For the sake of freedom, for the sake of democracy. And there were Aisha and me, the two most wanted people of the hour, standing in plain daylight in front of fifty windows, with only our flimsy disguises to protect us. We may as well have let off a skyrocket.

Then it got worse.

An old bus came lumbering up the street. It seemed to be packed with people, they were hanging out the windows. And a big banner was slung from the side. 'Hervey Bay Patriotic Society.' With a wheeze of brakes the bus pulled up right in front of us. The door puffed open. And, I swear to God, I could hear the passengers inside singing 'Waltzing Matilda'.

I glared at Harry. 'You're kidding.'

He considered the bus happily. 'No joke.'

'The Patriotic Society?!'

'Fully paid-up members, every single one of them.'

'But—'

'It's cover, you idiot. Now get on board.'

I had a thousand more protests to make, but before I knew it we were in the bus and on our way. It was all heat and sweat inside, people standing in aisles and crammed into overflowing seats, talking, singing, and slapping me and Aisha and Harry on the back like we were the oldest of friends.

I tell you, dear interrogators, I would have felt safer in the hands of the Federal Police. I mean, sure, the Patriots *claim* to be just a society for proud and loyal citizens, but even I know that they're really in cahoots with the authorities. It was the Patriots, after all, who were demanding the detention of all Muslims, even before the Canberra bomb. It was the Patriots who lobbied to get the death penalty reinstated as punishment for treason. It was the Patriots who helped run the campaign that introduced conscription. It was the Patriots who forced Christian prayers back into every school in the nation. And it was the Patriots who orchestrated the banning of abortion. 'Procreation, not immigration!'—that was their motto. (White babies please, not black, brown or yellow.) Even their name is a giveaway. Since when did Australians use a word like 'patriot'? They're my brother's biggest fan club, running dogs and informers one and all. And now we were with a whole busload of them.

Madness. But Harry shepherded Aisha into a miraculously spare seat halfway along the bus, and then ushered me onward, to where another two empty places waited. He took the window seat for himself, and then forced me down. 'Listen,' he said. 'This is our best shot to get you through the roadblocks. You and Aisha are just two faces in a crowd now.'

'But how can you trust these people?'

'They're not *real* Patriots,' he explained, head low to my ear. I noticed that, several seats ahead, Aisha was being similarly instructed by an elderly woman next to her. 'They're all members of the Underground. All we did was stack one of the Hervey Bay branches with our own people. Like I said, it's good cover. Not only does it give us an inside line to what the government's more radical policy ideas are, it's also bloody handy for travel. You flash a Patriot card at a roadblock, and half your worries are over. Which reminds me...'

He got up and went to the front of the bus. I stared after him. The crowd was chatting and laughing, waving little Australian flags like the good citizens they were supposed to be, and studiously ignoring the fugitives in their midst. Harry came walking back, paused to hand something to Aisha, then returned to me. He passed over a card that was red, white and blue.

'Your membership,' he said. 'Put it in your wallet.'

I tucked it away, then waved a hand at all the people on the bus. 'Just how many of you are there in the Underground?'

'Around the country, thousands. But this is nearly the whole Hervey Bay contingent, right here. And it's risky, having us all on the one bus. But this way the police at the roadblocks will be too busy vetting everyone else to be looking closely at individual faces like yours. More to the point, travel is restricted in the area right now. We'd have no chance getting anywhere as just average people. But there's a big Patriot rally going on in Brisbane as we speak, and no one fucks with the Patriots, so a group like this will be let through.' He glanced around at the crowd, smiled wanly. 'You know, you owe these people, big time. Not only are they risking their lives for you and Aisha, they'll actually have to attend the rally. Three whole days of it. And those things are like bloody Nuremberg.'

He fell silent. The bus had laboured through the back streets of Hervey Bay, and was now turning onto the main road out of town. There weren't many people about—and there wouldn't be, if travel was restricted—but otherwise it looked like the normal world out there. Petrol stations. Fast food restaurants. But then the bus began to slow. Harry tensed beside me.

'First checkpoint,' he said. 'Just go along with everyone else and don't do a damn thing to draw attention to yourself.'

Through the window I saw flashing lights, police cars, army vehicles, and black and yellow barricades. Then the brakes squealed as the bus came to a stop.

And I could hear the sniffer dogs barking.

THIRTEEN

Roadblocks. Checkpoints. Citizenship Verification Stations, to quote an official title. Or another—Designated Freedom Access Points. Call them what you will, we've all had to deal with them these last years, in ever-increasing numbers. This one, however, was far bigger than most—not just your half-platoon of bored army conscripts with stop signs and a few barriers. The army was there, sure enough, but I could also see AFP cars, Department of Citizenship vans, and several other vehicles that were unmarked but obviously secret service of some kind. The authorities really weren't kidding around in their search for Aisha and me.

Uniformed men advanced on the bus from every direction, some already checking under the chassis with mirrors, others opening the luggage compartments, and others again leading the sniffer dogs about. But the weirdest thing was that, when the doors opened and the first inspectors climbed aboard, the whole bus broke into polite applause.

Hidden away at the back, I glanced questioningly at Harry. He was clapping too. 'Remember, we're all Patriots here. We approve of the roadblocks. They keep us safe from terrorists. We think the inspectors are heroes.'

I nodded. It made sense... although it took some effort getting my head around the logic. Still, to give the inspectors their due, they weren't disarmed by the reception. Their faces remained blank as they waved away the applause.

'Ladies and gentlemen,' the leader called. 'Ladies and gentlemen, please. This is a federal checkpoint. Have your Australia Safe cards at the ready.'

He was in a suit, not a uniform, and his two colleagues were the same. Of course, under current law, no official is required to identify himself, so it was impossible to know which body these men represented precisely. But they had the look of Department of Citizenship to me—and that was scary. The AFP might spy on our every move, and the military might have taken over our streets, but Citizenship (or Immigration, as they used to be called) are the ones who, ever since September 11 and its aftermath, have been making people disappear.

The reception for the inspectors died away to a hum, and a general digging into pockets and handbags for personal papers began. I didn't know where to look. Should I pretend to be talking to Harry? Should I be staring vacantly out the window? Should I be smiling at the Citizenship men? Nothing felt right, and my face had turned into a hot heavy mask.

'Relax,' Harry was whispering through an easy smile. 'They're not going to pay you any special attention. Trust me.'

And it did all seem very congenial up there at the front. People were cheerfully handing over identity cards, yarning and grinning. The three inspectors were staring at photos and comparing them to faces, taking thumbprints on their little computer scanners and running the results... But had their demeanour softened? Was it possible to be surrounded by so much goodwill without defrosting a *little*?

Then I was staring at the back of Aisha's head as the first inspector reached her. I could feel that Harry—despite the fact that he was now chatting about fishing with the man sitting just in front of us—was watching her too. This was her first encounter with the authorities since her capture by the OU, and who really knew what her plans were? She could betray us all with a word, yet when the inspector put out his hand, she passed over her papers and pressed her thumb on the scanner. Then, while the man studied the screen—amazement of amazement— she turned blithely to the old woman next to her, said something and laughed. Laughter! From Aisha! I nearly fell out of my seat. And the inspector, with that curt nod that all secret police use when they're satisfied with something, from the Gestapo on down, handed her papers back and moved on.

Closer to me now. I told myself there was nothing to fear. The OU sympathiser who'd created our new papers must be damn good if Aisha had got through, thumb print and all. We were safely in the system. So the only way we were going to get caught was by a direct identification. And they hadn't recognised Aisha, so they wouldn't recognise me. I had to believe that, and stay cool. Only what the hell was my assumed name again? What was my job? Where on earth was I born and raised and how many generations could I boast?

The inspector was in front of me, and I offered up my Australia Safe card.

Did the bus fall silent? It couldn't have, I know, but it was silent in my head. I thumbed the scanner and he stared at the computer screen. Then at me. Then at the screen. And then, long and straight it seemed, at me again.

'What happened to your nose?' he asked.

'Football injury,' I heard myself say, through a mouth stuffed with cottonwool. 'I was a ruckman. Years ago.'

He frowned. 'It looks recent.'

I opened my mouth, but nothing else came. He knew I was lying. Of course he knew. His gaze was hardening. The farce was over already.

'Oh *fuck*!' It was Harry, next to me, slapping his forehead in disgust as he stared at his own papers. 'Goddamn, I'm an idiot. Officer? Officer?'

The eyes flicked away. 'What?'

A distressed Harry was waving his identity card. 'I've only just realised. This ID has expired. It's a month out of date. Jesus, I forgot all about it.'

Annoyed, the inspector grabbed the card. 'That's an offence.'

'I know. I can't believe I let it happen.'

'Didn't you get the letter advising you to renew?'

'Sure. I think so. It's probably stuck to the fridge right now. How much trouble is this going to land me in?'

The inspector didn't answer right away, busy reading Harry's thumb print. Beneath Harry's card, he still held mine. Information flashed up on his little screen, and he punched some keys, got more information, then grunted. 'Well, you check out. But I still don't think I can let you pass with this.'

'Really? I know I fucked up, and I know you guys have to be careful, but isn't there a fine I can pay or something?'

'Oh, there'll be a fine,' the Citizenship man muttered darkly. 'In the meantime, you're a security risk.'

'But I can't miss the rally!'

There were murmurs of support from the crowd around. Someone from the front called out, 'Give him the Test! That should settle it.'

'Yeah,' someone else cried. And suddenly the whole bus was echoing it. 'The Test! The Test!'

The inspector seemed to puff up slightly. 'Okay. A CVT it is.'

Internally, I sagged with relief. Harry was taking the heat for me. And a part of me was curious too, because I'd never heard a CVT delivered first-hand—although, like everyone else, I'd driven through plenty of checkpoints where, off to one side, some hapless non-Aussie-looking individual was being grilled with that week's list of questions. Okay, maybe in this case it was only being applied to Harry for form's sake. Still, taking the Test is never just a joke. For those who don't pass, strip searches, beatings, or even detention have been known to follow.

The Citizenship man pulled a green paper from his pocket and read from it, all formality. 'I'm informing you now that I am about to apply a Citizenship Verification Test, which will consist of seven questions. Failure to answer all seven correctly will have consequences. Do you understand?'

'I understand,' Harry replied. Of course, it wouldn't have mattered if he didn't understand. Inability to speak English is certainly no excuse when it comes to the Test, as many luckless older migrants could confirm.

'First Question—What was Donald Bradman's batting average?'

'Ninety-nine point nine four.'

No response from the inspector. Supposedly they never tell you if you're right or wrong, until the end. Not that there were any worries about a Bradman question. Meanwhile, the bus really had gone silent. The other two inspectors were working their way down, but everyone else was listening eagerly.

'Second Question—What line follows this one from Banjo Paterson's "The Man From Snowy River": *There was movement at the station...?*'

'*For the word has passed around.*'

Another giveaway.

'Third Question—On what date does Anzac Week begin?'

Hmm. That was a harder one. After all, this is just the second year since the government upped the Anzac tributes from one day to seven, to fit in all the new ceremonies and the commemorative war games. (Not to mention the pilgrimage to Gallipoli itself. I heard somewhere that last year it topped a quarter of a million Australians. That's ten times the size of the original army we sent!) Still, it was only a matter of counting back a week from the old date...

Harry was way ahead of me. 'Nineteenth of April.'

'Fourth Question—Which country has repeatedly threatened the Australian environment by carrying out nuclear tests in the Pacific?'

A scowl from Harry. 'France.'

Ah now, this was different—not just a question about Australia, but also a check on political attitudes. It remains official policy, as everyone should know, to hate the French. And all other European types who won't join in the wars. But there was a trick in the question, too, because if some fool dared to mention the USA's nuclear tests in the Pacific, well, it would be off for re-education on those subversive tendencies, wouldn't it? Not that Harry needed to be warned.

'Fifth Question—What did most Aborigines die of after Australia was settled?'

'They died only of disease.' And was there a twinkle in Harry's eye? 'Not lead poisoning.'

The Citizenship man gave him a stare. This wasn't the place for irony. The new Australia has no sins to hide, no black armbands, and certainly no room for smart-arse doubters. Not unless they want a taste of the whip.

'Sixth Question—Where did the criminal bushranger Ned Kelly murder three innocent policemen?'

I nearly laughed out loud. Seems the government is still trying to paint poor old Ned black. You can't have a bushranger as a national icon anymore. Heck, by today's reckoning, he was a terrorist, pure and simple.

'Stringybark Creek,' answered Harry, without comment.

'Seventh Question—Who bowled the underarm ball, and was it legal?'

Chuckles all round the bus.

'Trevor Chappell. And yes, it bloody well *was* legal.'

Take that, New Zealand! But then, a little Kiwi-bashing was no surprise—our former allies across the Tasman are nearly as bad as the Europeans these days. Peace-mongering lunatics who haven't even locked up their Muslims yet.

'Finally—Recite the Australian Oath of Loyalty.'

Which was always how the Test ended, I'd heard—and not so easy to do, either. Sure, I'd recited the oath the last time I'd gone to get my Australia Safe card renewed, but they give you a sheet of paper with the words on it for that, and the woman behind the counter hadn't even listened.

But Harry was upstanding, hand to his heart. 'I swear loyalty to the Commonwealth of Australia, to obey its government, to uphold its laws and to preserve its values. I swear loyalty to our Prime Minister, and to our armed forces, wherever they may serve. I swear to report all traitors, and to respect all alliances, most of all, our great and good friendship with the United States of America. God bless Australia.'

Harry started the recital alone, but the bus couldn't resist, and by the end fifty voices were shouting it out loud. Patriots all.

'Correct,' the inspector intoned. He handed Harry his card. 'Get that updated,' he warned. Then, without even a glance, he handed my card back to me, motioned to his colleagues, and stalked away down the aisle.

'Jesus,' I said, as the bus started up and Harry was assaulted by handshakes from all around, the faces genuinely relieved under all the mock bonhomie. 'Are we gonna have to go through this at every checkpoint between here and Brisbane with that dodgy card of yours?'

'God, no.' He pulled out another ID. 'This one is fine. I always carry an expired one too, though, just for tight situations. When the security boys are looking hard for a major crime, it's always a great distraction to give them a minor one.'

FOURTEEN

Citizenship tests... Could we sink any lower?

And as for loyalty oaths, time was that only new immigrants had to take them. For the rest of us sunburnt slobs, lucky enough to have been born here—well, that was all you needed. You didn't have to play the national anthem twenty times a day, or fly the Aussie flag in front of your house, or swear loyalty against a thousand enemies. We knew exactly who we were, and how good we had it, and there was no need to make an unseemly fuss in the meantime. Australia? Yeah, a great place, thanks, mate. Happy to be here. National anthem? Don't actually know the words, cobber, but shocking bloody tune. The flag? Funny thing with a Union Jack in the corner. War against Islam? Sorry china, not right now, the cricket is on.

Then came the Twin Towers.

I remember where I was that day. Or that night, actually. Late, Tuesday night, Australian time. I was in a Sydney hotel room, having my last drink of the evening and staring at the TV. I was watching, in fact, that old series 'The West Wing'.

(Not that I was fan—I thought the show was pretty far-fetched at the time, having known a few politicians in my day. And Christ, how ludicrous does it appear, looking back now? What a liberal wet dream of how the White House should be run!) Anyway, it was close to the end of the episode. There was an ad break, and I was flicking channels idly, and suddenly there was a picture of a burning tower on the screen. I assumed (and this happened to other people I've talked to) that the image was part of 'The West Wing'. A dramatic cliffhanger climax to the episode. And just another crisis for President Jed Bartlet and his faithful staff to deal with, in their considered and law-abiding and utterly fictional fashion.

It was a good thirty seconds before I realised that the burning building was real, not part of the show. And about thirty seconds after that, the second plane hit.

Still, I had no real concept of how much things were going to change. In the USA. In the world. And in little faraway Australia too. How could I? The years leading up to September 11 had been so balmy, so pleasant. Even my own fortunes were on the rise again. Where was I up to in this story? That's right, I was dangling about in Canberra, waiting for a meeting with Bernard, the new Minister for Local Government. And yes, the little bastard made me sweat on it, but the day finally came when I was invited into his ministerial office.

It was my first good look at the new Parliament House. Actually, I arrived early for my appointment and took the public tour. A lot of glass and steel, it felt to me. Almost like something *I* would have built, in my eighties heyday. The grand foyer could have been the lobby of a resort hotel in Surfers Paradise, and the rest of the place felt either overweight with its own self-importance or, paradoxically, as flimsy as a garden shed. But at least the two chambers—the House of Representatives and the Senate—were bigger than the cramped quarters of the old Parliament House. The politicians no longer had to suffocate together, jammed into the backbenches. Now there were deep, comfy leather seats for each MP or senator, tasteful green in one chamber, garish red in the other. And if they wanted fresh air, there was always the lawn-topped roof for a stroll, in the shade of the biggest, shiniest flagpole known to democracy.

Pure chintz, really, but off in the administrative wings and away from the public eye, things were more businesslike, and Bernard, as a departmental head, had a whole suite. I was held in the waiting room for half an hour or so, flicking through glossy Local Government brochures. Then I was ushered through to Bernard's office. And a glance told me that this wasn't my little brother anymore. Instead he was...

Well, put it this way. Power pumps up men like balloons, and while he was still nearly fourteen years away from the full size and pomposity that he would display as Prime Minister, when I walked in I saw a man who was just beginning to inflate. It was something about the way the collar of his shirt cut into his neck— the new, defiant out-thrusting of his meagre chin. And when he shook my hand, a moue of distaste on his lips, it was perfectly clear that he thought I was exactly the sort of disreputable prick that might burst his bubble.

Ah, but why would I want to do that? The only point of this reunion, remember, was to help relaunch my career as a developer. I needed him fully inflated. And Bernard, for his part, knew that if he was stuck with a brother determined to trade on his name, then it was in his interest to at least set some ground rules. Which he proceeded to do. There would be no special treatment for me or my projects, he insisted—but on the other hand, his government was entirely in favour of development, and he wouldn't do anything to stand in my way either, as long as I behaved with some decorum. And hey, I could read between the lines. If I kept my nose clean, he was telling me, he wouldn't object to me leaning on the odd local council by dropping the name of the man who handed out the grants. And yes, he'd even introduce me and my friends to *his* friends in the party, as long as in return... Well, cash donations to the election fund were always warmly appreciated.

So we had an understanding, and I was back in the trade, and for the next five years I soared. Relatively, anyway. It wasn't like the 1980s all over again, but still, it was good times. I had investors, I had developments on the go, I had my name in the paper. But it wasn't only me. Looking back, it seems like the whole country had it pretty good too. The economy was up, unemployment was down. And yet the period seems a dull blur now. Strangely lifeless. There must have been important things happening, headlines on the news every night, but to tell the truth, I can recall very little. There was the big debate about Australia becoming a republic. A year of fuss and fury that ended in nothing. There was all that stuff about apologising to Aborigines for taking over their country. More fuss, more fury, and nothing whatsoever as a result. There was the rise and fall of One Nation. The biggest fuss and fury of the lot, and again, so much rotting newspaper now. Is that really all we had to worry about? The introduction of a sales tax, a few skirmishes with the unions, an ever-victorious cricket team, the Olympics in Sydney?

And the world? What were the big international concerns? The death of Princess Di? Monica sucking President Clinton's dick? The Y2K bug? It's bizarre—why can't I remember anything important? There must have been wars and revolutions going on everywhere. There must have been warning signs. I suppose to anyone in the Middle East or the Third World, there were signs aplenty. But us westerners...lord, we were just sailing along. I do recall that al-Qaeda were active even then, bombing things here and there. But no one was really worried about them, were they? And sure, people talked about terrorism, and rogue states, and the evils of oppressive regimes. But it was only talk. I suppose everyone was still bathing in the afterglow of the collapse of communism, even a decade on. The big battle was won. There was nothing left to do but sit back and watch the money roll in. Easy to see the collective blindness now. A lot harder when you're part of the generation living it.

And yet it's curious. Australia had things rosy—but somehow, for Bernard and the Liberal Party, the times weren't quite so

good. They were in power, yes, but to many people they still
seemed a rather ordinary government, and John Howard only an
average Prime Minister. That's hard to credit now, when Howard
stands tall in the books as one of the longest-serving PMs in the
nation's history. But he was a bit of joke back in the nineties,
even to the people who voted for him. Who can forget him
showing up at that rally on gun control, out west—conservative
voters all, his very support base—wearing a bullet-proof vest in
case someone shot him! Then there were problems with his
ministers, sackings for incompetence, the messy union battles,
the endless cost-cutting. Between it all, after a mere three years
in government, he very nearly lost his second election. A few
more years passed without much improvement, and as 2001 rolled
around, yet another election was looming, and Labor was streets
ahead in the polls.

As for Bernard, he stagnated in Local Government for most
of that period. Very handy for me, but obviously frustrating for
him. To most of his colleagues, he seemed increasingly strange.
Even though it had nothing to do with his portfolio, most of his
utterances seemed to be about things like national security and
foreign affairs. And about the USA. He was greatly heartened
by the return to sanity in the States, with the election of George
W. Bush. From afar, he encouraged the Republicans to stamp
their authority on the world. Forcefully, righteously, and even
militarily, if necessary. Indeed, in retrospect, Bernard was talking
like a neo-con even before the term was much in use, and
preaching a hawkish line at a time when the likelihood of anyone
starting a new war was next to zero. But the White House—in
Bush's first year, at least—didn't seem to be listening. Like the
Howard team, they were floundering about in search of direction.
What both governments badly needed, Australian and American
alike, was a defining purpose.

Hey presto—September 11.

And no. Let me make this clear. I don't for a second think
that there was any grand conspiracy about the attacks, that
somehow the CIA or other Bush cronies were behind it. The

idea is lunacy. You have to remember, it was a more innocent era. Western administrations didn't slaughter thousands of their own citizens just for politics' sake. (Nowadays, on the other hand...Okay, we'll get to *that* all in good time.)

But my God, talk about synchronicity for the Bush camp. A crisis just when they needed it most, and a chance to shine forth with leadership.

Perfect timing for the Liberals, too, in Australia. Although, in fact, we already had our own little crisis going on here in the weeks before 9-11, which was doing wonders for the government—the wave of refugees that had begun to break across our unwilling shores, most of them Muslim. John Howard was joyfully whipping up hysteria about the invasion, and playing hard ball with the refugees themselves, locking them away or stranding them at sea. The voters were lapping it up, anti-Islamic feeling was on the rise, Labor was caught wrong-footed and, who knows, the refugee issue alone might have got the Liberals home. But then the planes crashed into the USA—all of them piloted by Muslims—and that was game, set, and match. Suddenly the Prime Minister was shoulder to shoulder with George W. Bush against the new Enemy, and only fools, pacifists and traitors would have dared to vote against him. *That's* when John Howard the political giant was born.

It was the true beginning for Bernard, too. No doubt he was sobered and mortified and sickened by the Twin Towers, just as we all were. On the face of it. For public consumption. But inside, I bet he was grinning from ear to ear. The neo-con nonsense he'd been spouting for years was suddenly the new gospel truth, and in Australia, at least, he was one of the leading prophets. In the ensuing election, the Liberals won in a landslide, and in the new cabinet, Bernard was elevated to a whole other realm of power and influence. A security portfolio.

But me...The day after the attack, I was wandering the streets of Sydney, trying to go about my business despite a head full of terrible premonitions. And you know, the thing that stuck with me most wasn't the planes crashing and the buildings falling.

No—it was the expression I'd seen in the eyes of the American news presenters in the first hours of the disaster. As the towers were followed by the Pentagon, and then the crash in Pennsylvania, and then by wild reports that other aircraft were circling up there somewhere, waiting to hit their targets—I saw something in the news readers' eyes that was astonishing to see on American TV. Fear. Stark and bewildered, not knowing where to turn for the next horror.

I had *never*, *ever* seen that expression on the face of the USA before, and it was their fear that scared the absolute shit out of me. Not because I had any concerns for Australia or for myself right then. I wasn't worried about planes falling out of our own skies. It was because I knew that, once America stopped being afraid, they were going be angry. Angry about the attacks, of course, yes, but absolutely furious at being scared and humiliated like that. They were going to be *outraged*. And when the most powerful country the planet has ever seen is in a rage—a red-faced, spittle flying, screaming fury—then it didn't matter who you happened to be in the rest of the world. Friend, enemy, neutral—all of us were going to be running for cover.

FIFTEEN

The mass meeting of the Australian Patriotic Society was taking place at the Brisbane Convention Centre—just across the river from the city heart. Something like twenty thousand people were expected, and the footpaths surrounding the centre had taken on a carnival atmosphere. It was early afternoon by the time we arrived, sunny and warm, and crowds were flocking everywhere amidst the booths and stalls and flutter of patriotic banners.

Security forces had closed the area to traffic, so our bus parked a block away, and we all climbed out to join the throng, waving our little Australian flags. Loudspeakers crackled noise. The smell of hot dogs wafted through the air. Children cried and laughed. It might really have been a carnival, except for the police and the soldiers who stood watching at every corner, guns at the ready. It was a peculiar feeling—the warm day, the crowd, the tall buildings of Brisbane all around—and several hundred armed men who, if only they'd known, would have shot me and Aisha on sight. Fortunately, they weren't really looking for us. (That was the job of the various roadblocks we'd encountered, and safely passed, on the trip down.) The forces there at the rally were more worried about suicide bombers or protesters. So, tucked away in the middle of the group, Aisha and I walked unnoticed by anyone, safe behind our disguises.

In the shadow of the convention centre we came to the major checkpoint for entry. Long queues had formed there, in front of the metal detectors, under an enormous banner that read 'A Loyal Australia. A Safe Australia. A Strong Australia'. Our own group of Patriots, babbling with pretend excitement, dutifully joined the lines—but Harry discreetly led Aisha and me away. We headed along a row of merchandise booths, then past the traffic barriers and off down towards Musgrave Park. The crowd thinned out, and we came to a taxi parked at the roadside, the driver lounging against the hood, smoking and reading a magazine. He and Harry exchanged a minimal nod, and we all climbed in, Aisha and me in the back seat. Then we swung away, heading south, and turned onto Vulture Street.

I studied the driver. He looked like an old hand behind the wheel—world-weary and unshaven, elbow out the window—and was ignoring us steadfastly. He had to be in the OU, however. Harry would never have loaded us into just any cab. Not when every taxi in the nation has been fitted with live cameras and microphones, all linked to a central AFP database with the latest in facial recognition software. True, the cab we were in was rigged with all the gear, lights blinking—but there was no chance that any of it was working properly.

No one said a word, and we moved along into Woolloongabba. Slowly. Indeed, the traffic seemed inordinately heavy for the hour, but it wasn't until we came over the hill near the Mater Hospital that I could see why. Up ahead was the Brisbane Cricket Ground, and another big crowd of people was swarming about outside the stadium, the attendant security forces blocking half the street. I sat up, interested.

'It's a one-day game,' Harry said, glancing back.

'Between who?'

His face was deadpan. 'Australia versus the USA.'

I sat back. Yes... I'd read something about this weeks before, in the papers. It was supposed to be a demonstration match, and the first official international fixture between the two countries. Although it wasn't a real American team—it was a military one, made up of players from the various US bases around Australia. Still, I was stunned when our driver pulled over across from the stadium and handed Harry a bunch of tickets.

'We're going in there?' I said, staring.

'It's all been organised,' Harry replied. 'Just follow me.'

Then we were out on the footpath, surrounded by cricket fans. We bypassed the long lines for general seating, and headed instead for one of the special entrances. Soldiers bearing guns stood watchfully along the walls. Some of them, I finally noticed, were US troops. Their eyes scanned the crowd steadily, myself included—but again, they were looking for the usual bombers or troublemakers, not fugitive individuals. We made the gate unopposed, ran our tickets through the machine, were sniffed by the explosive sniffers, then passed through the metal detectors and on into the bowels of the stands. From there it was up several flights of stairs and, finally, through a door that bore a placard reading 'AC, Exclusive Guests'.

And there it was, the Gabba, spread out before us, green and beautiful in the sunshine, pleasantly dimmed by a wall of dark glass. We were in a corporate box. Quite a nice one, too, with comfortable chairs arranged before the window, a television at either end, and a small bar and fridge waiting at the back. On the other side of the glass, some thirty or forty thousand people were gathering in the stands.

'This is the craziest thing I've ever heard of,' I said.

'Why?' Harry seemed perversely cheerful. He was rummaging through the fridge. 'I think it's pretty clever, actually.'

'Half the US bloody Army is outside.'

He found a beer, studied it with satisfaction. 'Take a look at the stands. The other half is inside. To watch the game. What d'you expect? Their boys are playing.'

I glared through the window. He was right, I saw uniforms

everywhere, Australian, American, air force, navy, marines, thousands of them.

'Relax.' A beer bottle hissed open. 'You want one?'

I took the beer—hey, it was a while since I'd had a drink—but I wasn't happy about it. Nor did Aisha seem to be. She was walking up and down before the glass, gazing out intensely at all of those sworn enemies in uniform.

'What date is this?' she wanted to know.

'The twenty-sixth.'

And something about that seemed to disturb her.

'Listen, both of you,' Harry said, flopping down in a seat. 'You're safe here. No one can see in, and no one would think to search for you in this of all places.'

'We'd be safer in one of your Underground houses,' I complained.

He shook his head. 'It's only for a few hours. Then we'll be linking up with our transport out of Brisbane. They're already right here at the ground.'

'And who is that?'

He only smiled. 'Sit down. Watch the game.'

I sat down and stared out impatiently. Things weren't under-way yet, but both teams were on the ground, warming up—the Australians in their green and gold one-day gear, the Americans in a stars-and-stripes get-up that looked ridiculous. A desperate attempt to create a spectacle. The whole event, in fact, felt ridiculous. But that's what international affairs have driven us to. With Pakistan no longer invited to play here, and with South Africa boycotting us for our supposedly inhumane treatment of detainees, and with even New Zealand frozen out, well, there are big holes to fill in the cricketing schedule.

Harry was watching Aisha as she prowled.

'You don't like cricket?' he asked.

'It's a stupid game,' she said, still preoccupied.

'But Islamic countries play too. What about Pakistan? Bangladesh?'

She shook her head abruptly and walked to the fridge. She

pulled out a bottle of white wine, unscrewed the cap, and poured herself a glass.

Harry gave her a look of mock astonishment. 'You drink?'

In answer, she downed half of it in one gulp.

'Some Muslim you are,' he laughed.

She perched moodily on a chair and said, 'I'm a new kind of Muslim. A kind you've never met or even dreamt of.'

Harry frowned for a moment. 'What kind is that?'

But Aisha had withdrawn again.

I drank. The beer was wonderful. But it, too, only raised more questions. Who was paying for it? Whose corporate box was this anyway?

I said to Harry, 'What does AC stand for?'

'AC?'

'On the door.'

'Oh. Australian Cricket.'

'The Australian Cricket Board? This is *their* box?'

'One of them.'

'How on earth did you get it?'

He gave a shrug. 'Through a friend.'

A friend on the board of Australian Cricket? I couldn't have been more shocked if he'd said the OU had contacts amongst my brother's cabinet ministers.

'It's no surprise, really,' Harry continued. 'Politically, the Cricket Board might be as conservative as they come, but the cricket is what really matters to them, and the way things are going with the game under this government...Well, certain members are deeply distressed. We can't just keep playing England and India and the West Indies for the next ten years. And games like this are a *travesty.*'

'Do they know who you've got in here?'

'Of course not. And they won't come looking either. We just said we needed a box for the day, and here it is.'

I had a sudden vision of our transport arrangement out of Brisbane. We would be travelling with the Australian cricket team itself, on their team bus. (They used to fly, but not anymore.

Too much of a risk for the national morale, if their plane happened to be one that got taken down by terrorists.) I would be sitting next to the Australian captain himself, and we would discuss batting averages and rebellion as we headed south.

But the fantasy vanished abruptly. I was gazing at the big video scoreboard. It had been showing the usual advertisements, but suddenly Aisha's face was staring back at me across the stadium, thirty feet high. I lurched up out of my chair in alarm. Was there a camera on us somewhere?

Harry's hand was on my arm. 'Don't panic. It's just the wanted posters.'

He was right. For a start, it was Aisha's *old* face up there on the screen, the long white hair, the crazy eyes. It looked nothing like she did now. And then it was replaced by another face—a man, no one I knew. And then more faces after that. All with their names emblazoned below, along with the words 'Wanted for crimes against the Commonwealth'. By that time I was sitting down again, heart thumping in relief. And studying the crowd, I could see that no one was paying attention anyway. This was standard stuff at sports venues now, and it always drew about as much attention from the fans as wallpaper.

I drained my beer, and got another.

Out on the ground, the teams had withdrawn to the dressing rooms, and now a US military marching band was doing some laps.

'Marching bands,' Harry observed. 'At the cricket. Honestly, they've probably brought bloody cheerleaders along as well.'

Meanwhile, ground staff were erecting a microphone near the pitch. The marching band worked its way over to it, then the two teams trooped back out and lined up on either side. 'Ladies and gentlemen,' came an announcement over the ground PA, 'please be upstanding for the national anthems.'

As one, the crowd, Australians and Americans alike, rose and put their hands to their hearts. An African American soldier in dress uniform approached the microphone and, in a quite decent baritone, embarked upon 'Oh say, can you see...'

'Oh God.' Harry was completely disgusted now, rising from his seat. 'Excuse me while I take a piss, will you? I can't bear this at the *cricket*.'

He vanished through the door. Aisha and I watched and listened to the rest of the rendition in silence. Then an Australian soldier stepped up, not looking nearly as shiny or splendid. He launched manfully enough into 'Advance Australia Fair', but there was no contest really.

'It never used to be like this,' I said to Aisha. 'When I was a kid you hardly ever heard the national anthem at sporting events. At international rugby games, maybe, but that was about it. Never at AFL games, never at the cricket. Now you can't even have two junior club sides meet without the whole damn audience having to get up and sing.'

'Enforced patriotism,' she snapped.

'Oh, I know. Otherwise we might forget what country we're in, God forbid.'

But Aisha had suddenly gone rigid. 'Look,' she said, pointing.

I followed the direction of her finger. Below us, and a few rows across, were some slightly less salubrious corporate boxes, open to the air. Most of them were currently filled by high-ranking American military officers. One of them, however, held only men in plain clothes. Suits, despite the warmth of the day. The men were all standing as the Australian anthem drew to a close, but they were chatting quietly, ignoring the singer below. And then I saw him. At the back of the box, standing alone, watching the crowd coolly from behind sunglasses. A tall, elderly man with a lean frame and a wave of grey hair. And a distorted, half-paralysed face.

'Holy shit,' I said.

'It's him, isn't it?'

'It's him.'

Our CIA friend. Or whatever he was. From the ambush. Relaxing now with his colleagues, it seemed, out for a day at the game.

Aisha bared her teeth. 'Good. I'm glad he's here.'

'Why glad?'

But that's when Harry came back. 'Is the flag-waving crap over yet?' he inquired, helping himself to another beer.

'Look,' I said, pointing out the man. Everyone was sitting down now. I hadn't actually seen the toss thrown, but America had won, and decided to bat first. The Australians were idling off to their fielding positions. A happy buzz of expectation ran through the crowd. But the secret service man only leant back dispassionately, his lips warped into that permanent half-smile. I remembered his accent. Light. Southern. Charming.

'It's really the same guy?' Harry asked.

'He's not someone you'd mistake.'

'No. But I wonder who the fuck he is?'

'You don't have any contacts in the CIA?'

'Don't be an idiot. We've got nothing on any of the American forces here. How could we? We're the *Australian* Underground.'

And inexplicably, Aisha was doubled up with laughter.

'What?' Harry demanded.

'You're sure it's the twenty-sixth?' she got out.

'Yes. Why?'

'I don't know if I should even tell you.'

'Tell me *what* dammit?'

She sobered. Glared with the old hatred. 'There's a bomb set to go off here today,' she said.

And down on the ground, the first ball was being bowled.

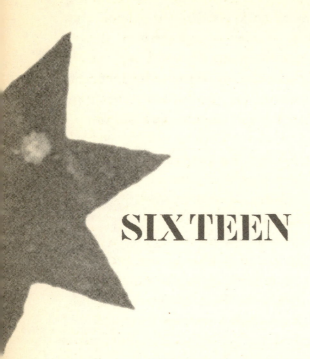

SIXTEEN

It was no game for the connoisseur.

Doubtless the American players had received some intensive training over the months previous in the subtleties of cricket, but there was still a faintly 'baseball' look to the stance of their batsmen—feet too far apart, bats held too high or too horizontal. As for their stroke-play... Well, they were two for three at the end of the first over. The three runs had come from an unconvincing slice over the slips cordon, to wild cheers from the Americans in the crowd. Hopefully, someone was explaining to them that while three runs for two outs might be an impressive score in their game, it was bloody hopeless in ours.

Not that we were paying much attention, up in the box.

Harry had put his beer aside in disbelief. 'What d'you mean, a bomb?'

'You know.' Aisha cupped her hands, then spread them wide. 'Boom!'

'Here? Today?'

'I think so.' She glanced out the window to the sea of uniforms. 'And why not? What better target than all this military?'

'It's impossible. This place would have been vetted six ways from Sunday for explosives.'

'What makes you so sure?' I asked Aisha. 'Is it one of *your* bombs?'

Harry was shaking his head. 'Her people don't have any bombs. Haven't you got that yet? Her people are a joke.'

'We have bombs!'

'Firecrackers. Is that all you're talking about?'

'No. I'm talking about something big.'

'But is it *your* people?' I insisted. 'Is it Southern Jihad?'

Aisha folded her arms and nodded serenely.

Harry was still deeply sceptical. 'You saw this bomb yourself?'

'No...but I meet with other cell leaders sometimes. And I heard rumours about this. A big bomb, on the twenty-sixth, somewhere public.'

'Somewhere public? That could be anywhere.'

'Somewhere public,' she repeated slowly, 'with a big crowd. In Brisbane. The twenty-sixth. Where lots of Americans would die. And where it would be seen on TV.'

All of our eyes turned to the stands. Television cameras hung from every vantage point. The game was screening coast to coast.

'I thought it might have been the Patriot rally,' Aisha went on. 'That's big, and public, and there will be TV cameras there too. But there are no Americans at the Patriot rally. It has to be this. Here and now. Today.'

'Holy shit,' said I.

Harry was considering. 'And who told you this exactly?'

Aisha only smiled at him.

'For fuck's sake, woman, whose side are you on? If there really is a bomb here, then *we're* the ones who might cop it.'

She nodded to the crowd. 'If they die too, then I don't care.'

'Motherfucker,' I added.

Harry stared at her in distaste. 'Christ, I can't wait until we get you into a proper debriefing.' He turned to me. 'She's got to be bluffing.'

'Doesn't sound like it to me.'

'But we studied her cell. They never had the capability to plant a big bomb—they didn't even have contact with the sort of people who *are* capable. And when *those* people do plant big bombs, they don't go telling lunatics like her about it. It doesn't make any sense.'

'If I was so useless,' Aisha observed smugly, 'then why am I the most wanted person in the country right now? Why was my picture on the scoreboard?'

And Harry had no answer to that. That was the big puzzle that none of us knew the answer to. That was the mystery behind this whole damn debacle.

'When is this bomb supposed to go off?' I asked.

'I don't know. Just today sometime.'

'Any idea where exactly in the stadium?'

Her smile floated up again. 'It might be right under this box, for all I know.'

'So why tell us about it?' Harry asked. 'If you're happy to die, why not keep your mouth shut?'

'To see you squirm, that's why.'

'And what if I raise the alarm? Get everyone out?'

'Go ahead. I dare you.'

'Why wouldn't I?'

She snorted in disgust. 'You call yourself an underground? Look at those people out there. All those police, all those Americans—every single one of them your sworn enemy. And you're going to save them?'

'If I believed there really was a bomb, then yes. There're civilians out there. Australians. Completely innocent.'

'No one in this country is innocent.'

'Oh, right, sure.'

'You know it's true. Otherwise you wouldn't be in the Underground.'

'Yeah? Well, I'd still warn them anyway. I'm sure as fuck not going to be the one who lets the Australian cricket team get blown up!'

They subsided a moment, each of them fuming. Out on the ground, a US batsman had just been hit on the head for the second time by a bouncer, and as the locals in the crowd roared with laughter, he was stomping off towards a bemused umpire, waving his bat in fury.

'Look,' I said, 'is there a bomb or not?'

'Yes,' replied Aisha.

'No,' said Harry, at the same time.

'So—what? We're just gonna sit here?'

And this time they were in agreement, both nodding stubbornly.

I gave up, went to the fridge and fetched myself another beer. I had decided—quite reasonably, it seemed to me—to get drunk. Certainly, back in my normal life, it's what I usually did when I ended up in a corporate box.

But it was hardly the same. Bad enough that I was waiting for a bomb to explode, so that every time there was the slightest noise from anywhere—a door slamming in the adjoining box—I jumped half out of my chair. Bad enough, too, that my companions were a sulking freedom fighter and a brooding suicidal terrorist who had no interest in getting drunk with me. Far worse was the game itself.

Oh, I admit it, I enjoy watching Americans get walloped as much as anyone else does in this single-superpower age. But it was hardly sport, was it. Nothing to stir the blood in the sight of flummoxed ex-baseballers swinging and missing at a nicely contrived off-cutter or deceptively looped bit of leg spin. Not that they were totally inept, but when they were all out for seventy-one after twenty overs, the writing was on the scoreboard.

And I couldn't focus on the action anyway. My eyes kept straying from the pitch to roam across the stands, taking in all those thousands of faces, and imagining what it would look like—a bloom of fire and smoke, the concussion, the glass wall in front of me shattering, the screams, the torn limbs thrown into the air, the mass panic in the stadium, the small and the frail and the elderly crushed in the rush for the gates. Assuming I was still alive to see it, of course, and that it wasn't my own limbs being tossed about. After all, our box was close to where the American top brass were sitting. They had to be the prime target, surely. My gaze came to rest upon the box with the suited men. The CIA box, I called it in my own mind. If I hadn't hated the look of those men before, I did now.

No way in a million years could you mistake them for Australians. They were all so neat. They might have been a bunch of Mormons sitting there, in their black ties and white shirts. Sipping soberly on their drinks and talking amongst themselves in tones that I just knew would be clipped and official and serious. Ignoring the crowd around them in a way that made it clear that this, from their point of view, was an inferior part of the world. Not as rich, not as smart, not as *right* as they were. It came to me, from some murky memory of studying ancient history at university, that this was how the locals must have felt— say in Spain or Greece or Syria—when they went to their regional amphitheatre and found the best seats reserved for Romans. The bosses of the world, with a God-given destiny to rule.

Ah, but forgive me. It's been illegal now for some years to compare America to the Roman Empire, hasn't it—by special act of Congress indeed, ratified by the governments of every allied nation. A criminal offence. America *cannot* be anything like the Roman Empire, because the Roman Empire collapsed, and to suggest any sort of similar fate for the US is pure treason. But fuck it, I'm a condemned man as I write, so screw all this neo-correctness. Those CIA agents in the box, and all the US military commanders in the boxes nearby, they looked *exactly* like the Romans must have. Slumming it in some imperial backwater, deigning to watch the local underlings perform some dreary ritual for their benefit.

And my friend with the half-paralysed face? Oh, he looked like the very governor of the province. No average Roman this one, he was the proconsul, or whatever the title was, like Pontius Pilate in Judea. A man with a direct line to the Emperor back in Rome. Who the fuck *was* he, and why had he been on that road in the aftermath of the ambush? Impossible to tell, but there was no denying it—the more I studied him, the more I could sense his utter disdain for the day. For the cricket, for the crowd, for Australia in general. And even, I became sure of it, for his own colleagues and countrymen. A superior bugger indeed.

Meanwhile, the half-time show was on. It took the form— and no surprise here—of an anti-terrorist drill carried out by a combined US/Australian squad. Black Hawk helicopters swarmed over the stadium and disgorged dozens of abseiling troops. Other troops dropped down from the stadium roof. Smoke grenades blanketed the ground in multicoloured clouds and, somewhere in the middle of it all, a group of presumably Islamic terrorists was rounded up and dragged away. Although what exactly terrorists were doing waiting as sitting ducks out on the pitch was never explained. But no doubt the crowd felt safer. Even though one of them, I was growing ever more certain, had a ticking bomb right under their seat.

'When the fuck do we make the transfer and get out of here?' I asked Harry.

'When the game is over,' he said. 'Which won't take long.'

And that was true enough. The half-time mess was cleared away, apart from a few unfortunate divots left in the turf by the armoured vehicles, and the Australian opening batsmen strode to the crease. This was a team that could regularly clock up scores of three hundred against quality bowling attacks. Seventy-one, against part-timers, was going to take them all of half an hour. I needed to drink faster. I dug around in the bar, found a bottle of red wine, and started guzzling.

'Watch it,' Harry warned. 'You have to be able to walk out of here.'

'Fuck you,' I replied, and carried on.

So the rest of the game was a little hazy for me, between my growing drunkenness and my distraction about the possible bomb. But there wasn't much to see anyway, beyond the comedy of the American bowlers, who had developed an ungainly cross between a baseball pitch performed at a sprint, and a legitimate cricket delivery. To be fair, they did generate some good pace. Even some swing. But what they hadn't quite got their heads around was the intricacies of *bouncing* the ball—of deviation, of the seam, of spin. Delighted, the Australian openers clubbed ball after ball to the boundary. The crowd was in fits. And even in the CIA box, faces looked unaccustomedly glum for a moment. After seven farcical overs, Australia was none for sixty-eight, and the only question left was whether the first ball of the next over would be hit for a six or a four to win the game.

Which was when the bomb went off.

It was on the other side of the stadium. I saw a flash of orange, and felt a solid clang that reverberated through the concrete walls. Then came billowing clouds of smoke, and the sound of forty thousand people screaming.

In the box, all three of us had ducked out of our chairs instinctively. But the glass didn't shatter, and Aisha was the first to rise again.

'Told you so,' she said happily.

Harry stared at her in amazement. 'I *still* don't believe it.'

Chaos had broken out below. Police and soldiers were running everywhere. The PA was bellowing instructions. People were surging from the stands, many of them overflowing onto the ground. The cricket players had already vanished. And opposite us, a whole section of grandstand, where maybe a thousand spectators had been sitting, remained enveloped in thick smoke.

'Fuck fuck fuck,' Harry was saying, gazing at the destruction with the guilty horror of a man who might have been able to stop it.

'What do we do now?' I demanded.

'What?'

'What do we do? The transfer? Do we go or do we wait here?'

'We wait,' he said, uncertain. 'We wait...'

His attention remained on the bomb site. An upwelling of air was wafting most of the smoke away, and figures were emerging. People. Coughing and dishevelled, but walking. And as more smoke cleared, I could see that relatively few actually seemed to be wounded or incapacitated. A little stunned, yes, but not hurt.

'What the hell is this?' Harry said, growing puzzled.

Outside our box, I could hear boots running and voices yelling about evacuation. Abruptly, our door burst open. We whirled around to see an Australian Army officer standing there, flanked by two privates.

'Clear this box!' he yelled, but then, bizarrely, all three stepped inside and closed the door behind them.

Harry didn't seem at all surprised by the visitors. 'Have you seen this?' he said to the officer, gesturing to the view out the window.

'Damnedest thing,' the officer agreed. 'Looks like it went off in a stairwell, not in the stand itself. And more like a smoke bomb than something designed to kill. Weird.'

'Aisha here said she knew something was going off today.'

Military eyebrows went up. 'Really?'

'I didn't believe her. Otherwise I would have told you. Sorry.'

'Later. Right now we gotta go.'

'It's safe?'

'Hell, in all this mess, we'd never get a better chance.' He glanced at Aisha and me. Nodded to one of his privates. The soldier tossed three bundles of clothes at us.

I stared at the clothes blearily. They were uniforms.

'Get dressed,' the officer ordered.

'Excuse me?' I said.

Harry was nodding urgently. 'It's our ride. Put on the damn uniforms.'

The officer winked a greeting. 'You just got drafted, son.'

SEVENTEEN

My brother's elevation, in the wake of 9-11, was to the newly created position of Special Minister Assisting the Attorney-General. Not an imposing title, perhaps, but in fact the Special Minister's role was to formulate Australia's response to the new threat of terrorism. This meant liaising between, and focusing the attention of, a whole range of different bodies—the military, the security groups, immigration, police and so on. The word 'assisting' meant that the Attorney-General was still officially in charge of it all, but effectively, Bernard was now Australia's anti-terrorist supremo, and chief enforcer to boot.

The appointment certainly came as a surprise to me. And an upsetting one, because it meant that I'd lost my free ticket into the portfolio of Local Government. There was no business or financial advantage for me in having a brother as a *security* minister. But other political observers were puzzled too. The Liberals had won the 2001 election largely by promising to defend the nation more aggressively than anyone else might. So this new portfolio was a big deal. It was the jewel in the 'war on terror' crown. Yet it had been given to a relatively obscure minister like Bernard. Why?

Insiders, of course, knew the answer. But it would be a couple of years before I really understood it myself.

That happened on the day the US President came to town.

Actually, we all got a clue that day—23 October 2003—our first hint of what sort of Australia lay only a few years ahead. The location? Nowhere else but poor, benighted Canberra. You won't remember the day, dear interrogators. A very minor event in your view of the world. But it was a huge thing here—President George W. Bush himself, jetting in to our capital city to personally thank our Prime Minister for standing firm in the coalition of the willing against Iraq. Okay, so George W. was on a whistlestop tour of the whole world right then, thanking allies left, right and centre, and Australia was getting less of his time than most. But still—the honour of it! And the kudos for John Howard, to spend a whole day at Bush's side, sunbathing in all that superpower glow and glamour.

For the residents of Canberra, the honour was a little more mixed. After a night rendered sleepless by the constant drone of helicopters and the shrieks of patrolling jets, they emerged at dawn on the twenty-third to find their city occupied by the US. Not that anyone was surprised by the basic fact. Everyone had been warned, after all. The President was terrorist target number one, and if we wanted to be blessed with his presence, then surely we understood the necessity of some inconvenience for the sake of protecting him. And truly, no one argued with that.

What amazed people was the sheer scale of it. Until that day, Canberra (and the rest of the country with it) had barely heard of things like roadblocks and security checkpoints and armed soldiers on the streets. Now the city inhabitants found all their major roads shut down, and Parliament House itself—where the President would be addressing a combined sitting of both Houses—locked off by a cordon a mile in diameter. Canberra was a small place, with a radial transport system. Block off a mile-wide circle right in the centre, and the city ceased to function. Commuters trying to get to work that day ended up hours late, if they made it at all, stuck miles out in the country on some insane detour around the no-go zones.

Everyone could have put up with that if they'd at least known that the Australian security forces were in charge. If *we* were calling the shots. We weren't. For that one day it was obvious to everyone that sovereignty of our national capital had been handed over to the United States. We were not to be trusted. *Their* forces were calling the shots, and they were doing so with a ruthless lack of apology. It didn't matter that we were their allies, their friends, their most fervent supporters on the international scene. Wherever the US President set foot was American territory, it appeared, and us Aussies could just get the hell out of our own country, thank you.

I was there myself that day, shunted out of my normal digs at Rydges by the US occupation and forced to endure a room in a cheap motel halfway out to bloody Queanbeyan. A bother, but even so, initially, I had no particular concern about what was being done to Canberra. I was only in town because I had a big-shot American hotelier in tow. He'd been touring my resorts pursuant to investing some much-needed capital, and to butter him up, I'd promised him a chance to see his own President in action. By some adroit pestering of Bernard I'd managed to obtain two passes to the public gallery of the House of Representatives. Not an easy feat, considering 'the public' had been strictly banned access to the chamber.

So it was with some satisfaction that my American companion and I sallied forth to Parliament House that morning, passes in hand. Overhead, helicopters and jets blanketed the town. It really made you feel that you were at the centre of things, for once, even in sleepy old Canberra. (Whether they were Australian or American aircraft hardly seemed worth quibbling about. Indeed, the night before, we'd driven to the lookout on the top of Mt Ainslie to view the whole circus. We even managed a glimpse of Air Force One as it dived steeply towards the airport. At least, we thought it was Air Force One, but there was a lot of talk about decoy planes and so forth, so who really knew.)

My first doubts about it all only came when our taxi was stopped at a roadblock well beyond the edge of the security cordon, our destination still so far off in the distance that even the giant flagpole was barely visible.

'Out,' said the cab driver, after conferring with a man in AFP combat fatigues.

'But we have passes,' I replied.

'Out,' repeated the AFP man. 'You walk from here.'

He might not actually have been an AFP man, of course. Rumour had it that the Federal Police (a modest department in those days) were so hopelessly stretched by the Americans' demands that they had dressed up clerical staff in uniform to fill out their numbers on the street.

Either way, we got out and walked. We'd taken a roundabout route from the motel, and so were now approaching the new Parliament House via the old Parliament House—a pleasantly quiet and grassy prospect in normal times, rich with memories of bygone days in Australian politics. Today, though, the lawns were jammed with masses of police and protesters, already lining up for the first skirmishes of the day. Not that any of the protestors were likely to catch the President's attention at that distance. Those with megaphones were being instructed to point them towards Lake Burley Griffin, directly away from the new Parliament House. And those with anti-American placards? Well, debate seemed to be raging about which way they should point as well, just in case George, by some act of preternatural vision, might glimpse one from half a mile off.

We sauntered through the crowd rather pityingly, and made our way to the major checkpoint set up in Federation Mall. Our passes were approved, and we moved on. I was assuming that there would be nothing more until we reached Parliament House itself. I was wrong. We were stopped at another checkpoint, and then by roving security personnel to boot. Each time, our passes were examined with increasing severity and unhappiness.

Questions were asked, other identification was demanded, enigmatic marks were scribbled on the backs of the papers. And while each checkpoint was manned, as far as I could tell, by Australians, I noticed a funny thing. Me, they didn't like at all. I was just a civilian who had somehow scored an invite, but who obviously had no pressing reason to be there, and so was suspect. My friend, though—as soon as they heard his accent, all suspicion evaporated. An American! Yes, sir! Straight through, sir! It pissed me off a bit, to be honest.

Then we were on Capital Hill, and the glassy walls of Parliament House rose before us. And here there was very little pretence about who was running the day. The security stations at the front doors were surrounded by US personnel. And once again, they were not happy with me. Who was I? Why was I here? How did I get hold of a pass like this? In the end, I resorted to angrily explaining that I was the brother of the Special Minister Assisting the Attorney-General. Which worked surprisingly well. The Americans knew who Bernard was—he had been liaising with them directly about the President's visit. So we made it through to the interior. And not everyone did. I saw one irate famous face—a Canberra correspondent for a TV network—being refused entry by resolute Americans because of some trifling error on his pass. And his cries of 'But this is *our* Parliament House!' were doing him no good at all.

There were even more checkpoints and roving inspectors inside, and by the time we neared the doors to the public gallery, I'd gone from pissed off to quite disturbed. 'Where the fuck do they all come from?' I complained to my friend. 'Your guys must have brought half of Washington along.'

He smiled in amusement. 'We've always got a lot of people in Canberra.' He voted, he'd already told me, strictly Republican, and had links in high places. 'I hear they've got tunnels and bunkers under the US embassy, stuffed with all sorts of secret service personnel. They reckon there's even a tunnel that leads direct from there to here.'

'I can believe it,' I said, staring around. They did look as if they were pouring from some hole in the ground. A short distance off, an Australian news crew was being divested of a video camera, and a fight was nearly breaking out. Of course, everyone knew that cameras weren't allowed in the House, so normally it wouldn't have meant anything to me. Except that twenty yards away, at the entrance to the press gallery, an American film crew was sidling through the checkpoint, one of them grinning as the video camera tucked at his side was politely ignored by all. And even that didn't really mean anything to me, at the time.

Then, after one last check of our passes, we were in. The House of Representatives, the seat of sovereign power. Okay, so most of the accents around me in the public gallery were American, but down in the chamber itself, reclining in their green leather seats, were the elected members and senators of the Commonwealth of Australia. No Yanks allowed. Except the President, of course. The sad truth was, Parliament wasn't even supposed to be sitting right then. They'd called everyone back, at immense expense, just for this moment.

'I gotta say,' my companion observed, 'I'm a little surprised that your government is standing for all this hoopla. I mean, it's a bit subservient, don't you think? A bit *too* willing?'

I agreed, some relic of national pride stirring inside me.

'It's one thing to be polite hosts,' he added, 'but I'm not sure this is really the right way to get respect for your country.'

Still, there was nothing to be done now except watch the show. And quite a show it turned out to be—to which the evening news here in Australia, and internationally too, later testified. Oh, the start was smooth enough—Bush swanning in to thunderous applause, with back pats and handshakes all round. A heart-warming speech from the PM (and a slightly less excited one from the Opposition Leader, who was getting no kudos out of this at all). Fine and dandy to that point, but then came the President's own address, and the famous interruption by two Greens senators, leaping up with questions about Australian citizens stuck in Guantanamo Bay. Chaos! Howling outrage from the Speaker. The attempt to throw the senators out of the chamber. The scuffle in the upper seats when the senators refused to leave. The fuming brow on the Prime Minister. The smooth wink of George W., and his laughing reply of 'I love free speech.' And then, at the end, the running battle as the government members joined ranks to prevent the departing President being mobbed by Greens with petitions.

My American friend was in hysterics. 'You'd never see *this* back home,' he said through his tears.

Indeed. And no one outside the chamber would have seen it at all, if not for that American news crew with their contraband video camera. Oh, the scandal about that—from the Speaker, because his ban on cameras had been circumvented; from the government, because the Greens had embarrassed the entire nation; and most of all, from the Australian media, because *they* hadn't been able to sneak a camera in, and had to steal the footage from American broadcasts.

My brother had been right in the thick of it, part of the human wall thrown up to block the Greens, and I'd been delighted to see him jostled and angry. I had no expectation of actually speaking to him that day, however, seeing I wasn't invited to any of the more intimate functions he'd be attending. But when we emerged from the gallery and made our way towards the exit, I was surprised to see Bernard wandering around in the public area of the foyer. He was in the company of another man—an American, I guessed, even from a distance.

'My brother,' I said to my companion, pointing.

'I see.' Then his eyes narrowed. 'Hey, look who's with him.'

'Who?'

'That's Nate Harvey. He's the Assistant Secretary for Homeland Security, back in the States. Making quite a name for himself.'

Ah. So Bernard was hanging out with his US counterpart, security specialists the both of them. Perfectly natural, of course. But the sight impressed me somehow. The two men were simply ambling about the floor, gazing at the departing crowd as they conversed, and yet it was a glimpse of my brother in a way I hadn't seen him before. He was with a high-powered American official, and yet he looked very much the other man's equal. Not the usual dull, insipid Bernard at all.

We met them in the middle of the foyer, and introductions were made. 'Nate,' said Bernard, hand on the Assistant Secretary's shoulder in an avuncular fashion. 'This is my brother Leo. My older brother. By fifteen minutes.'

Laughter all around. And this was weird, because I knew for a fact Bernard *hated* being my little brother. Still, Nate was pleased to meet a fellow American, and it turned out he and my friend had acquaintances in common, and gossip to trade. Which left Bernard and I to talk between ourselves for a moment.

'Bit of a mix-up, back there in the House,' I said.

Even that couldn't wipe the smile from Bernard's face. 'The Greens made fools of themselves. You wait. The papers will crucify them.'

(And he was right, they did.)

I had another dig. 'So meanwhile it's your job to be tour guide for Nate here, is it? Got nothing better to do than babysit Americans?'

He laughed at me. 'Nothing better at all.'

'You two do seem very friendly.'

'Oh, we go way back, Nate and I. He's staying at my place.'

And it was the way he said it—I had a flash of comprehension. They really *were* old friends. No doubt it stemmed from all those tours Bernard had made to the US, but his relationship with this American bigwig was a cosy one. They liked each other. And finally I grasped why Bernard had been appointed to such a crucial position. Not only was he a loyal advocate of the war on terror. He was *connected*—with the Republicans, with the White House, with US security. And in the new world order, there was no connection more useful or more important.

Intriguing.

But soon enough Bernard and Nate were called away to more august company, and my American friend and I were left to wade our way out of Parliament House, and then down through the barricades again in search of a taxi.

'So what did Nate think of the Greens?' I asked. 'Pretty disgraceful, from an American point of view, I'd think.'

'He thought it was a good thing, actually.'

'Really? How?'

'Well, it makes the whole process look robust, doesn't it? We might be monstering your government about the war and taking over your streets, but there's still free speech, right? Like the President said.'

'It's hardly free speech if you get dragged out of the chamber for your trouble. Or when your capital city has been turned into a fortress around you.'

He laughed. 'It's true, Nate was just saying how Canberra is a security dream. The easiest place in the world to lock down. Small population. Centralised design. Miles from anywhere, off in the bush. Only three highways in and out. It might have been designed for a day like this.'

'I don't think that's quite what Walter Burley Griffin had in mind.'

We were coming down to the lake, and ahead of us the Captain Cook fountain was spearing into the air.

My companion turned thoughtful. 'No. But he's a perceptive man, that Nate. You watch him. He's not destined to just be Assistant Secretary forever. I hear he's running for State Governor soon. And after that, who knows?'

Prophetic words, as it happened.

Sadly, the day itself turned out to be a waste of my time, because my American friend decided not to invest with me after all. Still, it was something to see the President in person, if only from up in the gallery. Moreover, events would reveal that I hadn't merely *seen* a US president that day—I'd actually shaken hands with one. And by the time Nathaniel Harvey had risen to the highest office in America, who would be holding the highest office in Australia other than his bosom buddy, my own little baby brother.

EIGHTEEN

A hangover was kicking in as we made for the Queensland–New South Wales border. Not a *proper* hangover, I hadn't drunk nearly enough at the cricket for that. This was more a slow and unpleasant sobering up. The creeping return—after all the fuss at the Gabba, and the frantic rush out of there—to the cold realities of life on the run. Another false identity, and another secret journey to who knew where.

We were riding through the night in a battered old Humvee. It was the property of the Australian Army, and it wasn't like any of the luxury Hummers I've ridden in over the years. This was no hotel room on wheels—this was the basic military model, as stark and simple as you can get. And hard on the backbone. But then we were soldiers now, not soft civilians, Aisha, Harry and I—all of us dressed up in fatigues, and each bearing the distinguished rank of corporal.

Our cover story was that we were a team of communications experts, setting out to tour satellite facilities in regional areas. To that end, we not only had new IDs in our pockets, we also had military transit passes that were good to take us through any roadblock we might encounter in the next thousand kilometres. We would never have got out of Brisbane without them. The explosion at the cricket had sent the whole city into lock down. But there we were, already clear of the outer suburbs and heading south-west on the Cunningham Highway.

I was in the back, with Aisha. She'd scrubbed off the ludicrous make-up of her previous disguise, and dumped the jewellery, but with her styled hair and pale skin and narrow face, she made an unlikely soldier. Not that I was any better—a fat fifty-nine year old with not an ounce of muscle on me. Harry, up front, at least looked the part. But only the fourth member of our group, the driver, was genuine—a shaven-headed, gravel-voiced warhorse of a staff sergeant whose first name, Daphne, gave a rare clue that she was, in fact, a woman.

'A bomb,' Harry was still muttering, shaking his head and turning around repeatedly to glare at Aisha. 'A fucking bomb.'

It wasn't the bomb itself that bothered him—it was that Aisha had known about it. Harry was regarding her with a whole new air of puzzlement and worry now. So was I. Ever since the detonation, she'd had a look of creamy satisfaction on her face, a sort of distant smile that seemed, to me at least (sex-starved old fart that I am), almost post-coital. It was downright sinister. And a timely reminder about who she really was—a terrorist, sworn to violence, mad, and kind of beautiful, but above all else, highly dangerous. And important. Both to the authorities who wanted her dead, and to people like Harry who were trying to keep her alive.

'Woman,' he warned, 'when the high command get hold of you, they're gonna *grill* your arse. You know a lot more than you're telling.'

Aisha merely considered him with languid contempt.

I said to her, 'Just for interest's sake, are there any more bombs we should know about? I'd prefer to avoid them, if possible.'

'There will always be bombs. Until we win.'

'Win what exactly?'

'A united world of Islam.'

'And then what? Are you going to put on that veil thing and become a good Muslim wife to some man and never show your face in public?'

A smouldering glance. 'A united world of *new* Islam.'

'There you go again,' said Harry. 'And I'd love to know where you're getting it from. None of your terrorist buddies are talking about a *new* Islam. They seem pretty damn stuck on the *old* Islam. And they like things like the veil.'

'Western propaganda.'

'Who are your mullahs, then? Where do they come from? The Middle East? Indonesia?'

'My teachers weren't Arabs. Or Indonesians. They were white Australians.'

'Like who?'

But Aisha was done with the conversation.

'Well, screw you too,' Harry said, and gave up.

We rode in silence for a mile or so. Then Aisha spoke, softly. 'There are no more bombs that I know of. At least, not where we're going.'

I followed her eyes to watch the highway rolling underneath the headlights, the night darkness all around. Where *were* we going? South, that was all we'd been told. Somewhere south, where the leaders of the Oz Underground were waiting for us, whoever they were. Then I found myself staring about at the interior of the Humvee, dully lit from the dashboard. I was sitting, in effect, in the very heart of the beast—the bosom of an army that was now my enemy—and yet I was safe. And the implications of that were only just starting to hit me.

'How on earth did the OU pull this off?' I asked Harry. 'How can the Australian Army be part of the resistance?'

He turned to look back at me. 'Not all of the army, just some of it.'

Our driver stirred. 'Those of us with any fucking balls, anyway.'

I said, 'But the military should love this government. Army, air force, navy—they've never been bigger or more powerful or better funded.'

The woman gave a snort. 'Size ain't everything, darlin'.'

Harry smiled. 'Daphne here is regular army.'

'Thirty years coming up next month. When I joined we had maybe sixty thousand personnel in the whole Defence Force. Small, but bloody professional.'

'Now look what we have,' said Harry. 'Over three hundred thousand personnel, but most of those conscripted, and next to useless. They're spread thin, too, with all these wars we're fighting, not to mention home security. The truth is the ADF is being run ragged, and morale is at rock bottom.'

The sergeant gave me a glance in the rear-view mirror. 'I've got mates overseas, and what I hear isn't good. It's the same old shit. Wars we can't win. Peacekeeping where everyone hates our guts. The troops mostly strung out on drugs or booze. Whole companies refusing orders. Officers beaten up or shot in the back or just told to fuck off. Discipline's a joke.'

Harry was nodding. 'Then there's the ideological aspect. The Australian military used to be completely apolitical. These days, though, if you aren't a vocal supporter of government policy, then you don't go up the chain of promotion.'

'Thirty fucking years served,' repeated Daphne, 'with distinction. I was in the first two Gulf wars. Then some secret service queer in a suit sits me down and says I have to take a loyalty test. Or else. Stick it up your arse, I said.'

'She's not alone,' Harry added. 'The military have been in on the Underground pretty much from the start. The navy was first. That whole asylum seekers scare, the boat people, back in the Howard days—the navy really didn't like what they were made to do. They're *sailors*, and sailors have rules. You don't ignore people in a sinking boat. You don't fire warning shots at them. You don't have debates about whether to save swimmers in the water. You sure as hell don't wait until you get approval from Canberra before you send in a rescue party. Those guys all know that one day *they* might be the ones in the drink . . . And they'll expect someone to help, not tell them they're breaching an immigration zone.'

'That's nothing,' Daphne declared. 'The things I saw in Iraq, second time around, no one in Australia would believe. It was like every fucking thief and liar in the world descended on that poor bloody country and ate the place alive.'

'So anyway,' Harry continued, 'there was a kind of Underground operating in the navy from day one. A certain resistance to government directives. And it didn't take long for the army and the RAAF to follow. Not after what they were forced to do in Iraq and in the other wars since. Like Daphne says. Bombing civilians. Torturing prisoners. Keeping all the government's dirty little secrets. And for what? They know that none of this has a damn thing to do with protecting Australia. Then there's the ultimate indignity—being at the beck and call of the US, as if we were just an auxiliary arm of their forces. Our people feel insulted.'

'Fucking humiliated, more like it,' the sergeant growled.

'So yeah, to answer your question, the Underground has plenty of friends in the military. Not very high ranking. No one at the top command levels, for instance, or in the intelligence arm. But there's anger in the ranks lower down. Like—just whose army is it supposed to be? Whose country?'

And as if to illustrate his point, we crested a rise in the road and there, spreading out across the valley, seemingly as far as the eye could see, were the lights and buildings and illuminated flagpoles of Base Amberly.

'Avert your eyes, ladies and gentlemen,' intoned our driver, 'and look neither to your right nor to your left. For what we are about to witness does not officially exist. And God bless the United States of America.'

Amen, sister.

Now, this is something I may not have told you, interrogators, but I actually helped *build* Base Amberly. It was only four years ago. Things were a bit slow in the resort trade at the time, and then I heard (through private channels, because it was never announced publicly) that the US military had decided to make Australia the headquarters for their South-East Asia operations.

Japan had just thrown them out, after all, and what with Indonesia full of Islamic insurgencies, and the threat of China ever looming, the Yanks needed bases *somewhere* in the region. And, frankly, Australia was the last place where they could insist.

Although God only knows why the Pentagon opted to build the first and biggest of their new compounds on the site of the old RAAF base at Amberly. It's hardly private, right there on the main road out of Brisbane. But that's where they chose, and the word went out that they needed to erect accommodation for nearly one hundred thousand personnel. Which sounded like a pretty juicy plum to me, so I put in a tender, and won a bid for part of the construction. But don't get too excited, interrogators. My company only built barracks and dining halls. I had nothing to do with sensitive areas like the airstrips, or the secret radar installations—let alone the silos for the nukes, if rumour is true, and the bombs really are down there.

The madness of it was that, even though the money came from the US, at no stage were we allowed to refer to it as an *American* base. Strict government policy has longed since declared that there are *no* US bases in Australia, and never will be. Just joint American–Australian training facilities.

Yeah. Right.

There were certainly no Australians around as we passed by Amberly that night. For twenty k or so the highway runs directly beside the base perimeter, and there were several checkpoints along this section to monitor the passing traffic. They were manned entirely by American troops. They had no interest in us, of course, with our Humvee and with our military passes. But in truth, they didn't seem to be examining anyone very closely, just lazily waving most of the cars through. Otherwise they were slouching about in boredom with guns at half-mast, smoking cigarettes, or reclining in their vehicles, feet out the window.

Our driver was disgusted. 'Look at these brainless turds!'

'Conscripts,' Harry noted. 'The US is as stretched as everyone else. They're not gonna waste crack troops in a place like this.'

'Exactly. So we get a bunch of jerk-off beer-gut national guards—and they're in command of Australian roads. It sucks!' She took a deep breath. 'But that's what we have to put up with, ladies and gentlemen, seeing we lost the war.'

'Which war was that?' I asked.

'The big one, sweetheart. World War II.'

'Um, we lost that, did we?'

'How else can you figure it? If a country ends a war with its soil occupied by the army of a foreign power, then it lost that war, pure and simple. Sure, Japan and Germany were the obvious losers in 1945. But England and Australia—we ended up under American occupation too. Just because we asked the Yanks in and called them allies doesn't mean a thing. We *owed* them big time after that, and they've never let us forget it. We've trotted off to every dodgy war of theirs ever since.'

'You'd rather we ended up under the Japanese?'

'Who says we didn't? The Japs sure came out of it all stronger than we did.'

'Apart from the fact they got nuked.'

'Yeah, well, we're almost level on that score now, aren't we?'

And she had me there.

'Okay,' Harry conceded, 'we were stuffed either way in that war. We just weren't capable of real independence back then. But the point is, things have changed. We *are* capable now.'

Daphne spat out the window. 'I don't see any sign of it. Used to be the poms calling our shots, now it's the Yanks. Obviously we're a dipshit little country that needs great and powerful friends around to stop us wetting ourselves. Only—and forgive the fucking language—we don't need to get on our knees and suck their bloody cocks too, do we? We aren't *that* pathetic, are we? Jesus, even fucking New Zealand has more balls than we do these days, and that's a dipshit little country if ever there was one—no offence meant to the poor buggers.'

And Harry was laughing.

But eventually the road began to climb up into the hills of Cunningham's Gap, and the lights of Base Amberly sank behind.

Daphne mulled away into silence, and after cresting the range, we rolled without speaking across the lush highlands of the Darling Downs, aiming for Warwick. I'd been half-expecting that at Warwick we would turn left and head down the New England Highway, towards Sydney. But we didn't turn at Warwick. We drove straight on, westwards, for another two hours, and it was only at Goondiwindi that we turned south and finally crossed the border.

'Where the hell are we going?' I asked, as Queensland slipped out of sight.

'Bush,' was Harry's only reply.

NINETEEN

I was never much one for the Outback.

The stunning vistas, the colours, the sunsets, the history and the characters, the wide open spaces of desolation, the grandeur of the oldest land on earth...Oh yes, I'd read all the brochures. But there were no beaches, you see. No golf courses. No casinos. And hence, no need of developers like me. I wasn't about providing *adventure*, I was about providing luxury spa tubs and twenty-four hour room service. Most of all, I was about providing ocean views. 'Going bush' for me and my kind usually meant no more than straying too far inland to smell the salt air.

So this trip was all new ground to me. From Goondiwindi down to Moree, then a right turn across to Walgett, and westwards on to Bourke, which we hit around dawn, after a long night in the Humvee, and something like twelve hours since leaving Brisbane. But we didn't stop there. It was onwards still, south-west, along an interminable sandy track that followed the banks of the empty Darling River, three hundred kilometres and more with barely a sign of life except a lone pub at Tilpa, halfway, and an encounter with a rock which did something to the gearbox that took Daphne several hours to repair. We hit the highway again briefly at Wilcannia, but after that it was back to more dirt roads, and south-west still, all the way to a little place called Menindee. But we didn't stop there either. Late afternoon—coming up on twenty-four hours straight since Brisbane—found us jagging back to the south-east, towards somewhere named Ivanhoe, the road reverting to sand as it passed through terrain that looked to me like virtual desert.

The middle, in fact, of nowhere.

And really, I should have something meaningful to say about such a long drive—some sort of observation, perhaps, about this huge spread of country that I'd never seen; a recognition, in my moment of strife, of the imperturbable vastness of Australia, and of my roots in its soil. But for most of the time I was grainy-eyed with exhaustion, or half asleep. All I remember now is, I dunno...service stations. Stopping to fill up with diesel; always, it seemed, at broken-down little places with ancient bowsers and mangy dogs wandering about. And the smell of dead animals—kangaroos and cattle—by the road. And bad food from dingy takeaways. And no one talking much. And Daphne at the wheel eternally, sucking back can after can of Coke to wash down little white pills that had to be pure speed. And tall fences on the roadside hung with 'No Trespassing' signs that indicated military zones or secret installations—dozens of them out there, belonging to who knows which government. And the olive drab of the scrub, and red sand, and heat and flies...

What the fuck were we doing out there, that's all I cared about. And when were we going to stop? I badgered Harry with questions until, finally, after Wilcannia, he caved in and admitted that in fact we had hours ahead of us yet. Our ultimate destination, it turned out, was Victoria. And Melbourne.

Melbourne! They were taking me back to my home town! And this mind-numbing excursion, zig-zagging all over far-western New South Wales, hundreds of miles out of our way, was simply, Harry said, to evade the search for Aisha and me. A matter of sticking to the backroads, to avoid trouble.

Well, it was a nice idea.

But about an hour south-east of Menindee, with Melbourne still a good seven hundred k away, and with the sun near the horizon, trouble found us even so.

Flashing lights appeared ahead, and at first I thought it was a checkpoint, even way out there. But closer inspection revealed that it was an accident. A semitrailer had run off the narrow road and overturned. A white four-wheel drive was parked nearby with its hazard lights on. At a glance the situation looked innocent enough—the truck crashed, a passer-by stopped to help. But then I noticed two men standing beside the four-wheel drive. They were in uniform, one of them waving urgently at us to stop. And far more suspicious, about fifty yards off the road, thirty or so people were sitting in the sand.

'Shit,' said Daphne. 'What do you want me to do?'

Harry considered briefly. 'Pull over. It'd look strange otherwise.'

And as we pulled up, I saw that the group of people—they were all male—weren't just sitting there for the hell of it. They were under the guard of two more men who were brandishing what looked like automatic weapons.

'Thank Christ you guys came along,' the man at our window said. He had a bloody nose and an air of panic about him. 'We've got a fucking mess here.'

Harry cast an eye over the scene. 'What's the problem?'

The man produced a badge from his back pocket and displayed it a moment, his hand trembling. 'We're with Dextron Security, on contract for the Department of Citizenship, escorting this transport of detainees. The fucking truck had a blow-out, and now we got three dozen of these bastards out in the open with only four of us on guard. They've already made one run for it.' He wiped at his injured nose. 'It got ugly. Fights. Shots in the air. We barely held them back.'

So he was a security officer. A prison guard. And in the back of my mind the question had been hovering—where did all those men sitting in the sand come from? Not from the four-wheel drive. And the truck carried only a shipping container. But then I saw that the doors of the shipping container were split open, and that it was empty now, and then I looked at the thirty-six men again, and understood.

Harry's tone was hard. 'We can't really stop, mate. Army business.'

The officer blinked. 'Are you kidding? These men are a Grade One flight risk! We've radioed in for help, but that'll be an hour getting here at least. We need you guys right now!'

I watched the back of Harry's head, appreciating his dilemma. This was the last thing we needed to get mixed up in. But if we were genuine army, there was no way we could have just passed on by. The man would report it.

'All right,' Harry said tightly. 'We'll give you an hour.'

'Great,' the officer said, relieved, and turned back to his own vehicle.

Harry gave me and Aisha a look. 'Let me or Daphne do all the talking. Just act dumb and do whatever we tell you to do.'

We climbed out into the fading light. The smell of hot metal and burnt oil from the prone truck lingered in the air. We headed over towards the security officer, who was waiting by his four-wheel drive.

He stared at us in renewed astonishment. 'Don't you have any guns?'

Harry shook his head. 'We're communications, not combat.'

'Jesus. But you're still soldiers, right? You know how to shoot, don't you?'

'Sure.'

'Lucky we got spares then.' He dived into the back of his vehicle, and pulled out more weaponry. Two automatic rifles, and two hand guns. 'Who wants what?'

Daphne and Harry exchanged glances, then divided the guns between themselves, a pistol and a rifle each.

'What about those two?' the man asked, nodding towards me and Aisha.

Daphne shrugged. 'They're not rated for these firearms.' And even coming from a warhorse staff sergeant, it wasn't a very convincing lie.

'For fuck's sake! Who cares? We gotta form a perimeter around those detainees. I don't give a shit if they're rated, just give them a weapon.'

Another glance between Harry and Daphne. But what choice did they have? In the end, Aisha and I each got a pistol. And there was no mistaking the look in Harry's eye as he handed Aisha—terrorist and madwoman—a loaded gun.

'Right,' the officer said, leading us over towards the prisoners, 'We get in a circle, twenty yards out, and if any one of those fuckers makes another run for it, shoot them.'

Harry was staring at the truck. It had obviously been a slow roll-over, because there was no serious damage. 'You usually carry people in shipping containers?'

'These days, sure.'

'Why not a bus?'

'Too visible. You get a bus full of detainees, anyone can see it. We've had ambushes, rescue attempts. Those Underground pricks.'

'Ah.'

'So we bung 'em in a container, make sure that the escort vehicles are unmarked, and no one's the wiser. 'Specially if we stick to the back roads.'

'Clever,' said Harry, an odd lilt to his voice.

We spread out. One of the guard detail had remained back on the road to watch for the relief party, which left seven of us to form a circle around the detainees. Guns at the ready. Can you imagine it? Me—an armed soldier, standing guard over dangerous prisoners. Daphne was fine, and Harry too. Even Aisha looked perfectly comfortable with her hand gun. But *I* felt about as convincing as a kid with a water pistol.

Then there were the prisoners themselves. They'd already tried to escape once, so it seemed, and they were a desperate-looking lot. They weren't, I finally realised, the normal type of detainees.

They weren't Australian Muslims, or any of the other usual political undesirables from the ghettos. Every single one of them was bearded and Middle Eastern in appearance, and they were muttering to each other in a language I didn't understand. They were real Arabs.

'Who are these guys anyway?' Harry asked the security officer.

'Illegals. Came in on various boats. We got Iraqis, Iranians, Syrians. From the wars, basically. You'd think these people would have got the message by now.'

'They been processed yet?'

The man nodded. He was very young. 'Asylum denied. Suspected terrorist plants. We're shipping them to the maximum security camp up near Broken Hill.'

'I see.'

Some of the detainees apparently spoke English and had been following the exchange. 'We're not terrorists!' one of them yelled. 'We're refugees!'

'Shut it,' snapped the officer, lifting his gun.

The detainee thumped the ground. 'We're running *away* from terrorists! They killed our families! All we want is somewhere to live in peace!'

'Then you shouldn't have come here. Now shut up!'

Oh, this wasn't good. I glanced across at Aisha. Sure enough, I could see her eyes darting from prisoner to prisoner in fury. She was tapping her gun repeatedly against her leg. No, not good at all. Frustration boiled up in me. The security officer was right—what had possessed these people to come to Australia? I sympathised if their homes had been ripped apart by the wars, but everyone knew our borders had long been shut to unauthorised asylum seekers. Muslims in particular. They were bloody idiots— and we'd been caught up in their idiocy.

There were unhappy discussions between the detainees, and some of them were pointing to the horizon, where the sun had almost disappeared.

'It's sunset,' one yelled. 'We have to pray.'

'To hell with your goddamn prayer,' the security officer cursed. 'Just sit there and don't move and don't say another word.'

More angry murmurs.

'Fuck,' the officer continued, scanning the horizon nervously. 'We'll have full dark in half an hour, and we got no lights. This lot are gonna make another break for it before the relief gets here, I just know it. They'll cut our fucking throats.'

'The eight of us are more than enough to keep control,' Harry said, his voice level and calm. 'There's no need for things to get out of hand.'

The man was unconvinced. 'You didn't see them twenty minutes ago. Christ, you guys aren't even real soldiers. Communications, for the love of God!'

He laughed, sounding a little crazed to me—and I wondered if he'd received more than just a bloody nose in the earlier escape attempt. A blow to the head, perhaps.

The murmurs had grown amongst the detainees. Now several of them moved abruptly, rising to their knees and facing to the north-west. A cry went up, wavering and weird in the red evening, the Muslim call to prayer.

'Hey! Stop that!' The officer lifted his automatic rifle to his shoulder. 'Stop that fucking shit right now!'

Harry was saying, 'It's okay, it's okay, let them pray, what harm can it do?'

The men were bowing to the ground now, chanting in their own language, and more of them were following suit. The security officer stomped into their midst, his gun at the ready. 'I'm giving you a direct order!'

Harry was behind him. 'This isn't necessary. Let it go.'

'I'm in fucking charge here!' he yelled, without looking at Harry. Lifting a booted foot, he kicked and sent a bowed detainee sprawling in the dust.

Magically, Aisha was at the officer's side, her gun up against his temple.

'Let them pray if they want,' she said, into a sudden dead silence.

'Oh Jesus,' Harry breathed.

'What the fuck?' The security officer's face was as red with apoplexy as the sunset. 'What the fuck are you doing?'

'Aisha,' Harry said softly, 'put the gun down.'

'Let them pray, you dickhead.'

'Aisha?' the man echoed, his rifle still aimed squarely at the detainee on the ground. 'What sort of name is Aisha? Who the hell are you people?'

But the prisoners knew exactly what sort of name Aisha was, and they were all staring at her now in wonderment. And the rest of the security team were in such shock that their guns were still hanging at their sides.

Harry was almost whispering. 'Aisha. Please.'

For a few seconds longer the tableau held. Who knows what she would have done, if it hadn't been taken out of her hands. But one of the fool detainees made a sudden grab at the security officer's automatic. The officer fired in reflex, three rattling shots, and the detainee screamed. Then came another shot, and the officer's head imploded, his body toppling into the dirt. And standing over him there was Aisha, gazing placidly at the smoke coming from the barrel of her pistol.

Another split second of disbelief all round.

'Damn,' I heard Harry sigh.

Then the massacre got under way.

TWENTY

It was my own brother, of course, who passed the law forbidding entry of any Muslims into Australia—and Bernard, too, who declared that all Muslims already resident in the country would have to go into detention camps, or at least be restricted to the designated cultural precincts. In fact, they were two of the first Emergency Acts he passed after the bombing of Canberra.

He'd been in Parliament for twenty-seven years, by then.

And had been Prime Minister for just over one.

But I don't suppose I really need to detail the final years of his rise. It's recent history of which even you, interrogators, should be partly aware. After all, Bernard was internationally known long before he became Prime Minister—a key player in the world's security community, roaming the globe to decry terror. And then there was his great friendship with Nathaniel Harvey, erstwhile Assistant Secretary for Homeland Security, who had since gone on to a state governorship, and then, in 2008, all the way to the US presidency. That was the connection which really put Bernard in the spotlight. He ate, slept and no doubt shat at the White House several times in Nate's first year—giving my brother the imprimatur of Australian leadership even before his own party elected him.

But once the colossal figure of John Howard had departed the stage, it was inevitable that the Liberals would turn to Bernard sooner or later, especially after Tom Laurel's disastrous term in between. Okay, Laurel was all smiles and charm, which made a nice change, but he was an empty head in the end, a flash lair the voters didn't trust. For the worried Liberal Party, Bernard represented a return to the safe old ways of Howard himself. The two men were almost clones. Still, there were many who saw the prime ministership, by the time Bernard was appointed to it in 2009, as something of a poisoned chalice.

It wasn't a good period for Australia. The economy, after decades of boom, had finally gone stagnant. We'd been dragged into another three messy wars, and the Australian cricket team, after nearly twenty years of unbridled success, had just lost their fourth test series in a row. The mood was in the air that the country had taken a turn for the worse, that the Liberals were moribund, and that after so many years in the wilderness, the Labor Party might be worth a shot again. Bernard, declared the political pundits, was most likely to go down as a caretaker PM who oversaw the end of his party's long reign.

Instead, as we all know, Canberra was obliterated, the state of emergency was declared and my brother's transfiguration was upon him.

Actually, it didn't do Nate Harvey any harm either.

You shouldn't forget, interrogators, that prior to the bomb, the President's ratings in the US polls were no better than Bernard's were here. There'd been all those nasty race riots in the south, and all those mass protests in the northern cities, burning draft cards. It was all very well that the US should be overlord of the world—but was it putting food on American tables? Were the boys ever coming home from the wars? Did the wars serve any purpose anyway? Nate, the last in a long line of Republican hawks, was copping the blame.

The bomb changed all that. President Harvey could point to the ultimate horror—terrorists attacking the west with nukes—to reinforce the call to arms. And so, once again, the tired planet lined up faithfully to continue the fight.

And thus we have the world we have.

And where was I, while my brother soared to the top?

I was sliding towards the abyss.

To tell you the truth, by the day of that cyclone I was probably not long for this world, so deep and black was the hole into which I'd fallen.

But it was a long, slow descent, and it needs explaining. It began, clearly enough, in 2001, when Bernard left the Department of Local Government, and I lost my special access. From then on, even though I was always involved in some project or other, I never prospered. (Like my doomed attempt to get money from that American investor I took to see George Bush. My magic touch was gone.) But it wasn't just a financial decline. I was getting older, for one thing. A bit fatter, a bit slower, a bit less capable of recovering from the night before. But more than that...my spirit was flagging. Deep down, I'd somehow ceased to properly enjoy life.

And it wasn't just because I was slowly going broke. I'd gone broke before and still *enjoyed* myself. No, looking back, it was something about the times that was getting to me, something about my surroundings, about Australia in general. John Howard's Australia, as the newspapers of the day often called it. Which should have been my Australia too. After all, I voted for Howard all the way—even though he bored me rigid—and not just because I wanted Bernard in a position to do me favours. Hell, the Liberals were the party of business and money. Who else would I vote for? I wanted low taxes, I wanted the unions (the bane of my existence, when it came to building resorts) muzzled, I wanted the freedom to run my companies any way I pleased. The Libs promised all that, and delivered on it too. So Howard's Australia should have been a paradise for me.

Instead, when I looked around at the country, I felt a vague sense of disorientation. Where, to put it one way, had all the fun gone? Yes, we had the war on terror, it was no time for games, but that wasn't the whole story. We'd fought other wars before without losing our sense of who we were. This was something deeper, something that was missing from the character of the place. Where was all that irreverent energy that we'd once been famous for? Where was the vitality, the fuck-it-all brashness, the she'll-be-right flair? That was my Australia, the Australia of the seventies and the eighties. Not sophisticated, perhaps, and maybe not even really grown up. But at least the place was *alive*. Everywhere you looked—no matter what aspect of society, left, right, rich, poor—you saw people acting with gusto. Rudely, crassly, violently…but with colour.

You only have to consider what sort of Prime Ministers we had in the seventies and eighties. Now *they* were identities. Gough Whitlam—so enraptured and radical that he outraged half the nation to the point of civil uprising, and moved the other half to a fervour of worship so profound they deify him to this day. And Malcom Fraser, the man who toppled him—conspiring to freeze Parliament and then plotting with the Governor-General to depose his rival, the greatest constitutional crisis of the century. The nerve that took. The cunning. And then Bob Hawke, a raucous cockatoo of a man, a squawking dwarf with charisma to burn—and anyway, how could you not love a PM who once held the world record for downing a yard glass of beer? And then, finally, Paul Keating, the arch manipulator, an oily, stylish, backroom brawler dressed in designer suits, with a mouth that was both patrician and straight from the sewer. A man who was capable of the sneering remark that his own country was 'the arse-end of the world'. And meaning it.

Oh, yes. Liars, cheats and swindlers, every one of them, but they had *personality*, and none of them were afraid of anything, at home or abroad. The country they led seemed to be the same. Loud and boastful and too full of itself by half, but getting the joke, too; more than happy to take the piss out of itself, if need be. That's the country I remember living in. Okay, I'm looking through rose-tinted glasses, and I know it was far from perfect, but somehow during the 1990s everything changed. That breezy sense of confidence and of openness and of progress forward . . . it faded away.

I'm buggered if I know who or what to blame exactly. Certainly our political leaders—if not actually the cause of it—were at least symptoms. Take the dreary John Howard and his protégé, my brother. I ask you—can you imagine either of them (or Tom Laurel, for that matter) getting anywhere near the PM's office back in the wild old days? Whitlam would have roared his disgust. Fraser would have refused to dirty his hands with them. Hawke would have shrieked with laughter at the very idea. And Keating? Ah well, Keating was there to see Howard beat him fair and square, and so learnt the bitter truth—we preferred the bean counters to the visionaries. Lawyers and accountants, that's who we handed the country to.

And maybe that was the crux of my problem—somewhere in the Howard years, it all became about the money. I don't mean *my* kind of money—the sort of money that was made with such sinful ease that the only thing one could do was hurl it around gleefully. No, this money was different. It didn't matter that the country got rich again after the recession of the nineties, and then richer still—the weird thing was, this time around, no one seemed to be taking much pleasure in the process. It was grey, corporate money—that's why. A wealth that was nervous and greedy for more. A wealth not for sharing.

But we were happier than ever, apparently. Everyone said so. Safer. Smarter. Setting the whole world an example to follow. It was in the newspapers and on the TV screens every day. And that, too, I found disturbing. It felt as if that old bluff boasting of ours had turned somehow into a genuine arrogance. As if our old sense of humour had shrivelled up. Because if anyone dared raise a criticism about the new mood of the country, well, they were un-Australian, they were being negative, and we'd lost all patience with that. Instead, we were flying flags and singing national anthems. Even on Anzac Day—the crowds grew every year, but why were we there? Out of respect for dead soldiers? Or for nationalist glory? I honestly couldn't tell.

Nor, in my memory, had I ever heard so much talk about what exactly it was to *be* Australian anyway, or who had the right to claim it. 'I'm proud to be Australian!' we were suddenly declaring everywhere. Defiantly. Aggressively. As if to not say it was a weakness. And those declaring it the most were those of us who were white, who were born here. Which drove me mad, because what did we mean by it? Yes, we were born here—but why was being born somewhere something to be *proud* of? We might as well have said, 'I'm proud I have blue eyes.' Or, 'I'm proud I have two legs.' Or, 'I'm proud I wasn't born with congenital heart disease.' It would've made as much sense. Being born Australian wasn't an *achievement*.

We just inherited the place. Us, the baby boomers, and generations X and Y and the rest. The post-war generations. We made no great sacrifices to be called Australian. We rose above no great challenges. We weren't the ones who founded the nation. We weren't the ones who survived the Great Depression, or who fought the Second World War, when the nation really was under threat. We weren't even the post-war migrants who left their homes to make a new start in a strange land. We were just here. Sure, we all worked hard in our own lives, but the country itself, its institutions and liberties, its wealth and its lifestyle, basically, they were a gift. Which was something to feel lucky about. And grateful for. Absolutely. But why proud?

Indeed, if you ask me, we Australians have faced only one *real* challenge in the last twenty years, and that was the challenge of preserving what the previous generations handed down to us—quite simply, a free country. A small enough thing to ask, you'd think. But have we even done that?

I hardly need answer.

And maybe it all sounds strange, coming from me. Ludicrous that I, Leo James, fraud that I am, would ever have cared about any of these things, or have let them bother me enough to spoil my *joie de vivre*. But look at my life. In the seventies I did what everyone else did, I slacked off and dropped out. In the eighties, too, I did what everyone else did, I tried to get rich. I've always been a child of my age, I've always gone with the crowd. I would have liked to fit into the Howard age, too. But for once I couldn't. It was too hollow. Too grating.

Anyway, to finish the story...

I was heading downwards as it was, but then the economy went bust while Laurel was Prime Minister, and we were in recession again. Not a good time to embark on a major resort like Oceans Sands Green, but I was already committed, and it was my last throw of the dice, financially. Then the Canberra bomb went off, pretty much killing the tourism industry in Australia. International travellers weren't going to visit a country that was a nuclear target, and domestic tourists were too busy building bomb shelters in their backyards to go on holidays. Construction halted at Ocean Sands, and I sank into a stupor of defeat. A stupor filled with parties and endless drinking and as many women as my aging dick could handle—which was not so many, truth be told—but a stupor all the same.

I could perhaps have appealed to Bernard. Sure, he'd cut me off the night before the bomb, but that wasn't necessarily forever. And meanwhile he had all sorts of juicy government jobs and contracts at his personal disposal. I could have begged him. But my heart just wasn't in it. I was older and prouder now, and sick of seeing Bernard's face on every TV screen, day in, day out. Besides, I suspected that, now he was untouchable, he would have told me to piss off anyway.

No surprise, then, that I ended up at my empty resort— depressed, alienated, feeling about a hundred years old—half hoping that the cyclone might finish me off. It's a joke, really. Before Aisha's boys grabbed me, I wasn't all that worried about dying. But when people tried to actually *kill* me... Well, it saved my life.

Long enough at least for you, dear interrogators, to take it.

PART TWO

TWENTY-ONE

You know me well enough by now, I assume, to understand that, when the fire-fight started, the first thing I did was to drop my own gun, unused, and the second thing was to fall flat into the dirt with my hands over my head. And there I stayed, eyes shut fast, as all around me semi-automatic weapons sputtered flatly and voices yelled and screamed and swore. It was probably no more than a minute. One of those minutes that is measured in years.

Eventually, however, the shooting stopped, even if the screaming didn't. I opened my eyes. Bodies lay everywhere in the fading light. Wailing. Mourning. A figure violently kicking another figure that lay unmoving on the ground. Unreal, unreal, unreal. Except that I'd seen it all before, such an aftermath. This was my fourth time now. And as I rose to my feet, a part of my brain reflected with cold rationality that the nausea and the revulsion and the sweat of fear turning into a deep chill . . . it was all getting worse with the repetition.

I stumbled around in the dimness, smelling smoke and shit and blood. I saw many dead detainees, and others wounded, and others still unharmed, milling about as shocked and dazed as I was. I saw three dead security guards. I saw a body wearing an army uniform, and it was Staff Sergeant Daphne, her face set as hard and disgusted as it had been when she was alive. And then I heard someone calling my name. It was Harry, over by the Humvee.

'Move it, Leo, we gotta go!'

I stared at him. His face looked all black.

'Are you hurt?' he demanded, voice hoarse. 'Are you shot?'

'No.'

'Then come *on*, for fuck's sake.'

I walked over, still treading on ground that felt like rubber. I passed by the white four-wheel drive. It had been sprayed with bullets, and multicoloured liquids were streaming from the engine compartment. There was a body hunched in the driver's seat. The fourth guard. And from within came the crackle of a radio, and the urgent voice of someone in authority, calling and calling, unanswered...

Harry was beside me. Blood was streaming down his face from a gash on his forehead. Only his eyes stood out, furious and white.

'The bastard got to the radio before I could stop him,' he said. 'He put an emergency call into his base. In half an hour this place will be swarming.'

He was dragging me towards the Humvee. Behind us the wailing and moaning went on. Then Aisha appeared out of the gloom, pristine and untouched.

'We can't leave them here,' she said.

I glanced back. There were at least a dozen men still upright.

'Are you kidding?' Harry retorted. 'We don't have room.'

'Even so, we have to help them.'

'Help *them*? You stupid bitch—any second now they're gonna realise that we've got the only serviceable vehicle here, and then it'll be *our* arses on the line.'

Aisha sounded as mechanical as a robot. 'They have no chance without us.'

'Goddamn it! They never had any chance! They were all dead

as soon as you pulled that trigger. What do you think will happen when the reinforcements arrive? Who do you think will get the blame? Everyone here will be shot before dawn. And it's your fucking fault! You killed these people!'

She seemed to falter at that, staring wide-eyed.

Harry was dragging her then, too, his tone level again. 'The only important thing is that we don't die with them. We've got to go. Now.'

We climbed in, Harry behind the wheel. But even as he cranked the engine, I heard rising shouts from the detainees. A knot of them were moving towards us. Some were carrying guns, liberated from the dead guards.

'Run!' Aisha screamed at them. 'Run away from here!'

The engine roared, and the tyres spun wildly. Then we were fishtailing away. Angry yells came from behind, and I'm sure I heard shots fired, but we raced into the new night, and when I finally looked back, there was nothing to be seen but figures moving futilely to and fro against the horizon.

'Dammit dammit dammit,' Harry was saying.

I was in the front seat beside him, Aisha a pale shadow in the rear. For a long time no one else spoke. What could anyone say? There was just the hum of the engine as Harry sped faster and faster along the track. We skidded on sandy curves, and I didn't dare look at the speedometer.

'Christ,' I said. 'Don't get us killed—not after that.'

Harry wiped blood out of his eyes, scanning the half-darkness ahead. 'We have to get off this road. There'll be police or military coming along it before long. And as soon as they interrogate those detainees, they'll be looking for us.'

'You mean *us* specifically? They'll know who we really are?'

He shrugged bitterly. 'They might not guess who you and I really are—except that we're not genuine army. That's bad enough. But Aisha? Those detainees heard me say her name. You can bet your arse someone is going to work it out fast. And then the shit will really hit the fan.'

I glanced to the back seat, where Aisha sat glowering.

'So what now?' I asked Harry.

'We need to disappear. We need a side road.'

But there were no side roads. We were already *on* a side road. All around us there was nothing but bare wilderness. The time and the miles flashed by, and we met no one, saw nothing. The night deepened, the land fading to black. Was it twenty minutes since the disaster, was it thirty? Then I noticed that Harry was staring at the dashboard, tapping the dials.

'Shit,' he said.

'What?'

'The oil light is on, and the temp gauge is through the roof.'

My heart sank, and I pitched my ear to the engine. It was true, an ominous whine was emanating from it now.

Harry thumped the steering wheel. 'What next!'

I said, 'It must have got hit too, in all the shooting.'

'Either way, we're fucked.'

But my eyes were on the road. 'There's a turn-off!'

It was the merest trail, leading off to the right. Harry braked, swung the wheel. Then we were bouncing and swerving along narrow wheel ruts, the engine sounding horrible, the stink of overheated metal in our nostrils.

'C'mon baby,' Harry soothed, stroking the wheel. 'Not yet.'

And I suppose they really do build those Humvees pretty tough, because it ploughed on for what must have been another twenty minutes. But finally it began to hitch and choke. Sensing the end, Harry spun the wheel, and we leapt from the track altogether, plunging straight across the virgin desert. I knew what he was doing. If the thing was about to die, then better that it didn't die on the roadside, where it would be easier for the hunters to find.

Low bushes jumped up in the headlights, then disappeared under the bullbar. Rocks and the banks of shallow gullies tore at the vehicle's underbelly. The stench had grown awful, and the engine sounded like ball-bearings being tossed in a clothes dryer. Then there came the terminal clunk of something separating. The motor rasped and died. The Humvee limped along for maybe another fifty metres, and finally rolled to a gentle stop. Steam hissed into the silence.

'Everyone out,' Harry ordered.

We climbed out into what was now full night. I stared up at the stars, and at a sliver of moon sinking in the west. How far had we come since the massacre? Not far. Certainly not far enough. I gazed to the north. Somewhere back up there, the surviving detainees were probably already being rounded up. There would be army trucks—real army this time—and police and Citizenship men.

Harry was digging in the back of the dead Humvee, pulling out several dark packages. I heard the gurgle of liquid.

'Emergency rations,' he said. 'Every army vehicle has them, thank Christ.'

I looked at him, bloody-faced, his uniform filthy and yet, somehow, looking more and more like a real soldier every minute. The anger in him was still palpable, but it had never been anything like panic. Through it all, he'd remained in control. Absorbing each new set back, and moving on swiftly to a new plan.

I said, 'How do you know all this stuff?'

'What stuff?'

'About military things. About guns.' It came to me even as I spoke—and hadn't I noticed it as soon as he first donned the fake uniform? He *looked* the part. 'You were in the army yourself, once, weren't you? Before this Underground thing.'

Aisha, too, turned suddenly and stared, as if seeing him for the first time.

Harry shook his head. 'I was never in the army.'

'Then what was it?'

He gave a strange laugh, and for a moment it sounded like panic after all. 'Those people back there. The detainees. That's what I used to do.'

I gazed at him, not understanding.

'Jesus. I was a security officer. Guarding illegal immigrants.' He fixed Aisha with eyes that blazed even in darkness. 'Like the ones we just killed.'

A noise arose in the night, the distant drone of a helicopter.

We stared about—and there, low on the horizon, a light was lifting into the sky. We watched, transfixed, as it rose higher and soared almost directly above us, rushing into the north.

'What do we do?' I asked.

'We walk.' Harry pointed south. 'Out there.'

'But do you know where we're going?'

'Not a damn clue.'

And so we set off into the desert.

TWENTY-TWO

What did I say about not being an Outback person?

Okay, so I'm not even sure that a few thousand square miles of sand and scrub somewhere in the south-west corner of New South Wales *is* the Outback... But it sure felt like it to me. Especially as we set out into the middle of it, the sand still warm under our feet from the heat of the day, and our only landmark a dead Humvee behind us in the night. We had a mere scrap of food and a drop of water on which to survive, and we were alone in a place so big and empty that we could wander there until we collapsed and died, and our bodies might not be found by another passing soul for months—for *years*. To me, that was alien. That was scary. I felt more helpless and trapped in those first few miles of walking than I had in the back of the Australia Post van after my initial kidnapping.

Ah, but the sky! It's true what the brochures say, after all. In my entire life, I don't think I've ever spent a night so completely away from man-made lighting. There wasn't even the glow from some distant town beyond the horizon, or the shining of a single illuminated window in a lonely farmhouse. The world was a great grey shadow, unbroken—except for a flicker that came and went in the east, and that was only lightning shimmering amongst the tops of far-off storm clouds. A hundred miles or more over there it might be thundering and raining in the hills, but out in the desert the sky was clear. Just the warm evening breeze, the silence, and the stars.

And satellites. Glittering pinpricks, crossing far above us. Every time I glanced up in the early hours after sunset, my feet stumbling on the black ground, there seemed to be one moving stealthily up there. Military, civilian, who knew, but they were like an itch, like lice crawling about the globe, because they too were the enemy now. Spying eyes in the sky. It wasn't until the night deepened, and the satellites were no longer visible, that I could look up and simply see...well, the universe. Not so much something that was *above* me, it was more like I was walking upside down on a huge ceiling, and there was an immense gulf below into which I could fall, eternally, if the vertigo made me let go of my grip on the earth and launch off.

Ha! But maybe that's just an Australian thing, or a Southern Hemisphere thing, anyway—the arse-end hemisphere, to paraphrase Mr Keating. We're all down-under here, supposedly, clinging to the bottom side of the planet. In the meantime, the sky had more mundane uses, like navigation, and working out which way was south. Me, I just would have walked towards the Southern Cross.

'You'd be wrong,' Harry corrected. 'If you did that all night, you'd end up walking in a giant curve, because the cross describes an arc in the sky every evening. To head directly south, you take the long arm of the cross and extend an imaginary line from it downwards. Then you find the two pointers—those two bright stars a bit below the cross—and extend another imaginary line upwards from them, perpendicular to, and bisecting, the line between the pointers themselves. Where your two imaginary lines cross, that's true south.'

I took his word for it. He would know, after all, being in the

Underground, and with the Southern Cross being their symbol—
the five stars and the 'Free Australia' slogan.

'It's always upside down though,' I said to Harry as we stomped
along, side by side, Aisha a white ghost behind.

'What is?'

'The Southern Cross. Whenever you guys leave it as a calling
card, you draw it upside down, not right way up.'

He glanced at the constellation in question. 'Some people
thought we should use it upright. Problem is, the Southern Cross
has been used by dozens of little protest movements over the
years, and we are *not* some little protest movement. We're about
a complete overthrow of everything. So we flipped it.' He strode
on in silence for a time, staring up. 'Anyway, it's not always
upright in the sky, is it?'

'How did it happen?' I asked.

'Sorry?'

'You. All this Underground stuff. It's a long leap from hired
gun for the Department of Citizenship to resistance fighter.'

'It was called Immigration back then, not Citizenship. Anyway,
I worked for a private company that specialised in prisons and
remand centres. *They* were the ones who were employed by the
Department.'

'What's the difference?'

'The chain of responsibility, that's what.' He grinned briefly
in the dark—his cynicism baring its fangs. 'If the company
happens to brutalise the inmates, well, that's got nothing do with
the government, has it? Deniability.'

'So did you work in the actual detention centres?'

He hesitated a fraction. 'Yes.'

'Which one?'

'Woomera.'

'Ah…'

You won't know this, dear interrogators, but Woomera—
that's a name to strike dark and complex emotions in the Australian
psyche. A faint echo, perhaps, of what it might be like to mention
Auschwitz to a German. Our most notorious detention camp,

operating back in the early days after September 11, when the walls first went up and illegal immigrants from Islamic countries became public enemy number one. It was a pretty tame place, of course, by today's standards, and long since closed down. But Woomera was at the start of it all.

'I was just a prison guard once,' Harry went on, 'working in state institutions. But then, when the whole boat people thing blew up and all the new detention centres came on line, the call went out for staff. People like me with prison experience were high on the wanted list. It was more money than I was getting in the state system. So I took a contract.'

From behind us, Aisha spoke up. 'It was Woomera that made me become an activist. It was a war crime against the Muslim people.'

Harry glanced back. 'You couldn't have been more than fourteen years old.'

'I knew right and wrong when I saw it.'

'I didn't think it was wrong. Not at first. The people there had entered the country illegally. We couldn't just let them wander about in any way they liked. They had to be processed. We had to work out who was a legitimate refugee, and who wasn't. So in the meantime, yes, if they were detained somewhere comfortable for a while, where was the harm?'

'Somewhere comfortable?' I asked.

He nodded. 'That was the problem, of course. I'd worked in prisons, and the point of prisons is that they're supposed to be places of both detention and punishment, because the people in them have committed serious crimes. A detention centre is just supposed to be a temporary holding location, it's not supposed to be punitive. The only crime the people there have committed is to cross a border without paperwork, which legit refugees are allowed to do anyway. But Woomera was the most punitive place I'd ever seen. Murderers and rapists got far better treatment than the men, women and children in Woomera did.'

'I heard it was pretty hard on the staff, too.'

He shrugged. 'The whole place was a nightmare. Lack of

funds, lack of equipment, incredible heat, no shade, tin sheds, way out in the desert, a place designed for four hundred people holding nearly fifteen hundred. Then the Immigration Department stalled on the refugee applications and left us all there to rot. As far as I could tell, the unwritten understanding between the government and the company was just to make the detainees suffer—as an example to any future boat people who might want to come. After all, John Howard had sworn in public that no more illegals were getting in, hell or high water.'

'I remember,' I said.

'Everyone remembers. It's not as if it was a secret. But I saw it first-hand—innocent people, the vast majority of them completely genuine refugees escaping from regimes like Saddam and the Taliban—and this country punished them as if they *were* Saddam and the Taliban. You've got no idea what it was like to watch those people—who thought they'd found safety—gradually realise that they were even worse off than before. The way the hope turned into bewilderment, and then anger, and then just blank despair. So of course there was violence in the camp. Protests, hunger strikes, suicide attempts. The staff were helpless to stop it. And meanwhile the government was crowing: 'See? We told you these illegals were savages!'

'What was your job exactly?'

'Oh, I was just camp security. Manning the perimeter. It was harder for the medical staff—they really saw the worst. Me, I just had to keep the inmates in, and any intruders out. And intruders meant virtually everyone. Journalists. Legal Aid. United Nations inspectors. In the end, it started to get to me. I'd never had trouble in my old job. Crims were crims. But this...I mean, of course we had the right to control who entered the country. Even to send illegals back. But in the meantime, they were human beings. To deliberately neglect, imprison and dehumanise several thousand innocent people, little children included, over periods of years, simply to scare everyone else away...That we did *not* have the right to do.'

'Even though it worked? The boats stopped coming.'

'Oh, it worked all right. At least as far as most of the voters were concerned, come the next election. But not for me. After a year or so in that place—after seeing what this country was doing to people who had dared beg us for help—well, I'd walk around in a normal town or city and it all seemed surreal. It still *looked* like Australia. Sunny and warm and friendly, everyone going about their lives. But it was bullshit. I'd go back to Woomera, and see the filth and the insanity and the kids turned into zombies, and to me, that was the *real* Australia.'

'It was because they were Muslims,' Aisha intoned.

Harry waved a weary hand. 'Sure. Probably. Although some of the poor bastards converted to Christianity in there. Fat lot of good it did them.'

I said, 'Did you quit?'

'Not exactly. Do you remember the big break-out from Woomera?'

'Vaguely.'

'That's where it all began for me. Of course, there were always a few protests from the community outside about what was going on. There were marches and picket lines, even way the hell out there at Woomera. It was part of my job to secure the camp against them—although usually the government flew in extra South Australian police, or the AFP. Water cannons and the lot. But finally there was that one really big protest, and in all the running battles, someone got to the fence with wire-cutters, or threw them over the fence to the inmates—and the next you thing you know, the fence is down and inmates are running everywhere, mixing in with the protesters.'

TV images surfaced in my mind, old footage I hadn't really paid much attention to at the time—dust, and a fence buckling, and figures running, leaping.

'Complete chaos,' Harry said. 'The last thing I remember was some Immigration arsehole yelling at me to do something—to stop them, to shoot over their heads, maybe even to shoot *at* them, I dunno. But I just stood there stock-still for a minute and saw the raw joy on those people's faces. The ones escaping. It wasn't like you might see from a regular prisoner during a jailbreak. There was nothing furtive about it, nothing half-smart or clever. This was sheer liberation. This was people escaping a death camp, people who suddenly had their lives back.'

'So what did you do?'

'I dropped my gun and ran off with them.'

I gaped at him. 'Bullshit.'

He laughed. 'No. Seriously. I don't know what came over me—but in that split second, I wanted to be just as free as they were. That's what Woomera did to detainees and staff alike. It was a prison for all of us. And I wanted out. So I ran with them. Whooping, screaming, tearing off my uniform, hugging people I didn't know. I kid you not, it was about the best sixty seconds of my life. Then I sobered up a bit, of course.'

'Did you go back?'

'Hell no. Next thing I knew I was bundled into the back of some old hippie couple's car with two of the detainees, and we were racing hell for leather away from there. That's when I began to wonder what the fuck I was doing. And what the detainees were doing, too—'cause they were really gonna be made to pay for something like this, once they were caught again. But it was impossible to worry too much. I mean, the hippies were laughing and the detainees were grinning from ear to ear and it all seemed worth it, just for that moment.'

I searched my memory vainly. 'How many got away?'

'Thirty odd. Most of them, of course, didn't get far—they just ran off into the desert until the police caught up with them. But a good few got smuggled off by the protesters, like I did. And that's what really amazed me. Those protesters—they'd come organised for this. It wasn't just an impromptu dash. They'd planned the escape, and now they had plans to keep the escapees hidden. Those hippies, for instance—they weren't just any old fools. They had maps and supplies, and about fifteen k up the road they dropped me and the detainees in the desert, with instructions about where to go next. They couldn't keep us in their car. They knew there'd be roadblocks going up on all the main roads even as we spoke.'

'Didn't they care that you were one of the guards?'

'It threw them a bit, but they seemed to accept it. After all, I was half-naked by then and laughing like a maniac. It was the detainees I was more worried about. There we were suddenly, just the three of us running alone into the desert. Me, and two young Afghani guys. Now, they had no reason to trust me, let alone to like me. They could have told me to fuck off, they could have beaten the crap out of me and left me for dead. But they didn't. Despite it all, they understood what I was doing. And so we pressed on to the next rendezvous.'

'You actually got clean away?'

'Clean away,' he nodded. 'We hid during the day and walked during the night, for two nights, until we were out of the immediate search zone, then we hit a back road and got picked up, just as promised. By a couple of young greenies this time. They smuggled us to Adelaide, and handed us over to some lawyer, who hid us in his flat for a while. From there we moved to Melbourne, and then from house to house. Just with ordinary people, for the most part—a bit left-leaning, maybe, but nothing outrageous. And it dawned on me gradually. These were *safe* houses. And this whole system was an *underground*.'

'I get it. The Oz Underground...'

'Not quite. But the beginnings of it. I could scarcely believe it at the time. The government was screaming blue murder about the escapees. They knew we were being ferried around the country by sympathisers. And there were all sorts of threats being broadcast—anyone caught hiding an escapee was going to have the book thrown at them. They were gonna face prison themselves. Total hysteria. And yet here were everyday Australians, most of them just average middle-class folk, nice and secure, and they were risking it all to hide us. They were so disgusted by Howard and his mob that they were engaging in actual subversive activity against their own government. It blew my mind. Lazy old Australia—the most unradical place on earth—and we had a secret resistance movement!'

'And you stayed hidden? But you weren't even a detainee.'

'No. And once the real escapees were safely away and gone, I surfaced again. The AFP called me in, of course, and wanted to know where'd I'd been, but I just spun them some story about deciding to quit Woomera the day of the riot, and heading off on a holiday. They knew it was crap, but I didn't give them anything else.'

'And you've been in the Underground ever since?'

'Well, the name didn't come along until later. But I really think Woomera was the inspiration. That was the first time an actual *network* was set up. It took a lot of people to get those detainees to safety, and not just those doing the hiding. Some of the escapees were sick, so we needed doctors who were onside. We needed lawyers onside. We needed interpreters. We needed sympathisers from the Immigration Department itself. The incredible thing was that we could actually find people like that. And once all those individuals had discovered each other, and seen what they could do to circumvent some of the government's worst policies, hell, they weren't going to forget it. Especially later, when the government and the security laws got even worse. And so the Oz Underground was born.'

'And so here we are now.'

'Yes. Here we are.' He strode on in silence for a moment, boots crunching on hard sand. Then his head was shaking thoughtfully. 'It's funny. All these years in the OU, all the secrecy and the recruiting and the thousands upon thousands who joined us. And we're still losing. Losing worse than ever. And here I am again. Running off into the desert to get away.'

He stopped, stared all about at the night.

'At least back then me and the two Afghani boys knew what we were supposed to be doing, and where we were going. But us three...'

We had all stopped.

Aisha said, 'Allah will preserve us.' And the weird thing was, I didn't think this was just one of her ritual utterances. I think she really meant it—that she was offering, in her way, some sort of support and understanding for a fellow rebel.

But Harry just sounded deathly tired. 'You think so, do you?' He pointed northwards. 'Look.'

It was another helicopter, a blue light low on the horizon. It was too far away to hear, but a narrow search beam stabbed down from it towards the ground. And suddenly the night and the landscape did not seem so vast and empty anymore.

'By tomorrow they'll have found our tracks on that dirt road,' Harry sighed. 'Hopefully it'll take them a bit longer to find the Humvee—but once they do, they'll be right on our tail. It's just a matter of following our footprints.'

We watched the silent light hovering for another minute or more, no one speaking. Then we turned in unison, and fled on.

TWENTY-THREE

The three of us were still walking at dawn. By then, we'd left the sandy plain of the night behind, and were trudging across low scrubby hills. Dreary country, and hard. We hadn't slept in nearly twenty-four hours and, for me, the march had taken on a tone of exhausted delirium. Even Harry was flagging, and had begun to look for somewhere to rest—a hole, or thick patch of scrub, in which we might hide ourselves. But there was nothing. Only a few fences that crossed our path, and alongside them the faded wheel marks of seldom-used tracks—both reminders that we weren't in a real desert, but instead were traversing someone's property, a cattle or sheep station. But how big a property we couldn't hope to guess, let alone where it might end, or what lay beyond it, or where, at the last, we were headed.

'The Murray River,' was all Harry would say. 'It's south of us somewhere. And once we cross that, we're into Victoria.'

Yet even in my condition, I could see that crossing the border did not magically make us safe. This was not a matter of state jurisdiction. Besides, any bridge would have a checkpoint and soldiers. But Harry was past arguing.

'We'll swim across,' he insisted, plodding onwards.

The daylight grew, and the sun rose. Far away to the west, a tall line of dune-like hills blushed pink in the dawn, and cockatoos screeched in the scrub around us. There was not a cloud to be seen, and all of us were scanning the sky now, alert for the black dot of a helicopter, or even the sound of one. And indeed—just at the point were I was about to drop to my knees and demand to sleep, hidden from the searchers or not—there did come a sound. But it wasn't a helicopter. It came from ahead somewhere, and it was the rattle of a small engine.

Harry paused, his head tilted. 'Do you hear that?'

I stared at him blearily. He looked a mess. Bloody, dirty, unshaven, his eyes as red and swollen as mine felt.

'What is it?' I asked. 'A car? A motorbike?'

Already I was imagining army troops or Federal Police patrolling for us.

But Harry shook his head. 'That's a generator.'

We crept cautiously towards the noise. It rose and fell deceptively, and after several minutes we didn't seem any nearer. There were certainly no buildings in sight. It was as if the thing was underground. We scrambled up a low ridge, and from the crest looked out over a wide expanse of white sand—it was a lake bed, long dry, and a few miles across. The ridge upon which we stood formed its eastern rim. But the sound of the generator was loud now, and I stared, suddenly confused. At our feet, the ridge sank away into a gully—and the ground there abruptly turned from earth into some sort of *material*. A material littered with sand and clumps of dead scrub, so that it merged uncannily into the natural surrounds. For an instant I thought I really had started to hallucinate, but suddenly the picture resolved itself. The material was shade cloth, stretched across the gully, forming a roof. We were looking at it from above.

'What the fuck?' Harry wondered aloud.

He led us down, until we were standing at the foot of the ridge. Ahead of us spread the white floor of the lake, burnt sterile by the sun. But looking back into the gully we could see, beneath the shade cloth, a deep, dim covered space.

I almost laughed. 'Sweet Jesus.'

It was a greenhouse, full of the biggest and fattest marijuana plants I had ever seen.

I turned to Harry. 'Can you believe this?'

Harry, however, wasn't smiling. His face had gone wary, eyes roving, and from his belt he drew the pistol that he had kept from the massacre.

'What's wrong?' I asked.

'Shut up.'

'But it's just someone's dope crop.'

'Exactly. A big one. With power, irrigation and a camouflaged roof. And something like this isn't going to be just left here without—'

Two men stepped out from amongst the plants, rifles at their shoulders, aimed squarely at the three of us.

'—guards,' Harry finished, shoulders sagging.

'Drop it,' one of the men ordered.

Harry let his gun fall.

And I remember thinking—what the fuck is happening in this country? Supposedly we have some of the toughest firearms laws in the world. Officially, no private citizen is allowed to own a weapon of any kind anymore. And yet it seemed that *every single person* I'd met in the last few days was armed, as if the entire nation was swimming in ordnance. Where did it all come from? And then I was recalling things I'd read or seen on the news—how the army somehow manages to lose ten per cent of its rifles every year, allegedly to a thriving black market run by conscripted soldiers; how murder and armed theft and violent assault are at record highs; and how odd it is that the more peace and safety and security from terrorists we have, the more guns the bad guys seem to possess.

We stared at our captors. They were Aboriginal, and even

disregarding the rifles, they looked mean. Hard, hostile faces. Bare chests. Tattooed arms.

'Hey,' Harry declared, hands raised. 'It's cool. We don't want any hassle here.'

The men glared. 'You got it anyway, mate,' said one.

'We're lost. We're just here by accident.'

'Yeah? Since when does the army get itself lost?'

Harry glanced down at his uniform in frustration. 'We're not in the army. We just ... borrowed this stuff.'

The men exchanged puzzled frowns at that. But behind them, the marijuana crop waited, dense and tall, reaching almost to the shade cloth. I'd dealt a bit of grass in my younger days—and a plantation like this, it was worth big money. The kind of money that spoke of underworld gangs and crime bosses. The kind of money people killed for, puzzled or not.

'Just let us walk away,' Harry continued carefully, 'and you won't see us again.'

More hard stares over the gun barrels. 'No one's just walkin' away.'

'Look. We're no threat. We're out here trying to hide from the same sort of people that you are.'

'What sort of people is that?'

'The army. The police.'

'Police? You got cops on your tail? Right this minute?'

'Yes ...' Then Harry's face fell, already seeing his mistake as the men's eyes went deadly cold, their fingers tightening on the triggers. 'No ... I mean, not right behind us this *minute*.'

And it might have ended there, dear interrogators, all our days on the run—but at that moment an old black woman emerged from the plants.

'That'll do, boys,' she said.

The men stared at her. 'Mum, we got it covered ...'

She gave them a swift glance, and snapped out a rush of words in another language. She was barely half their height, a round figure in a faded floral dress, with skinny legs and horned bare feet. But there was no doubting her authority.

'No shooting,' she commanded in English.

'But they've seen the crop,' one of her sons protested. 'They'll report it!'

'This lot? Bullshit. They won't be reporting anything.' White wisps of hair escaped from under a tattered beanie on her head, giving her a half-mad look, but her eyes were perfectly sharp and aware, studying us. 'I know who they are.'

Harry was amazed. 'You do?'

'Not you, maybe. But these other two? You bet.'

'But...how?'

She rolled her eyes at him. 'I watch TV, don't I?' She was pointing at me. 'He's the Prime Minister's brother. He's supposed to be dead.' Her finger moved towards Aisha. 'And her...Oh, I've seen *plenty* about her lately.'

Harry could only shake his head. After all the roadblocks and checkpoints, after all the people who'd seen our faces and not recognised us for an instant, this old creature had seen through us like it was the most obvious thing in the world. And she didn't even have the grace to act surprised.

Meanwhile, her sons had not lowered their rifles. 'They got people after them,' one warned. 'They said so.'

'I'll bet they have. This little girl here is worth half a million reward, last I heard.'

The men regarded us with renewed interest.

'You all terrorists then?' the old woman inquired.

'No,' Harry answered intently, 'we're exactly the opposite. The things you've seen on TV—they aren't true. Look...I don't know if this means anything to you, but I'm with the Oz Underground, and we have to get under cover.'

'Ah. The Underground.'

'You've heard of us?'

'Yeah, I heard.' But she didn't seem terribly happy about it. 'These people chasing you—they close behind?'

'I don't know. We dumped our vehicle last night, north of here, off the road. If they've found that, they will have found our tracks leading here.'

'Dropped us right in the shit, haven't you?'

'We didn't mean to.'

'Don't give a fuck what you *meant* to do.'

She sighed, and then turned to her sons, muttering something in her own tongue. The boys responded in what was apparent disagreement, but after further heated discussion a decision was reached. They shouldered their rifles, gave us all a dark glance, then headed off up over the ridge.

She watched them go, considered the three of us. 'C'mon inside, anyway. No good you standing out here in plain bloody sight.'

We followed her in under the shade cloth and through the plants, the smell of marijuana warm and cloying.

'Where did you send them?' Harry asked.

'To keep an eye out. And to clean up your mess. They'll follow your tracks back a couple of miles, then see what they can do.'

'You mean hide the tracks?'

'Maybe. They can't work bloody miracles though.'

'Thank you.'

She was still displeased. 'I'm not doing you any favours. I just don't want the cops charging in here.'

The greenhouse seemed to hold hundreds of plants, and in the middle of them we came across the generator. It was powering a pump that stood at the head of an underground bore, from which water was diverted into black plastic irrigation pipes. The old woman hit the switch and the motor died. She frowned at us accusingly in the sudden silence. 'And now my damn plants will have to go thirsty.'

But she led us onwards, to where the gully ended in a half-formed kind of cave. Several swags were spread there, a table, some chairs, a gas barbecue, petrol drums, even a television set that was linked to a small satellite dish, a power cord running off towards the generator. All the comforts of home. The old woman, meanwhile, was scratching around on the table. She found a box of matches, lit the gas ring on the barbecue, and set a kettle down on the flame.

'Right,' she said finally. 'Who wants a cuppa?'

The tea was hot, sweet and an utter godsend. We sprawled about on the swags, exhausted, and drank. Our host made herself comfortable in a chair, stuffed a pipe with tobacco and began to smoke it. Her name, she said, was Frieda.

'You're a local?' Harry wanted to know.

''Course I bloody am.'

'Is this your property?'

'The station? Nah. It's my *country*, though. And the owner knows we're here.' She glanced pointedly at the crop. 'He gets his cut, fair and square.' Then she gave Harry a look. 'Whose fool idea was it coming out here anyway?'

'It's a long story.'

'It'd wanna be.'

'Right now, we're just trying to get south.'

'To where?'

'The Murray, for a start.'

The old woman gave a pitying laugh.

'Why? Aren't we even close? Where are we, exactly?'

'You're nowhere much. The Murray's a good fifty miles yet, straight south.'

'Oh,' said Harry, crestfallen. He took a breath. 'The thing is, we've been walking all night, we haven't slept. We need a place to lie low for the day.'

'What—now you wanna stay here all day?!'

'There's nowhere else. And tonight we need to cross the border.'

She scowled around the pipe. 'I'm not in your bloody Underground.'

'But are you against us?' And Harry sounded raw, pushing hard. 'Are you on the government's side?'

'I'm not on anyone's side.'

'So is there a way we can get to the river from here without being seen?'

'Depends how hard they're looking for you.'

'But could *you* help us?'

She puffed smoke doubtfully. 'Why do they want you so bad in the first place?'

'It's because of Leo and Aisha here—they know something that can damage the government. We don't know what that is yet, but it's gotta be something big. And something that big can maybe help bring this government down.'

Her eyes were mocking. 'The whole government, eh?'

'In the long term, that's our aim.'

'It's not my bloody aim.'

'Why not? You can't be happy right now—things are worse for your people than ever under this government. None of them give a shit about Aboriginal problems, not when they've got their precious war on terror to fight. Christ, they even closed down Uluru because they say it's a terrorist target.'

The old woman shuddered with laughter. 'Yeah. I heard about that. They put up a big fence, right around the Rock.'

'You think it's funny?'

'Hell, the blackfellas up there still get in. No fence is gonna stop 'em. And at least it keeps all the damn tourists away. But that fence has got nothing to do with terrorists. It's because the army built some kind of satellite base on top of the Rock, some spy thing they need and don't want anyone to see.'

'You're kidding,' I said.

She glanced at me benignly. 'Nope. Doesn't matter, though. Aborigines burnt it down. The poor old army can't work out how it happened.'

'Exactly,' said Harry. 'You see—you have to fight these things.'

She shrugged. 'The Rock's not my country. None of my business. And the government pretty much leaves us alone, this part of the world.'

'But the rest of the country...'

'Bad times, I know. But it'll all pass one day.'

Harry reared up. 'It'll *pass*?'

She fixed him with a stare. 'Listen, Underground man. You walk out the end of this gully and what do you see? That old lake bed. You would've been twenty feet underwater here once, before it dried up. There's dry lakes all around here, they've been dead for thousand of years. Lake Mungo—you've heard of that, the one where all the tourists go to look at the fossils? That's twenty-odd miles west of here. But even this little lake that no one's heard of—I can take you along this shoreline and show you campsites that my people were using forty thousand years ago. We've always been right here, my lot. We survived everything—the lakes drying up, the desert coming, even you white folk trying to wipe us out. And as long as we don't go and do something stupid in the meantime, like getting ourselves arrested and shot, then we'll still be here in *another* forty thousand too. And by then, not a damn soul is gonna remember any of this stuff you're talking about.'

Harry sank back, disappointed.

The old woman shrugged again. 'We got enough enemies of our own. We don't need to take on yours as well.'

I said, 'But you can't just send us back out there.'

'I didn't say I'd do that either. Just let me think, damn it.'

We sat in silence for a time. Beneath me, the musty old swag felt like the most comfortable bed I'd ever imagined, and sleep beckoned irresistibly.

Frieda was staring at Aisha. 'You don't say much, girl.'

Aisha looked almost too tired to glare back. 'I'm not a girl.'

'Oh no?' Her smile showed broken teeth. 'And it's not true what they say? You aren't a terrorist?'

'I'm not a terrorist. I'm fighting in a war.'

'One of them jihads, eh?'

'That's right.'

'And you kill for that, right?'

'If it's necessary.'

The old woman thought. ''Course, Aborigines could have gone that way too. We still got a few hotheads wanting to blow up white people, to get our land back.'

'You should. It would be a way to stand up for yourselves.'

'Ha! It would be a way to get ourselves killed, that's all. No, we do our standing up on the *inside*, girl. We might not look like much, us lot out here, but we could teach mad buggers like you a thing or two about it.'

From above and far-off, came a shout that sounded like a warning. Frieda was up in an instant, head cocked alertly.

'What?' Harry asked.

'My boys,' she said, holding out a hand for quiet. There came another shout, then, surprisingly lithe, she clambered up the side of the gully to the underside of the roof. A patch of the shade cloth was detached there. She flipped it back to the open sky and lifted herself out to look. A long moment passed in silence . . . Or could I hear, just on the fringe of audibility, a hum of some kind? Finally, the old woman indicated that we should climb up and join her.

Above the roof, the morning was well advanced now, the sky empty and blue. But Frieda pointed away to the west, and there, in the distance, a tiny black shape seemed to hang in the air. Not a helicopter, but a spindly thing, half plane, half insect, moving slowly south.

'Predator drone,' the old woman said.

Harry was impressed. 'You've seen one before?'

'The army's got bases out here. Australian Army. American Army. They test things. Those drones come over once in a while. Never spotted us here, though.'

'Christ,' I said. 'They've got to be close.'

Frieda shook her head at me. 'That drone's good news. They wouldn't be using it if they were anywhere near, or if they were on to your tracks yet. But it's no time to be walking out in the open, with those little devils about.' She ushered us all back under the roof, and pulled the flap over. 'Okay. You stay here for the day, and get some sleep. Only thing to do—otherwise they'll find you out there, and you people are so dumb you'd probably tell them all about *me*.'

'And tonight?' Harry asked.

'Tonight, we'll get you to the river.' Her faded eyes glinted wide a moment, sad and stern. 'You can fight all you like after that. Just don't do it here.'

TWENTY-FOUR

When I woke, groggy and thick, it was late afternoon. Nearby, Harry and Aisha still slept on their respective swags. There was no sign of Frieda, or her boys.

The heat was stupendous, and my bladder was full to bursting. I couldn't see anything that looked like a toilet, so I rose and shuffled blearily through the marijuana crop, until I emerged from under the roof. A dozen yards along the foot of the ridge, I unzipped, and let loose—noticing, belatedly, that my stream was washing away the thin sand, and that something white and broken was emerging from just under the soil. It was a calcified fragment of bone. A fossil.

I was suddenly fully awake, eyes wide. I looked at the sky. It was bleached colourless by the day's heat, dry and empty, as if it had never known rain. I looked at the ridge, a beaten, crumbled arc of abandoned shoreline. I looked at the lake floor, white and stark and dead, like the skin of the planet had blistered and peeled away. And just for an instant, all alone out there with my dick hanging in space, the *age* of the place hit me. The silence of it. The stillness. Twenty feet of water, burnt away by the sun so long ago that even the memory of it was gone. Except for that fossil in the sand . . . Animals had thrived there once, and forests, and grass. Fish had swum by their thousands in the water, and birds had hunted them from the air. And humans were there too, camped on the lake shore, waves lapping at their feet. Their eyes staring out across a landscape teeming with life—year by year, decade by decade, century by century, age by age—watching as the weather changed and the desert came.

And now only the humans were left.

It makes you think, dear interrogators.

I mean, how much of this mess that we're in right now stems from the old hatreds in the Middle East, and the ancient claims of Arabs and Jews and Christians? And yet all those disputes only go back a few thousand years. Most of us came in even later, and only because of the oil. How does any of that compare to forty thousand years, and those people at the lake? We'd have to keep this up for another thirty-five millennia! What the old woman said was right. Does anyone really believe that after so long we're still going to be fighting and dying over the same old arguments? Or that by then anyone will even remember that oil and Islam and Israel and Christianity ever existed? We humans might still be around, but all that we value now or think worthy of belief—all that will be long gone.

It's obvious enough, I know, but the bigger perspective really catches you occasionally. A momentary thought at a dead lake in the middle of nowhere. Or a longer thought—let me tell you— sitting in a giant prison cell, while you're waiting for either the next round of torture, or for execution.

The rank, short-sighted *stupidity* of it all.

Anyway, I zipped up, and headed back. And as I did so, I saw a figure out on the lake bed, a shadow against the sun, heading towards me. I caught a burst of language, and a low laugh. And indeed, as if I'd called her up with my thoughts, it was Frieda, the descendant of all that unimaginable length of history, hobbling across the sand in her ridiculous beanie, white hair a mess, talking rapidly into the mobile phone jammed against her ear.

I waited. Her conversation finished as she came up.

'You get reception on a mobile out here?' I asked.

She gave me one of her eye rolls. ''Course not. It's a satellite phone. Even then, you have to go out in the middle of the lake to get a good signal.'

'Who were you talking to?'

'What—you think I turned you in or something?'

Actually, that hadn't occurred to me. 'Have you?'

'Nope. I was just callin' home.'

'Home? This isn't home out here?'

'You crazy? I got a house in Menindee. Me and the rest of the family.' She nodded towards the marijuana plants. 'This is just part time.'

'Pretty lucrative, for part time.'

'Ah, the money gets spread around. And there's no other work out here these days. But this stuff—you can never grow too much. It's all these armies in the country. Ours. The Americans. Those soldiers just buy and buy. I tell you, all the bloody wars around the world must run on marijuana.'

We were walking back through the plants now.

'Have you seen any more drones?' I asked.

'A couple. Long way off, though. And the boys are keepin' an eye out. No one's comin' this way yet.'

'So we go tonight?'

She pondered, studying the phone. 'I been talkin' to people all over on this thing—and the word is out about you lot. Army. Air force. Police. They know you're round here somewhere, and they know you're trying to head south, so they got every bridge over the Murray locked down. And not just south, either. East, west, north. Every main road, every back road.'

'Shit.'

She didn't seem too alarmed. 'Ah well . . . We'll see what night brings.'

★

Night brought darkness, and—thanks to some friendly weather spirit—it also brought a sheet of high cloud that flowed in from the west, blotting out the stars and the narrow moon. Frieda was pleased, even more so when her sons checked in to report that all was quiet in the immediate vicinity.

'Okay,' she said. 'We go. There's a bit of the river south of Robinvale. Long empty stretch there, no bridges, no locks, no houses.'

'And if we get across?' Harry wanted to know.

'You're on your own. The Murray Highway runs along not far from the other side. You can hitch a ride south.'

Harry thought a moment. 'Can I use that phone of yours?'

'Why?'

'I want to call my superiors. Maybe they can arrange to have someone pick us up there.'

'Government listens in on those satellite calls,' she warned.

'I know. But we got codes. I won't give anything away.'

She acceded, and Harry went off with the phone. By the time he came back, Frieda had gathered four garbage bags, each full of processed marijuana.

'You got it done?' she asked.

Harry nodded. 'Someone will be waiting.'

'Good.' She looked at us all. 'Grab a bag each and follow me.'

'You're making a delivery at the same time?'

'Two birds,' she replied. 'You'll see . . . The way we always get the dope across, we'll get you three across as well.'

We took the bags, hefted them over our shoulders, then headed off into the night. It was black out there, and although the old woman had a little torch with her, she did not use it, so we stumbled and tripped after her sure-footed shadow. Back up over the ridge and away from the lake, and then down through the scrub and the sand. There was a breeze blowing, giving the air a dangerous, chancy feel. It was heightened by the knowledge that all around us, waiting on the rim of a vast circle of wilderness, hundreds (or maybe thousands now) of searchers were manning barricades and watching for us to try to break out.

But Frieda led us on, unhurried, and after maybe half an hour we came to a knot of scraggly old trees, looming up in the dark. She flicked on the torch briefly, and we could see, secreted beneath the trees, the hulk of an ancient Landcruiser. Passing it by on any other night, I might have thought it was a wreck, but the old woman instructed us to load the bags in the back and climb in. And it started up fine, when she turned the ignition.

From there, we drove. Still in total darkness, no headlights, through scrub and over hills, down into empty creek beds and across sandy depressions that sucked at the wheels. At times it seemed that we were following one dirt road or another, but never for long, the old woman would always turn off again into the scrub, searching out some winding path of her own. We saw no other sign of life—except for once, when Frieda, staring intently through the windscreen, made an alarmed noise, then abruptly steered the vehicle into a deep gully, and switched off the engine.

'What?' Harry asked, beside her in the front.

She was leaning forward to gaze at the sky. 'Another drone up there.'

Aisha and I were in the back. I craned my head out the window, but the sky was black ink. How on earth had the old woman seen anything?

'It won't be able to spot us, will it?' I asked.

Frieda was almost whispering. 'They got thermal imaging. But as long as it don't go right over us, we should be hidden down here.' We sat. And after a time, the old woman seemed satisfied. She started the engine again, reversed out, and we were on our way.

We travelled for several hours more, it felt to me, carving a painstaking route through the night. Sometimes we came to fences, but the old woman always seemed to find a gate through which we could pass. At another point she slowed the vehicle to a crawl, peering forward. 'There's a proper road up ahead that we gotta cross—runs between Robinvale and Balranald—before we hit the river. There'll be patrols on it. But it's a long bit of track. They can't cover it all.'

She came to a stop. Minutes ticked by in silence. Then, in the distance, lights appeared to the right. Headlights, three vehicles, moving in convoy along the invisible road. Trucks, by the look, going slow, and full, no doubt, of soldiers. But they sailed steadily by, maybe five hundred yards ahead of us, then dwindled away, tail-lights fading, to the left. 'Okay,' Frieda muttered, and gunned the engine. We lurched forward, bouncing over the ground. I had a momentary glimpse of the road itself—black tarmac, white lines dimly glowing, an instant of traction for the wheels—and then we were over into the scrub on the far side.

And onwards still, the last miles now, seeing nothing, and seen by no one. Until finally the old woman braked, killed the engine, and instructed us to climb out.

'We're there?' Harry asked.

'Close. Grab the bags.'

We unloaded the marijuana, then hurried through the bush. Frieda risked a flash of her torch, and suddenly we saw the ground drop away before us, and the glint of water below. The Murray River. Half guessed in the darkness, no more than a hundred yards away, was the shadow of the opposite bank. The old woman dropped confidently down the embankment, and hunted around in the tree roots and bushes down there. At length she gave a grunt. 'Here it is.'

She was dragging a small rowboat from its hiding place.

'We row those bags across,' she told us, looking up, 'whenever we get an order. On the other side, there's an old shack in the bush where we drop 'em. It's not far from a rest stop that the trucks on the highway use.' She slipped the boat into the water. 'Now hand that stuff down.'

We let the marijuana slide down the bank. But just before we could follow, a beam of light sprang out from the darkness. Frieda froze, captured in it. The light wavered, moved on, returned to her. And with it, the sound of a motor. Staring back to the source of the beam, I could see now the low shape of another boat, just coming around a bend in the river.

'You there,' boomed a voice through a megaphone, clearly American, even with the amplification. 'Don't move an inch.'

Frieda stood upright, bag in hand.

'Step away from the boat,' the voice crackled again. 'We have weapons trained and are authorised to use deadly force.'

The old woman bent to put down the bag. 'Get under cover!' she hissed to the rest of us, still concealed in the scrub on the high edge of the river bank.

We all dropped to the ground. I peered down through the bushes as the boat drew near. It was an inflatable dinghy carrying four soldiers—all heavily armed, and all in US uniforms. There must have been an American base somewhere in the area, and they'd been dragooned into the search. They ran up on shore next to Frieda and piled out, guns at the ready. And yet, like the troops at the roadblocks back at Base Amberly, these didn't look like top-line combat soldiers to me. Their uniforms were untucked, showing T-shirts and bellies, one wore thick glasses, and two of them were smoking cigarettes. And even in that moment of panic, it occurred to me how incredibly odd this must have seemed to them—a bunch of good ol' boys patrolling some muddy Australian creek in the dead of night. The mighty Mississippi it wasn't.

'What you got there?' one of them asked.

'Yeah,' drawled another. 'What's in the bags, lady?'

'Nuthin',' replied Frieda, sounding sullen and slow.

They had torches with them, and were shining the beams about. The lights flickered across our hiding spot, but didn't linger. And they really couldn't have been top-line troops, because they didn't bother with a physical search, nor were they equipped with night-vision goggles.

'You alone out here, old girl?'

Frieda nodded, eyes downcast.

One of them was going through the bags now.

'Whoa,' he whistled to his comrades. 'Check this out.'

They gathered around to leaf through the marijuana.

'Holy Christ, woman, you gotta have over fifty pounds here!'

'Primo stuff, too. Mother of mercy.'

'You smuggling this shit? Are you crazy or what, tryin' to pull this off on a night like tonight? Man, are you busted!'

But one of them, at least, was a little more serious. 'What's your name?'

'Grace,' she mumbled.

'Where you from?'

'Robinvale,' she lied again.

'You seen anyone else along the river tonight?' he demanded. 'Two men and a woman, trying to get across? You seen anyone else out here at all?'

'I seen nuthin'. No one.'

'No one, hey?' He stared along the river, dissatisfied.

The others had gathered all the bags into a pile. 'So what do we do now? We authorised to arrest someone for running weed?'

'Christ,' the leader sighed, 'we can arrest whoever we like.' He made his decision, nodded towards their boat. 'Get the bags on board. We're confiscating it. Contraband.'

The others got busy, exchanging glances.

'And you,' he addressed Frieda, 'you get on home. An old lady like you, messing around with this stuff. It's a damn shame. But we'll let it go this time.' He leant into her. 'You were never here, right? And you sure as hell never met us either.'

'Never here,' repeated Frieda. 'Never saw you.'

'Get outta here then.'

The loading done, he stepped into his boat with the others and shoved off. The outboard spluttered into life, and the spotlight sprang out again. Turning in the current, they moved further on up the river, laughter and shouts echoing back behind them. In a few minutes, they were out of sight around the next bend. Harry and Aisha and I emerged from hiding, and crept down the bank. We found the old woman sitting on the bow of the boat, her shoulders rocking with silent laughter.

'What did I tell you?' She was wiping her eyes. 'This whole world war we're in, it's fought on bloody *grass*!'

And when she had recovered, we climbed into the boat, pulled out the oars, and rowed silently across the muddy water of the Murray River, into Victoria.

TWENTY-FIVE

The shack Frieda had mentioned—a tumbledown old thing, empty and overgrown—was hidden in the scrub not far from the southern bank of the river. The Murray Valley Highway was only a few hundred yards further away through the trees, and we could hear occasional trucks and cars passing by. Harry put in another call via the satellite phone, and arranged the pick-up. Then it was time for Frieda to bid us farewell. We were out of her country, and out of her hands.

'We can't thank you enough,' Harry told her.

'No, you can't,' she retorted. 'Not unless you're gonna bloody well pay for those bags they stole off me.'

'Maybe we can, some day, if we make it through this.'

'Huh. They'll catch you sooner or later, I know that much.' She scowled impressively at all of us. 'But not a word about me and my crop, right?'

'Right,' we promised.

And with that, she clamped her beanie down over her crazy

hair, then ambled away back towards the river, her bare feet silent in the dirt.

But of course, I've broken that promise, haven't I, interrogators? I've told you everything about her, just like I've spilled my guts about everything else. And yet, you know, she's the one person involved in all of this for whom I have no fears. That old woman was no fool. I don't believe for a second that her name was really Frieda, or Grace, or that her real home was in either Robinvale or Menindee. She'll escape all your reprisals. Even if you find the empty lake, amidst all the other empty lakes out there, and even if you find the right gully, under its camouflaged roof... Well, I'm betting that she and her sons and her crop will have long since moved on.

We spent the night in the shack, and then, about an hour before dawn, moved to the rest area at the highway's edge. The stop was just a gravel clearing where weary truck drivers could pull over, with no facilities other than an overflowing rubbish bin and a tottering thunderbox toilet. But there we waited, secreted behind the bushes, until, just as the first hint of light was in the sky, a semitrailer came grinding in off the southbound lane. The cabin was emblazoned with the shapes of naked women, and the two trailers behind it were loaded with pallets of boxed fruit. The driver let the engine rattle down to an idle, climbed out, hitched up his shorts, and then, ignoring the derelict toilet, made for the bushes as if to relieve himself.

We stood up to meet him. Here was another unlikely member of the Underground—a wiry old truckie, smokes jammed under his T-shirt sleeve, and a sweat-stained cowboy hat on his head. I never did learn his name.

'You,' he said to Harry, 'ride up front.' He dropped a plastic bag on the ground. 'I got one set of clothes, and one new ID. The ID is a bit dodgy, maybe, but it's only gotta last until we get you to town.'

Harry took the bag. 'What about Leo and Aisha?'

The man's narrow gaze appraised us like a load of explosive cargo. 'They're far too hot. They ride in back.'

'How tight is the security from here on?'

'There's a few checkpoints down as far as Bendigo, after that it's plain sailing. They think you're still north of the river.'

He led us over to the truck. 'In back' turned out to mean a hidden compartment. What looked like eight pallets of fruit boxes packed together was actually a facade. The outer boxes were real enough, but they were piled around a metal bin that formed a hollow interior. The inside was only a metre and a half square, and I assumed it was normally used for smuggling non-human OU contraband. Still, there was room enough for Aisha and me to climb in and sit, side by side. The truckie dropped two bottles of water in after us, and a bucket.

'Five or six hours,' he said, 'and we'll be in Melbourne.'

He shut the lid with a bang, leaving us in total darkness, breathing in the smell of oranges. We could hear fruit boxes being piled above us. A few more minutes passed, then the truck was lurching into gear, and we were under way.

Ever been locked in a metal box, interrogators?

Actually, you probably have. No doubt it's part of your endurance training. And it's not pleasant, is it? No way to stretch out or stand up. Hardly any air, the suffocating heat, the blackness that makes your eyes ache and your head spin. But add to that the swaying of the truck, and the noise, and the overpowering smell of fruit, and the exhaust fumes... Well, I'd thought that the bucket was there for the usual bodily functions, but after an hour or so in that sweating, stinking darkness, my stomach heaving, I learnt what the bucket was really for.

'Sorry,' I said, as the sour stench of vomit flooded through the box. Aisha shifted next to me, but said nothing. 'No fucking way to travel, is it?' I added.

'Get used to it,' came her voice in the darkness.

'Why?'

'This is the way a lot of people in the world travel now. Those men out in the desert, the refugees we left behind to die—they were in a steel box too.'

And it was true enough.

But then Aisha herself was coughing and gagging and reaching for the bucket. I listened to her retch, and couldn't help smiling. 'Holy shit,' she gasped disgustedly when it was over, and for once she didn't sound at all like a terrorist or a religious fanatic. She sounded like a teenage girl who was drunk for the first time, and was suffering the consequences.

'How old are you, anyway?' I asked.

'What does that matter?'

'I'm just curious.'

'I'm twenty-four. Okay?'

'Okay.'

Abruptly the truck was slowing, air brakes hissing all around us. We came to a complete stop, and then there were voices, only half heard through the fruit boxes, but sounding official. We hunched motionless in the dark. Something thumped on the boxes, and there were other sounds of shifting and opening. I distinctly heard someone say, 'Oranges, all right.' And shortly afterwards, we were rolling again.

'Twenty-four,' I mused out loud into the blackness, speaking to keep my mind off a returning nausea. 'Why is it you terrorists are always so young?'

'It's our privilege,' she replied. 'The young are the strongest.'

'Bullshit. You're just the most gullible.'

'You have no idea...'

But neither of our hearts were in the argument. Aisha sounded distracted, like she was having trouble breathing. I listened while she drank some water.

'You okay?'

'I'll get by.'

Silence for another few minutes of misery.

'Tell me,' I said. 'I really do want to know. How did you get into this?'

And maybe it was just the kinship of suffering that made it

easier for us to talk. Or the blackness, and not actually having to look at each other. It certainly made it easier for me, to have that sharp, bitter face of hers hidden. And for her—it gradually dawned on me that perhaps she was a little claustrophobic. There was a hint of panic that fluttered from time to time in her voice. So maybe the conversation, the connection with another person, made it better for her too.

'I was recruited at Queensland Uni,' she said.

'What were you studying?'

'Law.'

'I might have known. But you had nothing to do with Islam before that? You weren't raised as a Muslim?'

'I wasn't raised as anything. My parents didn't believe in religion. My father was an English professor. My mother was an artist. They were soft.'

'You were the only kid?'

'Oh yes.'

And in the darkness I could almost see a vision of them, a settled, intellectual, middle-class couple, probably far too indulgent with their single precious child—a tall, striking girl who wasn't satisfied with mere wealth and comfort.

'I bet you were smart at school,' I said.

'I was too smart. I even scared my teachers.'

'And your friends too?'

'I was at an all-girls school. Most of the others in my class, they were pathetic. Completely empty-headed. I couldn't be bothered with them.'

Tall. Striking. Fiercely intelligent. And lonely. I suddenly remembered that Aisha wasn't her real name. What was it again? Nancy. Nancy Campbell.

'And did you hate Australia even then?'

'I hated the things it was right to hate.'

'Like what?'

'Like the smugness of this country. The self-righteousness. The greed. The obsession with trivialities. Celebrities. Sex. Money. Sport. We were supposed to be so wonderful, so fair and equal.

But if you were poor or black or ugly or a refugee, then the whole country shat on you every single day.'

Well, yes, and I've written down similar thoughts in these very pages. Even so, there is *something* to be said for trivialities. Better, surely, to be obsessed with sport than to be obsessed with war and religion. Indeed, in the old Australia, sport and sex and beer were about it—which was why I'd loved the place so much.

Still, I knew what she meant.

I said, 'You were hardly the only one who thought that.'

'I may as well have been. People here are in denial. The rest of the world can see how rotten the West is, how self-obsessed, how overfed, how destructive. Africa. Asia. The Middle East. They all know the truth. But here, we're blind.'

'Things are hardly perfect in Africa or Asia or the Middle East either.'

'That's *because* of the West. We have all the money, all the weapons; we're like an infection. We exploit everyone else, invade everyone else, ruin everyone else. We have to, to keep our own obscene societies afloat.'

'Then why does everyone want to *be* like the West?'

'They don't! They just want to be left alone. In peace, with their own culture, not caught up in some bastardised version of ours. But when they look at how we live—the wealth, the luxury—it's like a drug. People can't help wanting to have that too, even though it's bad for them. Bad for everyone.'

Oh, yes. Tall. Striking. Fiercely intelligent. Lonely. Restless. No fixed religion or philosophy. Possessed of a keen sense of justice and an overblown case of white middle-class guilt. Christ, these things were probably written down in a terrorist recruiting handbook somewhere.

'So you went looking for answers in Islam?'

'I didn't go looking. They came looking for me.'

'At uni? Some fundamentalist group there?'

'Not exactly. There *were* Islamic groups at uni, but even in those days they weren't liked. And they were already being watched by the government. They had spies taking down names and addresses. Even if I'd been interested in Islam at that stage, I wouldn't have gone near those people.'

'Then how?'

'A woman in one of my tutes approached me.'

'She was a Muslim?'

'Not in any way that you would recognise.'

'But she told you about Islam?'

'Not about old Islam. She was talking about new Islam. About the war and the revolution that were coming.'

I sighed inwardly, and said nothing.

'The war she was talking about is the one we're fighting now, against the West. The revolution is the one that's happening within Islam itself. And it has to happen, if we're to win the war. The old Islam can't do it. It's grown soft too. And corrupt. It needs new strength, new purity. And when it's ready, then it can *fix* the world.'

The inward sigh was now a groan. How did it happen that, just because an intelligent mind was disappointed by the society around it and searching for solutions, it would fall for the first hardline idiocy that it came across?

My mind went back to a conversation I'd had years ago with an old friend. He was a long-lapsed Catholic, but he had decided to send his son to a Catholic school. When I asked him why, he said one word: 'Inoculation.' His theory was this—all religions and cults were dangerous, and he did not want his son involved in any of them. The problem was, if he raised his son with no religion at all, then the boy might well fall prey to the first religion or cult that he came across later, just out of curiosity and naivety. If he was raised Catholic, on the other hand, he would at least know a religion from the inside. And in my friend's opinion, Catholicism was the laziest and most stagnant of the western religions, and hence the simplest for his son to rebel against while growing up. And having seen through the nonsense of one religion, he would never then fall prey to another. He would have had his inoculation shot, and would now be immune. And as crazy as the plan had sounded, it probably worked. I certainly never heard of that boy blowing anyone up.

Nancy Campbell though...

'So, this new Islam, it was some group of radical Muslims?'

'There were no Muslims in it. At least, none who had been born that way. We were all converts. And it was secret. That was the most important thing.'

'But what's the point of that?'

'The point is that Muslims were targets. Anyone who was Arabic, or openly Islamic, the government already *knew* about them. When the war came, they would be the first ones to be crushed. So we had nothing whatever to do with Muslims. We didn't go to mosques, we didn't go to Islamic bookshops, we didn't dress Muslim or talk Muslim, we didn't tell a single soul outside the group about what we believed. In fact, in public, we drank and smoked and fucked around. We prayed only in small groups, and in private. Allah understood the necessity. We had to be invisible, the most secret of the secret—and we were to stay that way until the day we were needed, when all the other Muslims of the world were victimised and oppressed and defeated. Then the new Islam would stand forth.'

Some of the fervour was returning to her voice, and it was weirdly powerful, there in the dark. But the saner part of me went chill. What she was describing, of course, was the ultimate in terrorist sleeper cells. All of them average white middle-class Australians who had never even expressed an interest in Islam. I thought of the boys who had kidnapped me in the Australia Post van. They could have been in the local footy team.

'And who was in charge of all this? Who was your mullah?'

She turned scornful. 'We're an underground organisation, and you should know enough about them by now. We operate in cells. I've never known the names of anyone higher up than the woman who recruited me. And the people I recruited have never known anyone higher up than I am.'

A point confused me. 'Those boys of yours, back in Queensland. If you recruited them, they must have seen your face. So why bother with that burqa?'

'I didn't recruit those four. I inherited them from another cell leader who was martyred, after the war started and the Great Southern Jihad went active. Lots of us have died for the cause since then. My own recruits know what I look like, obviously. But those men never did.'

Men? What a laugh. They were four repressed, mixed-up, angry boys. Desperately lovesick for their goddess in the far-too-clinging veil.

I said, 'So when exactly did you go active?'

'We had to wait and wait. We waited through September 11, we waited while Osama bin Laden cried out for our help, we ignored the Great Hero and did nothing while the enemy invaded Afghanistan and Iraq and then started all the other wars. Wait, we were told, the time isn't yet.' And it sounded like she was reciting a ritual passage of mourning. 'But then came the holy fire in Canberra. That was when the war finally arrived in this country. That was when the government looked at the Muslims in their midst and hated them all. That was when the mass detentions started and the new laws were made and no Muslim could walk the streets anymore. That's when *we* were needed. And the command came down. Begin the jihad.'

I listened, horrified by her, but torn with a certain pity too, because what, after all, was this great war of hers? Her little terrorist cells were never going to achieve anything. Osama bin Laden was dead, he was never going to learn their names, or thank them for saving the Muslim world. It was a delusion of grandeur. A smart, lonely girl, dreaming of an influence she could never have. A teenager running away to punish her mother and father for their crime of conformity. I said, 'And what did your parents think of what you were doing?'

'They thought nothing. They didn't know.'

'And they still don't?'

'They never will. They're dead.'

'Oh...I'm sorry.'

'Don't be. They died in a car bombing.'

'A bombing? But—'

'I was the one who planted it.'

'What?!'

She sounded hypnotically calm now. 'It was my first mission, after we went active. I knew it had to be done. The past had to be cut away. So that there could be no going back. They were weak. I needed to be strong.'

'So—you just *killed* them?'

I was staring, trying to pierce the darkness and see her face. But only her voice was there, disembodied, desolate.

'You didn't believe me, when we first met. Harry didn't believe me either. But I told you. There's blood on my hands.'

We rode the rest of the way in silence.

There were several more roadblocks, but we passed safely through them all. I even dozed for a while, jammed up against the side of the box in an attempt to get as far from Aisha as possible, my head full of nausea and bad dreams. When I woke I could feel that we were no longer on the open highway. The truck was moving slowly in heavy traffic. It was Melbourne at last—although there was no way to tell which part of the city we were in. Even when we finally stopped and the fruit boxes were removed and we climbed out, all bent and crippled and pale, I still didn't know our precise location, because we were parked inside a large warehouse.

'Hurry,' Harry was telling us.

We followed him as best we could across the concrete, through stacks of crates and machinery, then into a toilet block. In the floor of one of the shower recesses a manhole had been opened, leading down into darkness.

'Where is this?' I asked him. 'Where does this go?'

'The one place in Melbourne no one would think to look for us. The AFP, Citizenship, they never go there. They haven't needed to, since they put up the walls.' He was grinning. 'Somewhere Aisha will feel right at home.'

We climbed down a ladder into a tunnel than ran off into midnight. Harry had a torch, and led us forward. I thought I knew where we had to be going, although the very idea sounded like madness to me. The tunnel went on. A hundred yards. Two hundred. Then there was a light ahead, and a ladder climbing up.

'We're safe now,' Harry said.

We ascended. There were arms up there, waiting to pull us through. Into a small room, another toilet block, in another unidentified building. And all around us, faces. Smiling. Nodding. Reassuring. Aisha was staring in wonder.

'Welcome,' someone said, 'to the Brunswick ghetto.'

TWENTY-SIX

Ah, Brunswick.

The name probably doesn't mean much to you, dear interrogators, but it takes *me* right home to the Melbourne days of my youth.

Admittedly, it was never really my part of town. I was an eastern suburbs boy. But Brunswick and its main thoroughfare, Sydney Road, was very much the place to go in search of exotic Middle Eastern foods. There were some popular Turkish restaurants and bakeries, for instance. And it was a colourful area, a bit ramshackle and run-down, a bit foreign, but all in a good way—which was how most of the ethnic enclaves were, back in that far-off time when multiculturalism was not a dirty word. Not that everyone who lived in Brunswick was from Turkey or Egypt or Lebanon—you still saw lots of white faces on the street—but you certainly saw Arabic faces too. And scarves or veils on many of the women, even the occasional full-length burqa. If I'd been asked, before all the troubles, to find a Muslim community in Melbourne, I would've gone to Brunswick first.

It was no surprise then—in the wake of the Canberra bombing—
that Brunswick became one of the designated detention suburbs.
Of course, it's by no means the biggest Muslim ghetto in the world.
Brunswick is downright tiny compared to those in America or
England. Nor is it the biggest ghetto in Australia. That, I'm pretty
sure, would be Bankstown in Sydney. It's not even the biggest
ghetto in Melbourne—there are more people confined to the
northern suburb of Broadmeadows. Still, jammed into those few
city blocks of inner Brunswick are something like forty thousand
Muslim souls, the vast majority of them forcibly removed from
somewhere else.

Oh, they kicked up a fuss about it. As did the non-Islamic
residents of the area, who were compelled to move away. As did
Melbourne commuters, when a stretch of Sydney Road was cut
off by the new walls. But my brother was quite adamant. There
was, he declared, a poisonous two per cent of the population that
needed to be dealt with. Too many to deport (and besides, no
other country would take them) and too many to detain in the
regular way. So ghettos were the answer. Or, officially, 'cultural
precincts'. Not prisons, my brother said, but merely a convenient
method of collecting the Islamic community into central locations,
as much for their own protection as anyone else's, what with
anti-Islamic feeling running so high. In the precincts, Muslims
would be safe and sound amongst their own kind.

Sure. Absolutely. And never mind the walls and the
watchtowers and the spotlights and the heavily guarded
checkpoints leading in and out.

The irony, however, is that since the Muslims have all been
locked in—with only approved workers allowed out on daily
passes—it seems that the authorities have been content to leave
the inmates to stew in their own juices. After all, what harm can
any extremists do if they're never allowed outside their own
zones? Who can they blow up or terrorise, apart from themselves?
And so the ghettos have become the one part of Australia that
isn't constantly under surveillance. The police stay outside the
walls. There are no video cameras, no hidden microphones, no

phone tapping, no internal checkpoints, no rules, no laws. In fact, before I actually went into one, all I'd ever heard about the precincts was that they'd been left to run wild—an overcrowded chaos of poverty, violence and gang warfare.

You can see where I'm headed with this, can't you, interrogators? What more natural haven for an outlaw group like the Oz Underground can you imagine than in the heart of lawlessness itself? The Underground High Council certainly thought so. Brunswick was the only place in Melbourne where it was safe for them to hold their secret gatherings. Which was why Aisha and I had been brought there, so that we could be called before the OU hierarchy. Indeed, a meeting had been arranged for the evening of the very day we arrived.

It seemed they were eager to get a look at us.

In the meantime, we were kept out of sight. The tunnel had deposited us in another warehouse, this one much smaller than the one on the other side of the wall. Apparently it was the depot for what had once been a company dealing in eastern spices— the smell of them still lingered: cardamom, anise, turmeric—but for the moment the place held only piles of sacks containing government-supplied rice. And there we stayed until night fell. Not alone, of course. Harry had disappeared off somewhere, but Aisha and I were left with an honour guard of about a dozen young men and women from the ghetto.

And a strange lot they were. I mean, by their very presence I knew they had to be Muslims. And I won't lie, it felt *weird* to be sitting amongst them. You just don't meet Muslims en masse in this country anymore. True, there were those men we encountered in the desert, but they were foreigners. Aliens. These people in the warehouse, they didn't seem foreign at all. Okay, many of them looked vaguely Middle Eastern, but their accents were Australian, their clothes were Australian. Indeed, take them out of the ghetto and there was no real way you could have picked them. Which was the whole point, wasn't it? They were the internal nemesis against which we had all been warned.

Looking like us, sounding like us, existing as us—and yet hell-bent, according to the government, on our overthrow.

But they seemed perfectly friendly. They gave us cold Turkish pizza to eat and new clothes to wear and we all reclined on the rice bags, watching the windows as the daylight faded. And for once no one was yelling at me, or pointing a gun.

'Are you in the Underground too?' I finally asked one of them who was sitting near me, a young man with an air of some authority over the group.

'Sure, brother.' He was a squat, well-muscled youth, dark-skinned, with a shaved head and a restless manner, dressed in jeans and a faded Essendon football jumper. Gold jewellery hung from his neck and his wrists, and his accent was pure western suburbs—so much so that I could picture exactly the sort of sports car he would have driven in the old days, cruising down Chapel Street with a sub-woofer thumping in the boot. 'We've been waiting on you guys for days now.'

'Um... Are many of you members? In here?'

'What? You mean Muslims? In the ghetto?'

'Well, yes.'

'A fair few of us.' He was reading a folded newspaper, and glanced up from it. 'Fact is, we're all underground in here, aren't we, like it or not.'

It made sense, I supposed, although it still seemed unsettling—Muslims and the OU in alliance. But maybe I was just too brainwashed to imagine Muslims in alliance with anyone in Australia these days. They'd been the enemy for so long. Abashed, I found myself staring at the newspaper on his lap. It was a *Herald Sun*. The front page was taken up by the report of a crashed airliner in a paddock somewhere in New South Wales. One hundred and twenty dead. Australia's worst-ever civilian air accident, it seemed. Terrorism not suspected.

'You get papers in here?' I asked.

'We smuggle them in. This is a couple of days old, though...'

A couple of days. I tried to remember—where was I a couple of days ago? Lost in the desert somewhere? Riding in the

Humvee? But try as I might, I couldn't piece it all together. I was too tired. I needed to sleep.

Aisha, meanwhile, was engaged in an animated discussion with some of the others, over on the far side of the warehouse. *She* wouldn't be worried or confused. She was probably feeling fine, amongst her own people at last. But I didn't want to be anywhere close to Aisha. In fact, since our time together in that metal box, skin pressing against skin, my flesh crawled at the thought of being near her. I'd never liked her, obviously, because she was a fanatic who had wanted to kill me. Still, during those moments in the box, when I'd glimpsed the human being behind the terrorist, the girl named Nancy, I'd thought that my feelings might have softened. But the final revelation about her parents— that had crushed any such impulse. Could it really be true? Had she actually done it? It was unspeakable, even if it was only a story she'd made up to shock me. It spoke of a deeper psychosis than just religion or politics.

The truth was, Nancy the human being actually depressed and repulsed me more than Aisha the terrorist had. Terrorists you can at least fear and hate, and that's a kind of respect, really. A failed, mixed-up human being, however, with a hatred for her family, her background and probably herself... Well, the best thing you can feel is pity. But when that person has a gun and an ideology and a willingness to kill for it, then even pity doesn't work.

I looked away from her, lay back on the bags and slept a while. And somewhere in my dreams I'm sure I heard, from outside, on distant loudspeakers, a reedy voice calling the people of the ghetto to prayer.

God is great, God is great, I bear witness...

And I thought, if only it was that simple.

The boy in the Essendon jumper was shaking me awake.

'We're outta here, pal.'

'What?' I saw darkness through the windows. 'Where?'

'The council.'

'Right,' I said, lumbering up.

★

With the ghetto youths as escorts, we left the warehouse through a doorway that led into a small alley. The alley was deserted, but only fifty yards along we merged into the residential streets of Brunswick. And while at first it all looked familiar—the little old houses, the tree-lined footpaths, the corner shops—a sense of dislocation soon swept over me. This was like no night I'd ever experienced in Melbourne before. The sky had the usual orange glow, but in Brunswick itself, the streets were black. There were lights on in windows and doorways, but not a single streetlight shone anywhere. It was like being in some erratic blackout. There were no cars either, not parked, not driving. But people were everywhere. A mass of shadows and voices, moving slowly up and down the narrow streets. Cigarettes flared in the darkness and, somewhere further off, I could hear what sounded like drums and flutes playing.

Aisha and I walked in the middle of our guards, a loose cordon around us, moving carefully at the crowd's pace. The Essendon boy was beside me.

'Does the whole place know we're here?' I asked him.

His eyes were dimly visible, scanning the streets. 'No.'

'We won't be recognised?'

'There's no reason why anyone should notice you. We got plenty of white faces in here. Albanians. Bosnians. Even fair-dinkum Aussies who were dumb enough to convert, and even more dumb not to convert back while they had the chance. Besides, it's dark out here. Don't worry.'

I stared at the dead streetlights. 'Have the authorities cut the power to them?'

'They didn't do it. We did. Smashed 'em all with rocks.'

'Why?'

'Choppers. They fly over once or twice an hour. Keeping an eye on us. So we thought, fuck it, no reason to let the bastards see what we're up to.'

And true, the darkness was comforting. I caught smells of food cooking, and then heard a burst of singing, and more laughter amongst the crowd. I was reminded of a kind of fete or street party. A poorly lit street party, but one with a pleasant hum, on a good, warm summer's evening. So where was the misery and poverty I'd heard so much about, where was the violence?

'There's no curfew? People can just wander around?'

My companion laughed. 'Shit, man, this ain't Warsaw under the Nazis. We live pretty much as we please. And it works in a way. Plenty of people still get out to go to their jobs, and bring in money, and food. And the government supplies us with most of the basics. It's crowded, sure. Two or three families to a house. But no one's dying in the streets.'

'I've read stories about gang wars...'

'Yeah, well, the papers like to pretend we're all animals in here.'

Indeed. We were coming up to Sydney Road now, and if you ignored the lack of street lighting, and the absence of cars, it might have been Sydney Road just the same as always. There were shops and restaurants and cafes open, and a steady stream of people moving up and down the footpaths. There was even, to my amazement, a single tram running along the tracks in the middle of the road, its bell dinging as the vehicle eased through the pedestrians. The faces of two old ladies, their heads wrapped in scarves, peered out from the front seat.

'I can't believe it,' I said, nodding at the tram.

Essendon boy was amused. 'Yeah. They left us one old rattler, and power in the overhead lines. The bloody thing just runs up and down the street, from the south wall to the north wall. But hey, we got no shortage of unemployed tram drivers in here. The poor buggers aren't allowed to work outside anymore. The government says their jobs are too sensitive.'

'Driving a tram is too sensitive?'

'I know. As if you could crash one of *them* into a building.'

We sauntered on, still loosely surrounded by the guards. I caught a glimpse, over roof tops, of the city skyscrapers only a few kilometres away, a whole different world. But there in Sydney Road, families walked in and out of restaurants, and children ran about shrieking, and groups of men sipped coffee and smoked and studied the sky. I still couldn't shake the image of a street party from my mind. Except that it was too peaceful. At a normal Australian street party there would have been beer, and drunks spilling out of pubs, and sausages and steaks frying on barbecues. Here the cooking smells were of spices and rice, and there was no beer, no drunks reeling about—indeed, the one pub we passed appeared to have been converted into a coffee house. Brunswick had become a 'dry' suburb at last, just like dear old leafy Camberwell had been in my childhood.

And then, as the street ran down towards the city, I saw ahead of us the south wall of the ghetto. It was a rigid barrier of upright concrete slabs, maybe three times man-height, topped with barbed wire, the inner side of the wall festooned with graffiti. There were two guard towers visible, about a hundred yards apart, and I could see men up there—soldiers or police, I couldn't remember right then who was responsible for the precincts. But even as shadows they did not appear threatening, they were just shapes leaning on railings, seeming to stare out in indifference. And amidst the throng, still far away from them, I had no fear of being seen.

A yelling voice caught my attention. It came from an old man standing outside a brightly lit shop. He was bearded and dark and dressed in some sort of traditional Middle Eastern garb, and was declaiming to his audience in bad, heavily accented English. A kind of street preacher, I decided, reminded of the Christian ministers who always ranted and raved on the steps of Flinders Street Station. I couldn't really catch what he was saying, only that he was angry, and that the shop behind him was the source of his anger. It was a music and video store—and the music pulsing from inside was unmistakably modern. Young folk were coming and going through the door, and the preacher glared at them one by one, pointing and shaking and promising—so it sounded—all kinds of eternal damnation.

The Essendon boy was watching me with a knowing expression. 'He's here every night. He thinks dance music comes straight from Satan. They find it the toughest in here, the old hardliners. They can't believe that, seeing we're all Muslims in the ghetto, we haven't brought in shari'a law yet.'

'Are there many like him around? Extremists?'

He didn't seem to like the word. 'Not so many. How could there be? Anyone like that the government had marked down years ago. They're in the high security centres now, or they're dead. They're not in places like this.'

'So, it's mostly just the average Muslims left?'

'I dunno. What's "mostly"? What's "average"? We've got about fifty nationalities in here, and about twenty different languages. We've got Shiites and Sunnis. We've got all five major legal schools. We've got a dozen mosques and just as many colleges, all with different imams. We've got conservatives and moderates and liberals and everything in between. It's a mess, really. The only thing anyone in here agrees on is that God is great, and that your brother is a total dickhead. And you could probably find people to argue even that.'

'So what are *you*?'

He thought, and then shook his head. 'I'm sick of this, that's all I am. It's so stupid. Ninety-nine point nine per cent of these people are completely harmless. The government knows that. They could open all the ghettos tomorrow and not a thing would change. It's all just for show.'

'You think it'll ever happen? Opening the ghettos?'

'Why not? This isn't the way Australia is meant to be. The rest of the country just let itself be taken in by a prick of a Prime Minister. People will wake up. That's why I'm in the Underground. Overthrow this joke of a government and get a proper one in, and half the problem would be solved.'

I wasn't convinced. 'What about Canberra? I don't think anyone outside is going to be forgiving or forgetting that event any time soon.'

He frowned. 'That was a fuck-up, I won't argue. I knew we were stuffed when that mushroom cloud went up.' He stared about in perplexity at his fellow inmates. 'But it's the weirdest thing. I'm not one of those conspiracy idiots who think that the

West is behind everything bad. I know it had to be fanatics from our side that did it. But I've met a few of the militants left in here. I've talked to them. And hey, they loved the bomb. They thought it was great. But they don't have any idea who actually did it. It wasn't any of their own people.'

I glanced back at Aisha. 'She says her people did it.'

He followed my eyes, startled. 'Her lot?'

'It might not be true. Harry doesn't believe her. But either way, it all goes back to Islam in the end. And that's what scares the rest of the country. As long as cells like hers remain, they'll never let you out of here.'

'Maybe,' he said, disheartened.

We walked on. A thudding sound rose in the air, and a helicopter hove into view over the wall, flying north along Sydney Road. The crowd barely paused to acknowledge it, but a few eyes turned up, cold and disapproving. A spotlight beam leapt down from the aircraft, probing the street, but it seemed almost disinterested as it flicked about. There was nothing to be seen anyway. Except people. Life. Normality.

The Essendon boy spoke again. 'I'll tell you this, though, that girl of yours is a puzzle. Okay, so she's supposed to be some sort of Islamic activist. But I've been listening to her this afternoon. And like I said, I've met militants before. They're crazy as loons, no mistake, but they *are* Muslims. They've warped it and twisted it into something else entirely, and what they do is far more political than religious, but at least you can recognise their starting point.' He shook his head. 'But that chick there...I don't have the remotest clue what she's on about.'

TWENTY-SEVEN

The meeting took place in a church hall.

Of course, the church to which the hall was attached—St Ambrose's Catholic Church on Sydney Road—had been abandoned by its parishioners when the ghetto walls went up. It had since been converted into a mosque. My Essendon friend gave me a look through the doors as we passed by. The pews were all gone, along with the altar, as well as any statues of Jesus or Mary—and the stained-glass windows were hidden by wall hangings that bore verses from the Koran.

'We haven't done any permanent damage, though,' he said. 'Like, we haven't removed the crucifixes from the roof.'

'Why not?'

'It's just polite. The Catholics will be wanting this place back one day.'

'Ah,' I said.

One happy day when the ghetto was thrown open, he meant. And it was good to see him optimistic again, even if history would suggest that ghettos didn't often get thrown open—usually they just got liquidated.

But I let it go. We moved around to the rear of the church and entered the hall. And church halls, let's face it, are never inspiring places. The echoing wooden floors, the peeling paint, the dusty windows, the memory of a thousand dreary functions that have taken place in years previous. This one was no different. As for the High Council of the Australian Underground—well, at a glance, they looked for all the world like a meeting of some church fete cake-stall committee. There were about twenty men and women waiting there for us, perched on plastic chairs arranged in a circle, sipping tea and coffee from old chipped cups. They could have been anyone. It was only on closer inspection, when their faces turned as we entered...

But I don't really need to go into names here, do I, interrogators? I mean, you *know*, don't you? Harry was there, of course. It was the others, however, that surprised me. The faces I recognised. The famous investigative journalist. The famous football coach. The famous film director. I mean, I hadn't expected celebrities. Not to mention the High Court judge, or the three serving senators from the emasculated Federal Parliament— two from the Labor side, and a Green. And even the people that I'd never seen before—they weren't just your average street-level resistance fighters. They were older, sober figures, most of them in suits, as if they'd come to the ghetto straight from their work in the high levels of state bureaucracy, or in the senior financial realms, or in the law.

This was no bake sale committee. These people represented money and influence. And that was a shock. I suppose I'd got used to the idea of the Underground being a collection of anonymous nobodies. Like Harry. Like the wiry old truck driver. Like Staff Sergeant Daphne. Like the bus full of fake Patriots back in Hervey Bay. Small folk—in useful positions, perhaps, but basically just angry individuals thumbing their noses at the authorities. It had never occurred to me that the Underground would include members of the establishment. Or that they might represent—in embryonic form, at least—an actual alternative national government.

That awed me a little. As did their expressions, as they studied Aisha and me. Because there was no doubt about the hostility in their eyes.

Harry indicated seats waiting for us.

'I won't make any introductions,' he said. 'Those you don't know, it's better they stay that way.'

I looked around at the council. 'So what have I missed?'

Harry didn't smile. 'I've been filling everyone in on our adventures so far. And catching up on other developments.'

'There's bad news?'

'There's no good news.'

'Why? What's happened?'

'You two happened,' said a man from across the room. He was no one I recognised, but he had gaunt gloomy features, and the look of academia about him. 'Ever since you first came into our hands, the Federal Police have launched an all-out attack on the Underground. Following pretty much in your wake, as it happens. The Patriot cell in Hervey Bay has been arrested. Our sympathisers in the army are under investigation because of that whole debacle with the refugees. Our contacts in Citizenship have disappeared. And our other networks are in trouble right across the board. Raids, arrests, ambushes, cell after cell going down. It's like we stirred up a hornets' nest out there. All for the sake of keeping you two alive.'

'They're hoping,' said Harry, fixing me with hollow eyes, 'that whatever it is you know, it was worth it.'

I swallowed, spoke to the circle. 'I've told Harry all along, I don't know anything. If I did, I'd help. I've got no reason not to. I'm no friend of my brother's government.'

'We don't mean you,' the man across the room replied. 'We mean her.'

The whole room was staring at Aisha.

My heart fell. One young girl. And a lunatic at that. If all their hopes were pinned on her, then I couldn't see what chance any of us had.

Aisha herself inflated with the attention. 'I have nothing to say to this council.'

'You claim to support a Muslim cause?' the man across the room asked.

'I do support one,' Aisha said.

'Then why wouldn't you help us? We're the best bet that Muslims in this country have.' It seemed that he was a spokesman of some kind for the group, even if he paled in comparison with the other luminaries present. Not the *leader* of the Underground, I couldn't believe that, but perhaps one of the philosophical driving forces behind it. Maybe a university lecturer. In radical political science, or some such field. 'It's the government persecuting your faith, not us.'

'You're still the enemy.'

'Then what about me?' asked another man sternly. He was robed and bearded and dark-skinned, but with a deep Aussie accent, and a casual toughness about him that made me think of prison somewhere in his past. 'I'm not the enemy. I *am* a Muslim. I live in this ghetto. I represent its interests here.'

Aisha hesitated for only a moment. 'If you're a true Muslim, then you shouldn't be associating with these people.'

'And who are you to say what a Muslim should or shouldn't do? How do I even know you're Muslim yourself?'

'I belong to the Great Southern Jihad.'

'Good for you. I've never heard of it.'

'You wouldn't have. You're soft. You're corrupt.'

The man's expression hardened—and it had been hard enough before. He had the body of a wrestler not long retired. 'One of the first things a true Muslim is taught is respect for their elders, girl. And don't pull that hardliner shit with me. I *know* the hardliners. I used to be one. I've probably had contact with every militant Islamic group in Australia, in my time. But I have never, anywhere, at any stage, met anyone who belongs to the Great Southern Jihad.'

Aisha's chin was out proudly. 'We're the new Islam.'

'There's a new one, is there?' The man shook his big head scornfully, looked to the rest of the circle. 'I wouldn't trust a word this woman says.'

'And yet,' said the famous journalist, speaking up thoughtfully, 'the whole government is after her. That alone proves she's somehow important. Plus, she knew about the bomb that went off at the Gabba. That proves she has connections with genuine terrorists. I can't believe it was her people that nuked Canberra—but they can't be dismissed entirely.'

'So where did they come from?' the ghetto representative demanded. 'Who runs them? And how come no true Muslim knows anything about it?'

Silence in the room.

I shifted in my seat. 'You aren't supposed to know.'

All the faces turned my way, including Aisha's. And over the next few minutes I repeated everything I remembered about our conversation in the metal box—about Aisha's recruitment, about Southern Jihad's secrecy, about its plans for war and revolution, and about the killing of Aisha's parents.

The room considered her anew.

'Bloody hell,' said the Greens senator.

'Genuine Muslims or not,' agreed the Labor man, 'they sound like a real enough terrorist group to me.'

'Is it possible we've got this all wrong?' asked the football coach. 'Maybe her people really did do Canberra. And maybe that's the only reason the government is after her. To drag her in for questioning. In which case, maybe we should never have got in their way. We could've just let them have her.'

'Would've saved us a lot of trouble,' someone muttered.

'No,' said Harry, firmly. 'They don't want to question her. They want her dead. When the federal agents had hold of Aisha, they were about to execute her, there and then. They weren't asking any questions. Which makes no sense. It never has. If she's for real, then the government should want her alive for interrogation. If she's not for real, then they shouldn't want her at all. But instead, they're moving heaven and earth to catch her—and then shut her up.'

'And let's not forget Leo,' said the journalist. 'He's not just a passenger here. Look at the chain of events. The government has apparently known about Southern Jihad for ages, but they never worried about them before—not until Aisha's boys kidnapped the Prime Minister's brother. That's when it all changed. That's when Aisha suddenly became a target. And when Leo himself, who's never mattered at all, suddenly mattered enough to be declared dead.'

'Which can only mean one thing,' the man across the room, the lecturer, concluded. 'One of these two knows something dangerous, and this something is *so* dangerous that the government wants them eliminated before they can tell anybody about it. Especially, I assume, before they can tell us.'

Harry nodded sadly. 'But neither of them has a thing to say.'

Silence again.

We were back to square one. But I was uncomfortably aware of something in all their faces as they stared at us. These were powerful people, desperate in their own way, and hardened to necessity. And I could sense—even though no one had said it, or threatened it yet—that a far more strenuous form of questioning lay in our immediate future. An interrogation, in fact. Possibly not to the point of torture, not like your own tender ministrations, my dear interrogators, but something close. It was the look on Harry's face, most of all. I'd come to regard him as, if not actually a friend, then at least as someone whose prime concern was my welfare. But there was a withdrawing in him now. A resigned pulling back and washing of his hands. We had become the High Council's responsibility. And in their eyes I could see no concern for my welfare at all.

I turned to Aisha. 'For fuck's sake, if you've got something to tell them, then tell them now. These people aren't kidding.'

A cold pride was in her eyes. 'They're not worthy to know.'

Oh shit. Any minute now, the lecturer or one of the others was going to nod, and three or four heavy-set thugs were going to appear and drag us off to a basement somewhere, with a single hard chair, and a bright painful light, and a wire mattress on the wall, attached to batteries.

But the man from the ghetto was leaning back with his huge

forearms folded across his chest, studying Aisha narrowly. 'Tell us about this new Islam of yours. What's so new about it?'

'Destruction. Righteous bloodshed. It will be the end of the West and the old Islam alike.'

The man gave an ominous frown. 'True Islam doesn't teach violence,' he stated, sounding like he'd partaken in plenty of it himself, once.

'True Islam teaches purity,' Aisha replied. 'And purity can only come from a cleansing fire.'

'It doesn't teach the slaughter of innocents.'

'No one is innocent, unless they're with us.'

'Crap, girl. The Koran says no such thing. Neither does the Hadith.'

'I wouldn't know. I haven't read them.'

The ghetto Muslim stared in amazement. 'You haven't read them?!'

'No. The old texts will burn with the old Islam.'

'Are you mad? The Koran *is* Islam!'

'The word of Allah is a living thing. In our hearts, and in the spoken words of our teachers. It has nothing to do with a book.'

The man spat on the floor. 'You're no Muslim. You never have been.'

A blush spread across Aisha's white face. 'I'm the only real Muslim here. I know the duties, and I follow the commands!'

'Is it a duty to murder your own parents? That's an obscenity. No real Muslim could ever do that. No teacher would ever command it, either.'

And it was that word, I think—*teacher*. It triggered something in Aisha. A man of her own chosen faith was challenging her credentials. A man who had once, it seemed, been a militant and an activist, like her. She couldn't let that pass. And maybe too, somewhere deep down, the human being was still there in her, ashamed of her actions and needing to justify them. Or maybe she just couldn't keep the secret inside anymore. I don't know. But she made the decision.

'No teacher?' she inquired softly. 'What would you know about *teachers*? I follow the greatest teacher Islam has ever seen.'

Her opponent sneered. 'And what great teacher is that?'

'You'll see, when it's too late for you. He knows about the Great Southern Jihad, and he approves of what we're doing.' Aisha was scarily calm. 'He's coming to be with us. Coming to Australia. Soon.'

'So why not tell us his name?'

'It doesn't matter if I do tell you. There's nothing you can do to stop him. Not you, not the government. The Great Hero goes where he wants.'

'The Great Hero?' The man faltered, looking puzzled. 'You can't mean...'

'That's exactly who I mean.'

'You're insane!'

'Wait and see then. And burn with the rest of them.'

The ghetto Muslim was shaking his head, disgusted, but Harry was leaning forward now, staring intently at him. 'Who's she talking about?'

'It's ridiculous,' the man replied. 'She's fucked in the head.'

'Who's this Great Hero?'

'Well, some of the hardliners and militants... It's a name they use for him sometimes... But it's complete bullshit.'

'Who, dammit?'

The man looked around the room, almost reluctant. Then he shrugged. 'Well, bin Laden, of course.'

TWENTY-EIGHT

The room broke into laughter.

It came from everyone around the circle, long and bitter, and somehow despairing, too—because if the High Council had needed a final demonstration of Aisha's delusional state, or proof that they had wasted their time in rescuing her and smuggling her all the way to Melbourne, then this was it.

'Osama bin Laden?' the journalist managed to say at last, marvelling at her. 'You really think he's coming to meet you? You actually *believe* that?'

Aisha was bright red. 'He is.' But the laughter had hurt her, I could tell. She had revealed her great and deep secret...and it was pathetic.

'He's dead, girl,' the ghetto representative said flatly. 'It's been years now. The Americans got him fair and square.'

'You did see that, didn't you?' the journalist asked, mockingly polite. 'You and your crazy friends do read the papers occasionally, and watch the news? The pictures of his body were only on the front page for about two weeks!'

More bitter laughter, but I was watching Harry, who was staring at the floor in abject misery. I knew what he was thinking. All the people who had died to bring Aisha to this point, all the networks that had been unmasked...

'He's not dead,' Aisha said.

Resigned groans came from around the room.

'He's not!' Aisha insisted, glowing. 'That wasn't him! That was just a man with a beard that looked like him! The Great Hero is alive!'

'Yeah,' a voice said dully. 'And so is Elvis.'

The ghetto Muslim was blunt. 'We've all heard that nonsense. Bin Laden is alive, the Americans didn't really get him, he outsmarted them again, the Great Hero marches on... It's a fairytale. The body was identified.'

'It was a trick,' Aisha retorted. 'He fooled them.'

'Sure he did. And when is this casual visit of his supposed to happen? And why, exactly, of all the places in the world, would he be coming here?'

'He's coming to meet the faithful, to lead us himself into the new Islam. We were promised. And he's coming soon. You'll see, and then you'll all die!'

To this, no one even bothered to respond. The council members just stared at each other in bleak acknowledgment, and a dismal silence stretched out. From the distance came the sound of a helicopter. The noise grew, as if the machine was flying directly over the hall, and then faded again.

It was the lecturer who finally spoke for everyone, his eyes turned to the ceiling. 'Well,' he said, 'we're fucked.'

The football coach had his chin sunk in his hands. 'I say we clear out of here and forget this ever happened.'

'Forget the whole damn Underground, frankly,' added the Labor man. 'Another week like this last one, there'll be none of us left anyway.'

'It isn't that bad,' the Greens senator protested.

'Isn't it?'

Harry lifted his eyes. 'What about these two?' he asked, indicating Aisha and me. 'What are you going to do with them?'

The group regarded us like the embarrassments we were.

'Well, obviously we can't let them go,' said the lecturer. 'Not after what they've seen here. I suppose they'll just have to stay hidden in the ghetto.'

The ghetto representative was shaking his head. 'I don't want that woman in here. She's an abomination.'

'There's nowhere else they can go. We can't get IDs or travel papers for them anymore. They'd be caught at the first roadblock they came across.'

'So *you* take them and hide them.'

A squabble broke out across the room.

Harry interrupted, his expression pained. 'No. Stop it. Look, we haven't finished with this yet. Nothing has changed. We still need to know why the government wants them so badly. Aisha is still the key. She has information, I know it.'

'Information?' demanded the lecturer, caustic. 'Osama bin Laden is alive and well after all, and now he's coming for a holiday in Australia? You think the government wants her dead because of *that*?'

'Okay, so it's nothing to do with bin Laden. But we can't ignore her completely, just because her head is half full of rubbish. There must be something genuine in there, something valuable. That's why she needs a proper interrogation. Covering everything. Over days. Weeks, if it takes that long.'

The plea had an effect. 'He's right, of course,' the journalist sighed. 'We'll have to keep her here, and get a proper debriefing team to work. We owe the people who brought her through that much of an effort, at least.'

There were supportive murmurs from around the circle, and nods of agreement.

'What about me?' I said, piping up at last.

Harry was rueful. 'You're a dead man already. You don't have any choice but to stay. And there'll be questions for you too, I'm afraid.'

Damn it. 'But how long can you keep me here?'

'You asked me something like that once before, and it's the same answer. How long is any of this going to go on? How long will the war on terror last? How long will your brother be in power? You tell me, Leo.'

He stood. Other people were also rising to their feet, forming little knots of conversation. The council, for what it was worth, seemed to be breaking up.

'So that's it?' I said to Harry. 'I'm a prisoner?'

He shrugged in half apology. 'You aren't seeing us at our best. It's been an appalling week. And you two haven't helped.' He breathed out, gave Aisha a look. 'Osama bin Laden? Christ, woman—did you have to say that?'

She was unrepentant. 'I've told you the truth.'

'Well for your sake, I hope you've got something else to tell us, eventually.'

I was mustering another protest—knowing there was no point to it—but just then the youth in the Essendon jersey, who had remained outside on guard duty with his friends during the meeting, hurried into the hall.

'There's a man here,' he announced to the room. 'He's just come through one of the tunnels, and he's demanding to see the council. He's out front.'

'What man?' asked the lecturer.

'I don't know him—but he's one of us. He knows all the passwords. He says he's just arrived from Sydney. On the run, by the sound of it.'

'Sydney!' several people exclaimed.

'He said he had nowhere else to go.'

'Nowhere else?' The lecturer exchanged an alarmed glance with the journalist. 'C'mon, we'd better check him out.'

They strode together through the doors.

Harry stared after them, hesitant, as if he wasn't quite sure what to do with himself. And I remembered—he really had nothing *to* do. He wasn't in charge anymore. The decisions were no longer his. His job was over.

'So what's with those two?' I asked him.

'I don't know. Except that it sounds bad about the situation in Sydney, if an operative from up there had nowhere else to come but Melbourne.'

'You have cells up there too, right?'

'Of course. Or at least we did, but the reports we're getting say this last week has been as bad in Sydney as anywhere else. And Sydney is the base for some of our major resistance programs. That's why we're so worried.'

I looked around the drab little hall. People were draining cups of tea and eating the last biscuits. A few had started stacking the plastic chairs away, but others were lingering, not certain if the meeting was actually over or not. Confusion and disappointment drifted in the air like cigarette smoke.

I said, 'You know, I'm surprised that the OU headquarters are here in Melbourne. I would've thought Sydney was the obvious place.'

'It would've been. That's why we're not there.'

'Ah.' I considered the man, his depression and his exhaustion, and just for once I forgot about my own pile of troubles. I said, 'So what happens to *you* now? You don't live here. Is it back to Queensland?'

'I dunno.' He ran a hand through his thinning hair. 'I suppose I have to get back to my job soon.'

'What do you do anyway? I never asked.'

He blinked at me for long, nonplussed moment. 'I'm a nurse in a retirement home.' And then he was smiling, in a small, sad way. 'Believe it or not, I used up the last of my annual leave to get you two down here.'

We looked at each other.

Then the journalist came rushing back into the room.

'No one go anywhere! This meeting is reconvened right now!' People stared at him, wondering at his excitement. 'This guy outside—you gotta hear what he has to say!'

Harry perked up. 'What?'

And Aisha was on her feet. 'Is it about him? Is it the Great Hero?'

The journalist gave her a cutting glance. 'Christ, no. In fact, Harry, get these two out of here. They're not part of the council.'

Harry was shaking his head. 'But—'

'Get them out, Harry! I'll fill you in later.'

Harry gave way. As the council members reorganised themselves in a clatter of unstacking chairs, he led us towards the front doors. Passing through, we encountered the lecturer—looking anything but gloomy now. He was bringing in the visitor from Sydney. I actually brushed shoulders with the newcomer, and for a moment we stared at each other. I smelt sweat on him, and something electric passed between us. His expression... I don't think I've seen one quite like it before. Exhausted and unshaven and dirty and bruised, as if he'd fought every step of the way from Sydney, and yet there was an elated kind of *knowledge* there too, filling him to bursting.

'Jesus,' commented Harry when we were outside.

'Who was he?' I asked.

'I've got no idea. I've never seen him before.'

The doors slammed shut behind us, and we wandered aimlessly into the churchyard. The guard of ghetto youths was waiting for us. They were staring, I realised, at Aisha.

'Osama bin Laden,' one of them said. 'My hairy arse.'

Harry sought out the boy in the Essendon jumper. 'We have to get these two under cover.'

'Righto. Although no one's gonna want *her* in their house.'

Harry wasn't interested in Aisha for the moment. 'That man they just took in—you know anything about him?'

'Like I said, he came in through a tunnel. He's from Sydney.'

'But who is he? *What* is he?'

'The only thing I heard is that he's an air traffic controller up there.'

Harry frowned. 'An air traffic controller?'

'Supposedly.'

'So what the hell does that mean?'

I said, 'In the paper. There was a plane crash in New South Wales.'

'That's right,' the Essendon youth said, nodding. 'A couple of days ago. Straight into the ground. One hundred and twenty dead.'

Harry looked back at the hall. 'A plane crash? But what could that have to do with us? Was there someone important on the plane? Someone big from the government maybe?'

'They didn't mention anyone special,' said the boy.

'Was it a terrorist attack?'

'Not according to the article.'

'Then I don't get this at all.'

The discussion paused, as once again the thudding of a helicopter filled the air. We all stared up. The aircraft was coming over the rooftops and seemed to be headed straight for us. We pulled back under the eaves of the church.

'Busy tonight, the bastards,' the Essendon youth observed.

A spotlight flickered over the yard. We waited for the chopper to move on. It didn't. Instead the thunder grew deeper, and another helicopter appeared.

'Two of them?' Harry shouted. 'Is that normal?'

The Essendon boy was gazing up. He shook his head, puzzled. The two choppers circled only a hundred metres above us. Then, abruptly, they seemed to bow towards each other. Only they weren't bowing...

'They're armed!' the youth cried. 'Rockets!'

And even as he yelled, jets of fire burst from the sides of both aircraft, and four fingers of white smoke stabbed down to hit the roof of the church hall.

It exploded.

TWENTY-NINE

I found myself on top of Aisha.

She was convulsed with mad laughter, writhing under me as the air pounded with chopper blades, and a rain of wood splinters and broken tiles tumbled down around us. I shoved myself away from her in complete loathing, and rolled over to look back at the hall. It wasn't there anymore, there was only a confusion of smoke and fire. Shapes were moving, and people were screaming, and there were gunshots. The young men and women who had been our escort—from somewhere they had pulled out hand guns and rifles (how could I not have noticed before that they had them?) and were firing wildly up at the helicopters.

Harry was running towards the ruins.

I stared after him. He disappeared through a twisted frame that had been the front doors. And then I realised that someone was shaking me violently. It was the Essendon boy.

'We've got to go!' he was yelling.

'Troops are coming up the main street!' someone shouted, dashing by.

'See? This is a full-on raid. We can't stay here.'

He was right. The helicopters had swung away out of sight for the moment, but the sound of their rotors still reverberated in the night. And from further away I could hear other cries, and gun fire, and explosions.

'Get Harry,' I gasped.

The boy looked up in exasperation. But even then, Harry himself came backing out of the fire, and he was dragging a body behind him. Galvanised at last, I climbed to my feet and ran over to help. At least, I tried to run, but one of my legs didn't seem to work. Looking down, I saw a shard of wood about half the size of a cricket stump, sticking out of my calf. I reached down, yanked it free.

Harry was covered in soot. But the man he was dragging looked far worse, his clothing mostly burnt off, his limbs all mangled and bloody. His face, though, was miraculously clean and white and staring palely. It was the man from Sydney.

'Help me with him,' Harry croaked.

I took the man's shredded legs, but my own leg gave way immediately under the weight. Some of the ghetto youths shouldered me aside and took up the burden.

'Where's the nearest tunnel?' Harry demanded.

The Essendon boy's football jersey was barely recognisable beneath a layer of grime. 'Not far. Under a chemist's shop. But there's troops in the streets.'

'We split up then. You take Leo and Aisha.' He was already moving off with the Sydney man's body, three of the ghetto youths helping. 'We'll meet you there.'

The choppers were back, search lights flickering through the smoke, and we scattered. I found myself running with the Essendon boy and Aisha. I couldn't say now which way we went, or how far it was. The night and the ghetto had dissolved into chaos. People were milling everywhere in panic, and gun fire rang out from all quarters. I remember glancing up as we crossed a side street, and framed between two walls I could see a section of Sydney Road. A line of soldiers, in full combat gear, were hurrying past, fire spurting from automatic weapons.

Then we were in the darkness of the back alleys, darting this
way and that. Helicopters circled above, and at one point we hid
frozen for long minutes in the bushes of someone's back garden
while spotlights danced around us. At another point we were
running through a thinning cloud of tear gas, eyes stinging, noses
streaming. All I could do was cling to the sight of that Essendon
jersey, thinking stupidly that I didn't even like Essendon, I was
a Hawthorn supporter, born and bred. And then suddenly we
were in the dimness of a small chemist's shop. In a rear room
there was a flight of stairs leading down to a basement. And in
the basement we found Harry again, and the other ghetto youths,
and the man from Sydney.

The man was dying, even I could see that.

'Did anyone else get out of the hall?' someone asked.

'No one,' another replied. 'They got them all.'

'There must be a whole fucking battalion out there.'

'I need ammunition! Has anyone got any fucking ammo?!'

'Shit. Fuck. Shit.'

Panicked, angry, frightened voices. The sour smell of
overworked bodies, of scorched flesh and gunpowder. A bout of
dizziness swept over me, and I collapsed into a corner. My lower
leg was black with blood. The room swam, and then one of the
youths was kneeling in front of me, wrapping the leg tightly in
bandages. My vision drifted to the far corner of the room. Harry
was there with the Sydney man, and another youth who was
cutting away the man's jeans, revealing muscle and bone, while
a third was drawing liquid from a small bottle up into a syringe.
Morphine, I thought, it must be morphine.

Harry didn't seem to be aware of the other two. He was bent
over the dying man, intent. He was listening. I could see the
man's lips moving, even as his face faded whiter and whiter and
his eyes roamed the room blindly. I couldn't tell if he knew that
Harry was there, but his last words spilled out regardless. Then
suddenly there was blood on his lips, and Harry was clutching
at the man's ragged shirt in some sort of wild desperation or
anger or disbelief, I couldn't tell. But it didn't matter. The man

was gone, and the youth with the syringe suddenly sat back on his haunches and let the needle fall to his side.

A detonation rocked the room, close enough to send dust cascading down upon us from the ceiling.

'We've got to get back out there!' someone cried.

'And do what? Get killed?'

'They'll find us anyway. They must know about the tunnels. They knew about the meeting, didn't they? They knew exactly which building to hit.'

But I had eyes only for Harry. I climbed to my feet again, reeled across the room. He was standing too, now, staring down at the dead body.

'What?' I said. 'What is it?'

He glanced at me with a look of rage so dark that I reared back, thinking he was about to hit me. 'I've got to go,' was all he said.

'Go where?'

'To see if it's true. To see for myself.'

'See what?'

He wasn't listening. He spun to the back of the room, and began tearing away boxes of medical supplies that were piled against the wall.

'Harry!'

'Fuck off,' he spat over his shoulder. 'You're not my problem anymore.'

'But you can't—'

'It's over, okay? It's finished. They've won.'

The Essendon boy was at my side. 'What is this, Harry?' He glanced down at the corpse. 'What did this guy tell you?'

All the boxes had been torn aside, revealing a trapdoor in the floor. Harry heaved it open. 'It was a lie. All along. He heard the pilots himself.'

'Heard what? Where are you going?'

Harry was just shaking his head. 'That plane crash. It wasn't an accident.' He set a foot down into the shaft, glanced back at us. 'I've still got one set of papers. Maybe I can make it out of Melbourne.'

Another detonation shuddered through the room. A voice yelled down the stairs: 'There's a squad coming up the street!'

The Essendon youth had no more time. 'Can we help?' he asked Harry.

'Keep these two here, I've got no use for them.'

'They can't stay here now. You know that. You have to take them with you.'

'I don't want them!'

'Neither do we. Look, we'll hold out here as long as we can. We'll cover up the tunnel. It'll give you some time.'

Harry stared back and forth between Aisha and me, anguished.

'All right, dammit!' And he dropped down the hole.

'Go after him,' the Essendon boy told me. 'It'll take you under the wall.' He slapped me once on the back, and then ran for the stairs, a gun ready in his hand.

I glanced back only long enough to see that Aisha had understood. There was blood on her face, I didn't know whose, but she was nodding. Then we were in the tunnel, and chasing after Harry, the sound of fresh gun fire echoing after us. It was narrower than the other tunnel, and black because we had no torch, and it stretched on forever. I felt sick and useless, with no idea of where we were going now, or why, knowing only that Harry no longer wanted us with him, but we were still there anyway, a dead weight around his neck.

In the end we came to a ladder, and climbed up to find ourselves in a mechanic's garage, a large shadowy cavern. There were vehicles everywhere, and Harry was already fumbling with piles of keys, hunting from car to car.

'This one!' he said.

I stared, almost laughing at the insanity of it. It was a little old campervan.

'In the back,' Harry ordered. 'And stay out of sight.'

He ran to the metal roller door, and hauled on the chain to lift it. The orange light of the city flooded into the garage. And with it came the sounds of the turmoil in the ghetto. Shots, explosions, screams. But heard from a distance now.

I climbed into the van after Aisha. There was a little table and a kitchenette and a bed at the rear. It even had lace curtains over the windows.

'On the floor,' Harry barked from the front.

We did what we were told. Harry started up, then roared, reversing, out into the street. I poked my head up for an instant. The other side of the road was residential. People—free people, on this side of the wall, everyday Australians—were standing on their front steps, staring towards the ghetto. A flash lit their faces, wide-mouthed and shocked, and then the thump of an explosion came. Harry worked the gears madly, found first, and peeled away down the street, the tyres complaining. With his free hand, he picked up something from the passenger seat. It was a tattered straw hat—belonging to the owner of the campervan, no doubt—and jammed it down on his head.

I gazed at him a moment longer, amazed at his presence of mind. It was the best he could do for a disguise, I knew, the van. And somehow, with that hat, and his plain, weathered face, it worked. He could have been anyone, a man off on a holiday, down to the lakes, maybe, for some fishing, with an esky full of beer in the back. At least to the casual observer.

But under the hat his face was still set black with fury. His eyes were roving, and caught mine in the rear-view mirror.

'I told you—get the fuck down.'

I dropped my head, and stared at the carpet.

THIRTY

And now, interrogators dear, I come to something that I can't explain. Any better than *you* could explain it, although I'm sure you're wondering how it happened. In fact, I'm sure heads are rolling because of it—maybe even literally.

Either way, by some miracle, we made it out of Melbourne without hitting a single roadblock or checkpoint. I can't tell you what route we took. I spent it all face down in the back of the van. Certainly, judging by the endless twist and turns Harry made, it was no direct path. And we must have come close to being caught, because I heard sirens wailing nearby several times, and even saw the reflection of flashing police lights through the windows. But nobody stopped us.

So maybe the little old campervan really was the perfect cover, with Harry at the wheel, in his hat. Or maybe the alarm didn't spread fast enough from the ghetto. I had no doubts that someone, somewhere, knew we'd got away. I could picture, all too clearly, the basement of the chemist's shop, and the bodies of the ghetto youths all dead from their last defence, and the tunnel uncovered by the soldiers. And that would lead to the garage and the open roller door, and the witnesses in the street. But how long all that took, I don't know. And how much longer it was before a call went out to search for us, I don't know either.

All I know is that we kept driving. After an hour we were clear of the city, and Harry let Aisha and me get up off the floor. He insisted, however, that we keep the curtains drawn over the windows. He also pulled shut the curtain between the driver's compartment and the rear. He was taking no chance of us being seen, or of anyone realising he wasn't alone in the van. So we simply rode there in back, me hunched on the little couch, Aisha curled up like a feral cat on the bed. In a box again, effectively, with nothing to see and no way to tell where we were.

But by the feel of it, we weren't on a major highway. We were on the lesser roads, winding and steep in parts. From that, and from some inner sense of direction, I guessed that we were heading north-east—up into the wild country above Melbourne, the maze of ranges and valleys that roll off towards the southern alps. Good territory to hide in, if that had been our aim—as bushrangers and outlaws throughout Australia's history have always known. But Harry didn't seem to be thinking of hiding. He just kept going. Two hours since fleeing the ghetto, three hours. We did finally stop somewhere for petrol, but locked away in the back of the van I saw nothing of the location. When Harry returned to the front seat, he tossed a bag through to us, full of water bottles and packaged sandwiches. I caught a glimpse of him feverishly studying a road map. And then we were on our way again.

It was a wretched time. My leg was throbbing, and I was expecting at any moment to be caught. Even the most cursory of roadblocks would involve someone looking in the back of the van. And while Harry might have a fake ID of some kind, Aisha and I had nothing whatsoever. And yet it wasn't even the fear of discovery and arrest that weighed down on me the most. Instead it was the sense of futility.

Whatever it was we'd been trying to do—and I'd never fully

understood exactly what that was—we'd failed. Worse than failed. My thoughts were still crowded with images from the ghetto, my nostrils still full of the stench of the violence from which we'd fled. Indeed, it seemed as if I could see a trail of bodies and blood stretching out behind us—a trail that reached back through Brunswick, and back past an overturned truck in the desert interior of New South Wales, and back to the bombed-out cricket stands in Brisbane, and back through an overgrown road cutting somewhere in the hinterland near Bundaberg and, yes, even all the way back to my ruined resort, ravaged by the cyclone. We were like a curse, the three of us, bringing death and disaster wherever we went, and to whoever we met.

And where were we going this time?

But Harry told us nothing. Indeed, he barely acknowledged our presence. We were no longer his responsibility, and he was no longer our indefatigable guide. Something amicable had broken in him. The collapse of the Underground, the destruction of the High Council, the words of the dying man...They had driven him into a silent and bitter place where he existed alone. Even when bodily necessities forced Aisha and me to demand a toilet stop, he gave no response. It was only some minutes later that he wrenched the van off the road, drove down a side track for half a mile, and then came to a stop.

'Here,' he said tersely. 'And make it quick.'

We climbed out into dead night, overcast. It was a narrow trail in the bush somewhere, not a house or a light to be seen, only the shadows of gum trees, and a fence running along a paddock. Aisha slipped away behind a tree. I did the same. And standing there, I could see no reason why Harry shouldn't just drive off and leave us. But he waited. I finished up and went back to the van. Aisha didn't reappear. I went looking and found her fifty yards up the track, standing at the fence and staring vacantly off into the night. There were mountains there, darker shapes rising against the sky. Her arms were folded as if it were freezing, even though it wasn't.

'I think I'll just stay here,' she said tonelessly.

I led her gently back to the van, and studied her once we were inside and under way again. The blood on her face was her own, from a jagged cut on her temple. She was concussed, I decided, pressing her back onto the bed.

We drove on, and I lost all sense of place. We went up hills and down them, and skidded on tight corners. Northwards, was all I knew, from my bones; we were heading north. Five hours. Six. At some stage, we must have crossed the border into New South Wales. Although how that was possible without meeting a checkpoint, I can't guess, even now. The fates were just with us that night. I slept for some time, and when I woke we were on a rough dirt track. I peeked through the front curtains and saw dawn growing in the sky. We seemed to be in the middle of some backwoods property up in the hill country. There was an old wooden shed ahead, leaning and forgotten. Harry steered the van into it, then switched off the engine.

'I have to sleep,' he said. Then he gave me his gun. 'Keep watch until I wake up. If anyone comes near—no matter who it is, even if it's a child—shoot them.'

And so we spent the day there.

There's nothing stranger, I think, than to be in your own country, and yet not know exactly where in that country you are. But waiting in that shed, I had to admit that I couldn't have pinpointed our position on a map even to within two hundred miles. It was such an alien feeling. Nor were there any clues. The sky was hidden by low clouds, with rain drifting across, and from the shed my only view was of a forested hill rising before me, its head wreathed in mist. The little rutted track by which we'd entered wound away behind the shed, and I didn't dare walk outside to see where it might lead. I could hear no other sounds of life, no cars on a distant highway. The land had simply swallowed us up, and we'd vanished.

Ah, but the peace of it. Harry had sprawled out on some mouldering hay bales, and Aisha was either asleep or unconscious on the bed in the van. So it was only me to stand watch. And although I was tired, I didn't feel like sleeping. The shed was dark and dry and safe, and so I just sat and stared, thinking that I might never have the chance to spend a day like this again, completely at rest, and in such solitude, listening to rain on a tin roof, and to the calls of birds under the clouds.

It was beautiful, and it was Australia, some faraway little piece of it where nothing had changed, and to which no trouble had come. It seemed impossible that I was still in the same nation in which thousands were confined to ghettos, or where terrorists exploded bombs, or where Citizenship and the AFP ruled at gunpoint, or where the US Army hunkered down in its bases of occupation. Or, indeed, that this was the same planet in which, even as I sat there, so many millions were fighting in so many wars, and scrabbling to kill or to die or to just survive.

But it *was* the same world, of course, and the same country.

The day progressed into afternoon. Harry awoke, and sat eating sandwiches as the light faded, his gaze dull. He said nothing, and I didn't ask the obvious questions. What are we doing? Where are we going? I knew he wouldn't tell me, that the very sight of Aisha and me made his mood all the worse. I tried to reason it out myself. It was to do with the dead man from Sydney. An air traffic controller, who knew something, it seemed, about a plane crash—an accident that was no accident. So were we perhaps headed for the site where the plane came down? But what could be the point of that? What could Harry want with smoking wreckage in a field somewhere? Or with dead bodies, and the smell of burnt jet fuel?

And if not the plane, then where? The man had come from Sydney, so was Sydney itself our destination? Was there some vital secret about the city that Harry had learned, some last Underground mission that he could save? The more I thought about it, the more likely it seemed. The more *right* it seemed. If the rest of Australia had gone bad, then Sydney would be its rotten heart, and if the evil root of our times was to be uncovered, it would be uncovered there. It was the city which my brother had made into his capital, after all. And where he had built his bunker, at Kirribilli House, overlooking the Harbour and the Bridge and the Opera House—the national icons. Each of them bristling with fortifications and barbed wire, defiantly, as if my brother was personally protecting them from the infidel.

Perhaps it was even Bernard himself that we sought. Maybe Harry, in his despair, had fixed upon some act of madness. Maybe the dead air traffic controller had revealed some hidden way by which we might reach the Prime Minister. And even if that wasn't Harry's intent at all, the idea still stuck with me, a lurid daydream. If we reached Sydney, I would leave Harry to do whatever it was he had to do, and myself, I would get dropped off at the front gates of Kirribilli House. And somehow, magically, I would get past the guards and the snipers. I would leap over the barricades, and evade the dogs in the gardens. And, finally, I would meet Bernard there on the front steps. The Great Leader, my brother, an ugly, empty man. And I'd proceed to beat his smug face to a bloody pulp.

Are you laughing at me, interrogators?

Aisha woke just on dusk, and the delirium seemed to have faded from her eyes. She crept gingerly to the door and looked at the misty evening. Her face—wan, thin and young—had been robbed of any sort of energy. She only stared out bleakly at a place she didn't belong—a place with no targets, no people, no ideology— then went and found a sandwich to eat. I had no doubt at all that she would leave us sooner or later. At some point she would simply slip away. What use were we to her anymore, or her to us? No doubt there was some other terrorist cell she could seek out and join, and then begin plotting our destruction anew, all the while preparing for prophets and madmen who would never arrive to congratulate her.

And so we waited there, the three of us—finished with each other, essentially, with nothing to say—until the rain stopped, and darkness fell.

'Let's go,' said Harry.

I commandeered the bed in the van for myself this time. For an hour maybe I lay awake as we drove, watching Aisha's narrow back. The van twisted and swayed, and it seemed that we were climbing more hills. And still the miracle held. No roadblocks, no checkpoints. But in truth I was falling asleep by then, so deeply and darkly that nothing could have woken me—not soldiers banging on the windows, not the smell of burnt jet fuel and dead bodies, not even peak hour in downtown Sydney. I didn't dream of anything, and I don't know how many hours I was unconscious. But in the end I was woken by the sudden silence of the engine switching off.

'This is it,' Harry said from the front.

Aisha was hunched at the curtains, peering out, and shot me a puzzled frown. I rose groggily and opened the sliding door, half expecting to find myself in yet another Underground safe house—a garage, a warehouse, a factory.

But I didn't see any of that.

I saw a clear night sky, and a plain of grass and shadows extending away before me, and hills in the distance, and not a single sign of civilisation.

It wasn't Sydney. And there was no plane wreck in sight.

Harry slammed the driver's door shut. 'We walk from here.'

THIRTY-ONE

The Southern Cross hung above us, like a great and cold Australian flag in the sky. The constellation was on our left, so I knew we were heading west.

But the direction hardly mattered. This was no place I recognised. It was a ghost landscape, the landscape of a dream. We were traversing a preternaturally flat plain, seemingly a dozen miles wide, and it was rimmed on all sides by tall, silent hills. It reminded me, on a vaster scale, of the dead lake we'd found out in the desert. Only this was no desert. The plain was covered with thick, knee-high grass, shining like water under the pale moon, and the hills were black with forest. And yet across the whole immense expanse there were no houses, no roads, no fences, as if no one had ever trod this piece of ground before.

Where on earth were we?

But Harry did not explain. 'We have to get there before dawn,' was all he told us.

Dragged in his wake, Aisha and I followed without a word.

★

The western hills drew closer. Harry paused suddenly, his eyes dark cavities, watching. Far off to our right, lights had appeared, moving along the edge of the plain. The headlights of a vehicle. They came slowly towards us. They didn't deviate, or rise or fall—and I formed the impression that the vehicle was driving along a wide, straight highway. But what highway? And why would such a road be utterly deserted, apart from this one slow car? As it neared, I saw that it bore an orange light on its roof, flashing steadily. It was the kind of light I'd seen on security vehicles. Military patrols. Harry tensed at my side, and touched the gun jammed in his belt. But a few miles from us, the headlights slowly curved away, following the unseen road, and began to climb into the hills. Then they disappeared, leaving the night even more empty and unreal than before.

Harry relaxed slightly, moved on.

At the edge of the plain we came finally to a fence. It was ten feet high, strong and sturdy and new, and topped with razor wire. It ran away to the north and south as far as I could see. On the further side, a dirt track followed along the fence line. And beyond that, a eucalypt forest swept up into the hills.

Harry touched the wire with the back of his hand.

'Arrogant bastards,' he said, half to himself. 'They haven't even bothered to electrify it. They're that confident that no one would ever come here.'

He searched about. There were a few lone gum trees on our side of the barrier, and at the foot of one he found a fallen branch. Taking it up, he climbed the fence and poked and pried at the razor wire until it came free in big loops, under which he could slip. He dropped down to the far side, looked back at us.

'Quick,' he said. 'There'll be a patrol along this track, sooner or later.'

Aisha and I climbed the fence in turn—not without some difficulty—and joined him. Then we plunged on, uphill, into the blackness under the trees. Walking was harder in there, stumbling over rough ground and dead branches and invisible holes. I was gasping when we crested the rise, and through the canopy I could glimpse the stars, but all around the world remained grey and featureless. We could be anywhere. Then it was down again, and onwards through the forest.

We walked for hours, leaving the plain far behind. Harry was setting a cruel pace for my leg. And the further we walked, the more baffled I became. At one point a sealed road crossed our path. It ran smoothly through the bush, but even though we waited warily for some minutes, there was no traffic. Hurrying across, I felt leaves and twigs crunch under my feet, as if the road had not been used in years.

Miles later the forest had faded away and we were hiking through country that was more open. In fact it was farmland, and yet it seemed overgrown and neglected. There were fields, and sheds, and even some houses, but the fields were deserted, and the houses were silent and dark, their windows smashed. We crossed more roads, all of them as disused as the first. The entire area felt abandoned. Derelict. But then, finally, we cleared a rise and I could see, faraway, a few points of light. They were off to our right and left. Distant houses. Or streetlights, maybe. Straight ahead, however, there rose a ridge of hills that terminated in a single low mountain, heavily draped in forest, and black against the sky.

Harry led us on. We were slowing down now, but eventually we crept to the mountain's foot. And here was another road. A highway. And as we paused there, headlights appeared, and a car went rushing by. Not a military vehicle, or a patrol car, just a normal sedan, unmarked. Two women inside.

Harry made no comment. We crossed over. On the peak above us, a tall structure of some sort stood out from the treetops. We began to climb.

My leg was on fire. We'd been walking for something like six or seven hours, and the sky was beginning to lighten, the first hints of dawn. Up and up we went, scrambling on the steeper slopes. Off to either side I could see lights again, many of them, widely spread over the hills like the sprinkle of outer suburbs.

Then the ground levelled out, and we were on the broad peak. There was a road there, and paved places for parking. The tall structure, I could see now, was a communications tower. There was decking built around it, like a viewing platform, with stairs leading up. And a creeping dread took hold of me, because I *knew* this place. I'd been here before at some point in my life, and something about the memory was very wrong. We stumbled across the car park to a stone wall that marked the far edge, where the mountain fell away again to empty air.

But even as we did so, a sound rose behind us. The growing roar of aircraft engines. I turned, and through the trees saw a huge passenger jet drifting out of the sky, off to the west and only a few hundred metres above us, wheels down and landing lights flashing. It soared across the hilltop, losing altitude steeply as it did so, the engines whining, and then sank from view beyond the further rim of the mountain.

Harry was already standing at the wall, facing south and staring down. Aisha and I hurried to join him, the view below us springing up as we approached.

'Fuck,' Harry was breathing, over and over. 'Fuck.'

I could see the jet again, below us in the middle airs, lowering towards an airport that was off to the left, only a couple of miles away. But everywhere else there were lights, orange and white, the expanse of a whole city, complete with traffic moving sparsely in the pre-dawn streets. From our vantage point, we were directly in line with a wide, sweeping avenue that split the town in two. The avenue began at a hulking domed building on the slopes of the hill below us, and then ran away, ablaze with illumination, lined with statues and memorials, to the shores of a narrow lake. On the far side of the lake was a sprawling grass concourse, at the back of which stood an imposing white building with two outstretched wings. And behind that lifted another hill, one that had seemingly been excavated and consumed by a half-buried building of glass and steel. And over that building rose a gigantic metal edifice, four great beams that vaulted inwards to join into a single spar, which then rose high above the hill, and above the entire city. A flagpole.

I recognised it all in an instant. The War Memorial, Anzac Parade, Lake Burley Griffin, the old Parliament House, Capital Hill and the new Parliament House.

We were standing at the lookout atop Mt Ainslie.

And before us lay the supposedly dead city of Canberra.

Alive and well, after all.

THIRTY-TWO

Ah, interrogators. I know that all through these pages of mine, you've been marvelling at my stupidity. My sheer gullibility. And the only thing I can say in my defence is that the rest of the nation shares my blindness. Canberra is gone, it was wiped out, we all saw it—what possible reason is there for anyone to doubt it? After all, what sort of madman would conceive of such deception, let alone carry it out? I *still* find it difficult to credit.

Even as I sit here in my prison cell, at Canberra's very heart.

But all that aside, I'm embarrassed. I should—at the very least—have realised that we were in the Canberra region long before we reached the lookout. As soon as we stepped out of the campervan and saw that unearthly plain before us, surrounded by hills, I should have known. How could I not have recognised Lake George? I've driven along its shores dozens of times, riding the Federal Highway on my way to or from the capital. Oh, I know, it was night, and things can look strange and unsettling in the dark—but then, even in broad daylight the lake has a surreal air, doesn't it? And true, there was no water. But that's the mystery of Lake George—the water that comes and goes, so that sometimes the lake is like an inland sea, and at other times there's only a grassy expanse where sheep graze. People talk of underground rivers that connect to secret reservoirs, channels that alternately fill or drain the basin. Whatever the truth, I should have remembered the place.

And there were plenty of other clues to our location. The fence we climbed. The military patrol we saw. Those deserted outer roads we crossed. The lifeless farmhouses, the paddocks left to run wild. Even the shape of Mt Ainslie itself, rising in front of us. They were all warning signs.

But then again, even if I had worked out where we were, I would only have assumed that Harry was taking us to look upon the ruins of the dead city.

Nothing would have prepared me for a *living* Canberra.

We stared down at it, the lights glittering.

All I could say was, 'But it's impossible.'

Harry was gripping the railing on the stone wall, his fists clenched in rage. 'You see it, don't you? Believe it.'

I saw it, all right. I turned to him. 'How did you know?'

'I didn't. Not for sure. Not until now.'

'But you brought us here. You suspected.'

His eyes hadn't moved from the city. 'It was the air traffic controller. He told me. Just before he died.'

'The controller? He was involved in this?'

Harry gave a tight shake of his head. 'He only found out four days ago. And straightaway he ran, looking for someone to tell. He had friends in the OU. But people were on his tail. They got to his Sydney connections, liquidated them, so he had nowhere to run but Melbourne. And they followed him there anyway. I think it was him they were after with the attack on the ghetto. They must have tracked him to that hall. They mightn't even have known that we were there, or that the High Council was meeting. We were probably just collateral damage.'

I pondered the irony of that for a moment. Perhaps it even

explained the ease of our escape from Melbourne. But none of it mattered anymore, compared to the sight below us.

'That man was from Sydney, not from here.' I waved an arm at Canberra. 'How did he find out about this?'

'It was the plane crash.'

I stared. 'The crash?'

'I told you. It wasn't just an accident.' Harry took a deep breath to calm himself. 'You remember that night we were lost out in the desert? You remember there were great big thunderstorms way off to the east?'

I nodded, thinking of lightning on a desert horizon.

'That's what started it. The controller, he was in charge of the airspace in southern New South Wales that night. He had a plane, a Melbourne to Sydney flight, that was routed right through those storms. The pilots needed a way around, east or west of the bad weather. The problem was, the flight was immediately to the west of Canberra, and the airspace over Canberra has been closed since the bomb. A no-fly zone. So the controller wasn't allowed to route the flight eastwards. He should have diverted them further west. Only he couldn't do that either. The airspace to the west was off limits too, that night. Temporarily. For a military emergency.' Harry glanced at me with a thin smile. 'That was because of us. The army and the air force had dozens of planes and drones up over western New South Wales that night, looking for you and me and Aisha. They didn't want commercial aircraft getting in the way.'

A chill ran through me. 'So what happened?'

'He sent the plane east. He thought there was just enough room between the storms and the no-fly zone for the plane to squeeze through. But the storms were moving faster than expected, and the plane was forced further off course, and the controller decided that surely it was no problem for just one flight to break the rules, if it was a safety matter. So he vectored them over the city. But suddenly the pilots were telling him something he couldn't believe. They could see lights below, lots of them. It was Canberra, and it wasn't a ruin like it was supposed to be.'

'Ah,' I said, beginning to understand.

'No one else heard this. It was just the controller and the aircrew, talking to each other. But a few minutes later the pilots were yelling something about being buzzed by military jets. And a few minutes after that, the pilots were screaming, and the plane vanished from the radar screen.'

I found myself staring down at the airport. The jet that had flown over us had landed, and was taxiing sedately towards the terminal. I could see now that it was no ordinary passenger plane. It was black, and without marking or livery of any kind. But my eyes were drawn to the far side of the airfield. There, amidst huts and hangars, stood a line of steely grey fighter jets.

'Holy shit,' I said quietly.

Harry nodded. 'The plane came down ten k outside the no-fly zone. And the controller ran. He was no fool. This place here—whatever the fuck it is—has been kept secret for a reason. And he knew that if they were prepared to shoot down a plane because the pilots had seen it, then *he* was on the hit list too.'

The insanity of the whole situation swept over me. 'But how can Canberra still be here? How could they get away with it? We all saw the mushroom cloud. It was real. So how did they fake it? And *why*?'

'I don't know.' He looked beyond me. 'Maybe she does.'

I'd forgotten all about Aisha. I turned and saw her there, on her knees against the stone wall, her face starkly white as she stared at the city.

'Well?' Harry insisted.

But Aisha didn't seem to comprehend him. She could only shake her head. 'It was destroyed. *We* destroyed it.'

'Who? Your fucking Southern Jihad?' Harry was behind her suddenly, his hands around her neck, slamming her body against the wall. 'Look at it, you stupid bitch! Look at it! Does it look destroyed to you?!'

She was choking, coughing, not even resisting.

'What the fuck is going on here?!' Harry screamed.

I dragged him away from her.

Aisha sagged against the wall, gasping. 'I don't know,' she got out. 'They told me it was us. That we set off the bomb. I thought it was true.'

'We all thought it was true.' I still had Harry by the shoulders. 'She was lied to,' I told him. 'Just like we all were.'

The fury went out of him, and I let go.

'Christ,' he said. 'What a mess.'

'What do we do now?' I asked him. 'Why did we come here?'

He looked at me blankly. 'Why? There's no why. I just had to see it for myself. The bomb was the whole excuse for what's going on in this country. The state of emergency. The arrests, the detentions. And it never even *happened*.'

'So we tell people, right? We get out of here and let everyone know.'

'Tell who? The Underground? The Underground died back in the ghetto. You saw it. There's barely anyone left.'

'Then we tell the media.'

He gave a painful laugh. 'Three crazies walk into a newspaper office and start raving about Canberra still being in one piece. Oh, that will work.'

'It might, if one of the crazies is the Prime Minister's brother. Who's supposed to have been dead for the last week.'

That made him think, but then he shook his head, rejecting it. 'Even if we could get to a newspaper, and even if we could make them believe us, it wouldn't help. The government has security advisers embedded in every single newsroom. They have to clear every story, every investigation. They'd pass the word back to the authorities, and we'd be dead in hours. Us, and half the newspaper staff too.'

'So you're sure the government is in on this?'

His look was withering. 'Are you kidding? The government had to have *organised* this. There's no other way it could be done, no other way the secret could've been kept. And not just our government. Governments the world over. You can't hide a whole city just by putting up a fence and a no-fly zone. There're satellites.

American. Russian. Chinese. A whole shitload of people must
know that Canberra is still here. And none of them are talking.'

'But there must be *something* we can do.'

He searched for an answer, then seemed to give up in despair.
He walked back to the wall and gazed down for a time. 'If only
we had a video camera with us. Some way of proving it. But
even then, who could we show the footage to? They'd only say
we faked it. People aren't going to throw up their hands and
just accept that we're telling the truth. It's too insane.'

The sound of more jet engines grew behind us.

We all turned. But when the plane appeared, it sailed over
us as serenely as the first one had, descending towards the airport.
It was another large passenger jet, but whereas the first one had
been black and anonymous, this one was grey, with military
markings and national insignia on the tail.

'That's not one of ours,' Harry said, perturbed. 'That's the
RAF. What the hell are the British doing here?'

We watched the plane land, and then taxi towards the terminal.
To our surprise, a convoy of black cars sped out to meet it. Stairs
were moved to the aircraft door, and a line of people—just tiny
dots at this distance—climbed out of the cars and waited to
welcome the descending passengers. A guard of honour.

Harry and I exchanged a glance of complete bewilderment.

'We have to get down there,' he said.

'Shouldn't we just get away? Before we're seen?'

'We can't just *go*. We have to find out what's happening here.'
He pointed to the lower slopes of the hill. 'Look, we can stay
under cover in the scrub almost right to the edge of the airport.
We can at least get close enough to see what all these planes are
about. And to see who's on them.'

I stared down, worried. Yes, we could make the airport, but
what then? Were we just going to walk into the streets of
Canberra and ask the first person we met? Ask them what?
Who the fuck were these people anyway?

'C'mon,' Harry said, already moving off.

I looked at Aisha, who was still gazing down bleakly. I felt a momentary stab of pity. Even if she was evil and crazy, I still knew it must hurt to have every belief you've ever held proved utterly and concretely wrong.

'What about you?' I asked her. 'You coming too?'

She rose to her feet, bedraggled and dirty. She wiped a slightly bloodied nose, looked at me, and nodded. 'I want to know who did this,' she said.

And so we descended the mountain.

THIRTY-THREE

The sun rose as we climbed down. The day was going to be hot, and we were out of water, out of food, and my leg had swollen stiff. I had no idea how we were ever going to make it back to the campervan, all those weary miles away. But nobody seemed to be thinking that far ahead. We were still engrossed by the glimpses of Canberra below us through the trees. It all seemed so normal—the traffic moving in the streets, the distant city noises floating up, the tiny figures of people jogging along the footpaths around the lake. In fact, there was only one thing missing from my memories of an average Canberra morning. No flag was flying from the gigantic pole over Parliament House.

Meanwhile, every ten minutes or so, passenger jets crossed low above us, landing gear down, heading for the airport.

'It's a busy fucking strip,' said Harry, staring up at one of the planes, 'for a city that isn't supposed to exist.'

Indeed, it could almost have been a typical morning's air traffic, back in the times before the bomb, with politicians and bureaucrats commuting in for the day's business. Except that none of the flights were commercial airliners. They seemed to be mostly military carriers, some of them grey and mysterious, but others with the clear markings of various nationalities. We spotted one that was Chinese, and another that was German. And then there were the two fighter jets that came roaring in to land—returning, I assumed, from a dawn patrol of the Canberra airspace. There was no doubt about *their* nationality. They belonged to the Royal Australian Air Force. And if I wasn't mistaken, they were two of our brand-new, only recently delivered, multi-billion-dollar F-35 Joint Strike Fighters.

'What do you think?' I asked Harry. 'Could the whole city be some sort of military base now?'

He shook his head. 'It wouldn't make sense. There's already a huge base over at Yass. That's only half an hour away. Why go to all this bother just to create another one?' He paused, troubled. 'And yet, obviously the military is involved.'

'I'm surprised your Underground contacts in the army never said anything.'

'No, but like I told you, we never penetrated the senior levels.'

'And no one else in the OU ever got any hint of this?'

'Not that we understood at the time. But there was one guy, I remember now. He worked in the power industry, a maintenance worker on the New South Wales grid. The OU used him to sabotage power supplies to government installations. But he turned up one day with a story about how the Yass base was using immense amounts of electricity, for its size. He thought that something strange had to be going on there, maybe some kind of military industrial complex we might be interested in. We investigated, but the base seemed perfectly normal. I'm just wondering now if what he saw was actually power being diverted to Canberra. They have to get their electricity from somewhere. It's another thing about a city you can't hide.'

'If only he'd dug a bit deeper,' I said.

'He might have,' Harry replied flatly. 'He disappeared, shortly afterwards.'

We trudged on, and kangaroos leapt out of our way.

★

And it's an ironic thing, interrogators. In the old Canberra, it would have been impossible to walk from Mt Ainslie to the airport without being seen by *someone*. True, we were safe in the scrub until the foot of the mountain, but between there and the airport, squarely across our path, lay the halls and playing fields of the Australian Royal Military College. Duntroon. In normal times, the very last area we could have hoped to pass through unobserved. The campus would have been swarming with cadet officers. Australia's finest. Except that now, of course, thanks to you, the college is abandoned, the cadets have long since moved to Sydney, and the native bush has been left to reclaim the grounds. So we were able to creep unmolested past the empty barracks, and arrive at the perimeter of the airfield itself.

And again, interrogators, the very nature of this secret Canberra of yours made it so simple for us. Because when an entire city is fenced off and protected, what need is there of any special security around an airport? Other airfields around the world might be bristling with barbed wire and patrols and cameras— but not Canberra International. The place is virtually unguarded. No one has even bothered to maintain the perimeter fence, and so it took us only moments to find a hole in the wire. From there we hurried a few dozen metres through the long grass, and then a drainage channel, deep and dry, opened at our feet. We dropped down, and waited.

So blame your own secrecy, and your own proud belief that you were completely secure in your hidden city, for the fact that we got in.

And for the disaster which followed.

'Well,' I said, 'we're none the wiser.'

The three of us were peering over the lip of the ditch, studying the scene. Fifty yards or so away were the outlying maintenance buildings and hangars of the terminal complex and, further off, the terminal itself. A few people were visible there, moving about, but for the moment the airport was between arrivals, and there was little else to be seen. We sank back below the rim.

'There'll be another plane,' said Harry.

'Then what?'

'We see who gets off it.'

I sat there uneasily, staring up at the sky. I wasn't happy about this, or with either of my companions. Harry seemed possessed by a reckless curiousity, overriding his native caution, and that wasn't good. What we were doing was dangerous. As for Aisha, well, she was an unpredictable element at the best of times. She hadn't spoken since the top of Mt Ainslie, but it was a brooding silence. The reality of Canberra, the lies she had been told— sooner or later, her anger about it all was going to come out. And then who knew what she might do.

But finally a grey airbus thundered over us and landed on the strip. We raised our heads above the ditch again and watched. The plane taxied over towards the terminal. This time, there was no honour guard waiting to greet it. Stairs were rolled up, baggage handlers attended to the cargo hold, and the passengers disembarked without fuss. At a glance, they looked like ordinary civilian men and women—some in suits, others more casually dressed, toting hand luggage—and they filed off into the terminal, for all the world like normal travellers.

The only notable thing about them was that they were all Japanese.

'So?' I asked Harry.

'So...' he replied, chewing his lip in confusion.

We sank back into the ditch.

'This is all a western conspiracy,' Aisha suddenly declared. 'Muslims are being blamed for the destruction of this city, and it never happened.'

Harry stared at her. 'A few hours ago you were convinced it was Muslims who blew Canberra up. And you were *proud* of it.'

'If we really had done it, I would be proud. But it was a lie. A lie told so that Muslims in this country could be locked away in the ghettos.'

Harry considered. 'I don't think that all of this was done just as an excuse to put Muslims in detention.' He thought some more. 'Anyway, who was it exactly that told you your own people were behind the bombing?'

Aisha adopted her non-cooperative pose and said nothing.

'C'mon. Whoever it was, they were bullshitting you, so why protect them?'

She frowned at Harry for a moment more, and then her expression dissolved into one of genuine perplexity. 'There was a man I was introduced to, from another Jihad cell. I never knew his name. He told me he was one of the team that smuggled the bomb in. He had proof. He showed me photos of it.'

'Yeah, well, we all saw the photos. They were made public. They were front bloody page.'

'No, these weren't *those* pictures. The man was in them himself. Standing next to the bomb. They were real. They weren't copies or fakes.'

'But there *was* no bomb.'

'Who was he then? And what was in the photos?'

'I don't fucking know. Obviously he was just some guy who saw the mushroom cloud footage on TV, and thought he'd claim it for himself. So he built a fake bomb and took some photos. So what? It doesn't prove anything.'

Aisha smiled. 'My meeting with him was before the bomb went off. Weeks before. He told me it was going to happen. He told all of us. Even the date.'

Harry opened his mouth, then shut it again.

'Damn it,' he said eventually, to no one. 'That's crazy.'

But at long last, a suspicion was forming in my mind. (And how *slow* had I been, interrogators? How *dense*?)

I said, 'This man Aisha met—what if he was working with the people who arranged the whole charade? What if he was working with the government?'

The two of them looked at me.

'Think about it,' I reasoned. 'We know that the authorities, for some purpose, wanted to fake a nuclear bomb going off here in Canberra. Obviously, they needed someone to blame it on. They needed a terrorist group. So they pick Great Southern Jihad, and they infiltrate one of the cells with a team of double agents. Those agents have photos of themselves with what looks like a bomb, and grand plans, they say, to destroy the capital city. They show the photos around to all their terrorist colleagues, like Aisha. Then, apparently, the bomb goes off as planned. And everyone in Great Southern Jihad thinks, yes, wonderful, it was us who did it.'

'That's ridiculous,' Aisha uttered.

'Why?'

'There were no government agents in the Jihad. We were too secret.'

'Maybe you weren't as secret as you thought.'

'Or maybe,' said Harry, his eyes lighting with an idea, 'you were never secret at all. Maybe you were being run by the government the whole time.'

Aisha glared. 'What?'

Harry sat up, excited. 'No, listen. Maybe they didn't need to infiltrate the Jihad, maybe they created it in the first place.'

Aisha shook her head furiously. 'The government was our sworn enemy!'

'Well, that's what they'd tell you, isn't it? You had to think it was for real. You people at the bottom, they'd fill your head with all sorts of anti-government stuff. Along with all that new Islam rubbish you keep spouting. Stuff no proper Muslim has ever heard of.' He was nodding. 'Christ, it makes sense. It would explain what we saw back in Queensland. Why the government always knew about you people, but didn't seem to care. Why the AFP were told to keep their hands off.'

'But why create a terrorist group?' I wanted to know.

'Don't you get it? This government, your brother, the state of emergency—it only works if there's a constant threat. What better way to keep it all bubbling along than to have some terrorists of your own doing the dirty work?'

Aisha was outraged. 'We were messengers of Allah!'

'Sure. Of course. But how could you tell? You were the faithful little cell leader, doing what your superiors told you. But you never even knew who those superiors were.' He gloried in the concept a moment. 'It's perfect, really. Tame terrorists to carry out an attack or two when it's needed, the population stays scared, and the security regime remains in force. With the bombing of Canberra the crowning glory of it all.'

'It's madness,' Aisha insisted, flushed red.

'Look around you. How mad is any of this?'

The air filled with the whine of aircraft engines. I looked up, and was suprised to see a small private jet crossing above us. Not a military transport, but a slender Gulfstream. One of the high-end luxury kind. This was something new. Harry raised his head above the rim of the ditch to watch it land.

'It's not enough, though,' I said to his back. 'It doesn't explain why they want me and Aisha dead. If she was really working for the government, even unknowingly, then why didn't they just instruct her to let me go after I was kidnapped? Why go through the pretence of rescuing me in that ambush?'

'That I don't know,' said Harry, without turning. 'But take a look at this.'

I climbed up to join him.

The Gulfstream was ambling across the tarmac. And racing out to greet it was another cavalcade of black limousines.

'This is more like it,' Harry said. 'This is someone important. Look. On the hoods of the cars. Those flags.'

I could see them. They were American. Fluttering bravely.

'This we gotta see,' he said.

And without another word, he was out of the ditch, and moving through the grass at a crouch.

'Wait!' I hissed after him, but he didn't stop. I glanced back at Aisha.

She was frozen, her mind working. 'It can't be true.'

There was no time for this. 'Why not?'

She stared at me. 'Because we were *promised*!' But I heard the doubt there—deep and terrible, now that it had been planted.

'C'mon. We can't lose Harry.'

I dragged her upright, and we followed Harry's track through the grass.

No alarms sounded, no guards came running. We caught up with Harry behind some small sheds. Then together we crept on, slipping from building to building, until we found ourselves behind a large hangar. At the far corner was a jumbled pile of empty oil drums. We crept in amongst them and peered out through the gaps. The main terminal was close now, and between us and it, some airport workers were busy servicing a refuelling tanker. They were not ordinary ground staff. They all wore uniforms. They were soldiers. Australian Army.

The Gulfstream was parked a little further out on the tarmac. The limousines had lined up beside it, and men from the cars had arranged themselves along a red carpet that had been unrolled. Most of them were in black suits, and wearing sunglasses. A secret service security detail if I'd ever seen one.

Harry gripped my shoulder. 'Look,' he said softly. 'There.'

He was pointing to the foremost man in the line. An older, heavily built individual, with a bull head, and a close-shaven scalp. The only one not wearing sunglasses.

'Don't you know who that is?' Harry demanded.

'I've seen him somewhere…'

'It's Carl Holbrook.'

'Who?'

'The US Ambassador to Australia!'

He was right. It was.

'I knew it,' Harry whispered. 'The US had to be behind all this. There's no other way it could work. But who the hell is he welcoming?'

The plane's pressure door swung open. A step unfolded down, and men emerged from the interior. They were all Arabs, in flowing white robes.

'Are they Saudis?' Harry wondered. 'Is it Saudi royalty?'

At my back I could feel Aisha squirming for a better position from which to see. The robed men formed a guard at the foot of the stairs, and the Americans still waited patiently, watching the doorway.

Then, after a pause, a last figure stepped out.

Harry's hand fell from my shoulder. 'Oh, fuck.'

It was a ghost. A vision. A tall man, slightly stooped, with a look about him of one prematurely aged. Plain peasant dress, a robe, a long wispy beard gone grey. Intent eyes, oddly peaceful, and a serene half smile on his lips. A face that had stared out from a billion television screens and newspaper front pages. A man who couldn't possibly be there. A man who was supposed to be dead ... Just like I was.

'The Great Hero,' came Aisha's voice behind me, choked.

'Jesus Christ,' Harry moaned faintly.

'It's not him,' I found myself saying. 'It can't be him.'

And yet, sedately, bin Laden descended onto the tarmac. I was blinking. It looked like him, it had to be him, but it couldn't be him. I knew that for a certainty. Not here. Not now. Stepping down from a plane into the Australian sunshine.

The American Ambassador strode forward to meet him.

'You were right,' breathed Harry in amazement, and I sensed (though I did not turn) that he was looking at Aisha. 'You were fucking well right.'

On the tarmac, the two men came together. Each was smiling warmly. They shook hands. They bent their heads together in a moment of conversation.

Quiet laughter drifted across the concrete.

And then Aisha was up and running.

Harry made a despairing grab for her and missed. She was out in the open, sprinting madly towards the plane and the tableau of the two men, talking while their retinues stood by. She was past the refuelling truck before anyone saw her.

Screaming, 'Osama! Osama!'

It was a cry that seemed to contain everything about her.

Adoration, and fanatical hope, and the fulfilment of those long-suffering years she had dreamt of meeting him. Yes. But there was confusion too. Anger. And a raging question—how could this be? After all the other lies and deceptions, now, there at last, was the Great Hero himself, just as she had been promised. Only he was standing hand in hand, and cheek to cheek, laughing with a representative of the Great Satan.

'Osama!'

The Ambassador glanced her way. So did bin Laden. And the Australian soldiers. And the Americans. And the Arabs.

There was a surprised beat of silence. Then the Arabs were reaching under their robes, and the Americans were reaching under their jackets. They all fell upon her in a flurry of limbs and guns, and the only amazing thing was that no shots were fired. When it was over, bin Laden and the Ambassador had been hustled safely aside, and Aisha was on her knees, held down at one shoulder by an American bodyguard, and at the other by one of the al-Qaeda men.

She was still screaming.

Bin Laden came strolling back. He stood before her, calm, and said something that I couldn't hear. Aisha abruptly fell silent. And then...

Then they just *talked*. They were too far away for me to understand any of it, and Harry and I were too stunned to do anything but watch. But I could hear the soft insistence of bin Laden's questions, and the fierce accusatory tone of Aisha's replies. She was shaking her head throughout, struggling against her captors. Was the girl actually berating the terrorist leader? Was she reminding him that he was supposed to guide her into the united world of new Islam, not indulge in friendly chats with the American enemy? Was she the faithful disciple unmasking the false prophet? And if so, then what could bin Laden make of her in his turn? Who was this mad young woman, ranting about a new Islam of which I'm sure he'd never heard, let alone approved? Who was this Muslim who was no Muslim at all? And who was she to challenge *him* on matters of faith and holy war?

Whatever they said, and whatever Aisha told him, about herself, about the Great Southern Jihad, or about her pain and her betrayal, it lasted only a few minutes. By then, bin Laden was frowning with impatience. He turned questioningly to the US Ambassador. Holbrook had been speaking urgently on a mobile phone, no doubt discussing Aisha's appearance with some higher authority. Now he broke off the call and addressed bin Laden in a low voice. The terrorist leader replied, gesturing in annoyance. They both considered Aisha. Then the Ambassador was on his phone again, asking a last question. Finally he shrugged, looked at bin Laden and gave an indifferent nod.

The Great Hero didn't hesitate. He issued a curt order to one of his men, who in response lifted a gun, put the barrel against Aisha's tangled hair, and blew off the top of her head.

It was only then that one of the Americans shouted a sharp command, and pointed right to where Harry and I were still kneeling behind the drums, dumbstruck.

Suddenly there were jeeps racing towards us, and sirens wailing, and bodyguards and Australian soldiers running everywhere. Harry and I were running too, back along behind the hangar, even as bullets peppered the empty oil drums.

Of course, we were never going to be fast enough. Especially not me, with my leg. Harry was already ten yards ahead. He had his gun drawn. 'The bastards!' he was yelling, to himself as much as me. 'The bastards!' And despite everything I somehow had faith in him still, a belief that he would find a way out of this. That he would save us both again, one last time.

He cleared the hangar, and I heard shots. Harry spun suddenly, as if stung, his mouth open, his gun firing. More shots answered, and his face seemed to shatter, spraying red. Then he was a shapeless thing tumbling to the ground.

I stopped running. I limped out into the open, my hands in the air. A dozen different guns greeted me, and stony faces of three nationalities.

'Down on the ground, motherfucker,' someone ordered.

I lay down, not far from Harry and the pool of blood beneath him. I watched his body heave and twitch a few times, and then stop.

They were not kind to me. But to be honest, I don't remember much of the next twenty minutes. The kicks. The abuse. The body search. The questions. (And God knows, there were far more of them to follow, right, interrogators dear?) No, I was off in some faraway place of horror and sadness. Thinking about...Oh, I don't know. The taste of beer on a hot day. Of how beautiful human bodies are, when they're young and smooth and strong.

I won't even try to explain.

Finally they dragged me, hands tied behind my back, across the tarmac towards the terminal. Yet another black limousine was parked there. They opened the doors, shoved me inside. I wasn't alone. A man was waiting, sitting comfortably. Mature. Dressed in a superb suit, and shining leather cowboy boots. Lean and weathered of countenance. A wave of bountiful grey hair. And yet all of it spoiled by the left side of his face, which hung slack and twisted. And when he spoke, it was in a slightly slurred American accent, almost drunken. It hinted wistfully of the bayous, and of the warm humid evenings in the deep south.

'Ah Leo,' he sighed. 'What a merry dance you've led us on.'

THIRTY-FOUR

The limousine rolled smoothly through the Canberra streets.

Not that I knew where we were going. The American had slipped a hood over my head, so I sat in darkness, on plush leather, surrounded by the whisper of air-conditioning. I was aching and bloodied. But I was reviving a little too, because it seemed that, for the moment, *I* at least was not destined to die.

'Why the hood?' I croaked. 'I've already seen all there is to see.'

I was sitting directly across from him, and could hear leather creak as he moved in his seat. Crossing his legs casually, I imagined. 'That's hardly true,' he said. 'Besides, I'm only acting under instructions.'

'Ah.' And didn't that just excuse everything. 'So who the fuck are you, anyway? I remember you. From back in Queensland. What are you? CIA? NSA?'

Amusement lilted in his voice. 'Something like that.'

'You got a name?'

'You can call me Sam.'

'As in Uncle?'

He laughed. Perfectly genuine and charming. 'If you like.'

And God, I hate charm. I said, 'We would have beaten you, you know. That day in Brisbane, the cricket, at the Gabba. Australia would have whipped your American arses, if that bomb hadn't gone off.'

'Oh, I know. Everyone knew. That's why the bomb was set for the time it was. It's one thing to promote US–Australian relations through sport, but no one wanted an embarrassment.'

I pondered that a moment, tasting blood on my lips. Fuck, I thought.

I said, 'And how many people died?'

'Hardly any.'

'Was it *all* you guys? All the terrorist attacks we've had? All the kidnappings and assassinations these last two years? The whole fucking lot?'

'Well, not *all* of it.'

'Aisha's group? The Great Southern Jihad? You ran them all along?'

'Not me personally. Not even my government. That was worked from the Australian end. But generally speaking, yes.'

'Why?'

He didn't answer for a time. 'Come on, Leo. You must know.'

And curse the bastard, I did.

'Why Canberra though?' I asked.

He chuckled. I pictured him staring out the windows, proudly. 'The funny thing is, it was you Aussies who gave us the idea. Years and years ago. Do you remember it? Back in 2003? When George W. Bush came to visit?'

'I was here.'

'Really? So was I. And you were so *accommodating*, you Australians. You shut down the whole town for us. I was part of the security detail. And we liked what we saw.'

A long-ago conversation came back to me. 'I met your President that day. Nathaniel Harvey. He wasn't President then.'

'You met Nate? Wonderful. Because this was his inspiration. He just couldn't get over how convenient Canberra was. How secure. A nice, small, modern city, but off on its own, miles from anywhere else. Only three roads in or out. A place you could evacuate without fuss. A place no one would even miss.'

'But *why*?'

'It's simple. We needed somewhere, Leo. A place away from all the troubles. I'm not just talking about the States here. Or Australia. I'm talking about all the major nations. And the major corporations too. All the players.'

'A place to do what?'

I could tell he was smiling. 'To run the world, I suppose.'

I laughed, felt blood in my mouth, spat it out. Which is a futile thing to do, when your head is wrapped in a hood.

'No, seriously,' he said. 'You don't understand how it's been lately. You can't get anything done anymore. Not in decent privacy. You try to hold an economic summit, and the venue gets overrun by protesters. You try to keep the oil flowing, and environmentalists and pacifists are rioting in the street. You try to put a motion through the United Nations, and a few tin-pot dictatorships derail the whole thing. It's unproductive. The only way to get results is to quietly gather the important people together and let them talk, away from the public.'

'So book a hotel. What do you need a whole city for?'

'You can't do it with just one *meeting*. It has to be ongoing. You need offices, you need diplomatic staff, you need the bureaucracy, you need standing committees and commissions. What you need, in fact, is a world government. The UN was supposed to be that, but it's a farce. You can't organise over a hundred and fifty different regimes into anything coherent. No—what you need is the dozen most powerful nations, along with their respective militaries, plus all the top corporations and money men...Then you can really get down to business, without having to worry about protests, or riots, or opinion polls. And Canberra was so *right*. All the infrastructure was here. All the bureaucratic space, all the diplomatic space. The city might have been built exactly for this very purpose.'

I said, 'So America and Australia run this place together?'

'Only as hosts, Leo. It's open to all our friends. The Europeans.

The Chinese. The Japanese. The Russians. The CEOs of the major transnational corporations. Oil traders. Arms dealers. You name it. The place is a convention centre, really.'

'You even invite the terrorists.'

'Terrorists?'

'I saw him. Bin Laden.'

'Oh. Well, all in the name of peace and order in the world.'

'Peace? I thought we were at war with him.'

'We are, Leo, of course we are. With him and others like him. But understand. War isn't as simple as one side versus the other.'

'What is it then?'

Sam was silent for a time. I had a vision of him, his withered face creased in earnest thought. Because that's how he sounded. Earnest. Sincere.

'Take the United States, for example,' he said. 'We've developed into a certain kind of country lately. In many ways—socially, racially, economically—we're quite a mess. It's not really possible for us to survive with stability as a nation anymore—not unless we have a unifying purpose. In short, Leo, we need an enemy. The blacks, the Hispanics, the poor, the left wing, the religious crazies—they're a big problem for us, even now. But they'd be burning down our cities if we didn't keep them busy fighting someone *other* than their own government.'

'Next you'll be telling me you did 9-11 yourselves.'

He laughed again. 'No, Leo. That wasn't us. But it was a godsend, no mistake. And that's really the point. September 11 was useful, sure, but it was too random. We had no idea what else al-Qaeda might be up to, or where they'd hit next, and that's not good for business. So of course we declared war on them and invaded some countries. But in the meantime, we put out feelers, and we talked, and we came to an arrangement. An alliance of kinds, actually.'

'Al-Qaeda were willing to make a deal? With *you* people?'

'Good heavens, yes. They're in the same boat. Maybe the US can't survive without an enemy, but the terrorist groups *certainly* can't. Lord, if we ever actually pulled out of the Middle East and left the Arabs to themselves, then who would they have to blame for all the fuck-ups in their countries? How would bin Laden recruit any followers or have any power, if the Great Satan wasn't around? No...He needs us, and we need him.'

'Then why do you pretend bin Laden is dead?'

'Oh, that was his idea. He was sick of the publicity, sick of hiding out in caves. The man likes a hot shower as much as the rest of us, Leo. So he was generous enough to throw us a bone and let us say we got our man. Even posed for the photos. And now he can run his side of things in peace.'

I heard him fumble in a compartment of the limousine, and then heard the click of a cigarette lighter. He puffed out smoke luxuriously.

'What it comes down to, Leo, is a kind of double war. On one level it's the official war—the West against the Islamists. But neither the western governments nor the Islamists want that war to end. What they both want is to stay in power, and to keep control over their own people. The people are the real problem, the civilians caught in the middle, the ones who are doing all the dying. *They* don't want the war. Muslim or western, they'd happily see it all stop tomorrow. The governments don't want that. The terrorists don't want that. The arms dealers don't want that. The oil companies don't want that. The big media bosses, they don't want that either—nothing sells papers like the war on terror! So by default we all have to form an alliance against the people in the middle, just to keep the war going, and the status quo intact.'

'And that's why they shot Harry and Aisha? To keep the status quo intact?'

'Well, you and your friends—your sudden appearance was incredibly unfortunate. Today isn't just any ordinary day here, you understand. All these flights coming in—it's the opening ceremony. We're about to start the biggest international conference Canberra has hosted to date. A month-long working party to sort out exactly who is doing what and where and to whom over the next three years. The world's a cake, if you will, and in the coming weeks we're going to slice it up.'

I couldn't take it in anymore. 'This is insane!'

'It's practical. You'd rather just anarchy? You think the little wars we're fighting now are bad? Believe me, they're nothing. Hardly anyone actually dies, and business keeps ticking over. But you take away the system we've set up, then you'd have *real* wars. Governments collapsing. Millions dying. Economic ruin. Which is unacceptable. We're doing a good thing here.'

And he meant it. He really did.

'In fact, you should feel honoured, Leo. None of it would work if we hadn't created the neutral ground here in Canberra. Australia's right at the centre of it all. And if there's one thing I know you Aussies love, it's being in the thick of things. I know Bernard gets a kick out of it.'

And in my memory I was back in The Lodge, on the night before news of the bomb broke. I was in the Prime Minister's office. I was talking to Bernard. And the little prick knew it was about to happen. He *knew*.

'My brother—he had no hesitation about this?'

'Well, he took some convincing. After all, Canberra was already being used, wasn't it? But we came up with the scenario to clear the city. And there were bonuses for him. A nuclear bomb, an outrageous attack upon Australian soil—the man was dying in the polls, I understand. How useful then to have something to make the country rally around.'

'But the bomb,' I said, grasping at straws. 'We all saw it. On TV.'

'Oh, there was a bomb. A real one. But not as big as we told everyone, and not nearly as dirty. We detonated it fifteen miles south, up in the hills. The TV cameras were to the north. They could see the mushroom cloud. But nothing else.'

'Canberra in ruins. We saw that too.'

I could almost hear the shrug. 'Industrial Light and Magic.'

And there were no straws left to grasp. 'You bastards.'

He was offended. 'No one even got hurt.'

'No one? What about the people who found out the truth?'

'Actually, we've done very well at keeping the city hush-hush. It's not easy. Food and water and power have to come from somewhere. All those planes flying in and out. People will notice, sooner or later. The trick is to divert the eye.'

I nodded tiredly. 'The Yass base.'

He sounded pleased with me. 'Exactly. Purpose-built as cover. Lots of troops there, lots of supplies needed, lots of military flights coming and going. Then we just fudge the records. It seems to work, without too many people having to be in the know. And it's not as if Canberra is as big as it used to be. I think the population was about three hundred thousand, before the bomb? It's less than fifty thousand now, permanent residents. And in all honesty, we haven't had to eliminate more than a few dozen curious souls who figured it out over the last two years.'

'Jesus Christ...'

'I certainly never thought *you* three would get this close.'

I closed my eyes under the hood. 'It was an accident.'

'An accident?'

'That air traffic controller. He told us.'

'You mean you didn't know before? Honestly?'

'How could we have?'

'Ha! That's a joke on us then.'

'A joke?'

'Well, you have to understand how it looked to us. We assumed that the Underground at least *suspected* about Canberra. We've been watching them very closely. We could tolerate them up to a point, of course, but not if they were going to expose the whole deal. And then things were brought to a head by that stupidity with Aisha's boys kidnapping you in Queensland.'

'It was a mistake, wasn't it?'

'It certainly was. Frankly, my advice had always been that, after we'd used them to fake Canberra, Southern Jihad should have been eliminated.'

'But they weren't.'

'No. That was your brother's call. The last thing he wants is an end to the state of emergency, so he needs regular terrorist attacks to keep up the tempo. A few bombs every year. A few assassinations. And if the targets happen to be Bernard's political enemies, even from his own party, all the better for him. The Southern Jihad people had no idea what was really going on, they just thought they were some sort of uber-Muslims, fighting the good fight against the filthy westerners. So it all seemed harmless. Until some idiots up in Queensland decide, without orders, to kidnap the Prime Minister's brother.'

'So why not order the Jihad to let me go? Why stage a rescue attempt?'

He sighed. 'Machinations, Leo. People got too clever by half. It was thought that Aisha and her boys might get suspicious about their superiors if they were ordered to merely hand you over. You were quite a prize, after all. No *real* terrorist group would ever let you go. So the simplest solution seemed to be enacting a rescue. And if Aisha and her men died in the process, well, they were expendable anyway.'

'But it got fucked up.'

'Indeed it did. Things were all nicely taken care of—but then the Underground intervened, and suddenly it was a whole other ball game. For one thing, the timing couldn't have been worse, what with the big conference about to start, and half the world's leaders on their way here to Canberra.'

A dim light of comprehension began to glow. 'Aisha. She knew that bin Laden was coming. She thought she was going to meet him.'

'Precisely. The agents who run the Jihad had made a promise to her and her colleagues—an audience with bin Laden, their Great Hero. They weren't going to meet him here in Canberra, of course. It would've happened somewhere else, under the pretence that bin Laden had snuck into Australia secretly. But they would have loved it. It was just a silly gimmick, really, to ensure their commitment to the cause. The problem was, they were told in advance. That was an error.'

'I still don't see why that made Aisha so dangerous. Or me.'

'Concentrate, Leo. If we'd rescued you and shot Aisha, that would have been the end of it. You'd have been debriefed and told to forget it ever happened. Your brother may not like you, but he didn't want you dead. Not at first.'

'But after the rescue went wrong?'

'*Then* we were worried. Because suddenly you and Aisha were in the hands of the Underground. That was bad. We knew that the Underground would be questioning Aisha about her operations. And we knew that, eventually, she'd tell them about Osama coming to visit.'

'She did. But no one believed her.'

'They didn't?' He was almost laughing again. 'Oh, Leo. That's the problem with the covert world. We always give our enemies too much credit. We really thought the OU would put it all together. About Canberra and the big conference. About why bin Laden was coming. About the meeting between him and the President. Everything. And that was altogether too much for us to be comfortable with. So the order went out. Get Aisha. Get the Underground. And get you.'

'Why me?'

'You were there. We assumed that whatever Aisha knew, and the Underground knew, you knew too by then. And you're the Prime Minister's brother. If you ever got to speak out about these things, people might actually listen.'

'And Bernard?'

'Gave the order himself, I'm sorry to say.'

'Fuck!'

'But the punchline is—you're telling me the Underground hadn't worked it out anyway! We needn't have bothered with any of this! Hilarious!'

I would have kicked him then, if I wasn't blind, and if my leg wasn't completely useless. But in any case, the limousine was coming to a stop.

'We're here,' he told me.

The doors opened, and I was aware of other guards around me now as I climbed out. It seemed to be somewhere high and airy.

'Where's here?' I asked.

Sam was at my side. 'It's your home for the immediate future.'

I was guided up some stairs and we entered what felt like a large, echoing room. From there, we were walking through corridors.

I said, 'You mentioned the President before. You said "bin Laden meeting with the President." I didn't see Nate Harvey anywhere today.'

For once, Sam sounded annoyed with himself. 'Well, it's a long conference. There's a lot to be discussed. But yes, Nate will be here in a few weeks.'

'Is my brother here?'

'Not yet, but he will be. He may want to see you when he arrives. He may not. But don't think we're keeping you alive just for his sake. Having disposed of your two companions, you're the only one we have left to talk to about this last week. There're some questions we want answered.'

'I'll bet.'

'But Bernard did speak to me specifically about where we should keep you. This was his suggestion, not mine. Some sort of private joke, I suppose.'

We were going down some stairs now, and through another corridor. It seemed a long way, for just one building. But then we entered a chamber where there was soft carpet underfoot, and where the sound around me seemed deadened.

'Take it off him,' Sam ordered.

The hood came away.

I stared about. I saw a huge room, with banks of green leather seating sweeping up all around. I saw a long table at the centre, trimmed with more green leather, and surrounded by chairs. I saw viewing galleries high up on the walls.

All as it had been before the bomb went off. The only thing missing was the ceremonial mace, but I suppose the members took it with them when they evacuated. And yet for some reason, they'd left the bound copies of Hansard behind.

A private joke all right, Bernard, you fucker.

I was standing on the floor of the House of Representatives.

My prison cell, ladies and gentlemen.

THIRTY-FIVE

And that, my dear friends and interrogators of the US secret service, that is pretty much it. My story told. The incident at the airport, and my interview with your half-faced superior, whatever his real name is—that was nearly a month ago, by my reckoning. I've been here ever since, at your pleasure, holding court in the very engine room of Australian democracy. A Parliament of one. So. Any more questions for me?

Actually, maybe there aren't. It hasn't escaped my notice that your visits have been steadily declining in frequency. Two weeks it's been since I took up pen and paper to write all this down, and for most of that time I've barely seen your over-muscled faces in here. Even my cigarette burns have had a chance to heal. It's no surprise, I suppose. After all, what do we have left to talk about? I do wonder, though—what are your plans for me now? I'd expected that by this stage some final decision might have been made about my fate, a sentence handed down and carried out, but you appear content to leave me in limbo. I have a suspicion as to why that is. But we'll see.

In the meantime, I have become more familiar with the House of Representatives than I ever wanted to be. As I've said before, I'm deathly sick of the colour green. Green leather chairs, green leather blotters on the desks, green carpet...and walls that I *think* are green, or at least faintly so. But it's hard to be sure, they might be white, and just reflecting the tone of everything else. I can't tell the difference. And maybe 'green' is the wrong word anyway for the whole colour scheme in here. It's really a paler shade. Perhaps it's 'eucalyptus'.

Either way, it's an odd prison. True, all the outer doors are locked and I can't escape, so it serves its primary purpose well enough, but it feels like a dreadful waste of space, just to hold one man. I mean, if Canberra is now supposed to be some sort of international conference centre for evil, then it seems to me that a meeting hall like the House of Representatives would be in demand. Surely you people have a normal prison block somewhere that you could keep me in?

Still, as cells go, it's not all bad. I'm not confined to just the House, after all. I also have access to the members' lounge immediately adjacent—and a welcome refuge it must have been, too, in the old days for drooping pollies during the longer parliamentary sessions. There must have been soft couches in there once, and five-star food and drink on hand. It's all stripped bare now, of course, but the adjoining toilets remain, and no prisoner ever had more luxury in a bathroom. All that stately polished wood and marble and mirrors. And just think of the famous arseholes that have lowered themselves, bowels unclenching, on the very same seat that I use.

And overall—especially since the worst of the interrogations finished—I've been treated well enough. I'm provided with three perfectly decent meals a day. I have blankets, and I've made myself a nice bed out of the shadow front bench. A doctor was brought in to treat the wound in my leg, which has recovered nicely. And as for my other bumps and bruises, okay, I may be bitter, but I do understand about that, interrogators. I'm sure you only did it for form's sake. We all know I was perfectly happy to spill my guts, pain or no pain. But now that torture is the western way again, you'd be idiots not to use it. Right?

Otherwise, well, I've had my writing to keep me occupied. As I said at the beginning, there's plenty of waste paper here, left behind in their desks by the departing members. I've discovered all sorts of documents; schedules, memos, petitions from constituents. Even a few private letters—one, notably, from the mistress of a backbencher on the Labor side, lovingly recounting a weekend of passion they shared in Byron Bay. (She goes into quite some detail, and I'm not ashamed to say it's brought me comfort and stimulation on the lonelier nights. And how many ejaculations of *that* kind has this House witnessed, I wonder, before I claimed the privilege?)

There are plenty of pens, too. I have them spread across the table in front of me, from cheap plastic biros all the way up to a glorious gold fountain pen—dry of ink, alas. And speaking of this table—I must say, I couldn't ask for a finer piece of furniture. A lovely warm wooden grain. And hand-carved, no doubt. It probably even has a special name, seeing that the governance of Australia once took place across it. The Table of Commonwealth, maybe. The Table of Judgement. The Table of Doom. I don't know. And although I have over a hundred very comfortable chairs to choose from, including the high throne of the Speaker's Chair, I've opted for the Opposition Leader's seat, right across the table from where my brother used to sit as Prime Minister. But I hardly need to explain the symbolism of that, do I?

I'm even something of a celebrity, I gather. Every now and again, people come into the visitors' galleries (which are sadly just out of my reach) to gawk at me. I have no idea who they are, but there can't be much to do for fun around here, if I'm one of the big attractions in town. Or am I wrong? Do you have the cinemas running? And the pubs? The golf courses? I bet you do. Canberra is the most exclusive town in the world now. The residents would expect their amenities.

Even so, sightseers keep coming to look at the famous prisoner, alone in his dungeon. Sometimes I feel a little like that guy in the Bastille in all those old movies—the Man in the Iron Mask. And come to think of it, wasn't he the twin brother to the wicked king, just like I am? Or was he the real king? Or did he just look like the king?

I can't remember, and the only resource material in here is Hansard. Miserable fucking reading that is, believe me.

Although I *do* read it.

Most of it is dry as sawdust, of course, but if you're patient, and weed through the drearier passages, then sometimes it does manage to come alive. After all, here before me are the verbatim transcripts of the last one hundred and ten years of parliamentary sessions. There have been some fiery debates in that time, well worth perusal. Awkward questions and angry denials. Furores and uproars and members expelled. Resignations and accusations and condemnations. Truly, the House has seen some great rhetorical battles in its history, and the pages of Hansard record them all, invective by invective.

The great identities are there too, the prime ministers of ages gone. Barton. Deakin. Fisher. Hughes. Scullin. Lyons. Menzies. Curtin. Chifley. Holt. Whitlam. Fraser. Hawke. Keating. Howard. To mention but a few.

And, of course, the Honourable Bernard James.

All names—apart from the last two—of which I assume you Americans will probably know nothing. But I can tell you, I sit here sometimes at night, and the echoes of those men remain in this room. Oh, admittedly, most of them worked in the old Parliament House, not this one. But the place itself doesn't matter. The House is still the House, whatever building it might be in. Those men are here. And, if Banjo Paterson will forgive me the quote, their ghosts may be heard.

They don't sound happy.

Indeed, in the first few days of my imprisonment—when your treatment of me was much rougher than it is now; when you had me strapped to this chair, denied food and water and sleep;

when you plagued me with questions day and night; when the cigarettes came out, and when the 'positions of discomfort' were applied—well, I confess I became a little delirious there, once in a while. And I'd imagine that there were other people in the House. I'd see stern faces behind your own, men sitting in the Prime Minister's chair across the table. Faces I recognised from old newspapers and old footage. Barton, I'm certain I saw him. And Lyons. And Curtin. And others. They never spoke, they never frowned, they never shook their heads. They just watched on. But ah, the judgement in their eyes.

This is not what they built this chamber for.

But Hansard contains more than just old arguments and old prime ministers. There are other histories in there too, testimonies to the challenges the whole nation has faced. Depressions and recessions, bushfires and floods, droughts and cyclones. And yes, wars of course, endless wars, and internal threats from enemies of every kind. And at times, reading the old speeches, you can almost feel, beyond the walls of the House, the actual nation as it was in the past, and how the country must have pulsed and swayed in different eras. You can almost feel, behind the politicians and their rhetoric, the Australian *people*. The many millions of them. Their struggles, their suffering. Their anger, their hate. Their hope and their triumphs and their doubt.

But most of all, you can sense their *power*. It's not a thing that is ever mentioned happily, or comfortably, by a single politician that I can find. It's an uneasy presence in their speeches, a monster over their shoulders that needs to be placated. It's evidenced by the changes of government, the elections won and lost. It's evidenced by the many names that disappear from the records with brutal suddenness, without farewells or ceremony. It's evidenced by the referendums that are proposed, to be either beaten down or passed. And in certain moments, you get a sense that the monster is not to be fooled with, or taken lightly.

Open the Hansards from the First World War, for instance. You'll find Billy Hughes in there, blustering about the need to introduce conscription, about the profundity of our alliance with Great Britain, about the desperation on the battlefields, about how a vote against the draft would be akin to an act of treason, a vote to lose the very war. Even so, come the referendum itself, the Australian people voted no. Indeed, they did it twice. And both times they were saying, 'We'll fight your damn war, but we'll do with it volunteers. We're not going to force anybody into the trenches.' And with volunteers alone, they did it indeed.

Or skip ahead, to Robert Menzies, in the 1950s, when the cold war was at its height and, over in the United States, the House Un-American Activities Committee was in full hysterical swing. Hear Menzies in stentorian voice, decrying the Communist Party and demanding that the nation pass a referendum to ban it forever or be swallowed up by the red tide. 'Put a sock in it, Bob,' the Australian people replied. 'The Commies can stand for election like anybody else, and good luck to them, because they'll need it. But we don't ban political parties in this country.'

The *strength* of those decisions. The courage of them. I mean, World War I was no joke. The cold war and the Communists were no joke. People were scared. And yet the nation refused to be stampeded by its leaders.

Yes ... but that was the old Australia.

If I flip to the Hansards of the last fifteen years, then what do I see? I see the rise of the new nationalism. I see the declaration of the war on terror. I see the outlawing of refugees. I see security laws passed time and time again, each regime more oppressive than the last. I see dozens of organisations banned. Protesters locked away. Freedoms disappear. Coercion legalised. I see new standards being set almost every day for how a western democracy should operate. And every single one of those standards is lower. And then lower again.

But nowhere, anywhere, do I see the Australian people saying no. The monster is silent. We arrived at this position—this George Orwell nightmare in which we all now live—willingly, it seems.

That's what I mean about miserable reading.

★

But look at me, the great judge and critic.

What example have I set, even in these last weeks, that's so wonderful? At what stage in this whole sorry saga have I stood up and cried, *Enough*? Who have I helped? Harry? Aisha? The Underground? Anyone at all?

Not bloody likely. I sit here, and write, and turn the pages of Hansard, and I remember the deaths of virtually every single person I came in contact with after that cyclone descended on my resort. And frankly—when I look back over my role in these events—I feel about as useless and ineffectual as all the other men who have sat in this very chair, ever since 1996, when John Howard and my brother took power, and the country was set on this godforsaken path.

THIRTY-SIX

Well, well. My suspicions were right, interrogators.

All this waiting around, when clearly you had no further use for me. It was just so Bernard could pay me a visit.

He strode into the House not an hour ago, even as I was putting down my pen—as confidently as if it were Question Time in the old days, with the Opposition floundering on the ropes as usual. My brother, the Prime Minister. Tanned and fit and groomed. His suit immaculate, his shoes shined.

The pompous little shit.

I didn't get up.

A couple of bodyguards were with him, but he waved them back to the door, and then took his old seat, the Prime Minister's chair, across the table from me. And if he was aware of any significance in the fact that the last time he'd sat there was the same day that we'd last met—and the last day that Australia operated as any sort of democracy worthy of the name—then he didn't show it.

'Leo,' he said, his expression cultivatedly grave and concerned.

'Oh fuck you, Bernard,' I replied.

That raised a tolerant smile. He glanced at my papers. 'They tell me you've been writing your autobiography. Is it finished?'

'All the fun bits, yes. I don't really know how it's gonna end though.'

'Ah.'

'But there's a passage about you masturbating in the shed, when we were kids.'

He only looked at me, then shook his head as if disappointed.

I said, 'You're here for the big conference, I suppose?'

'I am.'

'And is President Nate here now too?'

'He is. The concluding ceremonies are tomorrow. Followed by the joint signing of all the new treaties and accords.'

'And you're centre stage, are you? We're playing a key role in everything, Australia? I mean, we're more than just the caterers here in Canberra, right? We're not just serving out the tea and lamingtons to the big boys?'

'Our voice is heard,' he said.

'Oh, I bet it is. The Americans must owe you big, if you've done all this for them.' Anger rose up in me. 'That night at The Lodge. When that agent came in and told you about the bomb, it was all just pretend for you.'

He inclined his head modestly.

'But why did you want *me* there? Why all the crap about Mum's will, and about cutting me off? You knew none of it was going to matter.'

He shrugged. 'I had the time to spare.'

The time to spare? Ha! I didn't believe that for a second.

In fact, you want to know what I think, interrogators? I think he wanted me there that night because, somewhere inside him, there was a tiny spark of guilt glowing in regards to the travesty he was about to enact. It might only have been subconscious, but I think he needed to break completely from his family before it happened. To finish burying his mother, to cast off his only brother, to sever himself from all connections of kinship, before taking the final step into depravity. Just like Aisha—ridding herself of her parents before the jihad could begin.

But then who really knows with a furtive prick like Bernard? His hands stroked the table. 'I'm here to talk about *you*, Leo.'

I ignored that. 'What's the name of this thing anyway?'

'What?'

'This table.'

He stared. 'The Table of the House.'

Well, that was a let down. I gazed up at the walls and the visitors' galleries. 'Why here? Why did you ask them to put me in this room in particular?'

'Well, I knew it wasn't being used.' He considered the chamber in satisfaction. 'Besides,' he added virtuously, 'I didn't want you in a *cell*.'

And that was a lie too. I could have been kept in a house, a motel, anywhere at all. But no, the prison had to be Parliament House, at Bernard's insistence. And this is just my theory, interrogators, but perhaps that's how Bernard, in his dark mind, actually views the House of Representatives—as a prison. His own days in here were not happy—hemmed in by laws, constrained by the necessity for votes and debates and compromises. No doubt he was glad to be finally free of the place. And then couldn't resist the urge to lock *me* in here, in his stead.

I said, 'But don't you need a meeting hall like this? Where do all the big ceremonies take place during this great conference of yours?'

'We use the old Parliament House. Everyone thought it was more comfortable. Not as roomy, but more...intimate.'

And perversely enough, I could see that. This new Parliament House is all sharp edges and steel and glass, but the old one, it's more like a well-worn gentlemen's club. All scuffed polished wood and cracked leather. The sort of surrounds that world dominators have gravitated to ever since Britannia ruled the waves. Poring over the maps with brandy and cigars.

'So this building is empty apart from me?'

'Not exactly. Some of the offices are used.'

'By who?'

And he didn't seem to want to answer that.

'It's the Americans, isn't it?' I said. 'This is *their* headquarters now.'

'It's no such thing.'

'Oh no? Then why haven't I seen a single Australian face since they captured me? Why are the Americans doing all the questioning? Why isn't it ASIO or the AFP? This whole debacle is their business, isn't it? So where are they?'

The old stubborn look was there. 'It doesn't matter who questions you. We have an arrangement for the full exchange of intelligence.'

'Oh, right. Absolutely. And God knows, you can always trust the Americans, can't you? Especially when it comes to intelligence.' Then the realisation finally dawned. 'But they don't trust *you*, do they? Not you, not ASIO, not the AFP. You guys fucked the whole thing up. Ever since Aisha's boys nabbed me, you've made a mess of it all. So they've shunted you lot aside. Cut you out of the loop. In your own damn country. In your own damn Parliament House.'

Bernard glared coldly. 'Either way, they've finished with your interrogation. And the question of what to do with you now— that's entirely up to me.'

Which shut me up, good and proper.

'So what *do* we do with you, Leo?'

I couldn't answer. That's the problem with—well, I can't think of anything else to call it but sibling rivalry. Of course, brothers fight all the time, younger and older. And, in any family, the little brother will eventually score some sort of symbolic victory over the bigger. That's hard on the older brother, to have to admit defeat, and yet it's all part of growing up. But when the little brother has won absolutely everything, and holds the bigger brother's life completely in his hands...Let me tell you, no amount of growing up can help you there.

Bernard sniffed. 'Under the state of emergency security provisions, the law allows only one penalty for your various crimes.'

And I knew what that penalty was, sure enough. I said, 'What are my crimes, precisely? What law did I break?'

'Trespassing in the Canberra Protected Zone is a capital offence, for one. But there's at least a dozen others. Using false identity cards. Consorting with known terrorists. Illegally entering a cultural precinct.'

'I had no choice in any of that. I was a hostage. Seems to me, all I did was get kidnapped. And that only happened because I'm the Prime Minister's brother. But that's my real crime, isn't it, Bernie? Being your brother.'

He laughed.

I said, 'What is it exactly that you can't stand about me? Is it just that I always had more fun than you? That *everyone* always had more fun than you?'

He smiled his dead smile. 'You should thank God you're my brother. I'm the only one who can get you out of this.'

'And will you?'

'I've always bailed you out before, haven't I?'

'You signed my death warrant!'

'Maybe,' he said. And then, offhand, 'But you don't have to die.'

'I don't?'

'Not if you're smart. Obviously, you can't just be let go. As far as the world is concerned, you died over a month ago. But that isn't necessarily a problem. Quite a few officially dead people are living and working here in Canberra.'

'Osama bin Laden, for one.'

'He's an extreme example, but yes.'

'So what—you let me live, but I have to stay in Canberra the rest of my life?'

'There are worse options.'

'I wonder. *You* never liked living here, I recall.'

He took the remark seriously. 'This city was a mistake. It

should never have been built. At least now it's being put to a useful purpose.'

He said it with such complacency, with such indifference about what he had done to Canberra and the whole country. And yet I could see that it was as much explanation as I would ever get on the matter. There was no question of whether it was right or wrong—simply that it had worked.

I swear I would have reached over and belted him in that moment, if only the Table of the House wasn't so wide.

Instead I said, 'And what would I do here?'

'Anything you like. You'd be monitored, of course. But you're not entirely without skills. I'm sure a job could be found for you somewhere. Meanwhile, there's plenty of nice houses to choose from. Make yourself a home.'

And the rage drained out of me. What use was anger to me now? He had me, and we both knew it. So, I thought, a life in Canberra. Could I do it?

In short, of course I could.

After all, the high moral ground was *not* my native habitat. The pursuit of pleasure had always been far more important to me than worrying about who runs the world and how it's done. Staying alive was even more crucial. And there was no reason I couldn't be comfortable in Canberra. Bernard was right—I did have some skills, and one of them was always keeping myself supplied with the little luxuries. There would be booze somewhere in the city. There would be good food. There would be women around who were prepared to fuck my tired old body, if I asked nicely. What would it matter if they worked for the CIA or ASIO or some other secret police force? What would it matter if their heads were full of laws and rules and self-righteousness? As long as their cunts were tight and juicy.

Bernard was watching me, half smiling.

Ah, but I'd seen so many people die. Some of them crazy and violent, like Aisha and her boys. Some of them pathetic, like the refugees in the desert. Some of them doggedly doing their best in impossible situations, like the people in the ghetto. And some of them simply striving for a fairer world, like poor old Harry. But all of them caught in the same web that Bernard and his friends had spun. And that wasn't supposed to matter? I was just supposed to forget it all?

Bernard's smile told me exactly what *he* thought I'd do.

And oh, how I would've loved to prove him wrong. How I would've loved to rail at him about freedom and justice and the value of life, to declare that self-preservation wasn't everything, that fear wasn't the only motivating factor for humanity, that my soul wasn't cold and shrivelled like his. But in the end, I refused his offer for no such noble reasons or sentiments. I would have said yes to Bernard despite all of that, and served out my sorry existence in this charade of a city, and lived with the humiliation of owing him my life.

No, what stopped me was the simple awareness—just by looking into his eyes—that my brother was lying his head off.

He had no intention of letting me live. He never has had any intention, not since declaring me dead. And it isn't just because he hates me. He's always hated me. The crux of it is, I've done the unforgivable. I've embarrassed him in front of *you*, dear interrogators. In front of the Americans. Even worse, I've scared him. His whole wonderful scheme—Canberra, the state of emergency, his dictatorship—it all tottered there for a moment, as me and Harry and Aisha fled up and down the country. How that must have terrified him. How he must have sweated, waiting for us to be caught. There's no way he could let me survive after that, the suggestion was always the purest bullshit. No, he just wanted to see me beg for mercy. To confirm for him, if nothing else, my complete cowardice.

So I performed the one defiant act of my life. Because I'm going to die anyway, and because it robbed the little turd of that one last pleasure.

I said, 'No thanks.'

If Bernard was surprised, he didn't show it. He's a professional politician, after all. The vote had been put, and the motion had failed, but nothing had changed. He pushed away from the table, and stood there a moment by the dispatch box, gazing around at the House of Representatives one last time.

'Firing squad,' he said. 'Tomorrow morning.'

And out he walked.

'American troops?' I yelled after him. 'Or Australian?'

He didn't answer.

THIRTY-SEVEN

I've just woken, and come straight to the table.

I'm amazed, actually, that I went to sleep. I didn't mean to, not on my last night. And dawn can't be far away now. There are clocks on the walls in here, but none of them work. Can I see the faintest glow, through the angled windows above?

No, I don't think so. Not yet.

So I have a little while still, to write this down. Because while I was sleeping, I had a dream. A vivid, coherent dream.

I was sitting here as usual at the Table of the House, and I heard an odd sound from outside—like the soft popping of a champagne cork. One of the doors opened, and there, incredibly, was my acquaintance with the half-paralysed face, cowboy boots and all. My own Uncle Sam. Holding a gun in his hand, with the long barrel of a silencer attached.

He said, 'You coming?'

'What?'

'I'm busting you out, Leo. So *move*.'

I moved. In the corridor outside were two of my guards, lying dead on the floor. Sam beckoned me on without a word, and we hurried through the empty hallways of Parliament House, until we came to what seemed an important suite of rooms. In fact, they were familiar. It was the Prime Minister's wing. I'd visited Bernard there once, in much happier days. But it was all dark and deserted now. US flags hung on the walls.

We came to the Prime Minister's office, and there was Bernard's desk, just as I remembered it. Apparently it was Sam's office now. He closed the door, and then reached for something under the far side of the desk.

'What are you doing?' I asked.

'Watch,' he said, his half-smile twisted, and I heard a button click.

The desk rose slightly, and then swivelled on a pivot to reveal a hole beneath the floor. Narrow stairs dived down into darkness.

I said, 'What is this?'

'Our way out. We could hardly go through the front doors.'

I followed him down. There were many steep steps, and then we came to a smooth concrete tunnel, dimly lit. It ran ahead for hundreds of yards.

'I don't understand,' I said, as we moved down the tunnel, Sam limping slightly at my side. 'Why are you helping me?'

'Can't you guess?'

'No.'

He paused at that, and held out a hand to introduce himself. 'Samuel R. Hopkins. American Underground.'

I stared at him.

'What? You think you Aussies are the only ones with a resistance movement?'

'But *you*? Aren't you in charge of the secret services here in Canberra?'

'That I am. Not bad going, for an Underground operative.'

'But—but if you're against all this, then how could you let it happen? How could you go along with it all this time?'

'For the greater good, that's how. It's all part of a plan.'

'What plan?!'

'You'll see. Very soon. Now come *on*.'

We continued. The tunnel intersected with another tunnel, and then others, running off at all angles. There were signs on the walls, pointing out cryptic routes.

'Who built these?' I asked.

'We did.'

'Who? The American Underground?'

'No! The CIA. You must have heard the rumours about the US Embassy and all the tunnels underneath?'

'I never believed them.'

'You should have. We had this town completely wired.'

'Is that where we're going now? The US Embassy?'

'Christ, no. Too many eyes.'

The tunnel started to descend gently, and somehow I knew that we were going under Lake Burley Griffin. Eventually it rose again, and then we turned off into a smaller side tunnel, and ascended a ladder that ended in a manhole. We opened it and climbed into daylight, hidden from sight in a pocket of shrubs. I looked about. We were on the shore of the lake, directly across the water from the old Parliament House. The time seemed to be around mid-morning, and yet the city was deserted, no cars moving, no people walking. A ghost town.

Sam led me up the embankment to the foot of Anzac Parade. A black limousine was waiting there, driverless. We sat in the front, with Sam behind the wheel. He started up, and then we rolled away, north along the parade, past the statues and memorials of Australia's long history at war.

'Are we getting out of Canberra?'

He nodded. 'But there's something I want you to see first.'

We wound through the silent suburbs. Before us, Mt Ainslie hulked against the sky. Up we went along the road through the scrub, until we reached the lookout where I'd stood with Harry and Aisha. We climbed out and went to the railing. Canberra spread below us, empty and grey.

'Look there,' my rescuer said, pointing to the airport. 'You see that plane parked off on its own? The one that's all black?'

I saw it. In fact, I'd seen it once before. It was the same plane that had flown over the three of us that first morning, just as we reached the mountain top, not knowing that two of us would be dead within hours.

'It's a CIA transport,' Sam went on. 'And that's how we brought it in. The crew, the pilot, the ground staff back in the States—they're all in the American Underground.'

'Brought what in?'

His teeth were perfect as he gave his deformed smile. 'A nuclear warhead.'

'*Another* one?'

He nodded. 'But bigger than the last one. Much bigger. And much dirtier.'

'What's it for?'

'We're going to wipe Canberra from the face of the earth. For real this time.'

I stared down. 'When?'

'One hour from now. Midday. At exactly the same time that the closing ceremony of the big conference is due to finish.' He pointed down to the old Parliament House. 'They're in there right now, all the negotiators and guests and dignitaries, congratulating themselves. And they're right next to ground zero. The bomb is in a catering van parked at the back.' He laughed. 'Do you see our plan now, Leo? What we've been working towards all these years?'

I looked at him, understanding. 'You wanted them all in one place.'

He nodded. 'And for the first time in history, here they are. The warmongers. The dictators. The spy masters. The arms dealers. The oil barons. The corporate overlords. The terrorist leaders. The whole cabal that's ruined this planet. All those obscene old men who expect the rest of us to do the dying in the wars they start. There's never been any way to get to them before. Not all of them at once. But here in Canberra—they think they're so safe in this city. They think they've built a fortress. But it's a trap. They've built their own death chamber.'

'And in one hour . . . ?'

'It's not going to be pretty, Leo. When the bomb goes off, and the truth finally comes out, it's going to be fucking chaos, right around the world. Governments are going to collapse, revolutions are going to happen, riots, wars, bloodshed. But at least there'll be a proper *reason* for it this time. At least this will give us another chance at getting it right, without those people down there perverting it all.'

'I can't believe it,' I said. I turned away from the city and faced him. 'I can't believe it's *you* doing this. Americans.'

He shrugged. 'Who else could have? You boys here in Australia? The English? The Chinese? The Arabs? They all have their resistance movements too. But no, it was up to us in the States, just like it always is. And don't misunderstand, Leo. We're all proud Americans, in our Underground. We know full well that the US is the most important country in the world, and that it's our responsibility to *lead* the world.' He gestured out over the city. 'But not like this.'

A wave of hope swept over me, like wind on the mountain top. Then a trilling sound broke out. It was the ringing of a mobile phone. Sam reached into his pocket, brought the phone to his ear, and listened.

'Goddamn,' he said, after a time.

'What's wrong?'

He hung up the phone, tight-lipped, and nodded towards the city. At the same time, a siren began to wail. And then another one. And then more. Like air raid sirens, rising and falling mournfully, trying to wake the dead town.

'What's happening?'

'There's been a fuck-up,' he said grimly. 'Word has got out about the bomb.'

'They've found it?'

'No. But they know it's somewhere in the city. Look.'

Lights were flashing outside the old Parliament House, and

suddenly a crowd of people were flooding through the front doors, and down the stairs. Cars appeared from everywhere.

'They'll get away!' I said.

'No,' Sam replied, sounding sad, 'they won't.' He was staring at his phone. 'Although I was hoping *we* would.'

I looked at him.

He said, 'An hour would have been long enough for us to get clear. It's a pity. But it hardly matters.' He puffed out a sigh and, with slow finality, punched a series of numbers into the phone. Then, to my amazement, he handed the phone to me. 'Executive override code to detonate the bomb instantly. All you have to do is press "Send"—and that will be the end of it.'

I stared at the phone, and then down at the old Parliament House. The crowd there was piling into the cars, and the vehicles were racing off madly.

From very far away, I could hear the screams of panic.

'You want *me* to do it?'

'You've got as much reason as any of us, don't you?'

'But...'

'You don't mind, surely? You were going to die anyway.'

'I know...'

'But just before you do...' Sam was pulling a pack of cigarettes from his suit pocket. 'I was down to only a few of these a day. But there's no harm now.'

He lit up. Offered the pack to me.

And so we both smoked a last cigarette, savouring the unique pleasure of living a few minutes more, while below the sirens droned on, and Canberra convulsed in its final terror. Most of the vehicles fleeing the old Parliament House were heading, I could see, for the airport. It wasn't far. A large passenger jet had powered up, and a stairway had been rolled out to its side.

'What's the lethal range of that bomb?' I asked, fingering the phone.

Sam thought calmly. 'Even up here, we'll be incinerated instantly.' He studied the speeding cars. 'The airport is even closer to it. There's no rush.'

'Good.'

It was my first cigarette in years, and I wanted to finish it.

Below, the cars had reached the terminal, and figures were leaping out, running around the side of the building to get to the plane. And somehow, even from two miles away, I could see them all clearly, even their faces, as they sprinted across the tarmac. The lords of this corrupted earth, grappling and shoving at each other in their haste, mouths contorted. Brave generals, and national leaders, and suited CEOs. Arab oil merchants and their terrorist cousins. All of them shrieking and swearing and fleeing for their lives. Nathaniel Harvey was in there somewhere. Osama bin Laden too. But ahead of them all, miraculously, was my little brother. Bernard 'Last Man Out' James. Determined to be the first this time. His stout legs pumping.

I took a long final drag, stubbed out my cigarette.

I looked to Sam. 'Well?'

He stubbed his out too. Took a deep breath. Nodded.

Down on the tarmac, Bernard was clambering up the stairs to the door of the plane. He was waving madly at the cockpit. Go, go, go.

Behind him a scrum had developed at the foot of the stairs. Bernard was shoving the whole structure away from the plane anyway, screaming all the while.

The jet started forward.

I pressed the 'Send' button.

And a white purifying flame filled the sky.

THIRTY-EIGHT

But that was just a dream.

Here in the House of Representatives, it feels cold for the first time since my imprisonment. The sky, the tiny fragment of it I can see, still seems dark. But the guards were here a moment ago. They said they'll be ready for me in one hour.

I asked them where it will be. Which part of this building, or of Canberra, do they use for the executions? Outdoors, I assume, if it's a firing squad.

But they wouldn't tell me where, or who would be behind the guns.

So, dear interrogators.

What is there left for me to say?

Except...that dream. It has me thinking. I mean, there really must be some sort of US Underground, mustn't there? God knows, not every one of you Americans can be happy with the way your country operates now. Of course, I doubt that my friend with the blighted face could really be a member of such a group. There's no double agent as masterful as that.

But what about you, interrogators? I've seen five of you over these last weeks. Is there any chance that just one of you—just one—isn't so sure about the way things are? I'm not imagining for one second that anyone is going to save my life here. But these memoirs I've written. What about them?

It would only take one copy of these pages, let loose on the streets.

The truth would be out. And then what would happen?

Just a quick trip to a photocopier, that's all that needs to be done. Are you listening, whichever of you is reading this, days or weeks or months after I'm dead?

Are you alone in your office?

Then *do it*.

And I'm going to break one last law before I go.

I'm going to talk about the Roman Empire again. Because I look back at everything that's happened, not just in these last weeks, but in these last years. And not just in my life, but in the life of the whole country. I look at the changes in Australia that made these events possible, the changes in *us*, all in the name of protecting ourselves, of fending off the threat beyond our borders. And I can't help but think of Rome, its decline and its fall, and whether or not we in this age share any similarity with it. As I said, I've studied some history. And I'm wondering. Those Romans living say about the year 350 AD—could they see what was coming?

After all, to most people, the Empire must have looked as strong as it ever had, and the city of Rome as supreme and as untouchable. The barbarians loomed on all sides, true, but they were still being held beyond the frontiers. And yet, did any perceptive soul see what it *cost* the Romans to keep those hordes at bay? Like the armies that demanded ever more men and money? Or like the autocracy of the emperors that grew ever more severe—stifling internal debate, corrupting law, imposing dogma over knowledge, reducing free citizens to serfs—all for the sake of unity and strength? Did anyone see how dangerous that was? Did anyone feel the withering of the very inspiration that had made Rome so great?

And did they imagine, in their darkest dreams, that it was all in vain? That by the time the barbarians did break through, the Empire would already be essentially dead? That instead of protecting their world, they had fatally weakened it? That in fifty years Rome would be a smoking ruin? That the Empire would have become a bloodied stamping ground for the armies of a dozen different sides and causes? And that within a hundred years a Dark Age would be settling over Europe—an era of war and poverty and enslavement that would last for centuries?

There must have been some who saw it. Some who yelled it out in the streets. And how they must have been scorned, and locked up as madmen.

Well, I'm no prophet.

I have no idea what the future holds. I won't even be alive to see it. But I'll say one thing. If—in this blind pursuit of security above all else—we poison our own society, and so decline, and fall, then we will be more culpable than even the Romans were before us. And such a fall, I suspect, would be followed by an Age so terrible, compared with the knowledge and the light which preceded it, that it wouldn't merely be called Dark. It would be called Black.

I hear marching footsteps in the hall outside. Orders yelled.

I think the fuckers are actually going to shoot me in *here*.

And God help them, they sound Australian.